The Kashallan Alliance

Tales of the Kashallans: Book Seven

By

Celu Amberstone

This is a work of fiction. Similarities to real people, places, or events are entirely coincidental.

KASHALLAN ALLIANCE

First edition. February 29, 2024.

Copyright © 2024 Celu Amberstone.

ISBN: 978-1990581137

Written by Celu Amberstone.

Prologue

<<We are of one mind,>> intoned Qwaltamis, the oldest among the Khutani Makers. Within the deep cavern that was their underwater Council Chamber, their sinewy bodies mingled in a tightening knot. Phosphorescent trails of light spun out in a halo around the writhing snaky mass.

<<We are of one mind and one purpose,>> the other Makers chorused, repeating the ancient invocation.

<<And, for those of us who can remember the beauty of Timorna before the Great Destruction, what is that purpose?>> Qwaltamis asked.

<<To re-make the world from the patterns of life we saved.>>

<<That was the task given us by Mother Timorna, and The Star Guardians. What is the charge?>> the Ancient continued.

<<To protect the land and the species we saved and remade to combat Umwira treachery.>>

<<So it has been and so must it always be,>> the Makers concluded the ritual formulation.

Dievris, the Maker making its home under Lake Ticca, began the proceedings. <<I bring to this Council dire news. Over the Sorins, Umwira changelings from the Ghostlands attacked and almost killed our first kashallan. And though their minions were defeated within Ticca Keep, another band of the foul vermin from the West have dared to capture one of this kashallan's mates.>>

The knot of grey sinewy bodies writhed with anger, vomiting out the fiery taste of outrage and the bitter after-taste of fear. <<The Hated Enemy grows far too insolent. Foul creatures, how dare they!>>

Before the communication could sour completely, Dievris spat a placating spice into the whirlpool it had stirred up. <<There is more, my Amsi (age mates). When one of my hunting packs was sent to retrieve the

woman, the hunters' efforts to kill the Enemy were blocked by one of our number.>>

The Makers froze, unable to savor such a thing. A Khutani Maker a traitor, forsaking their Holy Charge and allied with the enemy, how was this possible?

<<I wouldn't go so far as to name that one traitor,>> Dievris hedged, dripping a soothing spice into the maelstrom. <<But certainly I would say misguided.>>

<<You are speaking of me and my involvement in the recovery of the woman. Who, I might add should be safely back at Ticca with your hunters by now,>> Tinguss announced before Dievris could do more than hint at accusations. <<While they were in pursuit of their quarry the Ticca hunting pack came into the lands over which I hold sway. I had every right to become involved in this matter.>>

<<But not to stop my hunt leader from carrying out his duty,>> Dievris accused.

<<I did not stop him from doing his duty, as you put it. Have you talked to your own symbiont child, who was also there? Your hunt leader himself was reluctant to kill those people if another way could be found to resolve things. I merely offered them another way.>>

<<Before you accuse me of anything savor the whole truth of the meal. My kashallan, at the urging of the Demon your people invoked, I might add, told him to come with her to intercept them and stop the slaughter. It seems the Spirit has taken an interest in that particular clan of the Western Umwira.>>

Once again the swirling mass froze, savoring the meaning of this new information. <<Yes, the Demon has taken an interest. Did you know, Amsi? Did you leave that tidbit out to add a tart spice to the flavor of your sending?>>

<<It doesn't matter,>> Dievris snarled. <<They are all Hated Enemy and should die.>>

<<They were starving women and children, not a hunting warband out for slaves and plunder,>> Tinguss countered. <<Even your own hunt leader had no wish to kill them when he saw what he had ensnared.>>

<<This is most disturbing news, Amsi.>> another of the pod said. <<What is happening to our world that one of our own created species should defy a Maker!>>

Gladdris rumbled a laugh. <<I believe I heard he is one of the new host people, and as we all can savor the Speir'dina have minds of their own and don't take direction easily.>>

The sweet taste of amusement dripped into their sending after that comment. Recalling Dunnagh's resistance to their attempts to prepare him for the Transformation, they all could agree on the truth of that mouthful.

<<But you did more than prevent the killing of women and children,>> Dievris spat out bitterly. <<You want an alliance between us and the Western Clans of the Enemy.>>

<<I offered sanctuary only to that one clan in the lands over which I have some power; that is true. If, and only if, they agreed to stop warring against us,>> Tinguss said calmly.

<<I say they are all vermin and can't be trusted.>> growled Sherigus, a scarred maker from pools deep in the Yeyen Banai Valley.

Several of the others regurgitated up their agreement to that sentiment. The pod writhed whipping the water to a foaming phosphorescence in their agitation. <<Can't trust the Hated Enemy! They will destroy the world as they almost did before!>>

Refusing to be swept away by the torrent of fear and anger flooding its pallet, Tinguss vomited the sour taste of its disgust into the collective soup. <<Stop this! Did the Long Sleep rob us of our reason? Are we only animals now, allowing our emotions to rule us?

<<Think! We will need them and the other western clans beside us in our fight against the Ghostlanders. The wizards, like Barak and his cabal, I fear have grown far more powerful in our absence than we dreamed.>>

<<Nonsense,>> Dievris scoffed.

<<Is it? I was told by your own hunt leader that an Umwira changeling had been the Ima Matri's trusted advisor at Ticca for many years before a kashallan discovered her. How was that possible, Maker?>> Tinguss challenged.

<<Perhaps we have grown too complacent—too careless,>> Gladdris mused, adding a soothing agent to the growing heat.

<<Stayed too long within our dreams in the Long Sleep,>> another agreed.

<<Yes, we did, and that is why I offered this band of the Umwira an alliance with us. Think, Amsi, why were they hiding and starving in the caves near the lake in the first place? Because they, too have suffered at the hands of the Ghostlanders, that's why.

<<The reason they were in Khutani lands at all was because they were attacked during the Sorins by the very people they thought were their trusted allies, the Ghostland wizards.>>

<<But those tribes have been aligned with the Northerners for as long as we can remember. Why would the Ghostlanders do that?>> an incredulous Ancient asked drooling the spice of its disbelief. <<They must have done something vile to evoke such a punishment.>>

<<No. We did.>> Tinguss said.

<<Always you create dissention among us, Cousin. You are babbling nonsense,>> Dievris snarled.

<<Am I, Cousin? The Ghostland Wizards sent their warbands to attack them because they thought the Western Clans had betrayed their age-old covenant first. And that misconception, in a way, *was* our fault.>>

<<Our Fault? What are you talking about, stupid slimeworm?>> Sherigus grumbled.

<<Our fault,>> Tinguss repeated. <<They were attacked because the Ghostlanders thought that one of the Western Wizards had created a race of mutants that could host our symbiont children.>>

Startled, the pod drank in the spicy flavor of surprise.

<<They never considered we would call a new people from the stars to become our Chosen,>> Tinguss continued. <<The Ghostland Wizards thought what every Timornan thinks, that the Speir'dina are mutant Umwira. And since *they* didn't breed them, some wizard in the West must have, in order to make a new alliance with us against them.

<<Through the eyes of my Chosen I saw the remnants of this starving band. I heard some of their story and tasted their flavor with my symbiont child. The Western Clans were hit hard; many of their war leaders and wizards tortured and then killed as the Ghostlanders looked for a traitor.>>

<<Hmm. As some of you may already know, our Dream-Chosen, our first kashallan-bonded was captured and tortured by some of the Umwira changelings in Riath,>> Gladdris mused. <<They asked the same questions of him.>>

<<True, he was near death when the hunting packs loyal to us captured Riath and the Umwira fled,>> Qwaltamis added.

<<How do the host and our child fare now?>> someone asked.

<<Host and symbiont are on the mend,>> Gladdris said. <<But it will take time for their healing to be complete, mentally and physically.>>

The Makers writhed, thinking of such a terrible fate and how they had almost lost such a precious gift as a host willing to bond.

<<This is just another reason why we need my proposed alliance with the West,>> Tinguss urged with a peppery bite to its sending. <<There isn't a traitor wizard among them, of course, but we can use their anger and need for vengeance to our advantage by making alliance with them.

<<Together we can war against our common Enemy—and this time maybe we will win, once and for all. That's what I hope to achieve by an alliance with the West,>> Tinguss concluded.

<<Your arguments have given us much to savor, Amsi,>> Qwaltamis said into the pause after Tinguss finished. <<For now, however, you will not go any farther with this crazy plan of yours. Not until the Council takes time to absorb and digest this proposal.>>

<<But we have no time,>> Tinguss pleaded, dripping the tart flavor of its frustration into the communication. <<The Umwira in the North are poised to attack our lands. Divided, and fighting among ourselves the Ghostlanders could achieve their goal and destroy all we have worked so hard to salvage from the Ancient Destruction.>>

<<Nonetheless, we will take the time to savor the broth made of everyone's words regurgitated here today,>> Qwaltamis intoned.

<<To prevent you from causing more mischief, Amsi Tinguss,>> Dievris said. <<I propose that you remain here confined, until we decide what to do about you and your absurd notions.>>

A chorus of burbled agreement answered Dievris's suggestion.

<<And what of my people, my descendants, and my land?>>

<<The Begta and your descendants can get along without you for a time. They can care for your precious Swamp,>> Sherigus growled

<<Did you not hear me? The Demon that was made to swear to protect our kashallans, sheltered this band over the Sorins from Barak's malice. It, too, wants an alliance with the West,>> Tinguss snapped. <<Would you ignore its obvious favor, just to spite me, Amsi Dievris?>>

<<This isn't about a personal challenge. Don't make it one,>> Qwaltamis chided. <<We will savor the Demon's involvement when we digest the matter, be assured.>>

Ah, but it was personal, Tinguss thought privately.

TINGUSS BRUSHED ITS sensitive mouth tentacles across the glowing Psy net that now enclosed its form and cut off all communications with its descendants in the world beyond its watery prison. In spite of what its age-mates claimed, it knew there was a sour taste of personal attack to its confinement no matter how Dievris and some of the others might try to sugar-coat its flavor.

Retreating to the center of its prison, it twisted its long snaky body round and round and then rested its head atop the massive coil. Conjuring an image in its mind of Dievris, it rumbled a laugh. <<Too late, old Mud Crawler. If my descendants have done what I assigned them, the shifting of alliances on our world already has begun.>>

Part One:

Chapter One

KASHALLAN PHILLIP-YOEY stood in the orange Thuulla grass overlooking the rocky beach. Below him members of the Blue Stone Clan's warband were hauling their long reed and rawhide boats from their concealment within a deep hollow in the cliff face. Savoring the salty tang to the sea air, he took in a deep breath and let it out slowly. Across the water to the west the far horizon lay vailed in purple mist.

<<It's beautiful,>> he said to the symbiont Yoey coiled in his middle.

<<Yes it is, Kasha. I have encoded memories of the sea before the wars, but now it is much different, yet still beautiful as you say. I wonder how long it will take us to get to the other side?>>

<<I don't know, Shalla, we shall have to ask our new allies the answer to that question.>>

Had that been a taste of anxiety he detected in the symbiont's mental voice? Well, he couldn't blame his bondmate for being nervous. Until recently when their parent, the Maker Tinguss, had formed an alliance with this Western Clan of the Umwira, these men had been part of the peoples known as, "The Hated Enemy," the ones that had raided Khutani held lands for slaves and booty for as long as anyone could remember.

Now of course these two former enemies shared a common foe, the Ghostlanders. So, here they were heading back across the Shallow Sea with the Blue Stone's warband, who had sought refuge in the caves near Ticca Keep, with their women and children in tow, in a desperate attempt to hide from Wizard Barak's wrath.

As a show of good faith Maker Tinguss had shared the language patterns for the Western Umwira Dialect, and then sent the bond-mates and a few Speir'dina, with their galactic weaponry, to gather the Western warbands in the alliance the Ghostlander's feared. If successful this united force, along with hunting packs going north from the Yeyen Banai Valley would make war upon the Ghostlanders and crush their power for good—they hoped.

"Kashallan?"

Phillip turned away from the view and smiled at the Avairei priest dressed in a travel-stained kilt coming up the trail through the grass. "Ata Doyan, how can I serve you?"

The good Ata looked nervous. He could detect the sour odor of the man's dusty brown fur. The priest was the companion of the Sweh'an Demon's mortal host Tessa. Oath-bound to the Khutani, the demon had seen something that meant Tess-weh and her household was also coming along on this little venture.

"Tess-weh and the War Leader say we will be ready to go soon. They want you to come down now."

"Of course, Ata, it has been so long since one of us has seen the Shallow Sea with our eyes," the Khutani symbiont Yoey explained. "I asked my Kasha to come up here so we could see." The Kashallan glanced once more at the view. "Unfortunately we can't see much through the morning fog," it complained.

Doyan bowed and started down the trail. Before he could get too far ahead, Phillip placed a hand on his shoulder. "I taste your fear, Ata, and to a certain extent share it.

"You were very brave not to abandon your charge and go back to Ticca with the Hunt Leader escorting Sairsa and the Blue Stone women and children. Like me, you aren't warrior-trained. I know it won't be easy for any of us, but we will just have to trust that Tess-weh has seen something in our future that makes all this necessary."

Doyan's lips twitched not quite able to offer a smile in return for Kashallan-Phillip's weak offer of assurance. "I'm sure you are right, Holy One."

Phillip chuckled and led the way down the hill. "I hope I am, too."

Back on the beach he could see that the Blue Stone boats they were taking were lined up in the shallows. Grim-faced warriors were busily loading them with weapons and their meager supplies. Finishing a hasty meal by the dying fire, the Blue Stone war leader, Ogwy, Tess-weh and her Warlinga guard Cadrach watched the preparations. Kashallan-Phillip, Doyan at his heels walked over and joined them.

Crouching by the smoky fire, Phillip poured himself the last of the tea from the sooty pot. His Begta apprentice Masonja handed him a piece of dry-meat from her pack. The tension between those at the fire was thick enough to be cut with a knife. What was the problem this time—did he really want to know? "I see we are about ready, War Leader," Phillip said as he ate.

The Umwira had been raiding the southern-held Khutani lands for so many years their genetic patterns were a mixture of Timorna's original inhabitants and those of the Khutani's introduced peoples bred to replace them after the great wars killed off so much of the planet's life.

Like many of the Blue Stone People, Ogwy was a blend of several heritages. A tall muscular man with brown fur and an Avairei cat-like face, he also had the Warlinga's whip-like tail and an extra pair of arms just above his hips like a Loti's six limbed body.

Without answering the Kashallan, Ogwy rose, kicked sand on the fire and stalked down to the beach shouting orders to his men. Tess-weh watched him go, a sly smile on her pretty heart-shaped human face.

"Umwira Mans stupid," Masonja muttered her mouth full of meat. That comment earned her a snort of amusement from the demon.

Phillip sighed. The wrangling between the demon and the war leader was starting to get tiresome. Just like Dunnagh-Tani, Ogwy always swallowed the bait she tossed to him.

"We should go, too." Finishing his meal quickly, Phillip fastened his battered metal cup to his belt and followed the demon and her Warlinga protector down to the boats, Masonja at his side.

When they drew near the Kashallan could hear a hissed argument between the war leader and his brother Lubwey. The men in the boats had stopped to listen. Tess-weh stood slightly apart, her arms folded across her creamy breasts, still looking amused.

<<What are they fighting about now, Kasha?>>

Phillip listened for a moment and frowned. <<It would seem that none of the crews want to take the Sweh'an Demon and us.>>

<<But how will we get there if no one will take us?>>

Phillip's mouth hardened. Their Amla Tinguss hadn't foreseen this little problem that the Sweh'an Demon was deliberately causing. Did these Umwira plan to abandon the alliance now that they were safely back to their boats and could escape? He opened his mouth to remind them of the consequences of that kind of oath breaking, when Tess-weh let out a mirthless laugh, drawing all eyes to her once more.

"How sweet, My Jewel, you and your brother fighting over who will have the pleasure of my company for the voyage." She smiled but there was no warmth in her dark eyes.

Laying a hand on Ogwy's scarred arm, she cooed, "Don't be sad, My Treasure, if I decline your offer."

Ogwy stiffened at her touch, his eyes flashing with anger at the implied intimacy of the gesture. "Leave me alone, Spirit! I have told you before. I am no Demon's play thing."

Tess-weh traced a ridge of scars up to his shoulder. "And I have told *you*, War Leader, you will be my play thing—if I want you to be."

With his kashallan-heightened awareness Phillip was aware of the Psy battle of wills going on, as the two adversaries faced off and glared at one another. Lubwey must have been aware of at least some of the tension, because with an oath he growled, "Enough, Brother this is dangerous—and pointless. The Warlinga and the demon can go with me."

Tess-weh turned to Lubwey and smiled. "Ah, your concern for me is touching, War Leader—"

"I am war leader here, Foul Creature—not my brother. I will decide who goes in which craft, and don't you forget that!"

"I will not forget, Umwira. You are war leader—but for how long I wonder? Think on that until I return, hmm?" Stepping closer to Cadrach she placed a delicate hand on his shoulder. The big Warlinga lifted her, cradled her in his arms and headed back up the slope.

"Where are you Going, Witch?" Ogwy shouted after the retreating pair. "We have to go now!"

Looking over her protector's shoulder, she grinned. "Missing me already, Umwira?"

"Honored Spirit, are you leaving us?" Doyan cried.

Phillip hoped the Umwira hadn't detected the note of desperation in the priest's voice.

"Don't worry, Ata, you will see me again—when I'm needed."

"I'm sure Tess-weh has her reasons for leaving, Ata Doyan," Phillip murmured, stepping close. I'm still here with you and our Speir'dina armachda."

When they reached a grassy rise Tess-weh turned for one last look down at them. Phillip raised a hand and waved goodbye.

Tess-weh threw back her head and laughed. "Oh, My Jewel, you surprise me once again." Then still chuckling to herself, she and the big Warlinga disappeared.

In a way he was glad to have a break from the demon's presence among them. The journey from their camp where they parted from the Speir'dina hadn't been a long one, but like Dunnagh-Tani, the war leader seemed unable to help himself from falling prey to her malicious humor.

While he'd been watching the Sweh'an, Moraga, Chang and Timma had come over to them. He could taste the battle alertness of his two armachda, but they remained silent, waiting on his orders, he supposed.

Returning his attention to the two war leaders, he asked, "If we are ready, Lubwey, does the offer apply to me and the others riding in your boat as well?"

Lubwey nodded, but before they could climb into any of the reed canoes, Ogwy made a cutting gesture with his hand. "No. you must split up. Too many in one boat sitting around doing nothing, is no good."

Chang snorted and reached to pick up an ore. "Who said anything about just lazing around? I was born on a Satsi Boat on the Galoom River back home. Without giving Ogwy time to protest he waded out with his gear and expertly climbed into a shocked Noi's boat, Timma a hesitant shadow in his wake.

Phillip chuckled and reached for another ore. "Though I doubt if I'm as skilled as my armachd there, I too can paddle. And of course so can Masonja." He gave Moraga an inquiring look.

"I used to race with a corrach team in school," she said.

"A corrach? I'm impressed, Armachd. I found those round boats a real challenge the one time I tried them."

She laughed. "They are that, Sir."

"Enough talk," Ogwy growled and waved her to his brother's boat. "The fog is lifting we waste time. The weather is treacherous this time of year for a crossing."

Moraga hesitated, her eyes going to the Kashallan and Ata Doyan. "Go on, Moraga, I'll keep the good Ata and Masonja with me. We'll be fine," Phillip-Yoey said.

"I'm afraid I've never been in such a craft before," Doyan confessed.

The Kashallan took his arm and ushered him to Ogwy's boat. "It's all right, Ata, just relax and enjoy your first boat ride. You can bail water if we need it."

"I'm not sure that makes me feel any easier in my mind," Doyan murmured as he passed the Kashallan to take his seat among the Packs in the center of the craft.

<<Will they be all right, Kasha? I don't like that we are split apart now,>> Yoey fretted. <<It would be much easier to kill or betray us when we aren't together.>>

<<I thought of that, too, Shalla. As our Amla has said, it isn't easy to trust. But I doubt if the Sweh'an would have left us if there was real danger. She would be foresworn if so.>>

<<I'd forgotten about that. I guess you're right.>>

IN A LOOSE FORMATION the warband set out across the indigo waters of the Shallow Sea. The wind and water were unthreatening for the moment at least; though he understood and shared Ogwy's fears for the crossing. Their delay in traveling here meant they had missed the early season's Calms when travel would have been more predictable. Now as the land and water heated with the warmer Sun Season, a storm could blow up out of nowhere in less than a sun-mark, making their passage unpredictable.

But for now at any rate, the yellow sun was a pleasant warmth at his back. Surrendering himself to the physical exercise Phillip allowed the symbiont's heightened senses to dominate their shared awareness as his body adjusted to the rhythm of the war leader's strokes. From one of the other boats a man lifted his voice in a rhythmic rowing chant that was quickly taken up by others in the surrounding boats.

Ogwy watched the Kashallan and the other Speir'dina for a time to make sure what they claimed wasn't just idle boasting. But no, they seemed to know at least the basics. They probably wouldn't tip them over with their stupidity. After a time his curiosity got the better of him, and he asked, "Speir'dina, your people already possess the power of the ancient magics. What could the Khutani offer that would make you want to come here and make a kashallan bond?"

Phillip barked a laugh. "In the end we had no choice but to come."

Glaring at him for such an uninformative answer, Ogwy muttered a curse and went back to his paddling. "I meant no offence, War Leader," Phillip hastily added. "We really didn't have a choice."

Overhearing them, Jebu asked. "Is the Khutani magic so strong that the Makers can bring people from another world to our own against their will, then?"

Gathering his thoughts before finally answering, Phillip said, "Men of the Real People, you are a wonder to me. Of all the peoples we've encountered since coming to Timorna, the Blue Stone Clan and the Begta seem to be the only ones willing to accept without question our Speir'dina assertion that we are from another world among the stars. Why is that?"

"Since you aren't from the Ghostlands, there is no other place you could have come from," Ogwy snarled. "The Ghostland Wizards say my people once wielded such weaponry as your Speir'dina use. They threaten us with their power constantly, though I've never seen them use the magic they claim to have."

To intimidate these primitive tribesmen with their spears and crossbows, the Ghostlanders wouldn't need to risk a demonstration of their power, the Kashallan thought. Whatever the wizards managed to salvage from their old technology would have to be carefully hoarded—as would their Speir'dina weaponry soon enough.

Returning to Jebu's question, Phillip said, "I have no idea the extent of the makers' power, but in our case it wasn't necessary for them to bring us here against our will. The Speir'dina, like your people, are a tool-using species. Over the centuries we developed our tool making to the point where we could travel from world to world in enclosed flying boats we call 'space ships' in our language."

He waved a hand to the sky. "Out there are many worlds where intelligent species live. And among them is a coalition of peoples on many worlds. In our language we call that alliance 'The Galactic Union.'

"The other kashallan you met is from a different planet than my home and Armachd Chang is from another planet within the Union. We travel from one world to another through the blackness of the Void.

"When our ship flew near Timorna we were fleeing a terrible war with another people not part of our alliance. Our ship was overcrowded with refugees fleeing the conflict on their planet. Unfortunately the ship was damaged during our escape.

"When we arrived near Timorna our technology—magics told us that we could survive on this world until the repairs were completed on our ship and we could go back to the Union. Many people were sent down to the surface of this world while others remained on our ship to repair the damage."

"It was said at the council that the Khutani brought your people here with their magic. Now you tell us you came here on your own. So your story is nothing but lies to fool us into making this hated agreement with you, Khutani." Another warrior said angrily.

Before Yoey could answer that accusation with an angry response of its own, Phillip said, "It's true we managed to find our way here in our ship, but I have never asked if the Makers had a hand in guiding us to this world and shielding us for a time from our enemy once we arrived.

"My kinsman, Dunnagh-Tani would know more about that. He was the first among us to make a kashallan bond; and I believe he was contacted in his dreams by them and agreed to the bonding before we landed. So in a way the Khutani did bring us here."

At the mention of Sairsa's kashallan-bound husband, Ogwy grimaced and put more effort into his paddling, making the others match his pace. Focusing on the task at hand, the crew fell silent.

Finally unable to resist, Jebu asked, "What happened to your boat? Once your kinsman was taken to the Khutani, why didn't the rest of you leave? Surely your home among the stars has many things to offer that Timorna can't give."

"You're right, Warrior, my home was a beautiful world with many advantages, but we can't go back—any of us, even if our ship hadn't been destroyed by the enemy who followed and eventually found our wounded craft and destroyed it. Nor could we go back to our old lives, even if a rescue ship were to find us someday."

"Why? Don't you want to?"

"Because of the kavay alignment we can never go back." At Jebu's puzzled look, Phillip pointed to the blue tinted water surrounding them and explained further. "The blue in the water, and our food and even the blue snows that come after the Sorins is caused by the kavay. This substance is unique to Timorna and once the alignment with it is complete, it changes the body in a way that makes it impossible to do without a constant source of kavay in your food and water.

The Kashallan smiled at the warrior's skeptical look. "It's true. When we first came everyone was very sick until the alignment was complete."

"Only in the most ancient of our writings," Ata Doyan said, "was there any mention of the alignment process. The Warlinga and Avairei the Dream-Chosen and a few of his kin met when they were captured, thought they were sick because of Begta blowgun poison, not a lack of kavay in their blood."

"Begta." Ogwy snorted in disgust at the mention of the Begta and their blowguns. He gave Masonja a baleful stare, promising a painful revenge for her people's aid in his warband's capture.

Her temper aroused now, Masonja blurted, "Starmans need go Sulas for bonding. Shaman help like Makers want. Begta got magics, too. Umwira mans no scare Begta."

The Kashallan touched her arm with a placating gesture. "Hush now, My dear, we all know the Begta have magic—and I know you in particular have Big Magic." Staring hard at Ogwy's scarred back his voice hardened as he warned, "No one is going to hurt the Begta or anyone else in this new alliance. Isn't that so, War Leader?"

Ogwy grunted a noncommittal response and continued to push the pace of his paddling.

"Even your people are aligned with the kavay—though I'm sure your wizards don't like to admit it," Yoey said. "All life on Timorna is dependent on the Khutani-created substance of kavay that protects us from the poisons left after the old wars."

<<Yoey,>> Phillip warned. <<Stop trying to provoke them.>>

Ignoring the symbiont's last salvo, the crew fell silent, straining to keep up. Though Ogwy set a fast pace, the warband after a Sorin Season of hardship couldn't maintain it for too long. When they resumed a more reasonable stroke, Phillip asked, "How much do your elders and wizards remember of the old days before the Great Wars?"

Ogwy shrugged. "Much more than a warrior like me. That kind of knowledge is a closely guarded secret. Only when a man has spent much time in the Holy Places to gain power would he be allowed such teachings."

"Provided he survives the painful mutations, of course," Yoey added.

Behind him the kashallan heard angry muttering from some of the warriors and glanced over his shoulder. "What? You don't think we know?" Yoey said. "I have encoded memories of this beautiful world. I know what Timorna was like. Your 'Holy Places' are really just dumping grounds for the old destructive weaponry. The things buried there were meant to kill life not bless it. The power gained by exposure to them comes at a terrible cost to your people."

"A cost willingly paid by our Wizards if it means protection from Khutani Demons sent to kill us to the last child!" Ogwy shouted.

<<Yoey,>> Phillip warned , having a pretty good idea where the symbiont was heading with this. Having to deal with centuries of entrenched hatred on both sides was going to be challenging, Phillip thought privately. <<The alliance is too new and fragile to be blaming anyone for the destruction of Timorna. This is pointless right now, Shalla. Please stop.>>

<<Sorry, Kasha, you're right.>>

"And as my parent has already told you, Ogwy," Phillip said in a quiet voice, "What was done to your people in the past was a mistake. That is why it offered you and any clan of the People who will join us, a new home in the land on the east side of the Shallow Sea where it claims dominion."

Chapter Two

They were far out into the indigo water now both shorelines only thin ribbons of purple on the east and west horizons. No storm clouds were looming, but he shared the war leader's desire for haste in the crossing. The weather at this time of year was unpredictable.

Tentacles extended, the Kashallan trailed a hand through the dark water and smiled at the wealth of information flooding his senses. Bringing his hand to his lips, he tasted its faint saltiness upon his tongue and then reluctantly resumed his paddling. The Shallow Sea was alive with life—and possibilities.

<<We will have to come back here someday, Kasha, there is so much here to taste and savor. Do you think our Amla will let us?>> Yoey asked.

<<Perhaps, Shalla, I agree with you, so much to study.>>

Sometime later noticing the western peaks disappearing into another fog bank, he asked, "How much longer till we reach the beaches of your home, War Leader? I smell no storm on the wind, but the afternoon fog is coming in to hide the land again. Wil that make it difficult for you to find a safe place to beach the boats?"

"It won't be long," Ogwy said. "The current is with us now. We will be there before the light dies and the fog thickens too much to blind us."

"That's good to know. Is all this stretch of coast Blue Stone territory?"

"No, not all this stretch of the coast is claimed by the Blue Stone Clan," Jebu supplied, "but others are allies and kin. If we land on a Sand Mountain or Bitter Water Clan's beach we offer them tribute for their 'hospitality.'"

"Mm, I see. What kind of tribute are we speaking of?"

Showing his long canines Jebu grinned. "Food if we have extra, otherwise we give our brothers slaves." His grin widening he motioned to Ata Doyan huddled among their few belongings. "We have no extra food so maybe we give them the priest—or maybe you, Khutani."

Displaying his own sharp triangular teeth, the Kashallan smiled. "That would be most unwise, Warrior. Though I carry no crossbow or spear I am not defenseless. Have you heard of the Black Kavay, Man of the Real People?"

"Enough of this stupid talk, Jebu," Ogwy snarled. "I can still see through the mist the cliff of blue stone that marks our boundary. We will be within our own territory when we land. I am War Leader here and I decide about tribute needed. So shut up and paddle, mewling slave."

Jebu grumbled. "I was only joking, War Leader."

"No more talk, paddle!"

IT WAS AS OGWY PREDICTED. As they came near a rocky beach, a large cliff speckled with patches of turquoise stone loomed up through the lavender mists on the shore ahead of them.

"A Blue Stone boundary?" Phillip asked.

Ogwy nodded without looking round. Steering their craft to run parallel to the cliff, he signaled for the boats to stay in deeper water to avoid the jagged dark rocks poking out of the surf at its base.

Phillip-Yoey laid his paddle across the gunwale and allowed his hand to trail in the dark water beside him. A short time ago as they neared the coast he'd become aware of a school of Dhuura swimming up from the depths for an evening feed. It would be nice to have something fresh and hot for their meal tonight.

Keeping his hand in the water with tentacles extended he savored the wealth of tastes available to him with his Khutani-heightened senses. <<Can we go down to them, Kasha? We're hungry,>>Yoey begged.

<<If you detect no Leongon or other predators hunting nearby, I think we can. And maybe the others would like a good meal, too. I think I saw someone loading a couple nets into one of the boats when we left.>>

<<Yes, there's a small one in the boat where Armachd Chang paddles.>>

Removing his hand from the water Phillip untied his kilt and allowed it to drop to the bench. The black knife he secured tightly in the sheath on the belt at his waist. Careful not to tip the craft unnecessarily, he stood.

The shift in the boat made Ogwy turn with a growled curse. "What are you doing, stupid Khutani!"

Phillip smiled showing lots of teeth. "Why, I'm going hunting. There's a school of Dhuura rising to feed nearly directly below us. Wouldn't you like fresh meat for our evening meal, War Leader?"

"They are too deep. We can't catch them now. Sit down and pick up your paddle."

"Too deep for your spears, true, but not too deep for a kashallan to hunt." Without giving Ogwy further time to argue, he dove into the indigo water. As he ducked below the surface he heard someone shout, "Where are you going, Khutani? Are you afraid? Can you swim all the way back to the Big Swamp?"

Actually he probably could, he thought privately, if he had to. Though it would be a dangerous undertaking for a lone swimmer—even a Khutani. The Shallow Sea like the Swamp had many predators.

Surfacing a short time later he swam over to Noi's boat and called up. "Noi, lend me that net I saw you pack in your boat. There are Dhuura nearby. I want to catch some for our meal tonight."

"No! They are too deep," Noi said, echoing his war leader's objection.

"Did everybody get stupid when you got into these boats? He is half Khutani. He can breathe underwater." Timma cried. Then without waiting for Noi's permission Timma picked up the bundled net at his feet and pushed it over the side to the waiting Kashallan.

Phillip gathered the net, allowing it to unfold behind him. Hopefully it wouldn't be too big for him to manage. As he was about to submerge, Noi shouted, "We won't wait for you, Khutani. So what will you do with all this food you are catching for us, hmm?"

"I will bring my catch to the beach on the other side of the point. That's where Ogwy plans to land, isn't it?"

"Yes, but—" the Kashallan ignored further protests and submerged, leaving the Umwira to stare at an empty patch of water.

As Noi picked up his paddle and shouted for his crew to get moving so they wouldn't be left behind, he gave Timma an angry scowl. "If he doesn't come back or loses my property, Priest, I will take that black Speir'dina knife at your waist in payment," he growled.

"You may try, Warrior." Timma shot back.

"Enough, Student!" Chang said. "You should have waited for permission, so if the net is lost you will forfeit the blade." At Timma's horrified expression he nodded. "A warrior must never allow his emotions to rule his words and deeds."

Then with a glance at Noi, he said, "My family were fishermen on my home world. I know to make such a net and keep it free of damage takes skill and many sun-marks of labor. I understand why you would value it so highly." then Chang's expression softened and he said, "But never fear, Young Timma, your knife is safe—this time. The Kashallan will do exactly as he said. He will return with fresh meat for our evening meal."

Giving him a noncommittal grunt, Noi went back to paddling. A while later he asked, "So, was this Speir'dina man who hosts the symbiont once a man of the sea, too?"

Chang laughed. "Dr Singey? No he was not."

"What was he then?" another man asked.

Chang paddled, thinking. At last he said, "Dr Singey was what we call, in our language, a scientist. He was...like one of your wizards maybe. I don't know what other word to use to describe him."

"And a healer, too," Timma chimed in. "Doctor Bennett told me he studied many years to become a healer among your people."

"That is also true, Student," Chang agreed.

Noi and his crew seemed impressed in spite of themselves, Chang thought privately. Well, that was all for the best. They might need it in the days to come.

FEELING THE COOL DARK water caress his body, the Kashallan dove ever deeper. The water like a tropical sea back home was clear, its unclouded surface due to the lack of pigmentation in the microscopic sea life immersed within it. The darkness from the surface he had observed was only an illusion coming up from its depths. The planet's weaker sun had already disappeared in the evening fog banks so Phillip's visual perception was limited, but Yoey's keener senses of smell, taste and hearing increased to dominate their bond in this watery world that was its natural home.

For a time he gave little thought to the task at hand just enjoying the freedom of movement this watery realm gave him and listening to the song of the Sea and the creatures dwelling within. He swam and danced to its wild rhythm.

The Dhuura were not exactly fish as a human would see them. Created for the Timornan environment, they looked more like a creature part frog and part shellfish, Phillip thought. They had a wide mouth and a frog's strong back legs for swimming but, they also grew a hard shell that increased in thickness over the Sun Season. Inside their shells they spent the Sorins buried on the sea bottom. With the Renewal of warmer weather the Dhuura abandoned their shells to swim free and begin the cycle again.

Floating lazily toward the surface after a particularly deep dive, he felt the Dhuura singing to him the joyous song of their feeding frenzy. The Nagril, the tiny, nearly transparent blue shrimp-like creatures populating this ocean in their billions were here to offer themselves so that others could live.

As he began killing them and pushing them into the big carry net, Phillip inwardly laughed. And now the Dhuura in turn would give up their lives to feed him and those waiting on shore for his return. Thinking of Dunnagh's Caldoni teaching about the Circle of life, he had to marvel at how different he was now than the arrogant rich prick he'd been before coming to this world.

Engrossed in his hunt the Kashallan was unaware of the others' approach till a sharp nip to his backside caused him to jerk, the opening of the carry net suddenly spilling wide and releasing some of his catch.

A sinewy body glided between his legs its sleek grey head rising to look him in the eye. There was a chorus of amused laughter in his mind as a few of the older adults from the Wild Pool Kindred circled and snapped up the Dhuura now floating free. <<All grown up, how nice of you to hunt for us now.>> another burst of squeals and laughter echoed their joking words.

In spite of himself Phillip-Yoey couldn't help smiling. He knew he'd been careless just now and that lapse could have cost him his life, but it was good to see them. Tentacles extended, Yoey brushed their tips over a smooth rubbery back and dripped its surprise and joy into the surrounding water. <<K'amsi it is so good to taste you. But what are you doing here?>>

<<Tasting you, what else?>> came the gurgling laughter again.

The Kashallan frowned. <<Let me rephrase that; *why* are you here?>>

<<To watch over you and keep you safe, Foolish Child,>> came a deep-voiced reply from Ro, Maker Tinguss's oldest descendant. The Khutani gave his shoulder a painful nip as it came up from the depths to coil itself around his body.

<<A task, I might add that might prove to be more difficult than our parent anticipated when it charged us with your safety. Why are *you* swimming these waters alone, Little One? Surely you must know how dangerous this is.>>

The Kashallan leaned his head on Ro's neck and murmured his agreement. His shoulder hurt but, the punishment was well earned. In spite of that, it was good to see them. <<We wanted fresh meat, K'amsi. And we were curious to explore and taste new things—and we forgot.>> Yoey said.

<<Forgot eh? See that you don't forget this then.>> Ro nipped his shoulder again. Then, deciding it had made its point the big Khutani nuzzled him and brushed its mouth tentacles over his face in a tender gesture of affection. The Kashallan relaxed, returning the love with his own tentacles extended, as the Khutani carried him into the depths.

<<We will let the cousins finish your hunt while you tell me what has been happening above,>> Ro said.

Chapter Three

Nearing the sheltered cove where Ogwy had chosen to come ashore, the Kashallan tasted trouble brewing like a storm cloud the moment he popped his head out of the water. Staring at the beach he could see several groups of people squaring off as if to fight. Ogwy, his brother Lubwey and some of the Blue Stone warriors were shouting and gesticulating angrily at a group of unknown Clan warriors facing them.

Nearby Ata Doyan and Masonja huddled, Timma, the two Speir'dina armachda and the rest of Ogwy's warriors standing guard around them with weapons ready for a fight.

<<Trouble already with them? My power isn't as strong as our Amla Tinguss, but I will be with you to help as best I can,>> Ro promised. <<We will follow and keep a link with you until our Amla returns.>>

<<Thank you, K'amsi Ro. That does ease my mind a bit,>> the Kashallan confessed.

With the help of the pod's young hunters, Phillip-Yoey was able to pull the heavy net into the shallows near the beach. As he rose, a dark figure dripping with seafoam, there was a shout from one of the strangers posted as sentry on the slope above. The arguing men fell silent turning to stare.

Recognizing him, Noi and a couple Blue Stone men hurried over to help with the net. Their eyes widened as they saw the bounty he had brought them.

"We should keep you to hunt for us all the time," Noi joked.

Phillip-Yoey laughed. "I had a little help from my cousins," he admitted, motioning with his chin to the sleek grey bodies now disappearing beneath the waves.

Noi hissed, his mouth twisting into an angry snarl. "Khutani in our territory! They dare much."

"We are your allies now, Noi," the kashallan reminded him. "Why shouldn't they swim here?"

"Did you call them?"

"I had no idea they were following until now, but I guess like any parent the Maker is worried about me," Phillip-Yoey confessed.

Noi grunted and motioned to lift the net over the sand and rocks at the water line. "I see we have company," Phillip said, changing the subject.

"Thieving Scum! They say this is their land now," Noi snarled in a low voice, so only he could hear. "They want us to pay them tribute. They say they will take the two priests as payment." Seeing Masonja approaching with the Kashallan's clothing, he added, "We can keep the Begta woman, if we want."

Masonja handed him his kilt as he stepped out of the surf. "Masonja glad Kashallan come back now," she said quietly.

Phillip took the kilt, but instead of taking the time to pleat it around his waist he left it folded and flung it over his shoulder. "Thank you, Masonja."

"Umwira mans—"

"I know. Noi just told me. I'll talk to them." Noticing the newcomers' women and children huddled among the rocks not far up the beach, he pointed with his chin to them and said, "Masonja, those people look hungry. Will you go over there and tell them I will gladly share my catch with them if the children and old people need a good meal."

She studied him for a long moment, her eyes widening at the angry bite marks on his shoulder. Her mouth twitched recognizing their significance.

"Yes," he said, answering her unvoiced question. "Some of my older siblings are near—and the eldest wasn't happy with me for hunting alone."

Masonja's eyes gleamed with amusement, but she only nodded. "Masonja will ask Umwira womans."

"Good." The Kashallan sighed. "And now I guess I'd better see to this other matter."

<<I am still with you, Little One,>> Ro said into his mind as he headed over to the waiting men.

Scarred with tribal markings and bone piercings, they were a fierce-looking bunch. Like the Blue Stone Clan, these people were a blend of the mutant descendants of the original Timornans and the Khutani-bred peoples they had taken as wives and slaves over the centuries.

As he passed, Armachd Chang with a hand near his sidearm fell into step behind him. "I'm here if you need me, Kashallan-Phillip," Chang murmured in Galactic Standard.

"Thank you, Armachd. But I hope it won't be necessary to resort to violence," he said in the same language. Then as they drew near the silent group, he switched languages and said to Ogwy, "I see we have guests, War Leader, it is a good thing my hunt was so successful. I've brought back plenty of Dhuura meat to share."

Ogwy scowled, but offered no other response. After a long silence that was growing painful the Kashallan said, "I'm Phillip-Yoey and this is one of my warriors, Armachd Chang. Somebody care to introduce me to the newcomers to Blue Stone Territory?"

"Blue Stone Territory, eh?" A tall well-muscled male with fur as dark as Phillip's own ebony skin folded his arms across his chest and snorted. "I am War leader Tesulu, and this is Sand Mountain land now. The Blue Stone People are all dead—or ran away like cowardly scum. You trespass, Stranger." Noticing the Warlinga-like death strand around Phillip's neck his eyes widened and he growled. "Who are you?"

"I am Phillip-Yoey as I told you, War Leader Tesulu. And as for the Blue Stone People being all dead, War Leader? I see several brave warriors of that Clan here with us right now."

That statement earned him another derisive snort from the man.

"There is no dishonor in fleeing a superior force when there is no chance of surviving," Lubwey said. "By the fact that you are here, Sand Mountain Warriors, tells me you, too, did your own share of running and hiding from the Ghostlanders over the Sorins, if we are talking truth here."

"The Ghostlanders favored us with their 'special' attentions," Ogwy snarled. "We had no choice. We lost our wizard, and so many warriors—"

"Where are your women and children, Begta Filth?" a thin elder with a dog-like snout and grey mane worn in a ragged tail down his back demanded. "I see only a warband out for plunder and a few strange mutant slaves. So I ask again, where are your women and children?"

The angry muttering, that had been going on in the background while the leaders talked, suddenly stopped. The warriors looked around as if realizing for the first time the women's absence.

After a long silence, Lubwey finally said, "They are safe and no concern of yours, Wizard Qwasigara."

The wizard laughed, but there was no mirth in the sound. "Where are they, Warrior?" He pointed with a clawed hand eastward across the Shallow Sea. "Over there? In the Khutani Demons' land? Why, what are they doing over there? Did you lose them? Or did you let this one," he pointed with his lips to the kashallan, "and his kin take them away from you? Are they slaves—are you all Khutani slaves now?"

"No we aren't Khutani slaves!" Ogwy shouted his temper sparking at last. "We are their blood-sworn allies—we had no choice."

"Had no choice," Qwasigara sneered. "So it is true what the Ghostlanders' claim. One of the clans of Real People broke faith with the Ancient Covenant and betrayed us to the Hated Enemy. We should kill you—all of you right now!"

"Not true!" Lubwey cried. "We betrayed no one. Yes, we fled to the Big Swamp after our grandfather Wizard Zeta was killed, but a Sweh'an Demon was the one who sheltered us both from the Khutani and the Ghostlanders. The payment for her protection was our alliance with the Khutani."

A Sweh'an Demon that too shocked them. "The host for the demon is my kinswoman," Phillip said into the silence. "I'm not sure what Tess-weh sees in our future that she offered her protection to the hunted Blue Stone People—she doesn't always tell us—I just trust it was important. The Demon has been sworn to our service."

"Sworn to who—you—this warband?" Qwasigara challenged.

Phillip's lip twitched into something not quite a smile. "That answer is—complicated." Addressing the wizard directly, he said, "Elder, it's obvious to me that you have seen my bondmate, the Khutani symbiont nesting in my physical body, but have you looked close enough to see the Guardian that is at present coiled about my spirit body, too?"

"I see well enough, Khutani. What magic did you promise these cowards that they would be foresworn?"

Thickening its form so that the warriors could see it, too. Ro leaned over Phillips shoulder its yellow eyes glaring at the wizard. Using Phillip's mouth it said in a deep voice very different from the kashallan's, "No one here is a slave or a traitor. We offered the Blue Stone Clan protection and an alliance because we share a common enemy now, the Ghostland Wizards."

"And what of these mutants that can host your foul children, Khutani, "A Sand Mountain warrior growled. "Where did they come from, eh? What did you promise one of the Ancients to breed you a host?"

"The Speir'dina aren't mutants," Jebu shot back. "Use your eyes; look at the weapons he carries." He pointed to Chang. "This one and the woman warrior over there carry knives made of metal, METAL! And the other object at his hip, has the power of the old technology, like is told about in the ancient stories."

"He also says that he and his people were guided here from their home among the stars by the Khutani to host their symbiont children," Lubwey added.

"What the war leader claims is truth," Ro said. "There are many worlds within the Starry River that have sentient life. We have seen them in our Dream conjurings. We called to this Chosen's kinsman and he agreed to come to us and make a kashallan bond. Through our link with this child and other Speir'dina who have chosen to make a kashallan union, we are no longer confined to our watery home. And through their eyes we don't like what we see, Wizard, so have a care how you annoy me."

"Big words, but can you prove it?" Qwasigara snarled.

"Chang," Phillip said in Galactic Standard. "Can you give them a small demonstration of your weaponry?"

"Certainly, Sir." Then as fast as a striking snake, Chang drew his sidearm and vaporized a large boulder near the Sand Mountain War Leader. Already aware of the power of Speir'dina weapons Ogwy smirked as Tesulu jumped high into the air.

"Do you need more proof, Wizard, War Leader?" the Kashallan asked quietly.

When he had recovered his composure, Qwasigara demanded, "If you control such power, Khutani why are we still alive? Why not kill us all and be done with it? Does it please you to toy with us before you strike?"

"No one is playing with you, Elder," the kashallan said. "Among my Speir'dina kin there is a saying, 'The enemy of my enemy is my friend.' I would like to think that at some time in the future both our peoples could set aside ancient hatreds and become friends.

“As my parent, the Maker Tinguss, has told our new Blue Stone allies, it feels a great wrong was done to your people in the past. It has offered this clan of the Real People sanctuary for that reason. Speir’dina and Blue Stone people are bound by both blood Oath and kinship now.”

Rounding on Ogwy, Tesulu growled, “Kinship? What does this foul creature mean? Has one of you traitors agreed to host a Khutani symbiont in exchange for this *sanctuary*?”

“No, we have not,” Lubwey snapped. “What he means is that to seal our alliance, and assure ourselves the Hated Enemy would keep their word, we gave my sister Yannan in marriage to the biggest and strongest warrior in this kashallan’s warband.”

“Yannan, the woman Wizard Zeta promised to me,” Tesulu said.

“Zeta is dead,” Ogwy said and smirked. “Nothing was said to me about a marriage contract. If the old witch knew, she didn’t tell me.”

After that revelation Ro studied Tesulu carefully through the Kashallan’s eyes. <<I wonder if we are going to have trouble with him over the woman? I hope not. He looks like a capable fighter. It would be a shame to have to kill him.>>

Phillip shivered, but agreed.

“If you have given these people sanctuary, Khutani, Why come back?” Qwasigara demanded. “This makes no sense to me. What do you hope to gain here?”

“We have come to the western shore seeking allies in our war against the Ghostland Wizards. For what they’ve done to the western clans, my Speir’dina People and many others,” The Kashallan said, “we hope to create a great alliance that will defeat them once and for all.”

Tesulu glanced around at the diminished Blue Stone warband and
The few Speir’dina accompanying them. He laughed. “I’m sure Wizard Barak is shaking with fear at the thought of your vengeance.”

“He may well be,” Phillip said, before Ogwy could answer with a blistering remark. “I believe the Sweh’an let him know of her presence.”

“Hah! I see no demon here. How do we know there really is one.”

"I don't care if you believe us," Lubwey shouted, his fists clinched in frustration. "That isn't the important question here."

"Will you join us in our fight against the Ghostlanders?" the Kashallan said. That's the question needing an answer from you Sand Mountain Warriors. We need your help to gather the other clans who seek vengeance for their dead at the claws of Ghostland monsters."

"Vengeance. A worthy plan when we are strong again," Tesulu growled, "but as you have guessed; we are in no condition to take on the Ghostlanders at present."

"I doubt if they will give you a chance to recover," Chang said. "I wouldn't in their place. Seasoned warriors with wrongs to settle, they will finish you off as soon as time permits."

"True as individual clans already ravaged by war you don't have much of a chance right now and that's why we've come. We offer alliance you aren't alone," the Kashallan said. "Other warriors in the Yeyen Banai Valley, Ticca and elsewhere seek revenge for their dead. They will be coming with us up into the Ghostlands."

"Warlinga Demons, no doubt." Qwasigara scoffed. "And what's to prevent them from attacking us when the Ghostlanders are defeated—if they can be defeated?"

"And what's to prevent you from doing the same thing to us," Phillip countered. "Trust in each other's blood-sworn word of honor is all we both would have." Phillip glanced from one grim face to another. "As a newcomer to this world I haven't endured long years of war and hatred.

"But I and some of my kin were slaves to a brutal and sadistic Warlinga K'San who killed and ate some of us when we first came here. What we endured was nothing I could have dreamed was possible in my old pampered life. I have tasted some of the bitter hardships Timorna can offer. I have few illusions left, but I as a kashallan have pledged my life in service to all the peoples of Timorna—and that includes the Western Clans if they so choose."

"Pretty words—" Qwasigara broke off, his attention snagged by the approach of Masonja, Moraga and an unknown Sand Mountain woman following reluctantly in their wake.

Turning the Kashallan saw them and smiled. "Masonja, what is it?"

Masonja placed her strong hands on her hips and glared, ignoring the scowls directed her way for the interruption. "Mans make too much talk. Food is done. Babies are hungry." She pointed with her jaw to the Umwira woman hanging back with downcast eyes. "Woman say no can feed babies till mans come. So mans come. No more talk."

Eyes popping with rage, Qwasigara snarled, "Insolent Begta Filth! How dare you interrupt a men's council—" He raised his hand as if to strike her down with his power

Ro becoming visible once more coiled around him, Phillip-Yoey warned, "I wouldn't do that if I were you, Wizard. If you touch my colleague, or anyone under my protection with your power," his eyes included the men of Ogwy's warband in that statement, "You will taste the power of *my* magics—Khutani and Speir'dina magic.

"Women are held in high regard among my Speir'dina people. We claim our descent through our mother's family line, not the father's as your people do," he said and looked directly at the woman trying to shrink back behind Moraga's bulk. "And for that reason they don't need any man's permission to do what is best for their children.

"I am the hunter who has brought food to this gathering. And it is me who decides that the women and children may eat whenever they so choose. If you have a problem with that; we can settle this here and now, Wizard, War Leader."

The two he name scowled, but chose not to press the matter. "Do as you like, Khutani. Feed them if you want," Tesulu grumbled.

The Kashallan laughed. "I would feed you, too. If you aren't too stiff-necked to eat with a hated Khutani like me, come have some Dhuura meat. I'm hungry and I'm sure your women are good cooks who will do you proud with the meal they have prepared for us."

Turning to follow Moraga, the Kashallan paused and looked back at the warriors. "We can continue this discussion as we eat with the women and children. Your choice."

Ogwy smirked and brushed past the wizard and his war leader. "We eat. Begta is right no more talk."

Chapter Four

Masonja led them away from the water up a winding trail to a sheltered hollow near the top of the cliff. A long narrow pit had been dug into the gravel there at some time in the past. At present a carpet of glowing rock smoked in its shallow trough. On top of the stones the Sand Mountain women were removing steaming purple seaweed wrapped bundles of cooked Dhuura meat. Nearby a cluster of big-eyed children watched the procedure hungrily.

Ata Doyan sat at a tiny fire, a cup of something in his hand. He seemed more relaxed as he watched the women as they cooked and did other camp chores. Timma was talking to a girl of about his own age with rich brown fur, a long golden mane and decidedly strong Avairei features. As the Kashallan and the others drew near she said something to Timma that made him laugh and toss his warrior's braid over his shoulder.

Walking beside him Chang scowled and muttered something under his breath that Phillip-Yoey didn't catch. Glancing out of the corner of his eye at Tesulu, he saw the warrior was watching the young people as well and wasn't any happier than Chang.

Sitting down beside Ata Doyan, the Kashallan noticed that he too was watching Timma. He and the girl had stepped away from the cooking pit and walked to a bunch of tall woody reed-like plants growing in a hollow up the slope. Timma was using his Speir'dina knife to cut stalks of the reeds while the girl gathered them into a bundle to bring back to the fire. Whatever they were talking about had their full attention. They hadn't yet noticed the newcomers' arrival.

When the laughing young people returned, Timma's eyes opened wide when he saw him sitting by the fire with Chang and the priest.

"Sensei, Holy One, I didn't see you come up. Niguiri and I were just," he dropped his bound reeds and motioned to the Sand Mountain girl to bring her bundle and lay it by the fire, "gathering more fuel for the night."

Hiding a smile Phillip agreed. "Yes, I can see that," he said. "That's very thoughtful of you to help her out."

With eyes lowered, Niguiri laid her bundle down then quickly retreated giving the kashallan a frightened look as she hurried away. Timma stared after her and would have followed, but Chang stopped him with a low-voiced command. Timma stared after her but took his place by the fire next to Chang.

Behind his lifted cup Doyan murmured so only the Kashallan could hear, "Our Timma is growing up. I think Ima Sagas should start looking for a wife for him when we get home."

Raising his own cup in acknowledgement, Phillip-Yoey nodded

The night closing in around them the evening meal was eaten in a tense atmosphere of mistrust. Blue Stone warriors and the kashallan's people at one fire, the Sand Mountain Clan huddled by another, each group quietly talking among themselves.

As they were laying out their bed rolls in preparation for sleep, Tesulu and one of his warriors approached the kashallan's fire. "Before your arrival we had word of a war council of the clans meeting soon. We will be leaving in a day or two. If you have more to say to us we will meet with you tomorrow when the sun is high." Without another word the Sand Mountain men stalked away into the night.

Watching their retreating backs Ogwy scowled. "Did you know about this war council?" Phillip asked.

Still staring out into the dark he shook his head. "No, I did not."

<<I wonder if, or when they were going to tell us about this meeting,>> Yoey said into Phillip's mind.

<<That is an interesting question, Shalla. And perhaps just as important, why tell us now?>>

Returning his attention to his companions around the fire he heard Ata Doyan say, "Is it normal for your people to gather at this time of year?"

Ogwy broke up some longer reeds and placed them on the dimming fire. With a hiss the new fuel caught and blazed with amber light. “No, it is not,” he finally admitted then laps back into a brooding silence.

“Our warbands would be—away right now,” Lubwey supplied. “Clan gatherings are usually later—just before the Sorin Storms come.”

“So this is a special meeting,” Chang mused. “Probably to see who has survived, and discuss what they plan to do about the Ghostlander’s attacks and betrayal.”

“I would welcome your thoughts on this matter, War Leader,” Phillip said into the silence. ”I can see advantages to attending. We can speak to more people than we could if we had to travel individually to so many clan territories. But I also foresee the danger to me personally—and to all of us.”

Lifting his lip to show his canines, Ogwy growled, “Do as you like, Khutani, but the Blue Stone Clan is going to this gathering with or without Sand Mountain as our allies. We have every right to be there; we’ve done nothing wrong.”

“So be it then,” the Kashallan agreed. “You haven’t done anything wrong by allying with us. We will come with you.”

“It would be a comfort to travel with the Sand Mountain People as our allies, though,” Moraga said glancing over to the arguing men by the Sand Mountain fire,

“Yes it would, Armachd,” Phillip agreed. “Hopefully we can convince them to join us tomorrow when we meet.”

A short time later as he lay curled in his Avairei cloak, the Kashallan noticed Ogwy arranging for some of his men to take turns on guard during the night. A wise precaution, he thought. He hadn’t tasted any of the Sand Mountain People and no one had sworn blood-oath to guarantee against treachery.

<<Have no fear, Little One,>> Ro said as he drifted near sleep. <<We watch, too.>>

THE DAY BROKE WARM and clear. With the ocean a siren’s call in his mind, the Kashallan rose early and headed for the beach. Noi and a few of the

Sand Mountain men were already by their canoes ready to launch a couple of their boats into the surf. Seeing him coming, Noi smiled and motioned him to his canoe. Phillip hurried over to help launch the boat.

"Ha," one of the Sand Mountain men cried. "Can't hunt on your own, Blue Stone; need your pet Khutani to help you?"

When they were settled and paddling out beyond the waves, he said, "I can't guarantee I can find a catch like I did yesterday but I will help as best I can."

Noi snorted and glanced at the Sand Mountain boat. "That would be good Khutani. Those Taba worms think they are such good sea-hunters that they can do better than we can even with your help."

Phillip tasted salt upon his tongue and felt a warmth on his face as Timorna's yellow sun cleared the purple mists shielding the eastern horizon. Trailing a hand in the water, he extended his tentacles to taste the wealth of stimuli available to the Khutani part of himself.

It wasn't long before Ro's colorless voice spoke into his mind. <<Hunting again, S'amsi? Come down to us and give me your news.>>

Checking to see that the Sand Mountain craft had disappeared behind the point, the kashallan reached for the net. "I'll be back," he said to Noi and tipped over the side.

In the blue depths he was soon enwrapped within the comforting swarm of his older cousins. <<Back again so soon, S'amsi? Shall we hunt for you again, Little One?>>

<<Hunt for him, Lazy Ones,>> Ro said, <<while I taste his news.>>

<<Be careful,>> Phillip-Yoey warned, <<A Sand Mountain canoe hunts nearby this morning and they haven't committed to the alliance.>>

<<How likely is that to happen?>> Ro asked as the Khutani enfolded him and drew him deeper into the inky depths.

<<We are to discuss that very thing today after our meal.>>

<<Mm, I would know your thoughts, Chosen. What is your assessment of these people?>>

Phillip took a moment before answering. <<As with the Blue Stone Clan, these people were hit hard by the Ghostlanders. The women and children especially appear to be suffering from malnutrition. They still have

their wizard with them, however, and their war leader is, I think quite fearless.>>

<<Hmm. If they still have their wizard that means one of two things. He is either too weak for the Ghostlanders to bother with, or he is extremely powerful and clever enough to evade their warbands and keep his people safe. Be careful of him, S'amsi,>> Ro warned. <<If he cannot be convinced to join us he will be a most dangerous enemy at our backs.>>

<<I am already aware of that, Elder. I will be careful,>> he promised. <<There is a war council planned soon slightly inland an a bit further north up the coast. It will be a good chance to talk to many more of the clan leaders. I hope before we go there to claim the Sand Mountain warriors as our allies.>>

<<Yes, that would be good—though its inland location troubles me. But you should go back now, Little One,>> Ro said as it swam towards the lighter water above.

Phillip looked around and spying Noi's canoe floating nearby he swam over to him, dragging the full net. Willing hands helped haul its heavy folds into the boat. Knowing his kin were still nearby the Kashallan remained in the water after the net was secured. Yoey still wanted a little time to play.

"Get in," Noi shouted. "We will beat the others back."

The Kashallan shook his head. "Go on in. I'll be along in a while."

As he started to swim away, Noi shouted, "Where are you going?"

"I'll meet you back at the beach. Don't worry." And without giving the warrior more time to argue, he slipped back beneath the waves.

Joining the cousins for a while he allowed himself to relax and play, the symbiont part of himself reveling in the familiar companionship of its kind. At last Phillip overruled his bondmate's pleasure and focused them back to the task at hand. <<K'amsi, can you help me do more hunting?>> Phillip asked the pod.

<<We can hunt, but you have no net now. How will you carry what we catch to the surface people?>>

<<As a gesture of good will I want to find the Sand Mountain boat and help the others with their hunt,>> he explained. <<Will you help me?>>

The pod twisted itself into a swirling grey knot everyone chattering at once. Finally they broke apart and dripped their agreement into the water between them. <<We see the wisdom in what you plan, Chosen. We will help you—this time. Come we will find the boat.>>

Grabbing on to a sleek grey body the Kashallan allowed it to pull him through the water at a much faster pace than he could have managed on his own. It didn't take them long to find the other canoe with its nets flung in the water slowly drifting on the swell.

So far the Sand Mountain boat hadn't managed to capture many sea creatures in their net's folds. Ordinarily this was probably a good spot. Phillip could taste the prey's essence in the depths, but he could also taste that several cruising Leongon, a Khutani created armored shark-like creature, had passed over this spot recently sending the Dhuura and other prey animals into hiding for the moment.

Popping his head out of the water near the bow of Tesulu's canoe, he said, "Several Leongon have just traveled these waters also hunting. The prey is deep and hidden in the rocks at the moment. Would you like some help flushing them into your net?"

For a long moment the men in the boat just stared, then with a sneer curling his lips one of the hunters said, "No we have no need of Khutani help."

"Really? Then you will be here a long time waiting for your prey," the kashallan snapped. "I know you plan to move on to the Red Rock Council Grounds tomorrow, by staying out here till evening do you hope to cancel our meeting with you today?"

Tesulu growled a curse. "No that was not our intent. We just don't want—or need help from you, Khutani Slimeworm."

In his middle the young symbiont writhed, its own anger starting to bubble. The host placed a consoling hand upon his bondmates coils. Refusing to be baited into an angry outburst, Phillip met Tesulu's eye and said in a calm voice. "I will not be drawn into an argument with your people and give you an easy excuse to cancel the upcoming meeting. Nor do I see this hunt as a competition.

"I can imagine how hard it would be to accept aid from a life-long enemy, but being a newcomer to this world I see only hungry people needing food and my help—nothing more. Now if you value your warriors' pride over your children's full bellies then so be it. I will follow the Blue Stone men back to the beach. I have told you the Dhuura and Sowika are hiding from the Leongon. It's up to you what you do with my information."

He waited just out of easy reach of their spears. Just as he was turning away, Tesulu called to him. "You are right, it isn't easy for us to accept your help. But you are also right; the children are hungry. What do you want us to do?"

The kashallan nodded. "All right, we will help. Hold the net wide and we will drive what we can into it."

"We?"

"Well, my older cousins actually. Alone I wouldn't be very good at this sort of thing," he admitted.

One of the men who hadn't been at their first meeting on the beach cursed and made a sign against evil. "Khutani here!"

The Kashallan pointed to the shoreline. "In spite of your claim that this is now yours that blue stone cliff says otherwise. And since we are now allies of the Blue Stone Clan me and my kin have every right to be here—maybe even more than you, Sand Mountain Man. Now get ready." Phillip ducked beneath the surface and dripped his call to the siblings waiting for him below.

With Khutani help it didn't take long for the net to grow heavy with squirming sea creatures. When the net was aboard he heard the men laughing about how busy the women were going to be drying their catch for the upcoming journey. Now in a good mood,. Tesulu motioned to the canoe. "Want to come back with us?"

The Kashallan smiled but shook his head. "It looks crowded up there and I have no wish to get my backside nipped by the Dhuura."

Tesulu laughed. "Suit yourself, Khutani."

"I'll be right behind you, never fear." Latching on to one of his escorts the Kashallan submerged and headed for the beach.

Chapter Five

After a hasty meal, the men of both factions gathered around a central fire. Up the slope the women and children were chattering contentedly as they erected racks over the long pit and began drying the day's catch. Cutting the Dhuura open to lay flat, the women laid them on loosely woven reed mats, which they placed atop the stick frames to cure in the hot air and smoke.

Never having seen such a process, Phillip watched with interest until Qwasigara rose and walked to the central fire. Carrying a carved bone from which several unknown objects dangled, he raised the wand and faced the barren rocky grey hills to the west. In a deep voice he began to chant in a powerful voice.

Repeating the chant and the wand waving he next faced south then continued around the circle in a counter clock-wise direction. Phillip could feel the hairs on the back of his neck rise as his Khutani heightened awareness traced the lines of power the wizard drew in the ether around them.

The enclosure of power he created was not as strong as the circle the Sweh'an had once made to confine and compel the Speir'dina to her will, but it *was* strong enough to threaten his Psy link with Ro and possibly keep out other spirit essences hovering nearby.

Frowning, the Kashallan wondered what exactly had been the old wizard's intent. Had he wanted to isolate him from Khutani intervention if there was treachery planned, or were these people more worried about Ghostland spying than they were letting on?

Finished with his invocation the wizard sat back on his haunches and glared across the circle at the Kashallan. There was a smug turn to his dog-like muzzle, the Kashallan thought. Phillip's eyes narrowed wondering what they were planning.

"We are listening," Qwasigara said into the silence. "Speak now and tell us what you have to say."

Unsure of the correct protocol for such a meeting the Kashallan held back, waiting for Ogwy or his brother to speak first. With a side-long glance at him, Ogwy stepped to the fire and picked up another carved bone lying nearby on the rocks and offered it to Sky and Ground in a reverent gesture. Still holding the bone he began to speak.

Everyone listened as he told them about the Ghostland attack, how their wizard had been tortured and killed and by combining their powers he and the old witch Hycla managed to deceive the enemy long enough so they could run to their canoes and escape across the Shallow Sea.

"But in spite of all our efforts Wizard Barak found us and even in the Khutani's own swamp he saw us and attacked."

Glaring at each Sand Mountain man he choked on the strength of his emotions as he continued. "You almost had your wish, Sand Mountain, for we would have all died that day if the Demon hadn't shown up to weave her protection around us.

"When the Ghostland wizard was gone, she guided us to the caves near the big lake called Ticca. We crawled into their dark places and starved, managing to stay barely alive throughout the storms."

Breaking protocol, Tesulu asked by interrupting the one holding the Speaker Bone, "Did the Khutani or the Warlinga living in the keep know that the demon hid you?"

Ogwy turned to Phillip-Yoey. He shook his head. "The people, and I assume the Khutani living at Ticca had their own battles with Barak and his minions during the Sorins to occupy them. I don't think Tess-weh told anyone about the Blue Stone Clan being so near the keep. But my parent, the Maker Tinguss lives in the Great Swamp itself. I know only what the Speir'dina hunt leader told me when he caught up to the Blue Stone Clan before they had time to reach their boats."

Tesulu snorted showing his disgust.

"We had our women, children, and old people with us. They were weak; we couldn't move fast," Ogwy cried angrily.

"Could you have done any better?" Lubwey challenged. "I think not if you had been in our place."

Tesulu glared, refusing to answer further.

Reaching for the bone Ogwy reluctantly gave him, Qwasigara fixed his eye on the Kashallan and asked, "If you live in the Big Swamp, Khutani, the war leader's story doesn't explain your presence if it was a hunting pack from the keep that found the Blue Stone People. Why are you here?"

Phillip-Yoey shrugged. "I am here because Tess-weh came to fetch me. She said that it was important. I trusted that she saw something in our future that made my presence necessary."

"Necessary." The wizard curled his lip showing his canines. "And what of this alliance, tell us more about it?"

"I can only tell you the basics at this time. What I do know is that all over Timorna clans are gathering and uniting to make war against the Ghostlanders. After what I was told happened at Ticca, another kashallan went with a hunting pack of Warlinga into the Yeyen Banai Valley seeking support for our alliance. The Real People and the Khutani-bred peoples all face a common enemy now, the Ghostland wizards and their monstrous warbands.

"If any of us try to fight them alone we will surely fail, but together we have a chance. That is why I am here, Wizard. It wasn't easy for my parent to send me with these warriors into the heart of our traditional enemy's lands."

He waved his hand at Chang and the blue stone men. "Even with Speir'dina weaponry and these brave warriors at my back I am vulnerable and may not survive this journey, as I'm sure you know. But the Maker knew that only a grand gesture of trust would be needed to convince your people of our sincerity. We need you, and you need us if you want to reclaim your honor and avenge your dead."

"Pretty words, but will the Warlinga in the Yeyen Banai feel the same?" Tesulu said. "Will they see us as allies or will they follow their breeding and turn on us the first chance they get?"

"Trust," Phillip said into the silence. "No matter how hard it is, we have to trust each other. If we fight amongst ourselves we will do the Ghostlander's work for them. I see no other way to achieve our goal."

Qwasigara grunted and then stood, the other Sand Mountain men rising with him. "We will discuss this offer among ourselves and come back to council with you before the sun has reached the western hills." Turning his back on the Blue Stone Men and the Kashallan the wizard released his circle of power and the Sand Mountain men walked to a sheltered place further down the beach.

Phillip let out the breath he had been unconsciously holding. <<What do you think they will do?>> the worried symbiont asked.

<<We shall have to wait and see, Shalla,>> he said.

Voicing Yoey's anxiety Lubwey asked the men still sitting at the fire, "What will we do if they refuse our offer?"

Phillip placed a few reeds on the flames and sat back. "We can go back across the Shallow Sea and meet up with our other allies—or"

"We go to the Red Rock War Council," Ogwy snarled. "These Begta slaves won't scare us away or set the other clans against us. We are Blue Stone People. We've betrayed no one; this is our land and we have a right to be there at the war council." Grumbling to himself Ogwy rose and stalked off down the beach in the opposite direction.

Phillip sighed and looked at the concerned faces of his armachda guards. "I guess we are going to this Red Rock War Council."

"It won't be easy to protect you, Sir, if the Sand Mountain men don't join us," Chang said.

The kashallan rose as well. "Then we had better hope that they choose to join the alliance. Now if you will excuse me I'm going to take a nap. I had a long swim this morning."

THE KASHALLAN AWAKENED with the afternoon's chill. Chewing on a piece of dried meat from his pack he wandered over to the main fire where Chang and Moraga seemed to be conducting a single combat lesson. Timma and a few of the Blue Stone warriors had taken their places on a level stretch of the shore not far from the center fire. His mouth twitched into a secretive smile as he noticed Tesulu and several of his warriors observing discretely from among the rocks just up the slope. Niguiri and some of the women had paused in their work to watch as well.

As he drew near Morag and Lubwey were just finishing a vigorous practice with their spears, holding them like a quarter staff as he'd seen Dunnagh use his, when he fought Gormach up on the mesa.

Now a weaponless Chang and Timma stepped into the circle of watchers. They bowed to one another, and then Chang barked a command and they began.

It had been a while since Phillip had seen them practice the traditional unarmed combat that Chang was noted for. Timma had worked hard, his movements almost as swift and graceful as his mentor's. They flowed through a controlled dance of kick, block, punch, thrust and parry.

At last they stopped and bowed to each other. But instead of leaving the circle Chang drew his Speir'dina knife and with a yell charged his student. Timma, without wavering flowed into the defensive moves needed to block his teacher's attack, then he went on the offensive, finally managing to disarm his mentor. Chang spoke to him and demonstrated where his defense and attack could use some improvement, then he put away his dagger and threw an arm over the boy's shoulder as they walked down to the water to wash and cool off.

That demo was nicely done, Phillip realized. It had been a subtle but calculated show to impress and perhaps sway the Sand Mountain bunch to their cause. When they were first thrown together during their slavery he hadn't liked Chang much. He was afraid of him, actually, for Chang like most of Dunnagh's armachda blamed him for their capture. How things had changed for all of them, he thought ruefully. As he got to know the man better on this journey he was starting to appreciate him and rely on his cool professionalism under stress.

After a hurried meal the two factions met once more around the central fire. Invocations to the Unseen Ones completed Tesulu picked up the speaker's bone wand and addressed the Kashallan and the Blue Stone Warriors. "We will accept your offer of an alliance and together we will war against our common enemy in the Ghostlands."

The kashallan breathed an inward sigh of relief. But the war leader wasn't finished. His next words left him more uncertain as to the outcome of their proposal.

Tesulu continued, "Like our Blue Stone brothers we feel that more than a blood oath is needed to secure this alliance and be sure it will last."

The Kashallan leaned forward, resting his arms atop his crossed legs. They were up to something but he couldn't puzzle it out as of yet. "And that assurance would be?"

"A marriage of your warrior," Tesulu pointed to Chang, "with my niece Niguiri." He motioned imperiously to an older woman who reluctantly pushed the girl into the circle of staring men. "As you can all see she is young and good looking. She can bear many healthy children. With this marriage we will seal our alliance," Tesulu concluded folding his upper set of arms across his scarred chest.

At the mention of a marriage Phillip glanced at Chang. For just a moment he saw the man's startled look, quickly masked by a cool facade of indifference.

<<I knew they were up to something, but this?>> Yoey said.

<<We should have expected something like this after Tarla's wedding, Shalla>> Phillip said.<<The old witch even told us how important marriage alliances are to these people.>>

<<I guess Chang's demo this afternoon impressed them too much.>>

<<Mm, maybe, but I won't force him to do it. Moraga has told me he is still grieving the loss of his wife and young son back home.>>

The Kashallan had opened his mouth to object, when Ogwy sprang to his feet his face contorted with rage. "Begta Filth I see your treachery. Do you hope to claim the Speir'dina and his weaponry for your warband? Well you can't have him!"

"Why not?" Tesulu shot back. "Is it because you have no control over your sister's husband that you oppose the union?"

"If you want a marriage to seal the alliance I will marry the girl," Ogwy shouted. "My wife died in childbirth. I have no wife or son. I will do it."

Phillip caught the note of anguish in the man's voice. In spite of the demon's efforts to release him from the magical compulsion that bound him to Sairsa, was he still grieving over the loss of her? That might go a long way to explain his moody silences and angry outbursts on their journey back to the coast.

"No, you will not! It is someone pledged to the Khutani who must be wed to the Sand Mountain girl," Qwasigara roared, "not you!"

In the uproar that followed the Kashallan asked in a low voice to Chang sitting beside him, "I won't ask or force you to do this, Armachd, but I would know your thoughts on the marriage."

"Thank you, Kashallan-Phillip. I have no wish to marry at this time, but I will do it if it is the only way to make an alliance." Then, his mouth set in a firm line he added, "But I will not join his warband if that's his game like Ogwy claims. Me and my weapons, as well as the girl if she becomes my wife, will go with us back to Ticca, so make that clear to them as well."

Before the uproar could deteriorate to blows Philip stood and took the speaker bone from a gesticulating Ogwy's hand. Startled the men fell silent staring. "Thank you," Phillip said. "If I understand your customs aright when I hold this bone everyone is supposed to be quiet and listen to me." Waving the combatants to sit, he held up the bone for their inspection.

"Say what you have to say, Khutani," Qwasigara grumbled.

Phillip had never been much of a gambler in his old life, but he would figuratively roll the dice on this one. Taking a deep breath, he said, "Among my Speir'dina kindred women, as the life givers, are held in the highest respect. We claim our descent through our mother's and a woman may have more than one husband if she likes." Out of the corner of his eye he saw Ogwy's smirk and the Sand Mountain men's shocked faces.

"That isn't our custom," Tesulu shot back angrily. "The girl will marry whom I say."

"Ah but if we are making an alliance of equals here then we must come to an agreement. It can't be just what *you* say, War Leader. "So if a marriage is what is needed to secure an alliance with you, then so be it. But in accord with our custom we will let the woman herself choose her mate."

The Kashallan folded his arms across his chest and looked each man in the eye, daring them to object. Crossing to the trembling girl, standing with eyes cast down, he gave the older woman, presumably her mother standing slightly behind her, what he hoped was a reassuring smile.

Crouching before the girl to appear less threatening, he said in a quiet voice, "Niguiri, I bet all this is very sudden and probably a little frightening for you. Do you understand what I told your men-folk? I am giving you the right to choose your partner as is the custom among my Speir'dina kin."

Startled she looked up, then seeing her uncle's murderous glare she hastily dropped her eyes again. She nodded shyly. "Take a moment to think about your answer, Little Sister," he advised. "You have some options and I will support you in your choice, so don't be afraid.

"My warrior is a good man, but he says he is still grieving the loss of his wife and son and doesn't wish to take another at this time. Then there is the Blue Stone war leader. He too is a good man and he does want a new wife. If you choose him you would be closer to your kin than marrying one who has other obligations and won't stay on this side of the Shallow Sea once the Ghostlanders are defeated."

Then in a low voice that only the two women could hear, he asked, "Or, perhaps there is another among my people whom you would like for your husband, Niguiri? Your uncle and the wizard say they want a marriage to ensure this alliance, and the forging of this alliance is important so we can stop the Ghostlanders, but I'm going to let you decide who your husband will be."

Niguiri glanced at the older woman, then back to the Kashallan. "Is this your Mother?" she nodded.

"I am Ishka," the older woman said and met his eye with a clear unwavering stare. "I am the widow of the war leader's brother Dolingo who died defending us from the Ghostlanders."

He studied the woman more closely. Like her daughter she had very Avairei coloring and features, and also like any haughty Ima she was watching him boldly, showing no fear. He gave her a slight bow in acknowledgment. "Then I'm sure you understand the importance of what we do here today." She nodded. "And do you understand what I am offering your daughter as well?"

"I think I do, Kashallan."

<<Kashallan? Kasha, I think she knows what we truly are. She must have been taken from a keep in the Yeyen at some point in the past.>>

<<Yes, I think you are right, Shalla. And she would have been well educated and high in rank to know what a kashallan is.>>

Returning his attention to the women, he caught the glint of a smile curving her dark lips. Yes, she knew exactly what he'd been doing when the two halves of himself were communicating just now. Acknowledging her discovery he nodded and said, "Then would you like a bit of time to impart your wisdom to your child? These men are too impatient to wait for long, but I can distract them for a while."

She gave him a secretive smile and said, so only he and the girl could hear, "Your will, Kashallan. Perhaps only one such as you could make these arrogant men do anything."

He returned the smile. "We can only hope—for all our sakes."

Ishka took her daughter's hand and led her from the fire without looking back. "Tesulu, sit down, they will be back soon. And while we wait can you tell me more about the clan leaders coming to this war council," Kashallan-Phillip said.

BEFORE THE MEN GREW too impatient with the delay, the women joined them hand in hand. The Kashallan rose to meet them and retrieved the Speaker Bone from the warrior who had fallen silent with the women's return. Coming to stand in front of Niguiri, he asked, "Have you made your choice, Little Sister?" Niguiri looked him full in the face for just a moment, then dropping her eyes she pointed to Timma sitting at Chang's side.

When her choice registered and they realized that she had chosen the Avairei student and not the seasoned master, Tesulu, the wizard and several warriors on both sides of the circle jumped to their feet shouting.

Rounding on the kashallan, Tesulu roared, "No, the priest won't do. A seasoned warrior is the only one worthy of our alliance. What need have we of another Avairei slave?"

"Ah, but our Timma is most worthy of such a match," Phillip-Yoey said. "He is a very special young man. As you have seen he is training with one of our most experienced warriors," he pointed to Chang with his lips, "but he is also healer trained by his mentor priest and a kashallan.

"My Speir'dina people have a type of warrior we call in our language a medic. A medic is one who is both trained in the skills of war and the craft of healing. Medics always accompany our warbands when we fight to help save the lives of the wounded that would surely die otherwise. Timma here is a medic. We have fought the Ghostlanders more than once since coming to your world and Timma has helped save many lives."

"Bah! Why take the student when we can have the master." Qwasigara snarled. The enraged wizard turned to the cringing girl and demanded, "Ungrateful Child, I should kill you for your disobedience!"

As the wizard raised his arm and pointed his bone wand at the girl, Timma leapt to his feet and placed himself in front of the two women. Dropping into a fighter's crouch he drew his Speir'dina knife. "Don't you try to hurt her, you evil old man!"

Suddenly there was the grating sound of mocking laughter from outside the circle, freezing everyone in place. Brushing Qwasigara's magical protection away like an annoying cobweb, Tess-weh with Cadrach at her back stepped into the firelight.

Mirth still curving her full lips, she chortled, "Since you will soon have lots of new Umwira relatives to challenge your fighting skills, it's a good thing, Young Timma, that you told me you weren't afraid of the Umwira anymore when I asked you to come along."

Looking directly at the wizard, she warned while continuing to speak to Timma, "And, My Jewel, I will give you my special protection so that no one will trouble your dreams."

Tess-weh smiled, showing lots of teeth, her dark eyes predatory. "You will need your rest to continue your studies with your sensei and Ata Temog back at Ticca. Won't you, My Treasure?"

"Good evening Tess-weh," Phillip said. "Glad you could join us."

Tess-weh grinned. "Why, I missed you, My Precious."

"Mm, I'm not sure that comforts me, Honored Spirit."

She laughed. "Ah but it should, Kashallan, for I always have your best interests at heart."

"Yes, quite."

Still chuckling she shook her finger at him. "Ah, Phillip, have a little faith. Isn't my advice always worth it?"

He bowed his head in acknowledgement. "Dearly bought but good advice true enough, Honored Spirit."

"And what of us, Demon, will your advice be as good for us as for the Khutani?" Qwasigara cried.

Turning her dark penetrating stare upon him again, Tess-weh remained silent for a long moment. At last she said, "I have no contract with you and your people, Wizard. Your fate matters nothing to me."

Leaning forward the Kashallan said, "Tess-weh, you are bound to me and my kin. So the Sand Mountain Clan—and any other western clans that join the Kashallan Alliance, would come under your protection, as well, wouldn't they?"

Reluctantly she nodded. "I *could* offer them protection if they ally with you, My Treasure, when you go to war with the Ghostlanders."

"Mm, thank you, Honored Spirit." Turning his attention on the still protective Avairei, he said. "Put your knife away, Timma. No one is going to hurt Niguiri for choosing you instead of your mentor. But tell me truly, are you willing to marry the Sand Mountain Girl?"

Timma glanced shyly at Niguiri then back at the Kashallan. "If it's like the Sweh'an says that I can continue my studies with Sensei Chang and Ata Temog then yes, I am willing."

The Kashallan nodded and then turned to the fuming Tesulu and the wizard. "And you? There is a proposed marriage to guarantee the alliance and some protection offered by the Sweh'an if you join us. What is your answer, Sand Mountain Men?"

Speaking for his people Tesulu took out his knife and stepped to the fire. Drawing the blade across his forearm he allowed his blood to drip into the flames. "With Unseen Ones as my witness I swear..."

Each man in turn went up to the fire and swore his own blood-oath to the alliance. Knowing what to expect Phillip-Yoey rose after they finished and gave his own blood-oath to the flames.

When they had finished and everyone was in the process of leaving, Tess-weh stopped the wizard with a gesture of power. "Mm, not just yet, My Jewel," Tess-weh said coming over to the Kashallan and the few men still standing around the fire. "I require more assurance from you, Wizard, than a drop of your blood."

Qwasigara raised his lip in a snarl. "You challenge me, Demon!"

Focusing her hard eyes upon him she let him taste a bit of her power. "Yes, I do challenge you, for I fear you may not have been totally honest when you gave him your oath." Qwasigara licked dry lips, and she smiled her predatory smile again. "So for that reason, I require that you repeat your oath while in the link with the Khutani."

"No! I will not let that foul creature touch me!" he snarled, his whole body quivering with outrage.

"You will do it or forfeit your power to me. "She said.

"Tess-weh is this really necessary?" Phillip-Yoey asked.

Tess-weh turned her hard eyes on him. "Taste him and see," she snapped.

The Kashallan made a placating gesture and extended his tentacles, reaching for the wizard's hand.

Qwasigara would have run, but she held him in place. The Kashallan took his unresisting arm and formed the link. Closing his eyes he allowed the symbiont half of himself to taste this complex man who had survived so long in this harsh land.

"When were you planning to send the runner to warn them of my coming?" he asked after a long moment.

"If you know so much Khutani, then you also know that I hadn't decided whether I would send the runner at all."

"Yes, I do know that, which is why you are still alive right now," the kashallan said.

Glancing at the Demon, then to the Kashallan, Qwasigara said, "You and your demon have made it very clear what will happen if I betray the alliance. So, Khutani, I will keep my blood-oath."

Releasing him from the link the Kashallan said, "Your people will need you, and even one such as I might benefit from your wise counsel in the coming days, so I hope you are able to set aside your mistrust and hatred and truly work for the success of this alliance."

As the wizard stalked away he turned to Tess-weh and bowed. "Thank You, Honored Spirit. My laps could have cost us many lives."

She touched his cheek with a tender gesture. "Stay alert, My Precious, all still may not be as it seems."

He would have asked more, but Moraga came over to them at that moment and held out a heaping plate of food to Tess-weh. "Tessa needs to eat," she announced in a no nonsense voice.

Tess-weh took the plate and laughed. "Always mother henning me, as that most annoying creature, Dunnagh-Tani would say."

Moraga smiled. "Someone has to. Now if you don't need Cadrach for a while I'll take him and feed him too."

Tess-weh sat by the fire and waved Cadrach away in dismissal. Reluctantly the big Warlinga followed Moraga to the cook pit where the women were just dragging more wrapped food bundles from the hot rocks.

<<I guess I will have to taste the young couple and make them some red kavay,>> Yoey said as the kashallan headed to the beach to consult with his Khutani relatives.

WHEN HE EMERGED FROM the surf a while later, Masonja handed him his kilt. As he thanked her and would have headed for their fire she stopped him, and said in a low voice, "Umwira womans is hiding in the rocks. Masonja thinks womans want talk with you."

Startled he peered into the shadows. There was definitely someone standing over there who didn't want to be seen by the people moving about the fires further up the beach. After tasting the wizard he was more alert to danger than he'd been before Tess-weh's warning.

The wizard and the warbands had given him their oaths, but did their allegiance apply to the women and children as well? A woman grieving over a lost child or husband could be a formidable enemy. As he pleated the folds of his kilt he asked, "Masonja, do you know who is there, or what she wants?"

The Begta shrugged. "Don't know what want. Woman mother of girl Timma marry, I think."

"Mm, I'll talk to her. And while I do that would you find a gourd or clay jar I can use to put the red kavay in the young couple will need for the wedding night."

Masonja grinned, her teeth bright in the dim light. "Masonja will do that for Kashallan."

"Thank you , My dear."

When she was gone Phillip-Yoey walked over to the rocks and sat on a flat-topped boulder near where the woman concealed herself. Without looking in her direction he stared out to sea as if watching Timorna's tiny moon rise above the distant cloud bank. Barely visible most nights through Timorna's hazy atmosphere it cast a weak yellow ribbon of light across the water. "Did you wish to speak to me in private, Sa?" he said after a time.

Still keeping to the shadows, Ishka let out her held breath. "Yes, I did, Holy One."

"I sent Masonja to hunt for a container to hold the red kavay I will make for the young couple, if that is your concern. I know Timma will need it. I'm not sure how things are done on this side of the Shallow Sea," he admitted. "It's been too many years since my relatives have concerned themselves with Umwira breeding practices, I'm afraid."

She let out a nervous laugh. "I hadn't thought of that, but it would be a good thing—for both of them."

Smiling himself, he said, "Mm, that's good then. But the red kavay doesn't explain your wish for secrecy. Is there something wrong? Is anyone threatening you or your daughter because of her choice?"

She hesitated then admitted, "They hint but at the moment no one has dared make threats openly either to me or her."

His mouth hardened at that. "How can I be of service, Ima? I would ensure your safety as best I can."

"Safety," she gave him an ironic laugh. "Such an elusive quality in all our lives. But you are right. Concerning our safety, I would ask a favor of you, Holy One."

"I'm listening, Ima."

"The Sweh'an mentioned that the young man will be going back across the Shallow Sea to continue his training. When you go, take me and my daughter with you. They will want to keep us—especially if she becomes pregnant before then. They will separate us after you go. And though I am older and at the end of my fertility cycle, Tesulu will try to use me as a pawn in his schemes to gain more power among the western clans."

"I take it this would not be to your liking?"

A note of steel was in her voice as she said, "No it would not! I despise them. I have only stayed so long because of my daughter."

Kashallan-Phillip was quiet for a time, watching the play of moonlight on the waves, thinking. At last he said, "A girl of such tender years shouldn't be separated from her mother so soon—especially if the mother hasn't had time to prepare the child for her duties as a wife and mother, and I will argue for that—perhaps with Tess-weh's backing, if there are any objections.

"But I will ask you to consider this as well. You have survived and created a place for yourself among these people, and are smart enough to turn Tesulu's manipulations to your advantage, I suspect."

Imagining what Sairsa might be facing now back at Ticca, he continued, "Think about what you want carefully, Ima. Your family and other Avairei in the Yeyen Banai may reject your claim of kinship. Your life may not be any better for the change."

"And what of my girl?" she snapped. "Would you want her to face their spite alone? Her new man won't be with her all the time to protect her as he did tonight. Who will save her—especially from the malice of women, who but me? Together we will be stronger than separated and alone, don't you agree?"

"So be it then, your argument is a valid one," he said, though he wasn't looking forward to another confrontation with the Sand Mountain men if they chose to object.

Chapter Six

Anxious to journey on to the Red Rock Council, the war leaders of both clans goaded everyone to eat and pack up as soon as possible. Marriage plans were postponed till later—possibly their evening camp.

The kashallan learned that the first part of the journey would be made in the canoes. Travelling over the rough inland trails would take too much time with the women and children in tow. Leaving them behind wasn't an option either, in case the Ghostlanders came back for another attack. The Sand Mountain people had with them some larger vessels with outriggers attached and most of the women and children crowded into them along with food and other belongings.

To his surprise, Timma led his new bride and mother-in-law to Noi's canoe and settled them in its middle, then he and Chang took up paddles and helped guide the boat into deeper water. Glancing around, he noticed that Tess-weh and Cadrach had disappeared again. Maybe they didn't like boat rides, he thought, but they would be back; he was sure of it.

THE CLANS BEACHED THE canoes in a shallow cove late in the afternoon. The older children were sent to gather dried seaweed and last year's aluutae reeds for the night's fires. Some of the women with Moraga acting as their guard headed off to gather roots and other edibles inland. Deciding to let the warriors do their own fishing for a change, the Kashallan strolled through the encampment searching for Timma. He at last found him and Ata Doyan with their medicine bags open and a line of patients waiting to see them. To his surprise Niguiri and her mother were helping the two Avairei, encouraging and talking to the Sand Mountain people if they seemed hesitant to be treated.

In Phillip's middle Yoey stirred and he could sense the symbiont's desire to join the healers. Phillip touched his bondmate, but held back. <<I know you would like to join them and offer your help, Shalla, but I don't think these people are ready yet to accept our touch. Maybe in time they won't be so afraid of us. And I'm sure Timma will consult us if there's anything he can't handle.>>

<<You're right, Kasha, but it's hard to just watch.>>

<<Then let's come back later.>> Deciding to distract his young bondmate he suggested they wander further inland. He was curious to taste how plants and animals had evolved in this harsh land over the years—and now might be one of the only times they would have to examine the evolution of life on this side of the Shallow Sea.

But before he got very far, Ishka saw him and came over to speak to him. "Is there something wrong, Kashallan?"

He shook his head and smiled. "No, I was searching for the young couple because I will need to taste them in order to make the red kavay for them; that was all." Then hesitantly he asked, "Timma is quite used to our touch. He has been giving the Blood-Gift to my cousin, Dunnagh-Tani since we fled Sulas keep not long after the first bond was formed. But, raised among the Sand Mountain People, I can't help but worry how Niguiri will accept my touch."

Looking back at the young people working together nearby she took a long time before speaking. "Each day I marvel that I have lived long enough to see the kashallan bond reformed. Someday I hope there will be time to hear more of you and your people's amazing story.

"As for my daughter, she will be nervous, after all the lies she has heard from her father's relatives all her life. But I think if she sees her bridegroom and, if you permit, me, to feel your touch first, she will understand there is no danger.

"I have told her since she was old enough to understand that the Khutani weren't the demons some would have her believe. Your presence here among us gives truth to that. When would you like us to come to you?"

The Kashallan glanced back at the healers and the waiting line, then on impulse he said, "My first thought was to go somewhere private and taste them, but if you think it would help the others lessen their fears about me, then perhaps we should do it now. And, I will gladly put you in the link if you believe it might help ease her mind."

"Hmm, I understand your reasoning. Let me go talk to her to see what she and the boy would like."

Phillip sat down in the sand and nodded. "Fair enough, I bow to your greater wisdom in the matter. I will wait for you here."

In a short while she returned and stood in front of him. "The young man agrees with you, and my daughter is willing to trust that her new husband to be knows what's best for them." Phillip-Yoey rose and followed her back to the healers.

When the people saw him approach they shrank back, some women clutching their young children to their sides. Ishka called out to them, assuring them that he was here to taste the young couple in preparation for the wedding night—nothing more. As he hoped, instead of leaving they stopped to watch the proceedings.

Smiling Timma rose and offered him a seat on the mat where he had been doing his examinations. When the Kashallan was settled, he knelt and held out his hands in the traditional gesture, inviting the link

Looking at Niguiri but pitching his voice so that the others could hear, he extended his tentacles and explained what he was going to do and why. Then, taking Timma's hands in his own, he formed the link. The Kashallan closed his eyes and allowed the symbiont half of himself to taste what it would need to make the red kavay.

In a short time he opened his eyes and released Timma from the link. The young man held up his hands and showed everyone that there wasn't any blood and that he wasn't hurt.

"By using my tentacles in this manner I taste the one in the link with me. What I 'taste' helps me make the medicines I need when I heal, or in this case, make the red kavay needed to ensure fertility," he explained.

Next he turned to the girl, and asked, "If you are nervous about feeling my touch, your mother has agreed to let me taste her first if it will help. Would you prefer that, Niguiri?"

Niguiri glanced at her mother and then at Timma. With downcast eyes, she said in a low voice, "If it won't give offence, Kashallan, that might ease my mind."

"All right." His eyes met Ishka's and she knelt on the mat in front of him as Timma had. Holding her hands out, he took them and formed the link. As she felt his touch her eyes opened wide. Phillip chuckled, aware now of the unease she had masked so well. In a low voice so only those standing close might hear, he said, "You were very brave, but my touch wasn't as bad as you thought, is it Sa?"

She shook her head and laughed. "No it is not."

Once again he closed his eyes to taste and consult. A wealth of stimuli flooded his Khutani-heightened senses. At first he examined her physical health to see if there was a hidden problem that he might detect and fix, but along with those simple tastings he became aware that she had relaxed and opened herself to him in a way few had done before.

Through their link he also tasted fragments of memory that resonated with the host's memories of his capture and early days on Timorna among an unknown people. Pain, fear love and joy flooded his duel awareness. Her life hadn't been easy among the Umwira, but her will to survive humbled him, filling him with admiration.

When he at last opened his eyes Niguiri seemed more nervous than before, and everyone was staring at him. "You were gone for quite some time. Is there something wrong, Kashallan?" Ata Doyan asked.

Startled, Philip blinked and released Ishka from the link. Ishka looked as dazed as he must by the unexpected depth of their communion. "N-no, Ata, nothing's wrong I-we shared at a deeper level than I had expected."

Turning to Ishka he bowed and said in a voice rough with emotion, "You honor me with your trust and sharing. Thank you."

She bowed in turn and would have risen, but he stopped her. "One more thing before you go, Sa, if I may? I can taste that your left knee is troubling you, a flare up of an old injury, I believe." Placing a hand to his mouth the Kashallan spat into his hand a gluey orange paste and plastered it to the aching part. "This should ease the pain for a time so that you can rest tonight."

Ishka smiled. "Orange Kavay. I haven't felt its healing balm since I was a girl. Thank you."

With a little coaxing from Timma, Niguiri at last knelt in front of him. Gently taking her hands the Kashallan formed the link. When she realized he wasn't going to hurt her, she relaxed and allowed him to discover what he needed to make the marriage gift.

Not wishing to probe too deeply and frighten the girl he couldn't help discovering that she wasn't as timid as he had assumed. Like her mother, Niguiri cloaked her true self as a means of survival among the Umwira. Both women would probably blossom in the more unconventional atmosphere of the alliance.

Releasing her from the link he bowed. "Thank you, Niguiri. I have what I need now to make the red kavay for your wedding."

"And how long will that take, Khutani?"

Startled Phillip-Yoey turned and saw Qwasigara observing him, a few of the Sand Mountain warriors at his side. <<Hmm, we had more of an audience than we planned.>>

<<I wonder how long he's been watching,>> Yoey said.

<<I hope they all learned something,>> Phillip said. <<And I hope what they saw helps break down the barrier of fear between us.>> Yoey remained stubbornly quiet on that subject. Phillip mentally sighed feeling caught in the middle and trying to make peace between two ancient enemies.

Returning his attention to the wizard he rose and motioned for the man to follow him as he headed back to the central fires. It was growing dark; his tasting of the young people had taken longer than he'd planned. There wouldn't be any time tonight for exploring and tasting plant-life.

"Not long. When would you like to hold the wedding?"

"Tonight after our meal. You can make them your red magic whenever. We will have a long hard paddle tomorrow. We enter Bitter Water Clan territory by midday. We will need to stay alert and focused after that. Now that we have changed our loyalties who knows what our former allies may decide to do?"

"Mm, since it's already getting late I had hoped to have at least until tomorrow evening, but I see your point. Perhaps we can do a simple ceremony now and something more elaborate for the young people later when there is time."

Qwasigara gave a noncommittal grunt and kept walking. "Do your people have a special way of marrying?" Phillip asked coming alongside the wizard again. "I can make the red kavay to help with Timma's potency—and

Niguiri could benefit from it, too, but I was hoping to bow to your knowledge where the actual ceremony is concerned."

Qwasigara halted and turned to face him. Surprised he at last said, "You will allow them to be married according to our custom?"

"Of course. As I just said I have no skill in such matters. I have tasted the couple; they are compatible. And, I will help with their fertility as is the custom on the east side of the Shallow Sea, but we are here, on the west side of the water, in your land and I will follow your customs in this."

"So be it then. After the meal the people can gather and I will call the Unseen Ones to witness the union."

Chapter Seven

As with the day before the war leaders had everyone up early. Dawn had barely tinged the eastern horizon when the canoes were packed and they set out north along the coast. Though he'd had little sleep the Kashallan took his accustomed place in Ogwy's canoe, eager to start. He found to his surprise that he was enjoying the vigorous exercise the day's paddling offered.

As the wizard predicted, the wedding last night had been a simple affair. When the people gathered Qwasigara stepped to the central fire and called the Unseen ones to witness the union. The couple exchanged tokens to ware around their necks and made a blood offering to the flames, as they repeated Qwasigara's coached vows.

Only able to cough up a mere dose of red kavay on such short notice, the Kashallan handed Timma his battered cup and promised him more when time permitted. All smiles, and maybe a bit nervous, the Kashallan decided, Timma thanked him and holding hands with his new bride headed for the soft bed of dried reeds and seaweed the women had made for them among the rocks.

Later when all was quiet and he was just drifting off to sleep, Phillip became aware of stealthy movement and watched as Chang concealed himself among the boulders just up the slope from the young people.

<<Is he worried about them, Kasha?>> Yoey asked. <<Are they in danger, do you think?>>

<<Armachd Chang lost his young family when we were stranded here, Shalla. On our journey across the Great Swamp as he trained the young man I believe Timma became a substitute for his lost son. Perhaps he is just being over cautious because he cares more for the boy than he will admit, even to himself.>>

THEY WERE WELL INTO the afternoon's paddle when the Kashallan became aware of a change in the unseen world around them. There was a new tension in the air. He opened his mouth and tasted salt, copper and a subtle sourness of decay stirred up from the depths. <<Yoey, what is happening?>>

<<A storm is coming, I think.>>

Suddenly an icy gust of wind slammed into his back, giving confirmation to the symbiont's words. Glancing over his shoulder he saw a ridge of purple storm clouds massing in the southern sky, churning the water to grey foam as it headed their way. What had they missed about the weather when they set out after the midday rest.

Nothing, he was sure of it. There hadn't been a cloud on the horizon in any direction when they launched. This storm had come out of nowhere. Ah, but was it a natural phenomenon? The Sweh'an had hinted before she left them again, not to be complacent. Being able to breathe underwater, and with his relatives nearby he could survive this storm—but the others...

How had the Ghostland wizards managed to learn of his plan to unite the west? Someone had betrayed them, either unwittingly or out of malice. Well those were questions to ponder later—when they were safe and ashore.

Sensing the growing storm nearly as soon as he had, Ogwy roared a command, "Row Lazy Slimeworms, or we will feed the Dhuura this day!" Shifting his paddle he guided his vessel to race parallel to the jagged dark cliffs along the shoreline.

Taking a moment to glance in that direction, Phillip could see no break in their formidable dark wall that would offer them sanctuary. This was probably the reason the Ghostlanders had waited till they had reached this stretch of the coast to spring their trap, he thought grimly, as he pushed himself and quickened his stroke.

Icy water crashed over the gunwales, drenching people and supplies alike. The war canoe rode high in the water its bow pounding out a wild rhythm as it tore through the angry waves. Nearby the Sand Mountain boats burdened with the men's families were not so fortunate. Even over the wind's demonic whine he could hear the frightened women and children screaming. The outriggers on the larger vessels helped stabilize some of them but they were having difficulty nonetheless.

Then one of the smaller Sand Mountain canoes capsized. High-pitched waling from the drowning people seemed to be echoed by mocking laughter in the howling winds. No one stopped to pick up survivors—they couldn't. The storm was gaining, jagged green lightning ripping apart the maelstrom followed by deafening claps of thunder seconds later. The air stank of burning ozone and rotting seaweed.

When she saw children sinking beneath the waves Masonja put down her paddle, rose and turned to face the oncoming gale. Throwing her arms wide she began to chant in a deep resonant voice as she drew sigils of power in the tumultuous air. Clear and unwavering her voice rang out quickly echoed by women in the other boats.

To the Kashallan's surprise, young Niguiri was one of the first to stand and add her voice to the song. Stowing his paddle, he saw Timma slide over and grasp her legs to steady her as the canoe bucked. Dropping his own paddle into the bottom of the canoe, Phillip did the same for Masonja. He could feel her drawing up power from the ocean floor to channel into a protective shield against the Ghostlander's malice.

Feeling its kindred swimming below them, Yoey drew upon encoded memories and added its own etheric power to the women's conjurings.

Knowing at last what the women were attempting, the men in the canoes took heart, and as they paddled they added their own voices in a deep guttural chant, punctuating the women's high-pitched song. Caught up in the exhilaration of the moment, Phillip shouted his own challenge to the Ghostlanders and mingled his voice with the men.

With the howling storm as a goad the canoes flew over the black water, the men and women screaming their defiance at the Ghostlanders, all fear forgotten. Losing track of time the Kashallan finally realized that the wind was lessening, the clouds breaking up and drifting harmlessly eastward. He glanced westward and saw that the shoreline had changed, no longer defined by impenetrable high cliffs it was now carved here and there by deep inlets and sheltered coves.

The light was nearly gone when Tesulu found what he'd been watching for and turned the lead canoe into a deep cove that appeared out of a cliff face without warning.

Out of the choppy water at last the exhausted men slowed their pace. Allowing the canoes to drift slowly toward a sandy beach near the mouth of the cove they searched for danger on the slopes above.

<<Chosen,>> Ro said. <<Many were too frightened to accept our help, but we managed to rescue a few survivors from the drowned boat, Warn the People that we are bringing them close enough to swim to shore or be picked up.>>

Calling over to the Sand Mountain canoes, the Kashallan relayed to Tesulu Ro's message. Not long afterwards several Khutani helping exhausted swimmers appeared in the cove following the canoes.

When the people were recognized many cried out in gratitude hurrying to help their relatives to shore or inside one of the canoes still waiting to be dragged onto the beach.

Trailing a hand in the water with tentacles extended Phillip-Yoey conveyed his thanks to Ro and the others.

<<I hope this will aid your cause and help convince them of our Amla's sincerity,>> Ro said.

<<I do as well, K'amsi, for I suspect the Ghostland Wizards aren't through with us.>>

<<Mm, and where was the demon who has pledged us her allegiance during this attack, I wonder?>> Ro grumbled.

Recognizing a note of delayed hysteria in his mental sending, Phillip laughed. <<Tess-weh definitely has her own ideas about when and where her intervention is needed, K'amsi.>>

On the beach at last the canoes were quickly unloaded and drenched supplies either discarded or spread out to dry. Men helped children gather fuel and soon several fires were lit to cook and keep the young and old warm. The kashallan helped with unloading Ogwy's canoe then seeing Masonja heading towards Timma and his bride helping to unload Noi's canoe he hurried to catch up to them.

As he drew near he heard Masonja asking Niguiri, "Where girl learn to make the wind magics?"

Setting down her bundle she dropped her eyes, but Phillip also saw the corner of her mouth curve into a tiny smile. "My father's mother was a weather witch; she taught me some things before she died."

Masonja smiled showing her canines. "Girl learn good. Masonja teach maybe. Know lots magics me. You want learn more magics?"

Niguiri glanced at Timma who nodded his encouragement. "Yes, I would like to learn more."

"Good we talk later. Now we work."

Helping her carry more damp bundles to the women unpacking by the fires, Yoey said, "Masonja, thank you for your help today. I doubt if so many would have survived without your magical skill. I'm impressed; we had no idea your people had evolved so well during our long sleep."

The Begta smiled again. "Old Majuma teach good. Shamanka use the magics to protect Begta when Sorin storms come."

"Mm, I am even more impressed."

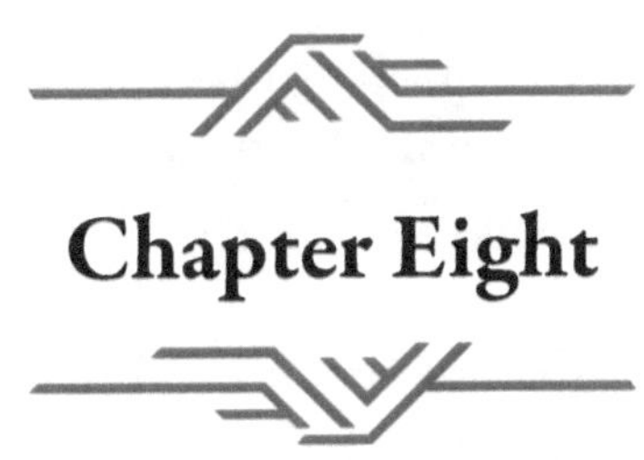

Chapter Eight

Next morning the war leaders and the wizard decided that everyone needed a day of rest before traveling on to the Red Rock Council. The storm yesterday had blown the canoes further up the coast than they could have managed on their own. They would still make it to the meeting on time—barring no more interference from the Ghostlanders.

Much of the food stores they'd managed to prepare for the trip had been made unusable by the storm, so the men decided that either on land or on the water they would hunt, while the women worked around camp or gathered roots and other edible plants from the nearby slopes.

Kashallan-Phillip already having demonstrated his skill in the water, was assigned to accompany Tesulu and the men going out in the canoes. Ogwy was told by Qwasigara to head up the hunters traveling inland to look for game. The Blue Stone men were outnumbered, but judging by the scowl on Ogwy's face his assignment wasn't to his liking.

Out of curiosity Phillip asked his young bond-mate if he knew why Ogwy was so angry. <<Maybe because in this season the hunting is much poorer inland,>> Yoey suggested. <<I suspect these people sea-hunt mostly at this time of year. If there are herds of larger animals living on this side of the Shallow Sea they will have moved to the grassy meadows on the slopes above the great desert further west.>>

<<Mm, I think I understand. Though outwardly Blue Stone and Sand Mountain are allies, personally the two war leaders are rivals, and this assignment is another move in the power game those two are playing.>>

<<I hadn't thought of it like that but you might be right, Kasha.>>

Glancing back at the shoreline where his Speir'dina armachda had remained to guard the camp he asked Tesulu, "My warriors are good fighters, but even so with so many men away is the camp safe? Where are we exactly; are we still in Blue Stone territory?"

Tesulu shook his head not breaking the rhythm of his paddle. “No, this is Bitter Water territory. They are allies, but I am wondering why they haven’t come to investigate our presence in the cove. This inlet is one of their main seasonal sea-hunting places.”

Phillip thought about that for a moment then asked, “Is it possible they haven’t come because they can’t?”

“All dead you mean? If they lost their wizard and their war leader—maybe—I don’t know.” Then with a snort of private amusement, he added, “Perhaps my brother war leader will give us some information when he returns tonight.”

Information indeed, the Kashallan thought when the canoes beached heavy-laden in the dimming light.

Ogwy had returned, and with little to show for his efforts, as Yoey predicted, but he was also accompanied by a group of bedraggled, starving people that the Kashallan learned were all that was left of the Bitter Water Clan. With a smirk Ogwy also introduced them to Kelga, the young widow of Madav, Bitter Water’s dead war leader, and his new wife. Along with her as bride price came the remainder of the warband. Bitter Water was no more. They were all Blue Stone people now.

In his middle Phillip tasted the symbiont’s rye amusement. <<I guess Ogwy’s hunting was better than Tesulu expected. The number of warriors each leads now is more evenly matched.>>

<<Yes, that may be true. The question we need answered, however, is how do these new people feel about the Kashallan Alliance? it is one thing for the two rival war leaders to vie with each other for dominance, but quite another if their machinations endanger the alliance.>>

After their meal the kashallan managed to catch Ogwy alone and ask him that same question.

“I have told them of the alliance, Khutani. They understand why we fight alongside you. Their hatred for the Ghostlanders is as bitter as the water found upon their land. And they have pledged their allegiance to me. Together we will appease our ancestors and obtain our revenge.”

“That’s good to hear, but I would still like to come talk to them and have them make blood-oath.” Seeing Ogwy’s angry expression, he added, “War Leader, don’t be offended. I believe their hatred for the Ghostlanders runs deep, but their hatred for my kind is also a deep well. I just want to assure myself that when they gave you personally, their fealty, they also intend no betrayal to me and the greater alliance."

Ogwy grunted his reluctant agreement and led him to the Bitter Water fire. As they passed his own encampment the Kashallan caught Chang's eye and motioned him to follow them.

When they arrived, the Bitter Water people were just finishing a meal of baked Dhuura and some small reptilian-like creature that Phillip hadn't seen before.

<<I think they might have been Oko—originally, now mutated to their present appearance these many generations later,>> Yoey supplied to his unvoiced query.

To Phillip they looked something like the stuffed armadillos he'd seen once in a museum on Dymar.

As they drew near those sitting around the fire looked up. Most met his gaze with a dull acceptance, displaying neither fear nor hatred. In spite of himself Phillip felt pity for these half-starved, traumatized people. Hoping his face didn't reveal his emotion, he crouched by the fire with Chang standing at his back.

"Good evening, I am Phillip-Yoey. I am one of the new kashallans War Leader Ogwy has told you about. My Speir'dina Chosen and his people were called to Timorna to host the Makers' symbiont children. We face a common enemy now. We seek vengeance against the Ghostland wizards and their monstrous warbands as do you, and so many others."

Rising he stepped to the fire, and drew his Speir'dina knife for them to see its alienness, sharp and lethal its dark metal absorbed the fire's light. Swiftly he drew the blade across his forearm and allowed his blood to drip into the flames. "With the Unseen Ones of this land as my witness, I swear to protect and care for, to the best of my ability, any who give me and my kin their allegiance."

When they finished Ogwy remained with his new relatives and Philip-Yoey and Chang walked back to their fire alone. Just outside their encampment Phillip stopped him. "Before we join the others I would know your thoughts about the new members of our alliance, Armachd."

Chang took a moment to gather his thoughts before speaking. At last he said, "They are smaller and probably still weak from the Sorin confinement. And they seem to have more Warlinga-like features than the Blue Stone Warriors. If there is time before we leave, I would like to set up some practice bouts so I can see how well they fight."

"You had better check with Ogwy and maybe Tesulu about that. We don't want to give unknowing offence, if we can help it," he advised.

Chang gave him a conspiratorial grin. "Already planned to do that, Sir. I'm aware of how touchy our new allies are about trespass."

Phillip touched his arm and smiled. "Forgive me for trying to tell you your job. Having you along is making my task much easier and I am very grateful for your help."

"Thank you for your confidence, Sir."

THAT NIGHT AS CHANG was keeping his self-appointed vigil over Timma and his new bride, Ishka came and sat beside him among the rocks. "What do you fear Warrior, that you deprive yourself of sleep each night? Don't you trust Tesulu's sentries?"

Chang scowled, then chuckled. "Maybe not—am I that obvious?"

Ishka shrugged. "No not really, but Niguiri noticed you last night and told me about your guard duty."

"Mm." glancing at the young couple wrapped in their blankets his scowl returned.

"So fierce you look, but don't worry I won't tell them. Your secret is safe with me. It's only that I trained Niguiri from early childhood to be alert to strange men attempting to conceal themselves near where she was going to sleep that she discovered you at all."

"Mm, somehow that doesn't comfort me. If Niguiri saw me then Timma should—"

Ishka laughed softly. "I can tell the boy means a lot to you, but don't be annoyed at him for his lack of attention. With red kavay flowing through his blood, he has other things on his mind at the moment."

Chang grunted his eyes still scanning the surrounding shadows. At last he sighed. "The lad though not of my blood is like a son to me—I wouldn't want them to be hurt... And after that unnatural storm I can't help wondering when and where the next attack will come."

"That is truly a sobering thought."

"It is what I would do in their place."

The pair lapsed into a thoughtful but companionable silence after that. Below them in the shadows the oblivious young people talked quietly among themselves the occasional giggle punctuating their chatter.

When the couple at last drifted into sleep Ishka sighed. "Ah, to be young and filled with promise again, I envy them somewhat."

Chang snorted. "Promise but also the threat of heartache."

Combing her fingers through her long ponytail she said, "Yes, there is always that possibility. I was newly wed to my betrothed when I was captured by the Sand Mountain warriors. I have borne my share of heartache, true enough. But when I accepted what the Unseen Ones had planned for me, and Dolingo took me as wife and gave me my beautiful daughter I found a measure of joy in my hard life among the enemy."

Thinking of the Blue Stone warriors' treatment of Sairsa and Briya Chang's voice hardened as he said, "Two of our women were captured by Ogwy and his warriors. One of them was our Ce'awn, our leader's wife. When we found them the women had been beaten and otherwise abused, so I can imagine how hard it must have been for you."

"It was hard; I won't deny it, but Dolingo had his admirable qualities. He was a good provider and seldom resorted to violence. I am sorry for his dying at the claws of the Ghostlanders, though I won't exactly mourn his passing. But what of you, Warrior? You said earlier that the young man is not of your blood. Do you have a wife and children waiting for you across the Shallow Sea?"

Chang muttered something in his native language under his breath, ignoring her question. He would have risen to go, but she stopped him. "I am sorry if I unknowingly gave offense. I meant no harm, Warrior. Ignore my foolishness, please."

Resuming his seat among the rocks his face contorted with his unexpressed emotion. At last gaining control of himself, he said, "I am sorry,

Ima. It is me who perhaps owes you an apology. You couldn't know—my wife and young son are waiting for me to return, but they wait not across the Shallow Sea, but up there," Chang pointed into the night sky, "in my old home among the stars. And it is my curse that I will never see them again."

His voice choked on the last of his words and he fell silent. After a long time of sitting and listening to the waves lapping on the beach and other night sounds, Ishka ventured to say, "You have chosen well with this adopted son of yours. My girl is fortunate to claim him as her mate. I will listen if you wish to tell me about the lost ones who also share your heart."

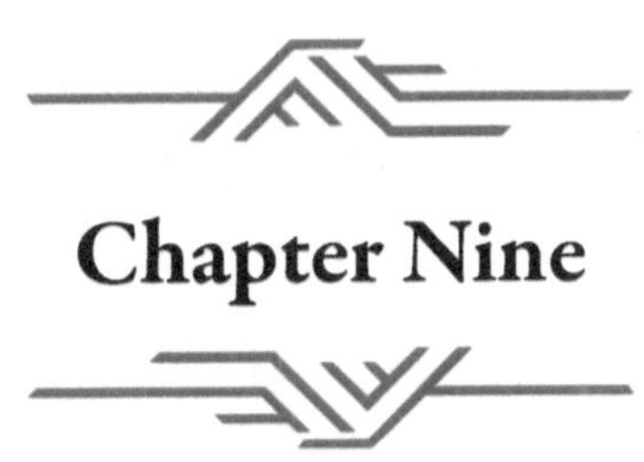

Chapter Nine

The Alliance's leaders decided to spend one more day in the sheltered cove in preparation for the rest of their journey. Still curious about the plants and animals along this side of the water Phillip-Yoey decided to remain in the cove and explore instead of going with the canoes.

Seeing her chance while most of the men were away hunting, either by land or by sea, Ishka approached him with another Clan woman in tow, before he could make his own escape. The newcomer had the usual six limbs common among the Westerners, but she also had strong Avairei features.

"This is Efosa. My son-in-law says that the healing of this woman's son, Mosi, is beyond his skill," she said by way of introduction. "He suggested we find you."

Inwardly sighing at another lost opportunity, he asked, "What seems to be the problem?" He had directed his question to the nervous mother but when she seemed unable to meet his eye and speak, he turned to Ishka for an answer.

"My son-in-law thinks the child might be suffering from the Ghostlanders' Mind Magic."

<<If that's true, Kasha, I can see why Timma would want us to examine the child,>> Yoey said.

<<Hmm.>> To the women he said, "Where is Timma? I want to consult with him first before I see the child."

The women took him to a mossy spot where Timma and Ata Doyan had set up their healing mats again. As they walked up, Timma was just plastering yellow kavay on a deep gash in a woman's arm. When he finished, he came over to the two women and the kashallan and bowed.

Taking the young man aside, Phillip-Yoey said in a low voice, "I assume you already know why I'm here. Tell me your opinion, my medic, how can I help this boy?"

"I am sorry to trouble you with this, Holy One, I know Yoey is still young—maybe still too young to heal the little one, but I think the child has been attacked by the Umwira mind magics. He won't talk, and barely eats, the mother tells me. He has the vacant look that-that we've seen before."

<<Since Timma himself was one that suffered at the Ghostlanders' hands, he would know the signs. For that reason I suspect he may be right in his diagnosis, Shalla,>> Phillip told his bondmate. <<But he also raises another question. If correct are we-you mature enough to perform a healing of such a magnitude?>>

A note of exasperation coloring the mental voice, Yoey said, <<I won't know till we taste him, Kasha. But remember our relatives are near to help us, if need be.>>

That was true, Phillip thought privately, but he would feel more confident if their parent, Maker Tinguss, was here to guide them. Ro was an ancient and wise creature, but he couldn't help worrying. Tinguss had been gone a long time—longer than it told them its council with the other Ancients should have taken.

Swallowing down his worry, he motioned for Ishka and her companion to join them. "Efosa, how old is your son?"

With an encouraging nod from Ishka, Efosa licked her lips then in a voice barely above a whisper she said, "He is three Sorin seasons old."

"Hmm... My medic and your friend Ishka think he has been afflicted with the Ghostlanders mind magic. It would be highly unusual for one of their wizards or warriors to take an interest in one so young. I will examine him, of course, but can you explain to me how this malady came about?"

Ishka looked around nervously then suggested, "Holy One, let us go somewhere more private and discuss this further."

<<I wonder what she's worried about, Kasha.>>

<<I wonder as well, Shalla. Perhaps there is more to this than the women are telling us. We will have to be careful, I think.>>

Nodding his agreement, the women led him away from the beach up a rocky trail. When they could no longer be seen from below, Efosa stopped by a clump of reeds and pushed aside a mat covering a dark hollow concealed by the taller vegetation. In the dim light he could see a small figure huddled against the wall of the earthen cave.

"Mosi?" Efosa called to the child. Wooly pelt matted, head crest and ponytail tangled and dusty the boy remained huddled with his back to them, ignoring his mother's entreaties, lost in his own misery.

Turning to the women he asked, "May I go in? If you don't think he will be too frightened by my touch I will examine him now."

"Touch?" Efosa seemed bewildered, but at last she shrugged. Ishka took her hand and nodded to him. "Do what you need to do, Kashallan."

Hopefully the young one wouldn't begin screaming when he formed the link, Phillip prayed. That might be awkward to explain to an outraged bunch of women coming to investigate the uproar.

Speaking softly the kashallan entered the hollow and crawled slowly over to the boy. Sitting down in front of him Phillip took one of the boy's hands, but didn't form the link. "Mosi, my name is Phillip-Yoey. I'm a healer. Your mother has asked me to take a look at you because she is worried about you."

Yes, Timma was right; he definitely had the vacant look assumed by those who had felt the Umwira mind magic. The child didn't even seem to be aware of his presence—or was doing a good job of ignoring him. Well he'd find out soon enough the truth of it, he thought. "Mosi, I am going to touch you in a special way now. You will feel a little prick."

Mosi looked through him as motionless as the stone at his back. Kashallan-Phillip closed his eyes and formed the link... Finished at last, he backed out of the hollow and stood, stretching to relieve a cramp knotted in his lower back from sitting in such an awkward position.

"Can you help him, kashallan?" Ishka asked anxiously.

Taking another deep breath, he let out a long sigh and said, "I will need to talk to my kindred swimming nearby before I can answer that, but first tell me more about what caused the boy to close himself off so completely."

"When our camp was attacked during the Sorins Mosi was very brave," Efosa said. "When he saw the monster torturing his father he-he tried to kill it. The evil creature grabbed him with his claws and-and—" She opened her mouth, but no words passed her lips. She swallowed and tried again but still with no success.

Phillip-Yoey patted her hand. "It's all right. I can guess the rest. Some of my kinswomen have also felt the wizard's foul touch in their minds."

She gave him a hopeful look, "Were you able to help them?"

"I personally wasn't kashallan-bonded at the time we fought the Ghostland warbands," Phillip said. "For those healings my kin were responsible. If you give us time to consult the Elder that swims nearby. My bondmate Yoey and I will see what can be done for your son."

As he headed for the beach, Ishka stopped him. "It would be better if your healing was done while the men are away, Kashallan. How long will you be gone?"

<<I knew it. These women are acting far too secretive for my liking,>> Phillip told his bondmate. <<Maybe we shouldn't work with the child at all, Shalla.>>

<<But the boy is suffering, Kasha, we can't just abandon him to die,>> Yoey pleaded.

<<No, we can't; you are right, Shalla. Let's see if we can learn more before we decide.>>

Returning his attention to the waiting women he folded his arms across his chest and gave them a stern look. "I sense there is more to this than you have told me so far. Why have you come to me with this problem? Why not ask Wizard Qwasigara to see to the child—or another healer from among the clans?"

"I have asked him," Efosa said, a note of desperation coming into her voice. "He says I must stop coddling my son. Mosi needs to stop whining like a woman and behave like a warrior. He won't help and none of our witches will defy him and help, either. Each day my son grows weaker and weaker until I fear for his life! Mosi is all I have left, Please help him, Khutani!"

<<There may be trouble over this if we interfere, Kasha, but the mother is right the child may die if we don't try to help.>>

<<I was afraid you were going to say that, Shalla.>> Sighing Phillip sat down on a nearby flat rock. "All right. We will help." He glanced longingly at the beach. He would love to go down there and swim out to them, feel the loving embrace of the kindred, and cool water flowing over him like a sensuous kiss. Ah, but that would take time, a pleasant distraction but not necessary if he swam to them in the dream instead of the physical world for his consultation.

"Ishka, can you go back to camp and find Armachd Moraga and Masonja for me? I will need them. If secrecy is important then it will be better if I'm not seen wandering about camp right now looking for them. I'd planned to go exploring anyway so if anyone asks..."

Next he turned to Efosa. "I will stay here and consult with my Elder. Can you bring some blankets and water and food in case this takes a while?" Seemingly eager to have some errand to focus on, she nodded and followed Ishka down the trail.

When the women left, his first thought was to lie down in the little cave beside Mosi and go into the Dream to speak to Ro. Then with the Sweh'an's warning echoing in his memory, he decided to wait until his guardians, physical and etheric, arrived to keep him safe.

Deciding to do a little exploring of the plant-life as he'd planned instead, he extended his tentacles and crouched to taste the nearby grey-leafed plant growing beside the trail.

The Kashallan barely had time to move on to examine a spiky purple shrub when the women returned with his guardians. Deciding that the tiny hollow was too cramped for a healing like he planned, Phillip asked if there was another place nearby where they could be private and yet more comfortable.

"Yes I think I know what you plan and what you need. The place isn't far," Ishka said and pointed up the slope. "There among the boulders is a sheltered spot covered with moss in the center. You and the boy can lie there while we witness and keep watch."

Kashallan-Phillip smiled. This enigmatic woman amazed him at every turn. She had had a harsh life since being captured, but who was she before the abduction? He already knew she was well educated; had she been an historian or some other type of scholar who had read about kashallan healings? Perhaps she would tell him one day.

When he started to crawl into the hollow to retrieve the boy Moraga stopped him. "I'll get the wee laddy." Handing a startled Kashallan the beam rifle off her shoulder, she crawled inside the hollow, murmuring some soothing words in her native Caldoni. She emerged a moment later with the child held in her arms, still talking to him in her soothing voice.

"I will take him now, Warrior," Efosa said, shifting the blankets she carried to one set of arms and holding out the other for her son. Moraga gently laid him in her arms, still talking to him in a soothing sing-song voice.

Efosa settled Mosi to straddle her hip. Phillip returned Moraga's weapon and motioned Ishka to lead the way to the spot she mentioned.

As they walked Masonja fell into step beside him. "Boy bad sick with Umwira magics. What want Masonja to do for Kashallan?"

"I need to go into the Dream to speak with my kin and try to release the boy from the foul magic if I can," he said. "Moraga can keep guard here in this world to see we aren't disturbed, but I need someone to watch in the Dream as well. The Sweh'an has warned me—will you do this for me?"

Masonja nodded. "I watch. Kashallan help boy."

He smiled and touched her shoulder. "Thank you, My dear that does ease my mind."

In the sheltered place among the boulders Ishka guided them to, he lay on the blanket covered moss and closed his eyes. By his side Mosi lay unmoving, breathing shallowly. Taking several deep breaths, the bondmates slipped into the Dream.

IN THE DREAM, YOEY coiled about Phillip's chest with head raised and mouth tentacles waving to taste the etheric currents. The bondmates swam deeper into the Dream, calling for their Amla, Maker Tinguss.

To Phillip's private worry, there was still no answer from that venerable Ancient. Ro and another cousin, however answered soon enough. <<We are here, young One. Why do you swim the Dream in these dangerous times? Is there trouble?>>

He laughed, but there was little mirth in the sending. <<There is always trouble, K'amsi, but for the moment we are safe. We come to ask advice about a healing. There is a young child who was attacked by Umwira mind magic. We seek counsel about his condition...>>

Without completely surfacing to wakefulness some time later, the kashallan reached out, took Mosi's hand and formed the link. Sinking once again into his deep trance, he searched for the boy's spirit hiding somewhere in the darkened maze of disjointed images and tortured sendings ensnaring the boy's mind.

They called out to him but received no answer. At last locating the dim silver cord of his life, the bondmates followed it until they came to a small cave the child had constructed in which to hide. The refuge was similar to the hollow in which he had been concealed in the Waking World with one exception.

<<Yoey, the opening is so small. There's no way we can enter. And if we try to force our way in I fear we might lose him to death itself,>> Phillip said. <<What should we do?>>

Uncoiling itself from around Phillip, Yoey swam towards the opening. <<Too small for you, Kasha, but not for me. Let me see if I can coax him out of his refuge.>>

<<Be careful, Shalla, I sense this is a construct of the child's own making. No telling what he may construct inside there if he feels threatened.>>

Yoey swam back and nuzzled his cheek. <<I know, Kasha. There is no Umwira magic here.>>

Before Phillip could protest further, Yoey slipped inside and swam over to the boy. Mosi seemed barely aware of him. He glanced briefly at the tiny silver Khutani, then returned his attention to a small window in the opposite wall of his refuge and focused his attention on whatever lay beyond the enclosure.

<<Want to come outside and play with me?>> Yoey asked. <<We could have lots of fun. I know many fun games.>>

Mosi ignored the symbiont, continuing to stare out the tiny opening. Yoey waited, and when the boy refused to acknowledge its offer, Yoey coiled itself around the boy and placed its head companionably on his shoulder. <<What are you looking at; may I see, too?>>

Mosi made room for Yoey, enlarging the window slightly so they both could watch the scenes of violent fighting and torture taking place among the red dust and thorny shrubs of a desert plain outside.

<<That's bad, very bad,>> Yoey agreed.

<<Big monsters come—lots of blood. Hurt everybody.>> the boy trembled. Yoey hugged him.

<<Don't worry; we are safe inside your sanctuary. And when we come out, my Kasha and I are here to protect and help you.>>

Mosi shook his head. <<Not coming out—ever! Bad Ghostland monsters will eat me.>>

<<You can't stay, Little One,>> Yoey said its mental voice gentle. <<If you stay you will surely die.>> Mosi continued to shake his head, refusing to budge. <<Who will take care of your mama if you stay here and don't come back to the Waking World? She will be sad and miss you. Do you want her to be sad?>>

Mosi stopped shaking his head. Now at least he was listening. <<I am little, too, but I have magic. I can help you kill these evil creatures that trouble your mind. Come out with me. My Kasha and I will help you—protect you if you show us the Evil Ones. Together we will defeat them. Please come.>>

When Mosi and the symbiont came out of the cave Phillip was there waiting for them. Mosi shied away, but Yoey still coiled about his chest and shoulders nuzzled his neck. <<Don't be afraid; that's no monster—even though he is quite big.>>

<<Hello Mosi, I'm Phillip. I'm Yoey's bondmate. I hear some bad monsters are scaring you.>> Taking the child's hand, he said, <<We want to help you. Can you show us the foul creatures that trouble you?>>

Mosi tried to pull away and run back into his self-made cave.

<<No Mosi, don't run away. We will protect you,>> Yoey said. <<Remember I told you; we have magic. No one is going to harm you. Come, you can show us.>>

It took a bit of persuading on Yoey's part but at last Mosi agreed to walk with them.

Suddenly out of the darkness ahead came the sounds of battle, women screaming, men roaring and cursing warriors fighting—desperately out numbered. Then, one of the largest Ghostland warriors, its asymmetrical face twisted into an angry snarl, was suddenly rushing straight for them.

Phillip raised a hand and the image the boy was projecting froze as if captured by a camera. <<Ah, I think I've seen this creature before, Mosi.>>

<<You have! When, Kasha?>>

<<When we fled Sulas through the hidden paths under the mountain, we were attacked by a warband of the Ghostlanders. I think he was among them at that time.>>

<<Did you fight him?>> Mosi asked.

<<No, Little One, I did not. I was neither a kashallan nor a warrior at that time.>>

<<But our cousin did fight their war leader and made him run away.>> Yoey chimed in. <<Didn’t he, Kasha.>>

<<Yes he did, Shala.>>

<<Tani was very brave, you told me, and it was just a baby much younger than you, Mosi.>>

<<Host Dunnagh and symbiont Tani worked together, combining their power to defeat the same enemy that attacked your family.>> Phillip said.

<<I’m too little to fight them,>> Mosi said with a sob.

<<Now perhaps you are too small, but you will grow up and be a strong warrior someday,>> Phillip said.

<<Wizard Qwasigara thinks I am a coward. Says he will give me as slave to the Red Wind People.>>

<<We don’t think you are a coward. Maybe you should talk to our warrior, Armachd Chang. There are ways a small person can learn to defeat a larger foe,>> Phillip said. <<Maybe he will teach you.>>

<<But I can help you too,” Yoey added. "I will show you my magic. Come.>> Yoey uncoiled and started toward the monster still savaging Mosi’s kin.

<<Yoey,>> Phillip warned, hoping his sending was to the symbiont alone. <<Be careful. This is no game.>>

<<I know, Kasha, but the phantasm troubling him is but an echo of the Ghostlander’s power. There’s no wizard here anymore. Qwasigara is right in a way, this construct is of the boy’s making. I can release it, Kasha.>>

<<Even if it is only of the child’s making, it still may be dangerous.>>

Then there was no more time for the bondmates to discuss the matter for the Umwira warrior roared and charged them. Mosi screamed and would have run but Phillip grabbed him crushing him to his breast where he clung whimpering. <<No, Little One, don’t be frightened. Watch Yoey use its magic.>>

As the Ghostland warrior loomed over them with teeth bared ready to tear them to bits, Yoey lifted its head and shouted, <<Go away, Evil Creature, or I will kill you dead!>>

The Ghostland warrior laughed and flexed his claws. <<You are too small to hurt me. I will kill you and the boy too!>>

<<No, you won't hurt my friend Mosi.>> As the monster lunged Yoey reared up and spat black kavay into its face. The monster screamed, clawing at its mouth and eyes as the etheric ultra violet light dissolved the Ghostlander's face and chest in a most gruesome an satisfying way before the boy's eyes.

When it was finally dead at their feet, Yoey said, <<See, my Khutani magic is much stronger than a Ghostland monster. The foul creature is gone and won't trouble your dreams or waking thoughts any longer.>>

Mosi trembled in Phillip's arms impressed, but he thought the child wasn't totally convinced the fiend was gone.

<<Are you sure, Yoey?>> Mosi murmured softly, in case the fearsome warrior could still hear him.

<<Yes I am sure.>>

<<It is time to return to our sleeping bodies, Little One.>> Phillip said, breaking off any further argument. <<In the waking world I will have my apprentice Masonja, who is a very powerful shamanka, make a charm for you to ware around your neck to protect you from any more Ghostland conjuring. Our magic will help keep you safe until you are older and strong enough to fight them yourself. Will that be agreeable to you, Young Warrior?>>

Mosi stroked Yoey's silver head and smiled up at Phillip. <<Yes, that would be good.>>

<<Then let's go back. Your mother and the others are waiting for us. One of my cousins will guard your sleep until the talisman is made.>>

The boy relaxed in his arms, Yoey coiling companionably about them both as they drifted up into wakefulness.

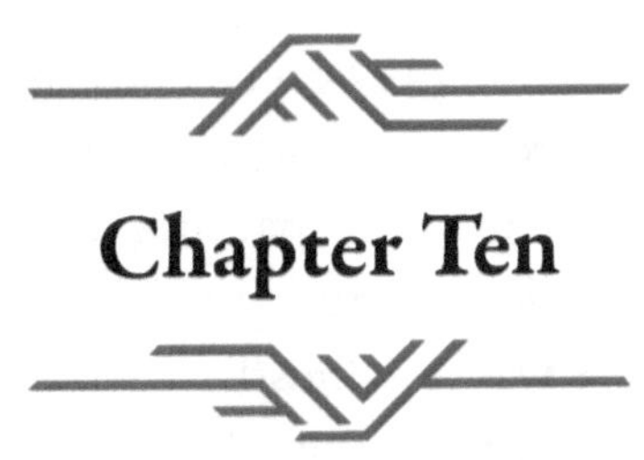

Chapter Ten

The clans left early next morning to continue their journey up the coast. Fearful of another unnatural storm, and with the canoes now overcrowded with the addition of the Bitter Water People, the leaders decided to journey only one more day hugging the coast northward. After that, they would be only a long day's walk from the Red Rock Council meeting ground. They might be safe from drowning, Phillip thought, but a land journey opened the way for a whole new set of possibilities for harm

It didn't take long for the news of his healing on little Mosi to spread through the combined camp. At the midday rest he couldn't help hearing the talk. Some were amazed that he would bother with a sniveling child, while others were angry that a Khutani, one of the Hated Enemy would dare touch one of their children. To his surprise, his strongest defenders were Ogwy, his brother and some of the other Blue Stone men.

The muttering festered throughout the afternoon finally coming to a head when Qwasigara noticed the charm around Mosi's neck that he and Masonja had crafted for the boy.

When the wizard tried to take it from him, the boy grabbed a bone knife and fought him, screaming his defiance and threatening to have his friend Yoey kill him if the wizard didn't leave him alone.

This defiance, of course, brought the angry wizard storming into the Blue Stone camp, radiating menace.

Chang and Moraga leapt to their feet hands by their weapons. Ogwy and the warriors by the fire stood as well forming a solid wall in front of him. Phillip sighed, swallowed the last of his sourwood tea and rose. <<I knew there was going to be trouble over this,>> he grumbled to Yoey.

Moving in front of the men he walked to meet his dog-faced adversary. Before Qwasigara could open his mouth, he motioned for the wizard to follow him away from the people by the fire. Signing to the others not to follow, he said in a low voice to Qwasigara, "I believe your dispute is with me alone, Wizard. No need to trouble the others with our concerns, is there?"

When they were far enough away that they couldn't be seen or heard by the others, Qwasigara rounded on him. Teeth bared, he snarled, "You had no right to interfere. There was no Ghostland wizardry—the young warrior needs to stop being foolish and be strong. Your coddling him will only make him weak in the future."

"Qwasigara, please I meant no offense. The mother asked me for help. I am well aware now that there was no Ghostland magic involved with his malady. The constructs were of the child's own making. But I am a healer as I told you and the others. It is against my nature to see suffering and not do something about it."

"Then what did you do to the boy? Did you cast a foul Khutani spell upon him? He attacked me—me! Was that your doing?"

<<Well now he knows the boy isn't a coward,>> Yoey quipped.

<<Mm, but foolhardy maybe.>>

To the wizard, he said, "No, that wasn't my doing as you put it. And, I didn't cast any spell. We took him into the Dream. My bondmate, who is also young, showed him that even tiny creatures can kill big ones. Yoey killed his Ghostland monster for him, a monster I might add that I personally have seen in the real world. Before I became a kashallan, my Speir'dina kin and I were attacked, I believe by the same Ghostland warband that came to massacre your people," Phillip added.

Qwasigara paused, his mouth open for another angry outburst, but seemed to change his mind. At last he said, "This is truth, not a lie?"

"I am speaking truth."

"How did your people survive, some foul Khutani magic?"

Phillip grimaced then laughed, but there was no mirth in the sound. "Sheer luck, I think. We learned later that the warband we came across were fleeing a recent battle with Warlinga and probably weren't at their best. Our Ce'awn, our leader was recently kashallan-bonded at the time. His symbiont was still young, but the host's people have magic of their own. Together the bondmates managed to defeat the Ghostland war leader with the war magics. They fled and so did we—in the opposite direction, of course."

Returning to the original topic under discussion, Phillip pleaded, "Qwasigara as I said, I meant no challenge to your authority. The talisman is a crutch for a time true, but I told Mosi when he's older he won't need it, because he is already a brave warrior."

Qwasigara grunted something in reply that may have been, "Don't do it again," and stalked back to the Sand Mountain encampment.

Kashallan-Phillip breathed a sigh of relief, hoping things were settled and headed back to the fire. He was cold—and needed a drink—but unfortunately sourwood tea would have to do.

NEXT MORNING AFTER a short paddle they came to the sheltered cove where the clans planned to store their canoes for the trek inland. Tess-weh and Cadrach were waiting for them on the mossy cliff above the beach. Some of the newcomers to the alliance reached for their weapons at the sight of the big Warlinga, but Ogwy roared at the men to put down their bows and keep at the work he had assigned them.

Everything stowed away to the leaders' satisfaction, the people headed up the rocky trail where the demon and her escort waited.

"Good morning, Tess-weh," Kashallan-Phillip said. "It's a nice day for a walk. Come to join us?"

Tess-weh laughed. "Good morning to you, too, My Treasure. But I don't plan on walking."

Phillip raised an eye brow, but Tess-weh didn't enlighten him. Hips swaying she passed him and flowed over to Tesulu who was just stepping onto the moss nearby. She gave him a coquettish smile. "Are you a gambling man, My Jewel?"

Tesulu grinned, giving her a fine display of his canines. "Maybe. What are we playing for?"

Tess-weh stepped closer. "Give me your Loti slave and I will show you a glimpse of your future in the coming battle with the Ghostlanders. Are you curious, My Treasure, hmm?"

Startled Tesulu gaped. He had been expecting something more—interesting. "You want a Loti slave?" He snorted a derisive laugh. "Is your Warlinga protector hungry?"

Tess-weh continued to smile but her eyes remained cold and hard. "Do you agree, or not?"

Tesulu waved a hand back to the people coming up the trail where the heavily burdened man struggled. "Have the Loti if you want, Demon. He is nearly worthless anyway. Show me the battle where I win glory."

She gave him a throaty laugh and motioned him away from the column. When they stood alone in the shade of a large boulder, she held up her hands, then placed thumb and forefingers so they were touching the same two fingers on the opposite hand. "Look between, My Jewel and see..." she said.

Tesulu bent and stared into the swirling opalescent mists suddenly revealed in the space. As he watched the mists cleared and he saw that a great battle was taking place on a dusty plain. In the center of the vision Tesulu himself was wielding his long obsidian-tipped spear surrounded by enemies. Two Warlinga and an unknown Speir'dina warrior were battling their way to aid him.

Before he could know his fate Tess-weh opened her hands and the vision dissolved. Tesulu growled and lunged for her. With a flick of her power she stopped him, freezing him in place.

"You tricked me!" he raged. "Qwasigara warned me—"

Voice as hard as the rock behind them she snarled, "I didn't trick you. We traded for a 'glimpse' of your future in exchange for the Loti and that's what I showed you a glimpse."

Releasing him from her power, she stroked his muscular arm, tracing his Sand Mountain tribal brand. "I could show you more if you pay my price, however," she cooed.

Boldly grabbing one of her ample breasts Tesulu squeezed then bent and ran his tongue over her now erect nipple. Tess-weh shuddered and arched her back to put more of the rosy bud between his black lips. When he saw she was enjoying his attentions, he stepped back giving her a mocking smile. "I will pay your price, Witch, but this time I will have more for my bargain than just a *glimpse*."

Her throaty laugh came again. "I will look forward to it, My Treasure, but be careful for what you bargain. You may not like all that you see."

He gave her his canine displaying smile again. "As you said, Witch, I am a gambling man."

"Later then, My Jewel."

When they returned to the waiting column Tesulu ordered his warriors to unpack the Loti and redistribute his load to other members of the clan. The people grumbled at the added burden, but were shocked into silence when they saw the war leader drag the reluctant slave over and hand his tether rope to Tess-weh.

Phillip laughed at their shocked faces. Glancing at Ogwy he saw him smirk in Tesulu's direction and suspected he had remembered how Sairsa and other Speir'dina rode the Loti and knew what Tess-weh planned.

Realizing at last that he had a new master, and that new master was a demon, the poor creature nearly fell to his knees with fright. Some of the people watching mocked him and laughed. Tess-weh ignored everyone. Turning to her new acquisition she ran a hand down his flank ensnaring him with her power. When he was calm and steady, Cadrach lifted her to his back and she settled herself comfortably looking around at her audience and grinned at their astonished faces. "I'm ready now, War Leader, shall we go."

Tesulu blinked. Then getting over his shock, he gave Ogwy a murderous look and shouted his orders for the people to get moving.

Throughout the day as they moved away from the cooling winds off the water, a choking cloud of red dust hovered over the column, adding to the discomfort of the baking heat. To Kashallan-Phillip's surprise he heard no complaints, even from the youngest children. These people seemed to accept the harsh climate as another of the tests they must endure. In spite of himself he had to admire their will to survive.

When he had first encountered Ogwy's clan newly captured by Ticca's hunters, he had felt only anger and maybe some contempt for the way Sairsa and Bri had been treated by their warriors. He had viewed Tinguss's alliance and his own role in fulfilling that charge as nothing more than a tiresome and difficult duty. Now, however, to his surprise, Phillip found that the longer he traveled among them he couldn't help feeling a measure of respect for their courage and endurance.

In his middle Yoey echoed his opinion when he conveyed that thought. <<Our Amla is a very wise creature to offer them sanctuary and an alliance,>> Yoey agreed.

To add to their difficulties, he had already noticed how random mutations affected the people. Phillip assumed they were caused by inadequate protection from the poisonous winds of the Sorin storms. Here and there were children with asymmetrical faces, one eye lower than the other or knobby growths on cheek or forehead. Men and women sported odd pigmentations of their fur or bald spots, others coped with one arm, or one set of arms shorter on one side of the body than the other. Some walked with a limp, but he wasn't sure if the malady was caused by injury or birth defect.

He supposed those affected with the most severe of the mutations would have been killed soon after they were detected, but he also knew that some courted the places where the Poison Fires existed, because they hoped for the power that mutations brought them. It was a gamble, true, but their wizards' tremendous Psy abilities were gained in that way.

BY LATE AFTERNOON, Phillip himself was wishing there was another loti among his new allies for whom he could do some trading. His feet, though not in as bad of shape as when he had been harvesting masa root as a slave at Sulas, were sore and a bit swollen. His watery life style in the Great Swamp definitely hadn't prepared him for this dusty trek.

With weakened women and children in tow, the column hadn't made as good of time that day as the camp leaders had hoped. Calling a hurried meeting as the light began to fade they decided to stop for the night and go into the council grounds the next morning when everyone would have had a chance to rest.

After a hasty meal Kashallan-Phillip was sitting by their tiny fire sipping at his cooling tea when Chang approached. Motioning for the warrior to join him, he asked, "Is there something troubling you Armachd?"

Chang squatted and tossed another chip of dung onto the dying flames. “Maybe,” he admitted. “I can’t help but wonder why the Sweh’an has joined us again.”

“Yes, I’ve been thinking about that, too. Even when we were threatened by that unnatural storm, she didn’t show herself. I know there certain limitations concerning her service. She won’t intervene unless someone’s life to which she is bound is dangerously threatened.”

Chang’s expression became even grimmer than before. “I suspected it was something like that.”

Phillip opened his mouth to explain more, when the warrior continued, “One other thing gives me cause for unease. I’ve been watching the Warlinga all day. His attention has been divided between you and the demon. If Tess-weh didn’t want to get her feet dirty she could have made Cadrach carry her. I think her getting Tesulu to give her the Loti had a more significant purpose.”

Phillip nodded his own expression suddenly as grim as his armachd’s. “I hadn’t thought of it like that, but she has freed her protector to act swiftly in case of trouble.”

“That’s how I see it as well, Sir. We are certain to be attacked—soon tonight or tomorrow I figure, before we reach the main encampment maybe.” They fell silent, each with his own dark thoughts. Finally breaking the silence Chang ventured, “Would Tess-weh tell us when and what to expect if you asked her?”

Phillip shook his head. “I doubt it. She can’t interfere like that. Remember how frustrated Dunnagh-Tani used to get with her when he tried to press her for more information?”

Chang laughed. “I do. The demon sure knew how to jerk his chain.” The men grinned at each other lost in their shared memories of their trek across the Great Swamp. Sobering after a long moment Chang returned to the current topic of discussion. “If you have no objections, Sir, I’ll find the leaders of our allies and tell them what we suspect.”

“Yes, that’s a good idea. I think we’ll need as much preparation as possible for what’s coming.” Rising, Chang bowed and disappeared into the darkness.

THE DOUBLING OF THE camp's guard and their restless night's sleep was for nothing, however. No attack disturbed them. Nor were they ambushed on their way to the meeting grounds. It was only later that Kashallan-Phillip appreciated the brilliance of the Ghostlanders true plan.

Located in a grassy meadow surrounded by high red cliffs, the allied clans reached the Red Rock Council Grounds by midmorning with no mishap. Noticing the Speir'dina, Tess-weh atop her Loti slave, and especially Cadrach striding boldly among the new arrivals, caused quite a stir among the people already gathered there.

With shouts of alarm men reached for their weapons and women screamed for young children to come to them as they fell back behind the warriors. The alliance leaders had been expecting trouble so they were right up front to show the advancing warriors well-known faces. Though visible, Kashallan-Phillip and the Speir'dina along with Timma and his new wife and mother-in-law hung back behind the allied clansmen.

Wizard Qwasigara's booming voice rang out over the chaos. "We are not your enemies, Clans of the Real People. Like you we come seeking vengeance for our dead. We bring powerful allies with us."

"The Warlinga is but a mindless slave to a Sweh'an Demon," Tesulu shouted, a note of contempt coloring his voice. "Are you blind, Stupid Begta? Can't you see the sigil of power carved into his forehead? He is the demon's protector, nothing more!"

In the confusion, and the shouted arguments that followed as the alliance clans moved into the larger encampment and claimed their traditional camping ground, The Ghostlanders closed the jaws of their trap.

Kashallan-Phillip and Ata Doyan were standing near Tess-weh, the Ata talking quietly with the demon when Tess-weh suddenly vanished, leaving the good Ata staring with his mouth open. At almost the same instant the kashallan felt the currents of the Ether about them rip apart. The illusion of peaceful uninhabited red rocks at the base of the cliffs dissolved to reveal screaming hordes of Ghostland warriors surrounding the encampment on three sides.

"Back! Go back down the path," Ogwy shouted to his people who hadn't yet unpacked to set up camp. "Get out before we are all trapped!"

Phillip saw little more of the unfolding battle for at that moment Cadrach grabbed him and Ata Doyan and leapt away from the fight . In great leaps he half dragged, half carried them down the steep trail they had just climbed, dropping them in a safer spot in an open space they'd passed a short while before.

Catching his breath Phillip sat down in the grass, a shaken Doyan beside him. Everything had happened so fast, he hadn't had time to warn Masonja or worry about Timma and the others. As if mirroring his own worries Ata Doyan asked the big Warlinga, looming protectively near them, "Cadrach, are you allowed to tell us what is happening back there? Are Timma, the Begta woman and our Speir'dina guardians safe?"

"My sister Warlinga is bringing many of the Umwira women and children out of the fighting. The Begta shamanka is with them. They will be here soon."

"And what of Timma and Armachd Chang?" Phillip asked. He was especially worried about the young man, recalling his trauma after his last encounter with the Ghostlanders.

"The warrior fights with the Blue Stone and Sand Mountain men. The priest-medic and his women have set up a place near the battle. They are helping the wounded brought to them."

"And what of your Mistress, Cadrach; is she safe?" Doyan asked.

"My mistress is well, Ata."

"What is she doing now?" Phillip asked.

"She is weaving a protective shield and giving battle to the Great Ghostland Wizard."

He was aware of the invisible battle going on in the realm of the Dream. He could sense the release of tremendous powers and shuddered. "Does your Mistress need my help or that of my kindred who swim nearby, Cadrach?"

"No, I don't need the help of you or your slimy relatives, Khutani," came the Demon's voice out of her slave's mouth.

Phillip shrugged. "Sorry, just trying to be helpful."

Neither Cadrach nor the Demon answered his last comment, and soon enough he was distracted by the stream of frightened women and children

Moraga was shepherding in his direction. Hurrying to meet them, he was relieved to see Masonja among them.

Taking her hand, he gasped, "Masonja are you all right? I'm so sorry I had no intention of abandoning you back there. Cadrach—"

She patted his arm silencing him. "Masonja not hurt." She waved her hand in the direction of the frightened people milling about them. "Umwira womans and children hurt. Masonja Lesala and Kashallan help maybe."

She pointed to an older woman with a grizzled pelt and ragged ponytail, her two sets of arms weighed down with baskets and bundles. Taking his arm she led him to the elder just setting down her burden. "Woman is witch. Her know lot magic."

Hoping he wouldn't be rebuffed when there was clearly a need for his services, Kashallan-Phillip bowed. "Elder how can we help you?"

SEEING THAT HER CHARGES were being taken care of for the moment Moraga approached Cadrach. "Can you protect them if I go help Chang and the warriors, Brother Warlinga?"

"Yes, Sister Warlinga. My Mistress says go help them."

Hurrying to Kashallan-Phillip she handed him her sidearm. "Just in case you need it. I'm going back to help Chang and the other laddys." He tried to hand it back murmuring something about Cadrach and black kavay, but she was already speeding back up the slope.

TIMMA SWORE ONE OF Nathan's favorite Caldoni oaths when he saw Niguiri and her mother hadn't obeyed his shouts to follow the rest of the women to safety. Rounding on them, he demanded, "What are you doing here? You should go with the others, my dear One. I don't want you hurt or killed!"

"And I don't want you hurt or killed either," Niguiri shot back. "I go with my husband. You said I was your apprentice, so I'm a medic, too. We will do this together."

Timma had meant his comment to flatter his new bride, but the middle of a battle was no time to argue the point. Motioning for them to keep close, he led them through the clumps of fighting to the centre of the encampment. There a small number of unarmed people huddled under or near a thatched shelter with open sides where a ring of stones had been laid for the coming council fire.

Directing the women to lay out one of the mats in the shade, he crouched beside a wounded man bleeding copiously from a deep gash in his side. Pushing the weakened warrior onto the mat, Timma rubbed a handful of the cauterizing powder, normally used for stopping bleeding after a Blood Gift, on the bubbling flow. The man jerked as the burning medicine closed the gash.

Without him asking Niguiri handed him a jar of the yellow kavay to cover the wound. The warrior grunted and would have risen, but Timma shoved him back. "Lie still till it dries," he instructed.

The man swore at him. "Get away from me, Khutani slave. Who do you think you are to order one of the Real People what to do?"

Timma slammed him down before he had a chance to sit. "I'm no one's slave, but I am the man who just may have saved your worthless life, Begta puke. Now lie still until the kavay dries, because if you start bleeding again I won't waste my medicines on you again."

By the time he had finished with his first unruly patient there were other wounded being helped to his healing mat.

STILL OUTSIDE THE COMBAT, Moraga slowed as she neared the fighting to get her bearings. Red dust clouds swirled above the combat making it nearly impossible to tell friend from foe. The stink of coppery blood and dying men and monster's wastes choked her nose and mouth. Where was Chang? Beam rifle tucked against her hip she skirted the fighting men, searching for her partner.

They had talked late into the night, discussing how best to deploy themselves and their off-world weapons. Instead of wading into the fray, Chang would be looking for a way to circle around the Ghostland troops and pick them off from behind. Seeing flashes of green light explode off to her left she headed in that direction.

Suddenly a Ghostland warrior loomed out of the dust haze in front of her. Long snaky arms with razor-sharp claws on each of its four-fingered hands, it reached for her, snarling. Moraga screamed a Caldoni war cry and incinerated the creature in mid lunge. Giving way to a berserker rage she shouted her defiance and fought her way to her Lann Gheal companion's side, a trail of charred Ghostlander body parts smoldering in her wake.

Chang gave her a grim smile and sliced a scaled monster with a rock studded war club in half with a beam from his side arm. The two halves fountaining gore dropped twitching into the red dust. Moraga shot another creeping up on them from the side, slicing off both arms. Guarding each other's backs they burned their lethal way through the Ghostlanders' battle formation, cutting them down from behind.

TIMMA WAS WORKING ON one of Tesulu's men when he heard Niguiri scream. Glancing up at the distraction, a bolt of fear stabbed into his heart. Niguiri was being dragged away by a fearsome Ghostland warrior. It was happening again; another he loved was being hurt by these unnatural creatures.

But Timma was no longer the terrified boy hiding in a rock crevice while his best friend Orlan was taken. His long hours of training with Sensei Chang had worked their magic. Tossing down his healing jars he drew his Speir'dina knife and charged.

Not expecting any resistance from a mere Avairei, the warrior was unprepared for Timma's fierce attack. He managed to slice a deep gash in the warriors arm and follow it with a bone jarring front kick to the monsters knee before the warrior let go his prize and went on the offensive.

Aware of the danger the Ghostlander's whip-like tail posed, Timma kept on the move, darting in to stab or kick at an exposed area then leaping nimbly out of the way before the enemy's claw or tail could touch him. The warrior roared in frustration as each attack was blocked, or met by empty space. But with his longer reach, Timma knew it was only a question of time before the monster grew wise to his tactics and overpowered him.

Snatching up one of the wounded men's spears, Timma sheathed his knife and used the longer weapon to expand his own killing potential. They continued to spar, people hurrying to get out of their way. At last the monster growled through gritted teeth, "I grow tired of your games, Slave!" Snarling the Ghostlander came at him in a rush with teeth bared and claws extended.

As Timma raised his spear to block the frontal attack, he wasn't experienced enough to see that the move was only a ploy. When he raised his spear, the Ghostlander whipped his tail around and tripped his adversary. As Timma fell, the warrior snatched the spear from his hands and tossed it contemptuously away. "Now you die, Little Worm," the warrior roared and lunged for him.

Snatching out his knife Timma propelled himself upward to bury the blade hilt-deep in the man's groin when he loomed over him for the kill. At the same moment Timma struck, an obsidian-bladed spear plunged into the enemy warrior's back with force enough to pierce his armored scales.

Covered with acrid purple blood Timma rolled aside as the Ghostlander crashed to the ground beside him. Wiping the mess from his face, he blinked and stared up at a grinning Tesulu. Flipping over the body the war leader retrieved the knife and considered its lethal sharpness. He started to put it in his belt then happened to see his niece huddled in her mother's arms and reluctantly handed it to Timma.

"So, Nephew, you can actually fight. Your Speir'dina teacher has taught you well. Your little dance performances on the beach weren't just for show. Maybe we keep you after all."

Timma grinned, catching his breath. "Thank you for the help, Honored Uncle. I think maybe I still need more lessons."

Tesulu smirked. "Maybe." Then he grinned again showing his canines. "Now if you have caught your breath, I need you to use some of your other skills." He pointed with his chin to a bloody warrior leaning heavily on the shoulder of another man. "This clumsy Begta forgot how to use his spear and now look what's happened? Maybe I give him to you as a slave, hmm?"

Through gritted teeth the wounded man swore. Tesulu laughed again and helped him to sit on the now bloody mat. Retrieving his medical supplies from a still shaken Ishka, Timma was dabbing green kavay on his fingers as Tesulu and the warrior left them.

LOSING TRACK OF TIME Kashallan-Phillip was absorbed in his healing work when he heard Cadrach wail in anguish. Lifting his face to the sky the big Warlinga cried out for his Mistress and there was such a note of despair in his voice that the Kashallan shuddered in fear, icy chills running down his back. Then the big Warlinga leapt into the air and disappeared.

At almost the same moment the world around him exploded, knocking him and everyone else to the ground. Overhead deafening thunder boomed, the sky igniting with blinding streaks of blue-white fire. Picking himself up at last Kashallan-Phillip stared open-mouthed with everyone else at the devastation around them.

Large boulders had been tossed about like pebbles. Thorny shrubs and other vegetation were scattered everywhere. It looked as if a giant child had had a temper tantrum and ripped everything in reach to shreds. In the direction of the Council Grounds clouds of dark smoke billowed into the lavender sky. The balance of the world had changed, and though he could sense it, Phillip-Yoey couldn't know if the difference was for the good, or foretold disaster.

Chapter Eleven

Kashallan-Phillip and the others who cautiously approached the Council Grounds found that the enemy was gone, leaving behind only their dead , their smoldering bodies often entangled with their western clans' adversaries. Dazed survivors wandered about aimlessly searching for friends and relatives. Women knelt beside fallen kinsmen keening.

<<This is terrible, Kasha,>> the horrified Yoey said. <<I fear this unexpected attack has left behind only a shattered remnant of a once fierce and proud people.>>

Fearing for the safety of his own people, Phillip-Yoey scanned the destruction for signs of Chang Moraga and Timma. The shaded canopy that had been erected for the coming council was on fire. Through the smoky haze he spied Timma and his wife and Ishka hastily trying to drag the worst of the wounded to safety. There was no sign of Moraga and Chang. Hurrying to help his medic, he prayed the others were unharmed.

Throughout the rest of the day Kashallan-Phillip amerced himself in the many tasks needing someone's attention. He hauled water from the nearby spring, helped extinguish fires and piled up the dead, separating friend from foe. When called for, he coughed up kavay medicines Timma ran out of and consulted on patients when asked by the other healers.

At some point during the afternoon a distraught Qwasigara found him returning to camp with a yoke with filled water gourds slung across his shoulders. "Where are the demon and her slave?" he demanded.

Setting down his burden, Phillip wiped the sweat out of his eyes and stared blankly at the wizard. Qwasigara angrily repeated his question. Its meaning finally penetrating the fog of his tired brain, he shook his head. "I have no idea where she is. She was battling the Ghostland wizard and then something went wrong, I think, because Cadrach disappeared, too."

He waved his hand at the surrounding destruction. "Then this happened. I don't know any more than you do at this point, and at the moment I'm too tired to worry about it." He settled the yoke back upon his shoulders. "She'll be back when she is needed—if she isn't dead."

PHILLIP-YOEY SAT AMONG Timma's replenished medicine jars, his head leaning against one of the four central posts surrounding the council fire. Nearby exhausted people went about their evening tasks, their movements only a series of flickering shadows behind his closed eyelids. Never since the early days at Sulas had he been this exhausted.

Crouching beside him, Masonja put a bowl of cool water in his hand. Glancing up he thanked her and took several long drinks of the draft. "Thank you, My dear." He finished the bowl and studied her more closely. "You are as tired as I am, I'm sure, you should go rest."

She shrugged. "Masonja rest soon. Starmans want see you." She studied him through narrowed eyes as if assessing his strength. Sighing, she finally added, "Him say important."

Phillip inwardly groaned. He glanced around but didn't see Chang among the warriors taking up a defensive position near the edge of camp. "Do you know what he wants? Can't he talk to me here?"

Masonja shook her head. "Him say better nobody see." Repeating herself she implored, "Him say important. You come now. Masonja help you if Kashallan too tired."

She meant give him some of her magic, which shamed him. She was as exhausted as he was. He was behaving like a pampered Dymarian, Phillip thought privately. This was Timorna—no one else was whining about being tired. Giving her a wan smile, he got to his feet. "Thank you for the offer, but I'll manage. Take me to him." Masonja led him through the shattered camp. No one challenged him, only a few aware of their passing.

Chang was waiting for them in the shadows about halfway down the slope where Cadrach had carried him earlier. "Thank you for coming, Sir. I have something to show you. I don't know what to do—and I need your advice to figure it out."

"This sounds very mysterious, Armachd. But couldn't you have—"

"Better I show you instead of trying to explain," Chang murmured and headed off into the brush away from the path. "It's not far now and Moraga is waiting for us."

Chang led them to a mossy spot above the trail. In the dimming light Kashallan-Phillip saw a huddled figure crouching protectively over a dark form sprawled on the moss. Nearby another charred lump smoldered, wispy blue smoke still curling lazily above the twisted corpse.

"Commander Tizu lent us one of the night scopes out of supply. So Moraga and I told Ogwy we would go on a scouting mission to help make sure the Ghostlanders that survived were gone and not lingering about planning another surprise attack," he explained. "Then we came across this." He motioned to the scene before them.

Phillip moved closer and stared down at what Moraga was guarding. He gasped when he realized that it was a horribly burned female human body sprawled on the moss. Tessa? Nearly bald, her charred skin blackened and peeling away from the raw flesh beneath she was almost unrecognizable.

Moraga looked up, tears streaming down her cheeks. "Glad you laddys have come back. There's been some creature snuffling about over there—had to frighten it away with a beam shot not long ago."

With a groan of despair the Kashallan sank down beside the wounded woman. As he reached for the burnt woman's hand, he asked, "Any signs of life?"

"I see her breath sometimes."

Oh Tessa, I'm so sorry—and curse the foul demon for abandoning you to your pain and death instead of staying to help. Well he supposed the damned creature would be back if they could save its host's life.

"We figured that for her safety—as well as our own, it would be better to keep this a secret as long as we can," Chang said. "There might still be Ghostland spies around. Better to keep them guessing, we thought."

"Good idea, but I can't continue to treat her way out here," Phillip-Yoey said. "We would be too vulnerable to predators if nothing else." The question right now was how to move her and treat her without his Khutani kin and the soothing waters of a healing pool. He felt frustrated with his inadequacies. He would do the best he could, but she might indeed still die.

"What wrong Kashallan?" Masonja said, crouching down beside him.

He contracted his tentacles and released Tessa's hand. Glancing at their expectant faces, he said, "She is alive—barely, but for how long I don't know. I need to wrap her in something and move her." He glanced down at his filthy, blood-stained kilt, and grimaced. It was the only piece of large cloth they had, it would have to do.

"But in order to do that I need to cover her burns with some kind of salve to protect her damaged skin before we try to carry her anywhere. Unfortunately, I'm too tired at the moment to make anything—"

Masonja patted his hand and rose to her feet. "Kashallan rest. Masonja can help. Old witch Lesala teach me." Motioning for Chang to follow her she headed into the darkness. "Come Masonja need big knife."

They returned in a few minutes with a carry net full of several purple round melon-like objects. The Begta shamanka directed Chang to set them one at a time on a flat rock and cut them in half.

Coming back to them she motioned for Moraga to turn Tessa on her side. Scooping a sticky gray mass out of the melon she plastered it liberally on the worst of the burns. When the melon was clean inside she motioned for the next one and kept covering Tessa until she was encased with a thick grey mass that like the yellow kavay hardened over the injuries to form a protective seal.

Unable to contain his shock the Kashallan reached for one of the empty melon shells and plunged his sensitive tentacles into its spongy inner shell. For the moment the excitement of a new discovery washed away his exhaustion and despair.

<<Kasha, our Amla may not know about this wonderful plant. I have no encoded memory of it,>> Yoey bubbled.

Phillip patted his middle, sharing his bondmate's interest. <<Living here for a thousand years or so it makes sense that these people have discovered medicinal plants to take the place of the kavays, Shalla. They couldn't have survived otherwise.>>

Using his kilt like a hammock they took turns carrying the still unconscious woman to the encampment. As they were leaving Chang glanced at the charred remains of the Warlinga, and said, "Guess I'll come back tomorrow and see if I can cut away a few bones for Cadrach's kin at Ticca, I'm sure they would like them."

Recognizing Chang and Moraga, the sentries let them pass with no comment. With so many wounded, some also badly burned, their return to the council grounds caused little notice. Those who could were already asleep, those still awake too exhausted to be curious.

At the Blue Stone fire an anxious Ata Doyan stood when he saw them. "Praise the Mother, you are all safe," he greeted them.

Timma, Niguiri cuddled against his side, and Ishka were also still awake and waiting for them. When Ata Doyan saw the burden they carried he gasped and hurried over as they set the blanketed form down in the shadows a short distance from the fire. "Who?" he breathed, then he answered his own question. "Tess-weh."

"For the moment just Tessa," Phillip said and couldn't keep the bitterness from his voice. "If she survives I suspect the demon will once more return, as well."

Doyan touched the grey cocoon enclosing her. "One of the Umwira witches shared some of her healing knowledge with Masonja," he said, answering his question before the Ata could ask. "There's a plant—" he broke off as he noticed that Lubwey had joined them and was also staring at the injured woman.

"Is it the demon?" he asked in a quiet voice.

"Just the Speir'dina host, Tessa, at present," Phillip said. Glancing around, he added,. "Where is Ogwy?"

Lubwey made a face and shrugged. "Off somewhere with his new wife. He left me in charge for the night."

"Keep her identity quiet for now. Chang thinks there might still be Ghostland spies among us. If the Ghostlanders know she is so badly injured and the demon has left us for the moment, they may attack again," Phillip warned. "Lubwey, we would be extremely vulnerable if that happened. She deflected a lot of the Ghostland wizard's power today. We might not have survived otherwise, I fear."

Lubwey considered then nodded. "I see your point. Where is the Warlinga?"

"Cadrach is dead. My warriors found them both lying in a burned patch of moss back down the trail."

"Can she speak; tell us what happened?"

"So far she has remained unconscious, and in her present condition that's a blessing." Kashallan-Phillip would have said more, but Ishka pressed a soothing cup of tea into his hand and urged him to come sit by the fire.

"Go, Holy One," Doyan urged. "I will watch over her. It is my duty to care for the H'an, please rest now."

The Kashallan allowed himself to be led back to the warmth of the fire. When he was settled someone placed a blanket around his shoulders and Niguiri handed him a couple pieces of warmed-up Dhuura meat. It was tough and chewy, but he didn't care, it was food and he was too exhausted to worry about not getting gourmet cuisine.

Before he totally passed out, he asked Ishka, "I know there's nothing like a Khutani healing pool on this side of the Shallow Sea, but is there another water source, near the spring where the camp has been getting its water, large enough to have a place where Tessa could lie in cold water while her burns heal and her body mends?"

"There is such a healing place in the mountains about a half day's walk from here," she said. "After the funeral takes place tomorrow evening, a party of wounded and their relatives will be going there. We can join them."

Chapter Twelve

As he was drowsily sipping his morning tea next to Chang, Lubwey sat down near them with his own clay jar of the bitter-sweet brew. "I have been giving some thought to what you said last night about spies, Kashallan. It is very strange that the Ghostlanders seem to know what we plan to do almost as soon as we know ourselves. There wouldn't have been time enough for even the swiftest of runners to reach one of their outposts."

"The spy wouldn't need to leave the clan he or she was traveling with," Chang said. "When we were attacked at Ticca during the Sorins Wizard Barak's changeling agent had been living at the keep as one of the Ima Matri's trusted advisors for years. We found out after her death that she had been communicating with her Ghostland master through a crystal communication device—something saved from the old technology of your people, before the Great Wars maybe.

"One of the Ima's own nieces was also ensnared by means of a crystal pendant she wore. Everyone thought it was just a simple piece of jewelry and that mistake almost cost Sairsa's and many other lives."

Phillip-Yoey hadn't heard from Tizu this part of the story when they caught up to the Blue Stone Clan. There were more important things to consider at the time to relate unnecessary information. Now however, that little tidbit of knowledge could prove to be very useful.

"If there is a spy still among us that wasn't killed in yesterday's raid," Chang was saying, "look for strange jewelry on someone you would never suspect. The spy will be someone well trusted and respected, but maybe has a grudge to settle. Someone not a leader, but close enough to the inner circle to have information about our plans."

Lubwey sat staring into the flames, thinking. Coming to some inner conclusion he nodded to himself and rose. "You have given me much to think about. I will speak to Qwasigara and a few of the others. We will find the spy and make him pay."

Yes, Phillip thought, think long and hard, suddenly glad it had been Lubwey here last night instead of the more unpredictable Ogwy.

"Lubwey," Kashallan-Phillip said before he could go too far. "Remember the Ghostland agents at Ticca were both women."

Glancing around after Lubwey left he noticed that Tessa was no longer resting near the Blue Stone fire. Chiding himself for being a self-indulgent lay-about this morning, he asked Chang where they had moved Tessa.

"The women erected a shelter for the Blue Stone wounded last night while we were—gone." He motioned to a grass thatched shelter nearby. "Tessa and a Blue Stone warrior are the only casualties needing extended care right now. Ata Doyan and Timma's wife and mother are looking after both patients. The Begta shamanka and Moraga went to get cool water from the spring for them."

Water, yes it was a never ending task, he thought, his arms already feeling the pull of the buckets. But first he would go check on the warrior and Tessa to see if she had regained consciousness.

Entering the shelter he found a dozing Ata Doyan, sitting beside a pallet in the dim interior. Closer to the entrance the wounded Blue Stone man lay on a similar mat, his torso heavily plastered with yellow kavay. He was also asleep. Stripes of orange kavay for the pain had been drawn down one arm, accounting for his rest. Certain that Timma had done the basics, he crouched and took the man's limp hand and formed the link.

The man hovered at the border between life and death, but the priest-medic had done everything he could have done for the man. Adding a further incentive to the warrior's own body's healing efforts; he broke the link and stood.

Careful not to wake the exhausted priest, Phillip-Yoey sat beside his other patient, uncovered a hand and formed the link. Finished with his initial exam, he opened his eyes, but remained in the link and studied her face. She was watching him with hard dark eyes. Phillip grimaced. It was as he had tasted: the demon was here, but not happy about it.

"A death for your H'an now will be an easy solution to dissolve a contract I know you dislike, Spirit. But how, I wonder, will those who oversee your contract with this woman judge your service to us if you allow her to die now?"

Anger flared in those dark orbs, but he met her glare and held it unflinching. "Wizard Barak is dead, Khutani."

"Mm, that is good to know, Honored Spirit, but I'm sure there are others in the Ghostlands who are ready and willing to take his place. For surely one such as you, who didn't need the help of a 'slimy worm,' such as me or my kin, couldn't be vanquished by just one mortal wizard?"

The kashallan tasted her searing anger as she snarled, "No, damn you; he was not. The wizard had help—lots of help."

The kashallan released her from the link and sat back. His voice hardened as he added, "Then you had better start helping me heal this woman. We still have work to do, and you, I'm sure, will want to extract vengeance on the ones who killed your protector, and almost killed your host. Is that not so, Spirit?"

She thought about it for a moment and then gave him a slight nod. "Good." Taking up Tessa's hand again, he closed his eyes and reformed the link. Together the demon and the Kashallan worked to mend Tessa's badly damaged body as the life of the camp flowed on about them.

When he finally released her from the link and opened his eyes the demon had retreated and Tessa was sleeping peacefully. To his surprise, Ata Doyan and several others were crammed into the tiny enclosure watching him. Qwasigara and Masonja were among his attentive audience. Using their spirit-sight they had probably seen much more than Lubwey and Ishka also occupying the space.

Suddenly exhausted and feeling smothered by so many people, he rose shakily to his feet. Addressing Ata Doyan, he said in a tired voice, "Tessa is healing. The Spirit and I have worked together to save her life and begin the healing process. She will sleep for some time now, Ata, so get some rest yourself. Someone can fetch me if she is still in pain when she wakes."

Outside he breathed in several great lungfuls of the cool desert air. He wanted nothing more than to crawl off somewhere and sleep like his patient, but there was too much to do to indulge in that luxury. At last he turned to the curious men waiting to speak to him

Qwasigara and Lubwey were there as well as Tesulu, Ogwy and some men he didn't know, but assumed they were leaders of the other clans who had gathered for the war council before the attack. Motioning them away from the hut he led them back to the Blue Stone fire, hoping he could find something to eat or drink there.

Masonja and Ishka had beaten him back to the fire and had already set a pot on the flames to heat so they could serve him and their guests the always present and favorite drink among the Clans, sour-wood tea. When everyone was served tea, strips of Dhuura meat were passed around, followed by a bowl of soft grease in which to dip the tough, dry meat.

When the men had eaten and the bowls of tea had been filled for a second time, the women retreated and Qwasigara began, "I sensed the demon has returned. What did the Spirit have to say?"

Phillip stole a look at the strangers to whom he hadn't been introduced, wondering just how much to tell them. "Tess-weh didn't tell me much about the battle itself. Mostly we used our combined power to help the host Tessa. She did say that the Ghostland wizard, Barak is dead."

That news brought gasps from many about the fire. "Then it is over," one of the newcomers said. "We have nothing to worry—"

"Cowardly Begta," Ogwy snarled. "Barak wasn't our only enemy. Is your head as empty as the clay pots your people bring to trade?"

The Green Clay warrior reared back as if Ogwy had struck him. Before things could go further down that road, Phillip said loud enough to drown out the man's angry protest, "The Demon did confirm that Barak didn't conjure alone. Others were with him and still are out there threatening our survival—as well as seeking to avenge their leader's death, no doubt."

"That is a sobering thought," Lubwey said. "Knowing that other Ghostlanders still seek my blood won't ease my sleep tonight."

"Ah, but it may give us some time to collect ourselves and plan," Tesulu said, his expression thoughtful. "After such a blow the wizard's subordinates will war among themselves for a time till one emerges as their new leader."

"Wise council, but don't count on a long war," kashallan-Phillip said. "The Ghostlanders have already demonstrated that they can work together and combine their power. Barak alone couldn't have come so close to killing the demon's host. There might be someone that has just been waiting for the opportunity that the Sweh'an provided to take over."

"Yes," Qwasigara agreed. "I can think of one or two, and there may be more, lurking in the shadows unknown to us."

When the meeting broke up and the men drifted away, Phillip called for the wizard to wait a moment. Qwasigara turned and he motioned for him to walk with him away from the more trafficked areas of the encampment. When they were out of hearing by a casual passerby, Phillip stopped and faced him. Taking a deep breath, he began, "This is difficult for me to say—and I don't know how to say this with proper clan protocol, so forgive me—"

Qwasigara made a cutting gesture with his hand. "Just come out with it, Khutani. Say what you want to say."

"All right then, as Lubwey probably already told you there is a spy for the Ghostlanders among us. It won't be long before Tess-weh's survival is common knowledge in camp. If the Ghostlanders learn of this they will strike again while she is too weak to aid us.

"We need to find that spy—and soon. And," He took a deep breath. This was the real hard part. "And someone from among the clans must come forward to become her mortal protector and slave."

Qwasigara's head snapped back as if the kashallan had struck him. His lip curled in a snarl, but before he could say or act on his anger, Phillip held up his hands and hastily blurted, "Though my situation isn't the same, I know what I'm asking of the warrior who gives up so much. As a bonded host, I know better than most what such a sacrifice will mean.

"But while she is so vulnerable she will need protection. And later when we war against the enemy her protector will gain much acclaim for the clan who offered up its brave son. Think about what I've told you, please. That's all I ask."

After a long uncertain moment in which Phillip maintained eye contact with the snarling wizard, Qwasigara relaxed and finally nodded. "I will consider your words and talk to others with—special gifts among us."

Phillip let out his breath and bowed. "Thank you. That's all I ask."

Chapter Thirteen

Tumpline pulled taught across his forehead, Kashallan-Phillip was just setting down a carry net of dry brush for the evening's council fire when Ishka came over to him and held out a bowl of cool water. Untangling himself from net and line, he took the bowl and drank deep.

"I have been looking for you, Kashallan," she confessed. "I'm sorry to trouble you; I know you have been busy, but Efosa is quite distraught and won't be comforted until she sees you."

Startled he lowered the bowl without drinking the rest. <<I wonder what this is all about, Shala, we barely know the woman. Why would she be so insistent to see us?>>

<<I don't know, Kasha. Maybe something has happened to Mosi.>>

Yes, that was it, surely. Her concern for the boy was the dominate focus of her life. Privately he hoped the child hadn't done anything rash like attacking the wizard again. Voicing his question to Ishka he asked if she knew what was the problem.

Ishka stared at him open-mouthed, then said, "I thought you knew—but maybe not. Last night you were gone from camp and today..."

He frowned. "No. Tell me what has happened."

Ishka nodded and started off to a part of the camp where he hadn't had reason to go before. "Come I will explain as we go." Telling the others on his work crew that he was needed elsewhere the kashallan fell into step beside her.

"Yesterday Efosa took Mosi and went to visit her Twisted Grass relatives on the other side of camp from our clan assigned site. She may have wanted to show her uncle and aunt that the curse of bad luck was no longer shadowing her. Mosi was doing much better since your healing.

"When the fighting started they were too far away to flee with the rest of Sand Mountain and Blue Stone. I don't know how exactly he was killed;

maybe when the lightning struck and there were so many fires—I don't know. Since his death her aunt says, all she does is cry—and ask for you."

As they drew near a group of hastily erected grass-thatched lean-to shelters clustered around a central fire pit they heard an angry man's shouting, punctuated by a hysterical woman's weeping. Ignoring the angry muttering when he was recognized, Kashallan-Phillip flung himself down in front of the distraught woman, Yoey's tears already blurring his eyes.

"Oh Efosa, I'm so, so sorry! Ishka just told me—I didn't know—truly I am sorry. He was a brave, brave warrior for one so small. I will miss him—he was my friend," Yoey said.

In her lap he noticed the charred wooly bundle held protectively. "Friend," she repeated in a dull voice. "He talked about his friend Yoey constantly as we traveled here, you know." Reaching out a hand she clutched the kashallan's wrist with an iron grip.

"Please, Khutani, heal him again—say I'm not cursed—bring him back to me. He is all I have. My husband, my older children—all gone, and I grow too old to have more now. Please, who will take care of me now, an old woman, cursed with such bad luck with no husband and children!"

There was such sorrow in her voice that it tore his heart to hear it. "No, no, My dear, you aren't cursed. We live a hard dangerous life on this world. These things just happen." Yoey's tears still flowing down his face, he reversed her grip on his arm and formed the link, sending a calming agent down their bond.

Head down Efosa shook her head, unwilling to listen. "Please, Khutani, heal him for me once again."

"I'm sorry I cannot. That healing would be beyond the skill of even the Ancient who made me."

"No, no, say it isn't so," she begged.

His voice choking on his words, he said, "Ah, Efosa, he is gone. You must accept what the gods—uh—Unseen Ones have given you to bear."

He looked up, catching Ishka's eye. She said in a quiet voice, her eyes glancing at Efosa's hand he still held in the link. "They need to take the young warrior away to prepare for the burial tonight."

Phillip gave a slight nod and increased the tranquilizing agent he was pouring into her blood. He understood. "Efosa, my dear, you need to let your relatives take him now. They need to prepare the young warrior for his journey tonight."

She shook her head as an older woman with a braided gray mane and white muzzle crouched and held out her arms.

"Yes, you must, my dear," he soothed, pouring more tranquilizer down the link. "You really must let go, but if you like I will sit with you. We will grieve together, and you can tell me about my friend when he was small." The woman held out her arms again, but still she hesitated.

"Who is this, Efosa? Can you introduce me to her," Phillip coaxed. She has a kind face. I would like to pay her my respects and maybe some of the others sitting and standing nearby. Can you tell me their names?"

Efosa sniffed. "This is my aunt Daylay. And my father Tego is over there," she pointed with her lips to the angry gray-pelted warrior who had been shouting abuse as he and Ishka arrived. Distracted by the task he had given her, Daylay gently removed Mosi's body from Efosa's now relaxed hold and took him away.

Still holding her in the link the Kashallan settled himself more comfortably beside her and listened as she related sad and funny stories about her lost son throughout the afternoon. When she broke down and sobbed in her silent Western Clan way, Yoey cried in sympathy, giving voice to the grief she couldn't express so openly. The symbiont also told her funny stories from its own early days as a child of the pools. Phillip doubted if she understood much of what a tearful Yoey shared, but she welcomed its concern nonetheless.

At some point during the afternoon an unnamed woman asked him why he made water from his eyes. "It is one of the ways my Speir'dina people show their grief," Phillip explained. "In this case it is a sign of our deepest feeling and respect."

The woman snorted, not believing him. "A Khutani, one of the Hated Enemy showing respect and for a mere child, I find that hard to believe. Why would you do that for one you barely knew, Khutani?"

Phillip heard the anger and bitterness behind her words. Refusing to be bated, he said in a calm voice, "I'm not your enemy, Woman of the Real People, nor is my parent, Maker Tinguss."

He didn't want to let this discussion deteriorate into angry accusations when everyone's emotions were so raw. He was framing a diplomatic answer when the symbiont blurted, "You're wrong! Mosi was my friend!"

Phillip sighed and patted his middle with a calming gesture. <<Yoey, Shalla, please,>> Phillip soothed. <<We are all upset right now this is hard for everyone. Don't let's make it worse.>>

To the woman and the others listening, Phillip said, "My symbiont is young as was Mosi. Within the Dream spirits touch in a way that here in the physical world we seldom achieve. The two young beings connected in a special way. This is the first time for my bondmate that it has tasted the death of someone it knew. It feels—we both feel the loss deeply. This is truth I tell you. By the Unseen Ones of this land I swear it."

AS THE AFTERNOON WANED, Daylay with the Kashallan's help persuaded Efosa to eat something and drink a bowl of sourwood tea. Giving her a slight sedative, the Kashallan stood and looked around for Ishka. He wanted to go back to the Blue Stone camp and rest himself. He predicted it was going to be a long night.

As they were leaving, Daylay called to him to wait a moment. "Thank you for being so kind to my niece this afternoon. She has lost so much—her life filled with nothing but misfortune since she defied her father and married that Sand Mountain man. We listened to your words and watched how you cared for one who is not your kin and were honored.

"We of the Twisted Grass people have talked it over among ourselves. As a mark of our respect for you the Family of Mosi wish you to sit with us tonight. We would like the Begta and the woman warrior to join us, as well. Ishka has told us how they protected his body and spirit when you took our little one into the Dream for the Healing."

Phillip-Yoey bowed. "I am honored by your regard, Elder. I and my people would gladly sit with the Family of Mosi." Thinking of his problem with Qwasigara after the healing he wondered if he would be breaking protocol if he accepted. "If it is permitted, that is. Some may object to my attending at all. I have no wish to cause more trouble for the Family—or anyone by my presence."

"Your concern, too is appreciated. Our head wizard Bahiem is aware of our request and agrees you should sit with us. Will you come then?"

Privately Phillip's instincts warned that there was more to this offer than appeared on the surface, but Yoey definitely wanted to go. What he sensed wasn't a physical threat to him, nor a magical one, but there was some unspoken motivation behind this flattery. He wished he'd had the Psy training of a Caldoni. Dunnagh probably could have figured it out by now. "Thank you again, Elder. We accept," he finally said.

Returning to the Blue Stone encampment he arrived as the wizard and the war leaders of Red Wind and Sand Mountain were just leaving. Qwasigara saw him and waited to intercept him before he reached the fire.

"I wanted you to know that we think we have found our spy."

Kashallan-Phillip's expression hardened, all tiredness forgotten for the moment. "Good. Who?"

Qwasigara shook his head strands of gray mane covering one eye. He brushed the hair aside and smiled. "Tonight the Wizard Council has placed protection about our camp while we mourn our dead. No communication with the enemy will get past our magic. Tomorrow is time enough to concern ourselves with spies and—other things."

"Mm, other things. Then your Council has discussed the equally pressing matter we talked about? Have you come to a conclusion?"

Qwasigara grinned, showing his canines. "Tomorrow, Khutani."

"How very mysterious of you." His grin only widened.

As the wizard turned to go Philip stopped him. "Since you're here I'd like to ask your advice on another unrelated matter."

Qwasigara turned to face him, arms folded across his chest, waiting.

"The boy Mosi was killed yesterday during the fighting. I've just come from sitting with the Mother and her kin this afternoon. They have asked me to sit with the family tonight for the ceremony. Her aunt Daylay said they asked their wizard, a man named Bahiem if it would be all right. He gave his permission, yet there is still something troubling me about their offer."

The wizard was silent for a moment then laughed. "Yes, I saw you over there sitting with *those people*." He laughed again, but Phillip could detect no merriment in the sound.

The kashallan's mouth hardened his eyes cold. "What are you trying to tell me, Wizard? Is there danger? Are they planning some treachery?"

Qwasigara snorted, some private amusement rumbling deep in his throat. "If you mean do they plan to kill you, or harm you with their magic, the answer is, no. With Sand Mountain and Blue Stone-Bitter Water and soon to be Red Wind sworn to your alliance those Twisted Grass people wouldn't dare. Bahiem is too stupid and weak to try anything like that.

"Sit with them if you want, Khutani, but be warned. Like an Oko hiding in the sand to catch its prey, he is a sly one. He probably has something planned for you and you may not like it." Still chortling to himself, the wizard left him to ponder the matter on his own, refusing to say more.

<<I still want to go, Kasha.>>

Chapter Fourteen

The booming of hide drums woke the Kashallan from a light doze. The sky had turned a deep purple while he'd rested. In the dim light he could see with his heightened senses the conjured web of faint green threads enclosing the encampment that Qwasigara said would protect them. By the fire Moraga and Masonja were waiting to accompany him to the ceremony.

Glancing about he noticed that most of the Blue Stone warriors were also readying themselves for the event. Suddenly fearful for Tessa's safety if so many left their camp, he murmured to Moraga, "I'm worried about Tessa if we all leave."

She handed him a bowl of some kind of pounded root mush and said just as quietly, "Chang and Noi are staying here to guard the healing hut. Several of the Blue Stone laddys are on patrol tonight. They will check in here with Chang and Noi, so don't fret yourself, Kashallan."

"That does ease my mind," he admitted and finished his meal.

"WELCOME, HONORED GUESTS." Daylay was waiting for them near the edge of the large circle to lead them to prominent seats near the front of the Twisted Grass Clan's allotment. Motioning for him to sit on a hair-filled cushion next to Efosa, she directed Moraga and Masonja to sit on mats just behind him. The light was dim, but his entrance and placement among the clans was noted and commented upon. Many weren't happy to see him here at all, let alone sitting up front with family elders in a place of honor. Ignoring the angry muttering at her back, Daylay seated herself calmly on his other side. Phillip glanced at Efosa sitting rigidly next to him. He took her hand but didn't form the link.

"How are you doing, My dear?" She gave him a wan smile, but didn't speak, returning her attention to the activity going on by the central fires.

As best Phillip could tell in the darkness while they waited for everyone to get settled, the circle had been divided into eight partitioned spaces. Each of the seven clans had their own assigned place, the eighth reserved for the shrouded bodies of the dead. Isles like the spokes of a great wheel divided one from another. Elders and heads of individual families sat near the center younger members and children further back in the darkness.

In the centre four fires formed a diamond that corresponded to the cardinal points of the compass. Near them several warriors stood warming the skins of their hand drums. Inside the cleared space Qwasigara and what he assumed were the Council of wizards and elders waited for the people to quiet.

At last an Ancient the Kashallan hadn't met walked to the center between the fires, raised a long carved stick decorated with bone ornaments and knotted hair charms, and began a call to the Unseen Ones in a booming voice. He invited the Powers to witness as the Real People gave thanks for their survival and honored their dead with offerings and the gift of song.

Throughout the night men and women from each clan in turn rose and spoke of their lost ones. The People lifted up their voices in song, the drums a haunting cadence to accompany their grief. For the first time he saw these usually stoic people openly screaming and crying in a cleansing outpouring of communal emotion. And he too was affected. Suddenly recalling Jemma's awful death when they were first captured and taken to Tragar, he found himself joining them in their displays of extravagant grief.

After experiencing the Sweh'an's manipulations in the grief ritual she conducted, Phillip wondered if the wizards weren't using a mild Psy compulsion upon the people as the demon had done to the Speir'dina when they traveled through the Great Swamp. In a way he regretted that Tessa wasn't well enough to attend. With her degrees in anthropology she would have loved this, Phillip thought. He hoped Ata Doyan was somewhere about taking notes for her.

Efosa shed many tears as she sat beside him holding his hand, but to his surprise she didn't walk to the center to speak of her loss, nor did anyone from the boy's father's lineage to which Mosi officially belonged. Finally it was her father Tego who mentioned the child when he spoke for his family, only mentioning Mosi after recounting the deeds of two warriors who died during the battle.

His expression hardened at the slight, but Phillip counseled patience to Yoey when he sensed its outrage, promising to find out more later from either Daylay or Ishka.

Unlike other peoples he'd encountered and rituals he had attended since coming to Timorna there was no feasting on their dead that night. Ishka explained to him later, when he asked her, that the People did practice the cannibalistic, "Feast of the Dead," but it was a more private affair for close family and lore keepers only. At times, when starving or maybe on the war trail a communal sharing might be held, but normally—and especially in warmer weather—the dead were burned or buried when possible. A communal grave had already been prepared away from the encampment where the dead would be laid later that morning.

Near dawn as the eastern horizon lightened to a russet and pink glow, trays and bowls of food were laid out on large mats in the center of the circle. Before the living were invited to eat plates were made up for the dead and arranged on the colorless grey mat in the section where the charred and mangled bodies had been laid out.

"This will be the last meal we share with our relatives who have entered the Realm of Ghosts," Daylay explained.

Prayers having been said over the offerings, younger members of each clan came forward and gathered wrapped bundles of warm food to hand out to the seated Elders and other noted family members, before they retrieved meals for themselves.

With the food sharing the mood of the gathering relaxed. Though still somber people talked among themselves and he heard occasional laughter coming from the knots of young people scattered here and there about the circle. Opening his food bundle when he saw the other's around him doing the same, Phillip saw it contained two soft orange pancake-like breads wrapped about strips of meat. They had a peppery flavor that was pleasant to Phillip's human palate, but unfamiliar to his symbiont bondmate.

"The bread is made from clamisa root," Efosa supplied when he asked her. "The first harvest is ripening just now. Someone must know where there is a field nearby."

<<I wonder if they are a wild mutated version of our masa root?>> Yoey said. <<There are so many new things to discover on this side of the Shallow Sea. I wish we had more time to explore...>>

<<So do I, Shalla. Later I hope we can return with some of our new allies to do just that,>> Phillip said.

While the assembled people finished their meal, a clan spokesman from each clan arose and announced the news of his clan since the last gathering. They spoke of the hard times during the Sorins, but also reported births and betrothals and other announcements that concerned all the Real People.

The Kashallan learned that in the next few days, those not going to the healing springs would head out into the desert further west. There the women, children and many of the slaves would harvest clamisa roots from the canyons while the men spread out to hunt qway and other big game animals on the open plateaus.

When it came time for the Twisted Grass Clan to speak, Efosa's grey maned father Tego rose to join the Elders in the center. With an imperious jerk of his head, he motioned for Efosa to join him. Hastily the kashallan and Daylay scooted back so she could get by them. Hearing the surprised murmurs from the people behind him, he glanced at Daylay for a clue as to what was going on.

He got no information from that quarter. She remained with her attention focused on the inner circle. If she knew, she wasn't sharing and that rekindled his unease. Well he'd know soon enough. In the confusion of resettling he murmured to Moraga in Galactic Standard, "I have an uneasy feel about this break in tradition."

He would have explained further but she nodded, as if already on guard. He turned to tell Masonja, but again she, too was ahead of him. She seemed to know there was something amiss. She patted his arm and motioned for him to pay attention to what Tego was now saying.

While he had been talking to his companions Tego had already related the clan's mundane news over the past few cycles. Putting his arm around his daughter he drew her closer and called everyone's attention to her. "This is my oldest daughter, People of the Clans. She is a woman to be pitied. The Unseen Ones have taken so much from her because in her youth she defied their will. They took two brave warriors that were her husbands, and now the last of her five children has also been taken from her. She is growing old—too old maybe for more children to take the place of the lost ones—too old for any man to pay her bride price.

"Who will take care of this poor woman now that she has no husband and no sons to provide for her? We cannot," he glared defiantly at the assembly. "There are young people with marriage contracts that are threatened if such an unlucky person should come back to live among us."

Like the best of showmen Tego threw up his hands then held them out to the assembly for suggestions. To the Kashallan's horror death and banishment were shouted out by some anonymous voices in the crowd. In his middle Phillip felt Yoey's anger coil, but he also sense the man was directing everyone's emotions towards a certain end. <<Be easy, Shalla. We won't let that happen.>>

Efosa had come to her father unsure what he wanted, but with head high. After his harsh words her head drooped, her eyes focused on the ground at her feet. With each shouted call for blood she seemed to shrink in more upon herself.

Tego finally held up his hands again, begging for silence. "My people, hear me now. True this woman has lost everything, but according to our law she can choose to adopt a son, someone to take the place of the one she just lost. Someone who will take her to his people and take care of her in her old age as any son of her own body would do for his mother."

Reaching into a pouch at his waist he held up a bone disk for the people to see. "This woman wishes to adopt the young Khutani Yoey as her new son. Wizard Bahiem and the family elders have talked it over and we would now like to welcome Yoey as a new son of the Twisted Grass Clan." He placed the disk in Efosa's hands and motioned for Daylay to escort Phillip-Yoey to him.

In the shocked silence that followed that announcement, the Kashallan stared openmouthed. *"Sly like an Oko,"* Qwasigara's words came back to him like a haunting prediction. He happened to catch the wizard's eye at that moment and saw the amusement gleaming there.

Phillip could think of a hundred reasons why becoming this woman's adopted son would be an unwelcome complication to his life. How would she like living in a Begta village; and would she and his colleague Masonja get along, to name a couple. But on the other hand neither he himself nor Yoey could allow her to be abandoned and mistreated, either. A very clever trap. The man was sly like an Oko indeed.

Then his thoughts turned down a darker path. A shaggy coated long armed man with a pronounced simian cast to his heavy jaw, this Bahiem was he an agent for the Ghostlanders? These people seemed very superstitious. By putting him on the spot to accept the adoption, and at the same time emphasizing how cursed Efosa was, did he hope to discourage other clans from joining the Alliance by claiming that her bad luck would taint the coming conflict?

Tego was already smiling and motioning for him to join them. Deciding he needed advice from a more experienced person in the field of magic and curses on this world, he hastily turned to Masonja. "Masonja, can you come with me in spirit when I go down there? I need to know what these people are up to. And, is Efosa really cursed?"

"Masonja see grey necklace on her neck. Maybe bad wizard put on her. Maybe want put on Kashallan too. It little thing Masonja come with kashallan. Can help. Can take it off Yoey's new mama. No worry. Masonja got Big Magics."

Big Magics, he hoped so. He patted her hand and rose allowing Daylay to lead him down to the waiting men.

As he stepped into the space between the fires Efosa was nudged forward to welcome him, still clutching the leather thong with its bone disk. As she placed it around his neck he saw there were unshed tears in her eyes. He gave her a slight nod, letting her know he wouldn't abandon her.

Alerted to its presence he now was aware of the sticky grey mass around the grieving woman's neck. He hadn't noticed it before so assumed it had been placed upon her that afternoon. Suddenly realizing that by putting on the disk with its clan symbol carved into it he would probably be infected as well. What was its purpose—how harmful? And, equally as important, would the contagion be spread to anyone who touched or came near them in his encampment?

Eyes flashing dangerously, he said pitched so only Tego and the wizard could hear, "Qwasigara told me that you were stupid, Bahiem, but I like to make up my own mind about people, so I thought I'd wait and see. Now I think I have to agree with him. You are stupid—both of you."

The wizard's eyes bugged wide at the insult, but before he could retaliate in outrage, the kashallan continued, "You have no idea what it means to make me your personal enemy—either of you.

"Don't try reaching for your knife, *Grandfather.* My warrior over there can kill you without moving from where she is sitting, so have a care. If I don't do it myself first—that is. Wizard Bahiem, have you explained to this man how the Khutani kill their enemies?"

Startled, Tego glared at the wizard. Phillip smirked; he guessed Bahiem hadn't. With a great show of bravado, he turned his back on them and faced the Clans.

Walking to the nearest fire he made a blood offering to the flames. "As the Unseen Ones as my witness, I am honored to be chosen as son by this woman whose spirit burns so bright with goodness," he said loud enough for the ones joking at the rim of the circle to hear.

"I don't believe she has been cursed by the Unseen Ones of this land. With my Khutani Spirit-Sight I see only the malice of jealous, angry men clouding her light. Anyone who has such gifts can see it as well."

With a gleam of amusement in his own eye he said, "You see it, the sticky grey strands that have been placed around her neck, don't you, Elders? Your Power is strong; you know what I am saying is truth, right, Wizard Qwasigara?"

Qwasigara blinked, then solemnly nodded. "I see it, Khutani. You speak truth."

Hearing the beginnings of angry muttering in the crowd, Phillip decided to demonstrate his own brand of showmanship. "Who would do such a terrible thing to a grieving mother—and for what purpose? Does the Evil One wish to infect me—am I already infected?" Phillip thumped his bare chest.

"How many other people of the Twisted Grass Clan—or anyone they have touched been infected? Does this Evil One wish to curse our war of vengeance upon the Ghostlanders?"

Forgotten by the men, Efosa sank to the ground putting her hands over her eyes she huddled rocking and sobbing. Daylay stood frozen beside her, unable to move or comfort her niece. The bondmates were aware of her distress but couldn't focus on her for the moment. He needed to finish what these men had started.

Looking squarely at Tego and Bahiem his expression as cold as ice, he demanded, "My new relatives, is there a Ghostland agent among us working to destroy us, do you think? Oh, the shame of it! How many more of the clans' warriors must die; who would do such a thing to his own kin?"

Out of the corner of his eye he saw Qwasigara smirk. The Red Wind head wizard had also taken an interest in their byplay and come to join them. Tego seemed horrified at the turn that his wish to punish an unruly daughter and inflict malicious spite upon a Hated Enemy—the Kashallan had taken. The muttering among the frightened people was growing louder. The situation was becoming dangerous. Someone had to tamp down the volcano of raw emotions that had already been stirred up once that night by the funeral ceremony and now once again were threatening to explode.

Qwasigara and the Red Wind wizard seemed to recognize the danger at about the same moment for they quickly moved back to the center of the space between the dying fires. As they raised their hands for silence several young drummers picked up their hand drums and boomed out a chant to focus and quiet the crowd.

As the song continued the Kashallan knelt beside Efosa checking on her. When he tried to put an arm around her and raise her to her feet she pushed him away. "Don't touch me, my son. I don't want to hurt you, too!"

"Nonsense, My dear. You aren't going to hurt me, and none of this is your fault. Come now, we will be infected with this grey thing and we will be healed of it together." Lifting her to her feet, he took her hand.

When the song ended and the people were quiet again, Qwasigara said, "Be at peace, My People. This curse is nothing to worry about. It is just a petty magic. Wizard Bahiem of the Twisted Grass People has agreed to remove it from his kinswoman—and her new son. Haven't you, Elder?" He smiled, showing long yellow canines. "This tiny magic isn't beyond your power is it, Wizard? Do we need to help you?"

"No, you do not," Bahiem growled his shaggy body quivering with suppressed rage.

"Good. I'm sure that will ease everyone's mind to know that this Malice can be cure by even a weak wizard like you," the Red Wind man said and waved the kashallan and the two women forward.

<<Masonja?>>

<<Masonja with you, Kashallan. No worry. Masonja protect.>>

Phillip-Yoey paid close attention as Bahiem unraveled the strands of his conjuring and flicked them into the nearest fire. As he did so it sparked with a satisfying blue glint to the flames. Next it was Daylay's turn and then his. He felt a slight tingling as something was pulled from his aura, Damn it, the sly old man *had* caught him, his rage suddenly flaring white hot. He was angry, but mostly at himself for his carelessness. Tess-weh had warned him. And now that she was hurt this was no time to get lazy.

When Bahiem finished and would have stepped away, Phillip-Yoey grabbed him. Shielded by the others the symbiont viciously stabbed its tentacles into the man's arm, before he could raise an alarm.

Looking the wizard straight in the eye, he pitched his voice so the Elders could hear. "Before I let you leave here alive, you need to answer some important questions."

Blustering with outrage Bahiem tried to pull away, his angry eyes begging for rescue from the other Clan Elders. He received none. The wizards surrounding him wore expressions as grim as the kashallan's. "Let go of me, Khutani Worm! I've done nothing to harm the People." Yoey firmed up its hold and sent a stinging burst of pain down the link. Bahiem staggered then steadied himself, still glaring.

"That remains to be proven," the Red Wind Wizard drawled.

"Nothing to harm the People," Phillip echoed. "So are you saying that your malice was directed towards me—and me alone? Was Tego's rebellious daughter only the lure to ensnare me in your conjured net, then?"

"And are you also telling us that you are so incredibly stupid that you couldn't understand that what affects the Khutani would also affect the warriors of the Real People who go with him to fight our Ghostland Enemy?" Qwasigara growled.

"He probably is that stupid, Brother," Eilo the Red Wind wizard said. "Aren't you, Begta Puke?"

"I don't believe the Ghostlanders are our enemies, Bahiem blurted once more trying to pull himself out of Yoey's hold."If someone hadn't betrayed us first by making this alliance with the Khutani then—

The man was strong enough to break him in half if he wanted, so Yoey sent a slight paralyzing compound down the link they shared to keep him from becoming too unruly while they finished their interrogation. Suspecting Bahiem had another motive for his magic, Phillip asked Qwasigara. "Is he the one?"

"No, but perhaps he is another we haven't caught yet. Can you taste the Ghostlander taint upon him?"

"Stop this!" Tego shouted. "This is all too crazy. Yes, I freely admit I asked our wizard to punish my daughter, and maybe by giving her to the Khutani I wanted to rid myself of another mouth to feed next Sorin Season, but that was all. We didn't plan to harm any of our people!"

Eilo of Red Wind snorted a laugh. "What you wanted and what this one," he pointed with his lips to Bahiem, "wanted may not be the same thing." Turning to the kashallan he asked, "What do you 'taste' Khutani, hmm?"

What did he taste? He closed his eyes and allowed the symbiont part of himself to savor the answer in all its complexity. At last he opened his eyes and looked around at the interested faces watching him. While he savored the wizard, the group had been joined by several more war leaders and clan elders. He took a deep breath unsure how to begin.

"If I am tasting him correctly, Twisted Grass territory is near the coast, but further north, much closer to the Ghostlands. They mostly live in the deep coves along the Shallow Sea and the sheltered canyons inland where the tall grasses grow from which the women make their beautiful baskets.

"So close to the North, they are in a vulnerable position and over the years have tried to maintain a certain amount of neutrality. They rarely go on raids with either the Ghostlanders or the Western Clans. All this has changed now, of course.

"Last Storm Season when the warbands came west they were warned—threatened actually, Bahiem's sendings were far too distressing for just a warning. The Twisted Grass Wizard was told to seek out, the traitors among you, or his clan would face the wrath of the Ghostland warbands when next they made war upon the People.

"Bahiem was instructed to mark the traitors among you in some way so they would be known by the warbands during a battle. Unfortunately for his clan, he hadn't found a way to carry out his Ghostland master's instructions until after their recent battle with us. In the hope perhaps that his action would deflect any future attack away from Twisted Grass, he saw his chance when Tego approached him wanting to punish his unruly daughter and took it."

"Many among the Clans died in this recent treacherous ambush; the question now is what do we do with him," the deep-voiced elder who had led the funeral ceremony asked.

"I say kill him," Red Wind snarled. "Do it, Khutani."

"Are you, serious, Elder?"

"I am. He may have failed his new master *this time,* but who is to say he won't try again to betray us, given the opportunity."

"He can't be trusted," Qwasigara agreed. "We can't afford to have him at our backs when we go north."

"Kill him? No!" Tego shouted. "You can't! He is our only wizard! Who will guide and protect us during the Sorins if we have no wizard."

"You should have thought of that before you agreed to his plan, Stupid Begta," someone shouted from behind Phillip.

"But I didn't know about the magic!" Tego pleaded.

"Doesn't matter," the Ancient said. "Stupid people suffer for their stupidity. Only the clever can survive on this side of the Shallow Sea."

On either side, Phillip thought. Life was hard on Timorna, period.

Incredulous, Tego looked into each elder's eyes. "Is everyone in agreement about this judgement?" he asked.

Ignoring the Twisted Grass patriarch, Qwasigara repeated, "You hold him with your power; finish it, Khutani."

Phillip glanced around the circle receiving nods of approval as he made eye contact with each man. "I would prefer you do your own killing. Just to prevent more bitter feelings directed toward me and my Khutani kin later," he hedged.

"Ah but you are one of us now," Tesulu smirked. "Didn't I see you make Blood-Oath and hear you say a while ago that you are now the son of my cousin's widow? Sand Mountain stands with you, Cousin."

Phillip made a face and sighed. "So be it then, *Cousin*." Turning to the Elders he added, "If you are also in agreement, then you should tell the people of your decision and why his death is necessary."

"You are right, Khutani. I will tell them," the Ancient said. Walking to the center of the circle he raised his hands for silence...

Later the Kashallan suspected they were all hoping to see him spit out black kavay so they could watch the man die horribly, but Bahiem didn't deserve that kind of torture, in spite of his betrayal.

Kashallan-Phillip inwardly shuddered at surviving another close call—and he would have Tess-weh check him over when she was well enough to bother—but he also felt sorry for the wizard. He'd been trying to save his people in the only way he knew how.

He'd been aware for some time as he held Bahiem in the link that others were blocking the wizard's Psy so he couldn't escape or harm anyone—especially him. Looking into Bahiem's dark eyes he saw the resignation pooling there. He had accepted his fate. "I'm sorry," he told him. "I will make this quick. I know you were only trying to save your people."

"Thank you."

Keeping eye contact with the man the kashallan sent a fast-acting agent to his heart. The man gasped, then dropped to the ground at the kashallans feet.

Tesulu stared openmouthed. "Is he dead?"

"Quite dead."

"I thought—black kavay?"

Yoey laughed, but there was no mirth in the sound. "You said you wanted him dead. You didn't say to make a spectacle of it. Next time do it yourself if you want a show for the crowd, *Cousin*."

Tesulu grinned "Next time maybe I will."

As the assembly broke up Phillip-Yoey stopped Tego before he could depart. "As your new grandson I want you to know that I take that obligation seriously. Efosa will go with me when I leave and I will care for her as best I can, but that commitment extends to Twisted Grass as well.

"When all this is over and before the next Sorin Season begins, if you are worried about your clan's survival bring your people across the Shallow Sea. The Maker Tinguss has promised sanctuary to anyone who wishes to stop warring and settle in the land over which it has dominion.

"The Blue Stone women and children are already there, protected by my Speir'dina kinsmen and their off-world weaponry. There are tall grasses there from which your women can make baskets to trade with the Speir'dina and even maybe those living in the Yeyen Banai Valley itself."

His eyes still smoldering with anger, Tego glared, then turned to go.

Phillip's mouth hardened, but he tried one last time. "Tego, you are also infected. I can see the grey film on your arms and hands. Before you leave you should have someone cleanse you as well. Don't be angry with me or the others. Bahiem would have let the Ghostlanders single you out for their 'special attentions' in their next raid, you know. With you gone he could continue to spy for them."

Chapter Fifteen

Mind alcrt, Chang sat motionless as a statue in the dim light of the healing shelter. Near the entrance the convalescing Blue Stone man snored peacefully in his drug induced sleep. Further into the dimness the demon-bonded woman lay wrapped in blankets dampened to cool the fire of her healing burns.

She was breathing rhythmically but was she asleep? And, more importantly at the moment, who inhabited that tortured body? He'd been trying to determine that for some time now. He could see through the grass thatch that the sky outside was brightening. The ceremony would be over soon and he would have missed a good chance to—

Chang tensed as he became aware of a light step approaching outside. He withdrew the sidearm at his hip and laid it across his thigh, then relaxed as a familiar dog-nosed face poked itself through the foliage at the entrance.

"Sleeping yet, Warrior?" Noi grinned, his eyes flicking to the black rod across Chang's knee. "I came to tell you they are almost finished now. And give you this." Noi bent and came into the shelter holding out a leaf-wrapped bundle. Never releasing his hand from his weapon, Chang took the warm package with his other hand.

"Feast food," Noi supplied, before he could ask. "They will be coming soon so you and I can finally rest."

"Thank you," Chang said to Noi's back as he slipped through the opening into the awakening day.

Setting the packet unopened at his side he resumed his vigil. He could wait to eat half-cooked Umwira. At the sound of a throaty laugh from Tess-weh his head jerked up. How long had she been awake and watching?

"You are running out of time, Warrior."

Yes, damn her, he was. Holstering his sidearm he went over to crouch beside her pallet. Bald head, cheeks and forehead plastered with a rainbow of kavay medicines, she no longer resembled the beautiful human woman Tessa. Only her lovely dark eyes gave promise to the woman behind the demon's hard stare.

Removing a rawhide pouch from his belt he opened it and showed it to her. Taking a deep breath, he said, "This is for Tessa, and maybe you, too, Demon." He held up a roughly carved bone bead for her inspection. "I made these to give to Cadrach's kin back at Ticca, but I thought you might want one as well." He motioned to the braided Death Strand around Tessa's neck.

Tess-weh stared at him for a long moment, her hard dark eyes revealing nothing of her inner thoughts. Chang remained motionless, waiting her out. The hot-headed warrior who had been the bane of his superior officers in Lann Gheal had been tempered by hardship and loss, transformed into a patient and much wiser man.

Tess-weh acknowledged his silence, her expression unreadable. "Death Strands, eh? I accept the gift, Warrior." As he placed the bead in her outstretched hand, she added, her voice thoughtful. "You have been kind to my H'an and I've been told you found us and helped guard us through this *difficult time*. For this I offer you a gift to ease your mind."

Chang's mouth twitched with his surprise then resuming control of his features, he nodded. "Thank you, Spirit. It was my duty—and for Tessa."

Tess-weh glared. "Do you want my gift or not, Warrior? You haven't much time. I will offer this only once. Choose now."

Did he? Her 'gifts' were often—complicated. But she had said it would ease his mind—and she did owe him. "Yes, thank you, Spirit, I do."

Tess-weh raised her hands and let her thumbs and forefingers meet to form a circle. Mist almost immediately formed within the enclosure. "Look within," she instructed, "The one that still holds sway in your heart is searching for lost relations, a father," she chortled. "Perhaps he will find him and unexpected siblings as well."

When the mists cleared Chang saw a young man with golden skin, black hair and many of Chang's own facial features. He was sitting at the console of what was possibly a star ship.

Chang gasped, his eyes blurring with tears before he could read the insignia on the young man's uniform. Cursing himself for his laps he blinked several times to clear his vision, but when he looked again her hands lay flat upon the blanket. "What of my wife," he asked, his voice rough with emotion. Tess-weh only gave him her enigmatic smile, and then there was no more time. The grasses at the hut's entrance were pushed aside to admit visitors.

"GOOD MORNING, ARMACHD, Tess-weh." As the kashallan crossed to the injured woman's pallet he noticed Chang's neglected packet of food lying on a mat. "Oh good, someone did bring you something to eat. The qway meat was very good wrapped in clamisa root bread. You should eat it before it gets too cold. At Chang's startled expression he chuckled. "No it isn't the usual funeral meal we've grown accustomed to on Timorna. It's just animal meat and bread."

Sitting beside the pallet he reached out and took Tessa's unresisting hand. "How are you feeling?" Tessa's black eyes watched him coolly, but she made no answer. Refusing to play games, he sighed, closed his eyes and formed the link. "Guess I'll find out myself, then."

A short time later he opened his eyes and released her. He gave her a toothy smile. "Yes, I taste that your body is on the mend, healing nicely. When we go to those healing springs—"

Tess-weh made a cutting gesture, stopping him in mid flow. "I know I am healing, Khutani. Don't babble. Time grows short. I need to get ready for this meeting the wizards will call. I must be there."

Phillip-Yoey sat back, startled. "Is that wise, Spirit?"

She snorted a laugh. "Wise or not I am going. So stop wasting time and send Moraga and your women to help me get ready."

Phillip's eyebrows rose. "My women?"

"Yes, your new mother and wife."

"Wife. And just whom might that be, Honored Spirit?"

"The one the Sand Mountain War leader is hoping to trade for more power in Red Wind affairs. You had better pay her bride price and claim her soon, if you still want to bring her with us when we go back across the Shallow Sea. She won't live past another Sorin Season otherwise."

She was speaking of Ishka, of course. He shivered at the tone of prophesy in that last statement. Bride price... He looked down at the ragged loin cloth covering his crotch and fingered the death strand and carved Begta necklaces around his neck. They were all his worldly possessions. Tess-weh herself had claimed his kilt and Avairei cloak as blanket and clothing to cover her burns. How could he pay anyone's price?

As if divining his thoughts, she laughed, the sound a mocking taunt to his ears. "Think, Stupid Khutani. You have plenty with which to bargain."

<<I think she means we can bargain with kavay, Kasha.>>

He rose and bowed. "Thank you, Spirit. I will consider your wise counsel." Before he could leave she called to him.

"Take the warrior over there with you. He is faking the pain of his injuries and our young medic is being over cautious. I want him out when the women come to help me."

Phillip-Yoey nodded and knelt by the injured man. He too was awake. His eyes followed the kashallan's hand as he extended his tentacles and formed the link. She was right, not faking exactly, his wounds were quite serious still, but he could be moved to give her privacy.

Asking Chang to round up a couple of the warriors, they managed to carry him on his pallet out to a place near the fire. Then he went to check on the resting Efosa and find Moraga.

Easily found, like most of the people in the encampment Moraga and Ishka were awake and keeping busy. Men talked and joked with one another as they checked over weapons and other hunting and fishing gear. Women worked to prepare the evening meal and supervise children.

When he found Ishka coming back with heavy buckets of water from the spring he asked her why only a few of those who kept vigil last night were sleeping.

She laughed and then shrugged. "It's better to wait until the next sleep cycle, the Old People say, and that's how we've always done it."

He told her about Tess-weh's request and she promised to go help the injured woman right away.

Efosa was lying on his sleeping mat as he'd left her, her eyes closed, her breathing steady and rhythmic. Tess-weh wanted her, too, but he didn't have the heart to wake her.

<<I think I like having a mother, Kasha,>> Yoey said, as they slipped away. <<I am the only one of our siblings to have one. The Amsi are going to be so jealous when I tell them.>>

Phillip chuckled and patted his middle. <<I suppose they will, Shalla.>>

<<Kasha, you have a mother, right?>>

<<Yes, I do—or did. She may be dead by now; she was quite old the last time I saw her.>>

<<What was she like?>>

What was his mother like? To his surprise, Phillip found he could barely remember—couldn't even recall her face all that well. An only child of two busy professional people he'd been left in the care of servants much of the time while growing up.

It had been a lonely life with few friends, he thought upon reflection. But how could he explain all that to Yoey, a child always surrounded by loving relatives. <<I don't remember her well, Shalla. It's been too long ago. But like you, I think I will enjoy having a mother now.>>

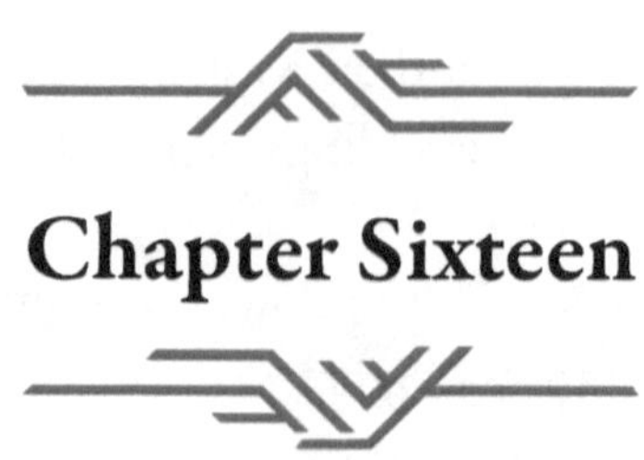

Chapter Sixteen

Kashallan-Phillip was summoned to the wizard's conclave in the early afternoon. When he turned to tell Chang to let Tess-weh and the women know, to his surprise he saw that she was already being helped by Moraga onto her Loti slave's back.

The Loti, named Toben had run away during the Ghostland attack, but with no food and nowhere to run he had drifted back to the clan encampment. Resigned to his fate, he allowed some of the older children to drag him back to the Blue Stone camp. There the always kind Moraga fed him and put him to work until Tess-weh had need of him.

When Tess-weh emerged from the hut she was covered from head to foot. His russet kilt had been washed and sewn into a loose-fitting garment that reached to her ankles. From Moraga or Chang's pack the women had cut and stitched some article of clothing to make a head scarf to cover her bald head and a veil to conceal her lower face. Only her inhuman, piercing dark eyes were visible above the cloth.

Coming over to them Phillip-Yoey bowed. "Spirit, do you need my assistance with the pain?"

"No. I do not," she snapped. Then softening her tone she added, "Maybe later, Khutani. Let's get this done."

Nodding he fell into step beside her. Juba, the Sand Mountain man acting as their escort led them out of the encampment where they took their place among other grim-faced men and women heading in the same direction. Finally they arrived at a small clearing back down the trail they'd taken up from the coast.

Many of the war leaders and clan elders were already waiting for them, seated by a fire in a half circle at the far end of the clearing. Off to one side several stern-faced men guarded two bound and hooded figures.

The kashallan and his shrouded companion seated themselves near the fire beside Ogwy and Lubwey. As the people fell silent the elder who had led the funeral stepped to the center and held up his hands.

"In order not to disturb the peace of the encampment once again, the Elders decided to hold this trial away from the camp and our mourning relatives." The Ancient waved his hand in the direction of the two bound figures, motioning for their guards to bring them forward to a place in front of the fire. "We have found more traitors among us."

At his signal, the guards pushed the captives to their knees in front of the wizards and pulled off their hoods. An old woman and a young man knelt blinking in the light.

"These two in this Bitter Water family have betrayed us and many have died for their black hearts." Qwasigara rose and held out a wrapped bundle. "Thanks to our Speir'dina and Khutani allies we knew what to look for when we realized there were spies among us."

He opened the bundle careful not to touch what it contained with his hands. He walked around the circle showing the opalescent crystals inside to the assembly. "This is how this woman and her eldest son communicated with their Ghostland master. This is how they called them to make war upon us once again, before we could unite and take our vengeance."

Waving for the people to step back, he went to the fire and dropped the entire bundle into the flames. The woman screamed and frantically tried to break away from her guards to rescue the bundle. Her cries were drown out in the turmoil that followed. As soon as the wrappings caught fire there was a deafening roar and blue tinged flames shot high into the air.

When the inferno died back to a normal fire the old woman lay sobbing on the ground where her frightened guards had dropped her.

"No, no, the Beloved Master promised. He wasn't supposed to die. The Khutani-bred devils the Warlinga killed my husband and my daughter, but the master promised he would protect my son—all my children—if I helped him destroy our enemies."

"So instead you betrayed the rest of us. Many have died for your selfishness—including your precious son." Eilo, the Red Wind Wizard snarled. Shouts of agreement came from the men and women summoned to witness the trial.

Phillip glanced at Ogwy crouched nearby, his face unreadable. Had he just married the widow of that very man? Her closeness to one of the war leaders of the Kashallan Alliance explained a lot. He idly wondered how much Ogwy had boasted to his new relatives or told his bride before sleep claimed him.

Then a more sinister thought occurred to him. Was Ogwy's new wife a widow at all when he married her? Realizing that Blue Stone, and Ogwy himself was at the heart of the Alliance, had the woman or her mother-in-law lured him into the match for just that purpose?

And more to the point, where did Ogwy stand now with these powerful men? This was certainly a coup for Tesulu in their ongoing rivalry, but Ogwy was still the Blue Stone war leader. If he was killed —or banished, what would his disgrace mean for the Alliance?

"Stupid old hag, you have condemned all your relations to death because of your evil," Qwasigara was saying as he focused his attention back on the proceedings.

Reaching a clawed hand into the mass of the woman's tangled mane, he jerked her head back and slit her throat. As her dark blood fountained, he dripped some of the flow into the flames.

"I call the Unseen Ones to witness my offering of a traitor's blood." Tossing the body aside, he continued, "And thus it will be for all in this accursed family and anyone else who betrays his kin."

As the wizard motioned for his guards to bring the young man forward, he shouted, "This one, Atahru by name, the younger brother of the dead traitor shall die along with all the members of his accursed line."

"No he will not," Tess-weh said. Her voice hadn't been overly loud but it was pitched so that everyone in the clearing heard it and froze. "Give him to me. I want him." Rising, she walked slowly to the center of the circle where the wizard stood openmouthed.

Phillip doubted if most of the people gathered in the clearing had been aware of her presence until that moment. They were now, he thought, as an icy chill settled over the assembly.

"I care nothing what you do with the others of his lineage but I need a new slave and the debt is owing," Tess-weh said.

"Why him?" the wizard stammered.

"Can you suggest another to become my protector then?" she pointed to Ogwy. "How about that one?" She chortled. "He would do nicely. The Blue Stone war leader is a man who is so eager to bury his blade in a soft warm sheath that once again he has chosen a woman unwisely. He is strong, and I can *make* him willing." She licked her lips in anticipation. "How about him?"

Or," she next motioned to Tesulu. "How about your own noble warrior, Sand Mountain? He is strong vigorous and craves glory in battle. I can give him that—and more. His family and clan can sing his praises for many generations, but unfortunately as my slave he won't know that."

She laughed and addressed Tesulu directly. "Do you want to caress my feminine charms some more and be my protector, My Treasure?"

Tesulu stared her in the eye, folded his arms across his chest and smirked. "No, I do not, Witch. I am too much of a man for even you to tame."

Tess-weh threw back her head and laughed. "Perhaps you are, My Jewel, but I would love to try."

Stifling her mirth she returned her attention to the matter under discussion. Meeting the eye of each Elder and Wizard she repeated, "Who will it be then?"

Qwasigara snorted. "If you want the traitorous vermin Atahru so much, you can have him."

Drawing his attention to the accused again, Phillip noted that unlike the massive Cadrach, Atahru was only a well-built medium-sized man of the Real People. He had the four arms and whip-like tail so common among the western clans. And as Chang had noted before, like many of the Bitter Water People, he had Warlinga traits in his appearance.

His grey skin resembled scales from afar, but closer inspection revealed that it was a type of soft hair resembling tiny feathers to Phillip's human eye. On his head was a small head crest like some forgotten Warlinga ancestor. His mane was parted to curve around the crest before being tied in the usual clan ponytail.

"No!" Atahru shouted. "I didn't know what my brother and mother planned. I only joked to my brother about new mutants I saw with Sand Mountain when I was hunting. I knew they were angry after my father's torture and death—but that's all. I didn't know they would betray the

People—I swear, please believe me and let me go. I will go to war against the Ghostlanders—all our enemies."

Tess-weh seemed startled and then amused by the young man's bargaining. She looked at the wizards and shrugged. "As I said, it matters nothing to me what you do with him and the rest of this one's kin, as long as you give me someone."

"Care to taste him, Khutani?" the Red Wind wizard asked. "I for one would like to know if the vermin speaks truth."

The kashallan stepped forward. "All right, if you wish." Phillip motioned for the man's guards to cut his bonds. They complied and dragged him to kneel at the kashallan's feet.

Taking one of Atahru's hands he formed the link. When he opened his eyes, he said. "He speaks truth as best I can tell, and it is nearly impossible to lie to me while in the link. He didn't know what his mother and older brother planned."

Releasing the man, Phillip said for Atahru's ears alone, "Be at peace. You will make your siblings proud by your sacrifice. And you will perform many great deeds in her service." Atahru stared at him blankly for a moment, then snarled, "But not if they are all dead."

Snatching up his distracted guard's knife, he held the point to his own chest. "I will kill myself first, unless you promise to spare my younger siblings. They are innocents. I won't become a demon's slave unless you agree to spare them!"

THEY ALLOWED HIM TO hug his two young sisters and little brother, barely more than a toddler before offering him to the Demon. The Elders told him they would be adopted into other clans. They assured him that the children would grow up with no taint of the traitor upon them.

Satisfied he knelt before her. Tess-weh took the blade he offered in her white hand and raised it to his forehead. Murmuring words of power she carved the sigil of bondage into his flesh.

Chapter Seventeen

The next morning the kashallan sat by their cook fire pondering his other difficult problem. Handing him a cup of sourwood tea while a breakfast stew simmered in the coals, Efosa asked, "What's wrong, My Son?"

He was quiet for a long moment gathering his thoughts, finally he said, "Are you and Ishka friends, Mother?"

Efosa paused in her stirring and considered. "She has always been kind to me, and never teased me about being bad luck, so yes, I would call her friend, I think. Why do you ask?"

He hesitated as Masonja joined them, setting down more sticks and dried dung for the fire. Squatting she poured herself some tea and studied his face. "Kashallan worried. What wrong?"

Phillip chuckled. "You two are far too perceptive this morning, so I might as well tell you."

Ladling out a bowl of stew Efosa handed it to him, and then served one for herself and Masonja. Moving the pot to the side of the hearth to keep warm she sat down beside them. Both women looked at him expectantly.

"Yesterday when I went to see Tess-weh, she warned me that if I didn't pay Tesulu's bride price for Ishka and take her as my wife she would be dead within the year. I assume that meant something bad was going to happen to her with this marriage the war leader plans.

"For Niguiri's sake I had hoped to take her with us, but now—well I don't know how to proceed. I find her good company and she offers wise council," he let out a nervous laugh, "but I really hadn't given any thought to marriage when I accepted this charge from my Amla, Maker Tinguss.

"So now what do I do?" he sighed and took another bite of stew before continuing. "Should I go ask Tesulu for her, pay him what he wants as bride price—" He shrugged. "I just don't know."

"Of course you should marry her," Efosa said emphatically. "But it isn't up to you to do the negotiations. You would appear weak and—needy, if you ask for her. He would double his price if you did—and he still might refuse you. As your Mother, it is my place to bargain for you. I will do it."

She glanced at Masonja who nodded. "Masonja help Big Sister. Kashallan not to worry. We fix."

Efosa smiled. "Yes, Sister, we will take care of it." Resuming eating, she added, "I think I know what the war leader plans. One of the Red Wind war leaders is looking for a new wife. A marriage with that family would strengthen ties between the two clans.

"Unfortunately, the man is a beast. He has no wife because he killed the last one when she didn't give him a son. The Spirit might be right; Ishka is nearing the end of her child baring cycle—as am I. she might not survive long among the Red Wind People."

They lapsed into a thoughtful silence after that as they finished their meal. As they were rising to go, Efosa asked, "What will you offer for your new wife?"

He held out his empty hands and shrugged. "I have nothing to offer—really—just whatever kavay I can make. I have nothing else."

The women looked him over critically as if they were buying a new race horse, Phillip thought privately, hoping his dark skin concealed his blush of embarrassment.

"Kavay is good thing," Masonja finally said. "But starmans knife good gift, too."

Startled, he touched the blade sheathed at his hip. He rarely thought of the knife. It was a useful tool, but he supposed he took its presence for granted. Not always remembering to oil and clean off the rust that collected in the swamp's dampness, he cared for it as if he could order another and have it delivered to his doorstep in hours. But on a world almost depleted of metals, his blade would be worth a king's ransom.

He sighed and nodded. "Keeping it wouldn't be worth a woman's life, but offer the knife only as a last resort."

A picture of the volatile Ogwy forming in his mind, he added, "I am aware of the personal rivalry between Ogwy and Tesulu. I have no wish to add fuel to that fire, if you know what I mean. A rift among the clans could cost us when we go up against the Ghostlanders."

They did know and nodded their agreement. "I will ask my Aunt Daylay for her advice," Efosa said.

"Witch womans, Lesala, maybe," Masonja offered. "Her very wise."

Efosa seemed startled, then nodded. "Good idea, Sister."

Both women patted him on the shoulder and told him not to worry. They walked off with a determined purpose marking every step. It was hard, but he recognized that the women probably knew more about these things than he did, so better to trust them and let go of his worry.

<<A new mother and now a new wife. So many new and interesting things to explore on this side of the Shallow Sea,>> Yoey bubbled. <<And we can play the fucking game with our new wife, too, can't we, Kasha?>>

Phillip froze. <<Yoey! Where did you learn about that game?>>

<<Tiel told me about the fucking game,>> Yoey said dripping its excitement into their communication and Phillip felt his member begin to harden. <<Conal-Tiel and our Amsi Tasheyna-Rinn play that game all the time. Tiel says it's lots of fun. Can we play it, too?>>

Making sure his loin cloth was concealing that unwelcome bulge, he rubbed his middle and soothed. <<Of course we will play the fucking game—if Ishka is willing, but we aren't married yet so let's not get too excited just yet. We still have work to do today.>>

In his old life Phillip hadn't taken much of an interest in sexual liaisons. His scientific research had been his passion. Now he chuckled and stroked his inner companion. Of course this wouldn't be just a marriage in name only. Yoey was curious and Ishka herself might be insulted if they didn't complete the sexual union.

Ah but what about Chang? The Kashallan had noticed that he had been spending a lot of time in her company. With Niguiri already married to his student Timma it was only natural that they would be thrown together much of the time. How was he going to feel about this upcoming wedding.

His assignment among the Western Clans was becoming far more complicated than even his Amla could have envisioned.

Maker Tinguss... Bringing that Ancient to mind got Phillip wondering again why there hadn't been any contact from the Maker. He didn't want to dwell too much on the subject for fear of frightening Yoey, but he suspected Ro was worried as well. Unfortunately he lacked the Psy skills to contact his older sibling on his own.

"You look troubled, Laddy," Moraga said as she helped herself to a bowl from the neglected stew pot and sat across from him.

He laughed. "Am I that obvious?" Glancing around, he noticed that Chang was teaching Timma and a few of the younger men further out into the open area behind the Blue Stone Camp. Good. "I need your advice, Moraga." When she nodded for him to continue, he blurted. "It seems I'm getting married soon."

When she put down her spoon and stared, he sighed and continued, "Yesterday Tess-weh told me I needed to marry Ishka or she would die. Efosa thinks Tesulu plans to marry her to a brute of a man in the Red Wind Clan to gain an ally.

"My new—uh—mother and Masonja just left to begin the negotiations for her bride price. I've seen Ishka and Chang talking and with the young people already wed I think maybe—but if Chang offers to marry her then Tesulu will want him to join his warband—and that won't work, but I can't just let her—" he broke off as Moraga began to chuckle.

"You may be right about his interest, but you are forgetting one important thing, Laddy."

"Oh, what's that?"

Still chuckling to herself, she said, "On the other side of the Shallow Sea where Speir'dina laws apply, a woman can have two husbands. If your new wife wants, she can marry him according to our ways, right?"

Phillip sat back openmouthed. "Yes she can indeed. If Armachd Chang is willing that would take a load off my mind," he babbled. "I wasn't sure how my new women were going to like living in a Begta village—which is where I must be much of the time. But if she could stay with Chang—and maybe Efosa, too—could stay with our Speir'dina kin it would be so much better—for all of us—maybe."

Putting down her empty bowl she rose. "When time permits, I'll let my brother warrior know what is going on. It will all work out. You'll see."

"I hope so—that's what the other women say."

Chapter Eighteen

Marriage negotiations continued as they traveled further into the mountains to the healing springs. It was hard not to fret, but he let the women handle all the preparations. Phillip suspected Ishka herself was aware of their plans, but she never mentioned it on the few times they ran into one another on the journey.

The trek was hot and dusty as before but he could see that they were climbing into the foothills, a range of purple mountains thrusting their jagged peaks into the russet and pink sky further to the west.

Thinking of Phillip's abused feet, Yoey asked Efosa on the morning of the second day, "Will we have to climb those mountains, Mother?"

She laughed and patted the kashallan's shoulder. "Be easy, My Son, the springs lie much closer. We will reach them later today."

Yoey sighed. "That's good to know."

As they walked the kashallan was aware of changes in the land about him. There was more vegetation here, unknown to him. There were grey and red patches of moss and shrubby clumps of grass growing in widening patches the higher they climbed.

Taller thorn bushes and twisted limbed trees reached for the light in sheltered places among the rocks. But the land wasn't healthy; he could see that as well. Evidence of the poisons blown by the Sorin Storms was everywhere. Ugly scabrous growths on the twisted trees, chalky patches of moss that gave off a foul smell that children were warned to stay away from were only a few of the scars still present as a reminder of the ancient wars.

<<I taste the land's pain,>> Yoey said as its tentacles brushed lightly over a grey-leafed bush. <<I have no encoded memories of this place, but I know Timorna was once so beautiful. This land...>>

<<It would have been beautiful, too, Shalla,>> Phillip said. <<And it still is, in its way. Life survives here, scarred but powerful and enduring—like its people—like all of Timorna, I suppose.>>

The Clans' healing place was in a bowl of a valley nestled between higher ridges of purple thorn. The familiar black willowy contours of kavalpa thickets were dotted here and there on the valley's floor, giving evidence of abundant water and more luxurious growth.

As they came down off the trail leading into the valley a plume of steamy water shot high into the cooling air. People cried out with joy. "Look, My Son," Efosa shouted grinning. "The Spirits of this place are welcoming us. Do you see?"

"I do, Mother. So the springs here are both hot and cold, then?"

"Yes they are; this is a most special place."

As he helped gather fuel for the ever-hungry cook fires the kashallan noticed how over the centuries the People had widened and deepened many of both the warm and cold springs so that now they formed little ponds similar to the healing pools in a Khutani inhabited keep. Dipping a toe into one of the warm pools, he couldn't wait to have a long soak.

But that wouldn't be for a while. There was work to be done setting up camp, Tess-weh and the rest of the wounded to care for, and Efosa had told him that there would be a short ceremony to ask permission of the Unseen Ones before people could freely make use of the site.

As he was hauling his basket of brush and dry dung for the fires, Phillip spied Ata Doyan staggering back to camp with the weight of full hide buckets from the nearby watering spring. Hurrying to help him he asked, "How are you managing, Ata? I'm sorry I've left so much of Tessa's care in your hands. How is she today?"

"The ride was hard on her, I think. We tied a pad on Toben's back for her to rest upon, but the travel rubs on the healing burns. Will you come see her soon? I think she needs something for the pain."

Falling into step with the priest he nodded. "Of course, Ata, I'll come right now. Let me help you carry one of those buckets," he offered.

Doyan stopped and gratefully gave him one of the brimming containers. "And how is Tess-weh's new slave and protector working out? I suspect Ima

Sagas is going to be quite shocked when you return to Ticca with an Umwira Wa'chassey'ul in Tess-weh's household."

Doyan chuckled. "Yes, they won't know what to think."

"And how about you and Moraga are you getting along with him? What is he like?"

Ata Doyan thought about it for a moment before answering, allowing a bunch of laughing children to race past before speaking. "He certainly is much different than Cadrach. The Warlinga I knew; he was—predictable. Atahru is very quiet when the Spirit isn't with us. I sometimes forget he is there, and then I look around—and for just a moment I see only the Hated Enemy and my bones quake. Then I recognize him and it's all right."

"Hmm, are you sure? He takes your orders, doesn't he? He hasn't hurt you or threatened—"

"Oh no, no, nothing like that. He is quite biddable, and quite solicitous when it comes to the care of his 'Little Mistress' just as Cadrach was. No it's just my own foibles. It's hard to overcome the teachings of a lifetime."

Phillip smiled. "And that's why that book you are going to write about your travels among the 'Wild Umwira' is going to be so important for future generations."

Startled Doyan almost dropped his bucket. Phillip chuckled. "I've seen you scribbling down little notes to yourself when you thought no one was looking. You, and maybe Tessa when you get back to Ticca, have your life's work cut out for you. But do be careful," the kashallan cautioned. "These people seem very superstitious. They might think you were writing an evil spell if they saw you."

"Mm, that's a sobering thought, Holy One. I will keep that in mind." The two fell into a companionable silence as they carried the heavy buckets and basket of fuel. As if still musing on a thought constantly on his mind, Doyan said quietly in the southern tongue, "These people aren't at all what I expected. All the stories—their warriors raiding and stealing our people our food—and that first day on the beach when Sand Mountain—I was so afraid—still am much of the time, but for different reasons.

"Traveling with them I've known hardship like nothing I could have imagined I would face, but I see how they accept their hard lives and don't complain. I've also seen fierce warriors playing with their children hugging their wives and joking with one another and our Speir'dina companions. And now having to care for Atahru as a part of my duty—everything is so different..."

Phillip gave him a reassuring smile as he put down his bucket by their camp fire. "Dunnagh said to me once, that he told the Makers that when they called the Speir'dina to host their symbiont children, they also got a people that would bring change to this wounded world."

Doyan chuckled and sat down his own burden, motioning for the Kashallan to precede him into the shelter. "The Dream-Chosen is a most wise creature. Change indeed."

LATER THE KASHALLAN was sitting by their evening fire finishing the last of his tea and trail meat. He'd been talking in Galactic Standard, reminiscing about their trek through the Great Swamp with Armachd Chang and Moraga when he heard footsteps. He stopped what he was about to say and waited as Efosa and Masonja drew near. They seemed excited and maybe a little nervous, Phillip thought as he watched them approach. At the last moment Efosa held back when she saw him talking with his warriors, as if not wanting to interrupt the talk of men. Masonja, on the other hand, took her hand and boldly marched in to crouch by the fire.

Phillip put down his cup and looked at them expectantly. Efosa took a deep breath. "Son, Tesulu and Qwasigara have agreed to give you Ishka for your bride. If you agree to his price." She took another deep breath "Please don't be angry with us. We tried—" she broke off unable to go on.

The kashallan felt a shudder rundown his back bone. What were they afraid to tell him? After a long pause when no one spoke he cleared his throat and said, "Tell me the rest of it, please."

Finally Masonja said, "Mama bargain good. Her say war leader can marry Red Wind girl to make new alliance. Girl young, not tested, but if kashallan make red kavay girl sure to give war leader a son. No need Ishka. Red Wind get mad Sand Mountain maybe, if no get baby for new husband cause woman too old."

He nodded his head and smiled. "A logical argument, My dear. How much red kavay must I make?"

"Three gourds," Efosa said. "One for Red Wind and two for Tesulu and Sand Mountain."

"Him also want two gourds yellow kavay and two orange," Masonja added not meeting his eye.

The kashallan sighed. "As long as he doesn't expect me to do all that in one day, I can manage. What else does he want? You two are too nervous for just that large amount of kavay. Come on tell me."

They were silent for a long time unwilling to meet his eye, finally Masonja gathered her courage and said, "Kashallan be angry, maybe. Him say marriage—

"Does he want my knife then? Though it might cause trouble I will give it to him if it means saving Ishka's life. I told you that."

Efosa looked up surprised. She shook her head. "No, he never mentioned your knife, My Son."

Trying to keep the exasperation out of his voice, he said, "Then what does Tesulu and the wizard want? I won't be angry with either of you, just tell me."

"Him want make mark on Kashallan." At his puzzled look she pointed to the twisted grass clan brand on Efosa's face. "Him want make kashallan Sand Mountain. Him say marry Sand Mountain woman, kashallan join Sand Mountain People."

Phillip-Yoey sat back stunned, his mouth hanging open. Closing his mouth at last he stared at his two Speir'dina companions. They seemed as startled as he was himself. In Galactic Standard, he mused, "Why in the world would he want me to do that? What game is he trying to play here?"

Starting to get angry in spite of himself, he said, "Surely he knows I won't stay with his people to fish for him and cough up kavay whenever the whim takes him? And I'm sure he knows he can't force me. And if he tries to hurt Ishka or Masonja—anyone I care about—I'll kill him with the black kavay he keeps wanting to see me use."

Phillip fell silent after his outburst becoming aware of the frightened women's faces. They hadn't understood his words, but they recognized his tone and knew he was angry. Switching languages he said in a calmer voice, "I'm sorry. I *am* angry, but not with you."

He reached out and took their hands, giving them a little squeeze. "You've done nothing wrong. I'm angry because I think the war leader is playing games with me, but I can't see his purpose." Glancing at the Armachda he raised an eyebrow. "I was a fairly eclectic reader back home, but I'm sure, Armachd Chang you've studied more of the ancient master's books on war tactics than I have. Can you see the meaning of this? Or, Moraga, can you?"

They shook their heads, thinking. Suddenly Chang laughed. "What?" Moraga said. Chang continued to laugh, unable to answer.

At last he got himself under control, and still grinning he said to Phillip, "Oh, you are right, Sir, he is playing a game—either him or that snarling old dog-faced wizard, but you, I think, are only the pawn. The Warlinga and maybe the Makers are the true opponents they battle."

At the kashallan and Morag's uncomprehending stares he started laughing again. "Think on it, Sir. You, a kashallan, a holy One, coming back across the Shallow Sea, sitting in an Umwira war canoe, your face marked by an Umwira clan tattoo, Aju'an, Fadir and the rest of the Warlinga hunters at Ticca—and the Yeyen, too for that matter, they will be so confused.

"Should they hold out their hands for the link, or flatten their head crests, pick up their spears and fight? Oh, Sir, think of it; nobody is going to know what to do with you?"

Chang grinned. "I can see Ima Saga's face now." He bent over chortling. "Priceless! They talked about us being wild, uncouth outlaws when we came out of the Swamp, but now..." he broke out laughing again and this time Moraga joined him. "We are going to piss off everybody, Sir!"

Phillip couldn't help smiling. Yes indeed they were going to piss everybody off, damn Qwasigara and Tesulu. They knew he wouldn't let Ishka die; they knew he would agree to their crazy notion. He could see the beauty in their plan. Sly like an Oko indeed.

Turning to the women, he said, "Tell my new brother-in-law I will be happy to become one of the Sand Mountain People."

He chuckled. "Mother, I'm a son of Twisted Grass, aren't I? So why not wear your clan's mark, too?"

Efosa thought about it and smiled. "I was afraid to ask you, but I would like that. Then everybody will know you are my son." She turned to Masonja,

"We should go tell them. There is much work to be done. Come, Sister." Talking excitedly they disappeared back into the twilight.

The Kashallan put more fuel on the fire and set the sooty kettle to boil. Still smiling he said to his companions, "They can mark me with the sigils for all seven damn clans if they want, because the first Ghostlander who sees me is going to know their covenant with the West is broken."

"It won't go well for those caught in the middle and not aligned with us," Moraga said thoughtfully.

Chang smirked. "I wonder if the old devil thought it through and that is part of his plan."

Chapter Nineteen

When the day came around for his wedding, his new mother and Masonja decided Phillip-Yoey looked far too scruffy with his dusty dreadlocks and ragged loin cloth to marry anyone in his present condition.

Taking him in hand, they led him to one of the warm pools for a bath and a relaxing soak. As he settled back in the bubbling blue water, Efosa knelt behind him and washed the dirt, dried leaves and sticks out of his hair. Confined to the deep cavernous pools in the Swamp for the Sorin Season, Phillip hadn't paid much attention to how his ebony locks had become a snarled mess of ropy clumps.

Once he had arrived back in the Begta village he had just confined the mass with a bright-colored headband that Masonja made for him to keep it out of his eyes. Now, however, he could hear Efosa clicking her tongue with dismay as she tried to create some kind of order out of the tangle and make him presentable.

Finally deciding it would be impossible to undo all the twisted knots she gathered them up and bound them with the headband into a spiky ponytail on the top of his head.

When he was allowed out of the water he found that his old ragged garment was gone. Instead a new fringed and painted soft leather loin cloth and cape were lying on the moss with his belt, cup and knife. Finally dressed, he stood before the women for their inspection. They smiled and nodded their approval. He fingered the soft cream-colored hide with its red and black geometric designs and smiled back. "Thank you. This is very beautiful. Right now I feel so blessed."

Efosa handed him a small bone disk on a braided cord. On one side of the disk was carved the Lann Gheal crossed swords and on the other a caduceus, the ancient symbol still used by human doctors throughout the galaxy. "Your warrior made this for you to give to your new bride," she explained.

Divining its deeper significance he closed his hand about the disk, a lump coming into his throat. Moraga must have indeed have talked to her fellow armachd. The disk proclaimed, in a subtle way, that Ishka would be marrying both men tonight. "This, too is a wonderful gift," Phillip said when he could speak. "I must thank him. I had forgotten about this part of the ceremony."

EARLIER THAT DAY TEGO showed up at their fire, and announced that he was there to burn the Twisted Grass clan mark onto his shoulder. The kashallan nodded and sat immobile as the carved stone was heated and then pressed onto his naked flesh.

When he finished, Tego studied his face for any sign of weakness. Satisfied at last that Phillip hadn't disgraced the family by crying out or flinching away from the pain, he put the cooling stone back into its sand-filled box and left with no more ceremony.

Reaching for his cup of tea, Phillip took a long drink and said to Chang, "I changed my mind about getting all seven of those clan brands. Two will be quite enough."

Chang snorted a laugh and toasted him with his own cup.

TO HIS SURPRISE IT was Tego and not one of Tesulu's warriors who came to escort him to his wedding when the drums boomed out their call for the people to assemble.

Leading him into the center between the two fires lit for the occasion, Tego told him to kneel. Then Qwasigara walked to him and announced in a voice all could hear, "This child of the Twisted Grass People has come here to marry a Sand Mountain woman. We now claim this Twisted Grass man as belonging to Sand Mountain."

Going to the fire he removed a glowing brand from the coals and smiling, looked Phillip straight in the eye. The kashallan stared right back once again as still as stone as the wizard press the brand into his left cheek. When he took the brand away Phillip took a deep breath and let it out slowly, the stench of his own charred flesh in his nostrils.

"Thank you, Elder," Phillip said as he got to his feet. "I am honored to be now a son of both Twisted Grass and Sand Mountain."

Qwasigara's mouth twitched, showing his canines in a mirthless smile.

Ishka joined him after his marking, taking his hand. Phillip stared, Yoey suddenly becoming excited to see the changes in her appearance.

<<She looks beautiful, doesn't she, Kasha?>> Yoey bubbled.

<<Yes, she does,>> he agreed.

Ishka's fur shone smooth and a rich brown in the firelight. She had braided her mane in the Avairei way in tiny braidlets with bone and shell beads on their ends. To satisfy convention, however, while still declaring her new loyalties she took the braidlets and tied them into a clan ponytail.

Instead of the beaded fringe most clan women wore around their waists she now wore a leather skirt painted with similar designs to the black and red markings on his own loin cloth. Her skirt wasn't an Ima's kilt but it was probably the closest she could manage on this side of the water.

The wedding itself was a simple affair as Timma's had been, a blood offering to the flames and an exchange of tokens and simple vows.

When he was about to lead his new bride away Ishka stopped him. "Wait, there is more," she announced in a whisper, and seated him beside her. At his inquiring look, she said, "Another wedding."

It seemed that Tesulu was also taking advantage of the assembly and his red kavay gift to marry the Red Wind girl and cement his connection with them. By doing so, of course, he was also adding them unofficially to the Kashallan alliance.

Tesulu waited between the fires as a powerfully muscled man with a four-armed torso, hard eyes and a jutting jaw, pushed a slim young woman ahead of him into the firelight.

Phillip-Yoey let out his breath slowly, a chill running down his spine. This must be the warrior Sand Mountain had wanted Ishka to marry. He wasn't sure the poor Red Wind girl would fare any better in Tesulu's bed, but he would have born the pain of those seven brands if it had meant saving Ishka from that brute.

Turning to his new bride he murmured the question.

"His name is Goro. His daughter is Keera," Ishka supplied.

The girl seemed healthy enough, the Kashallan supposed, only the odd mottling of her fur showing evidence of a benign mutation in her lineage. He secretly hoped his red kavay gift would ease the girl's life among his new relatives, giving the couple the son he knew Tesulu wanted.

Ceremony finally over, Tesulu threw an arm companionably over his branded shoulder and grinned. "Come, my new brother-in-law, we celebrate with clamisa beer while the women prepare themselves for our coming."

Phillip grimaced, but nodded his agreement, and motioned for Chang to join them. Phillip had always hated these macho displays of masculine prowess even as a youth at university. Nathan or Dunnagh would have enjoyed the debauch that was sure to follow. Unfortunately neither of them was here and just married, so there was no escape.

<<Don't worry, Kasha,>> Yoey assured him. <<I can digest the alcohol in the beer, you won't get drunk, unless you want to.>>

<<Thank you, Shalla, I do not. We will stay just long enough to not give offense; but that's all.>>

<<Yes it will be much more fun to play the fucking game with our new wife than remain at the drinking party,>> Yoey agreed. <<Though it would be amusing to see if Tesulu or anyone else starts acting silly when full of clamisa beer.>>

When they arrived at the noisy party already underway the kashallan noticed that it contained an assortment of war leaders and Elders from all seven clans. Goro and the Red Wind Wizard he had learned was named Eilo were there as well as his new grandfather Tego and many others from Sand Mountain and the other clans whose names he didn't know.

Lubwey and Noi were present representing Blue Stone, but Ogwy himself was not. Phillip had heard that because of his new Bitter Water wife his position among these men was uncertain at the moment. He had refused to kill her as Qwasigara and Eilo wanted, claiming she was now pregnant with his son.

Yoey had been consulted to confirm the claim. Reluctant to get involved, the kashallan was finally badgered into putting the frightened young woman into the link to find out. He could confirm that she was pregnant as she claimed, but told them it was too soon to say the sex of the child. Knowing

Ogwy wanted a son, Yoey nudged the growing embryo in that direction, at Phillip's suggestion.

With another son to occupy his attention, Phillip hoped he would remain on this side of the Shallow Sea, making Sairsa's life with him seem less attractive, should she still be thinking about leaving Dunnagh for the Blue Stone war leader. Yoey was also able to assure them that her part in her husband's and mother-in-law's treachery had been only the crime of obeying her husband and the old woman's orders. That, too he hoped would ease the growing tension between the clans.

If they had planned to get Phillip drunk and laugh as he acted the fool; they were sadly disappointed. Tesulu and Goro kept plying him with beer, which he dutifully drank with no change in his speech or behavior. To match them, and amuse himself, he proposed many toasts of his own, in their honor and watched the signs of drunkenness grow in their speech and actions. Tesulu and Qwasigara either forgot or didn't know that his symbiont bondmate metabolized food and drink for both of them. He could drink any of the brutes under the table—if they had a table.

Finally tiring of his game, he rose, and with an excuse to relieve himself he made his escape. As he turned to go Chang gave him a discreet hand sign not to come back. He would stay and regale the interested company with his own stories of wars among the stars.

Unsure where to find his bride, he wandered back to their camp's fire and there to his surprise he found a nervous Ishka, Timma, Niguiri, his mother, Masonja and the rest of the Blue Stone men, sitting companionably drinking tea. The women looked up and smiled at his approach, the warriors making joking comments about his eagerness to bed his new bride.

Ignoring the ribald comments, he stammered an apology to Ishka. "I'm sorry. Tesulu—I didn't want to, but I felt I had to at least make an appearance—"

She smiled and took his hand. "I know; it's all right. You would have given offense if you'd refused. Do you want some food—or tea?"

He laughed. "Nothing to drink. I've had enough liquid refreshment for a while—though I'm not drunk," he assured her as they headed back into the night. <<Yoey kept me from making a fool of myself, which I'm sure the war leader hoped."

She let out a soft chuckle. “Oh I’m sure of it.”

Ishka led him to a secluded nest within a daughter thicket on the edge of a large mother kavalpa grove.

Stripping off her leather skirt she climbed into the nest of soft moss and sweet scented grasses that had been prepared for them. She smiled up at him expectantly.

<<Now what do we do?>> Yoey asked, an excited but hesitant tone to the symbiont’s mental sending. <<Can we play the fucking game now?>>

<<Yes, I think she wants us to join her,>> Phillip said. <<But remember what I told you, Shalla,>> he cautioned. <<We want our Ishka to have fun too, so we can’t get too excited until she is ready for us.>>

Hoping the darkness hid his blush he untied his belt and dropped his loin cloth to the moss and joined her.

<<Now what do we do, Kasha?>>

What do they do indeed? Phillip wished he’d been able to talk to the more sexually experienced Dunnagh before tonight. Already having an Avairei wife, he could have given him instruction on how to please his nonhuman partner.

Sensing his hesitation as he just continued to study her without speaking, Ishka ventured, “Do your brands hurt you too much to complete our marriage tonight? We can just sleep if you like.”

Startled out of his contemplation, he shook his head. “No, my clan marks aren’t hurting over much,” he assured her. “Yoey is blocking most of the pain—though I don’t dare plaster them with orange kavay, as I wish I could. That would spoil my manly image, I believe.”

She laughed, the sound a musical trill in the darkness. “No, that wouldn’t be warrior-like of you, would it? With Tesulu and the old wizard it’s all about image. You must show them you are just as much a man as any of them, or they will think you weak and won’t trust you.”

He laughed too. “I figured it would be something like that.”

Tentacles slightly extended, he reached out a hand and began to stroke her soft brown fur. With Yoey’s Khutani senses heightening his awareness he fell silent still stroking her soft fur, enjoying its musky fragrance an the feel of its texture under his hand.

Becoming uncomfortable at last with his silence and inaction, Ishka broke in on his reverie. "Is there something wrong, Kashal—husband—do I displease you in some way?"

Torn out of his reverie by the note of anxiety he detected in her voice, he stared uncomprehending for a moment , then he laughed nervously. "No, no you don't displease us. I—we find you very beautiful tonight. It's just," a nervous laugh again. "You see Yoey and I are both inexperienced at this. We want you to enjoy our time together, too, but—uh—we don't know how to proceed.

"In my old life up there," he pointed to the night sky, "my research, my studies were my passions. I never seemed to find the time for more than the occasional relationship with women. I think we might need a little guidance from our more experienced partner to get started," he admitted.

"Ah, I see." She chuckled and pulled him down to cover her. "Then let us explore this new way of loving together."

Interlude

TINGUSS LOOKED UP AS two long sinewy bodies swam into view and paused outside his glowing prison. <<Come to gloat, Amsi?>> it grumbled.

Ignoring the comment Gladdris began methodically dissolving the Psy energies that confined the other Maker. <<You will need to feed soon. My descendants have brought you meat.>>

Tinguss slid out the opening as soon as it was wide enough to release its bulk. <<The council has decided to adopt my plan then?>>

Meyagus laughed. <<It doesn't matter what the Council decides now, does it, Amsi? Why didn't you tell us the charge you gave your child?>>

<<I would have, but I was never given a chance now was I? But how did you find out?>>

<<When your eldest Ro couldn't locate you it contacted Gladdris and I,>> Meyagus explained. <<It was worried that the Ghostland Wizards had captured or killed you because you sent your kashallan across the Shallow Sea to make your new alliance.>> Meyagus dripped the sour flavor of exasperation and ironic amusement into their communication. <<It told us what it knew of the kashallan's adventures.>>

No, it was my own kindred who chose to capture and confine me, not the Hated Enemy, Tinguss thought privately. Suddenly afraid, it fretted. <<Is my child all right; is he safe back on this side of the Shallow Sea?>>

Gladdris rumbled a laugh and looped a coil about the neck of the Maker with which it had once shared genetic patterns. <<Oh yes, Amsi, your child is well last we heard. And your new alliance is a reality and the mud crawlers among us are going to have to live with it. But even you may be surprised at what your bold offspring has done in your absence.>>

Part Two:

Chapter One

Traveling fast, the hunting packs of Warlinga and Speir'dina made good time through the ancient underground passages that led from Riath northward. Tobrach and his hunters were the most knowledgeable force for the area, so he headed up a patrol sent to investigate the Dingay main stronghold.

Nathan doubted that anyone of importance was left there, but they'd be fools not to check. The Changelings wouldn't have known how soon hunting packs would have been sent on their trail, so they might have left in a hurry, leaving important intel behind, he reasoned.

Next morning a runner had been sent back to tell them that the keep was theirs. Deciding to taste fresh air for a while, Kashallan-Nathan brought his hunters to investigate. Tobrach's messenger had also said there were prisoners. He would need to taste them, checking for the Umwira taint before they could know what to do with them.

They arrived at the keep as the purple shadows of late afternoon were streaking the thorny hillsides of the favored little valley where the keep sheltered amidst fields of masa root and dahalli bushes. From the open gate wafted the fragrance of frying mushrooms and meat. Torture!

He had teased Dunnagh mercilessly when they crossed the Great Swamp about his limited diet as a newly bonded kashallan...payback sucked. Masa gruel and the Blood-Gift would be his lot tonight. Torture! Oh well, at least his hunting packs would enjoy their first good meal in days. Thoughts of Dunnagh got his mind drifting down darker pathways. If they had lost him...

"Kashallan-Nathan, I'm glad you've come." Tobrach with head crest held high walked across the courtyard to greet him.

Nathan took note of the smoldering fires and a few bodies lying in lifeless heaps near the far wall. “Any of our hunters over there?” he motioned with his chin to the pile of crumpled dead.

Tobrach shook his head. “We have a few with minor wounds, but none bad enough to be sent back or slow us down. Truly I see the wisdom of having a priest—or as the Speir’dina call them, a medic, traveling with the hunting packs. Ata Fanon and his apprentice are seeing to them right now.”

“Mm, well let me know if there’s someone he can’t handle. He may not want to bother me, and that might cost a man his life.”

Tobrach dipped his head crest. “I will, Holy One, I’ve already noticed how nervous he is in your presence.”

Nathan grunted. “Do that.” Holy One, he wasn’t just Nathan anymore—not even Hunt Leader Nathan, but ‘Holy One.’ Once again an image of Dunnagh flashed into his mind. He hadn’t liked the honorific and the native Timornan’s deference any more than Nathan did now, but like Dunnagh before him, there was little point in fighting their tradition.

<<You know, Kasha, it’s me they are referring to, and through me our Amla, Maker Qwaltamis,>> Corha said in a hesitant voice into his mind.

Nathan patted his middle with a soothing gesture. <<I know, Shalla. I’m not used to being addressed like the top brass, as we would say. No, I’m just the lowly beast of burden good for nothing more than carrying my exalted bondmate from here to there.>>

<<Kasha, I love you! You aren’t just a beast of burden as you put it....>> the symbiont thought about it for a moment then said, <<Oh, you are joking with me, aren’t you, Kasha.>>

Nathan’s lip twitched. <<Yeah, Shalla, I am. I love you, too.>> and he did, damn it, much to his surprise, he did love the little worm nesting in his gut. As Dunnagh before him—and all the kashallans after him, Nathan supposed, he did love his inner companion.

<<I think it is going to take me some time to appreciate Speir’dina humor,>> Corha quipped.

Nathan snorted. <<We are a strange bunch, by Timornan standards, I guess.>>

The prisoners were a sorry lot, consisting of elderly and young Loti and low ranking Avairei. The wounded and older Warlinga left to guard the keep against 'Umwira mutants' were killed to a man before the main force arrived, taking that decision out of his hands.

Speaking gently to the Loti servants Nathan-Corha went among them, and with Ata Fanon's help he was able to put them in the link and reassure them that he was indeed a true kashallan

The Avairei, however were a different matter. One haughty Ata, who seemed to be the leader of this unhappy little bunch, looked down his nose at Warega and their Warlinga guards and blustered, "If you have come from the High Matri in Riath, as you say, then I demand to see Ima Enaju's writ of authorization for you and your hunt leader's outrageous behavior."

"Enaju Dingay and her brother are dead," Kashallan-Nathan said as he stepped into the room with Tobrach and Aju'an at his side. "It's me you will have to deal with now." Nathan smiled showing his new pointed Khutani teeth. "And you had better taste pretty sweet when I put you in the link or you're a dead man."

At the sight of his Speir'dina face the Ata staggered, nearly falling. The Warlinga closest to him thrust a clawed hand into his braids and jerked the priest upright. When he was over his initial surprise he growled, "Mutant Filth, K'San Drucas warned us to be on guard against the traitors from the West. So it is true what our Beloved Master said. The Ancient Covenant with the savages in the West has been broken.

"What did the Khutani promise your wizard, Mutant, slaves and the favored lands of the Yeyen Banai Valley that rightfully belong to us? Our K'San will return with all the might of the Ghostlands behind him. With the power of the ancient magics we will take what is ours and crush all traitors!"

Nathan glanced at the Warlinga surrounding him. All glared at the defiant man with head crests flattened and teeth bared, even Corah coiled ready to spit black kavay into that arrogant face. But what was the point? A martyr's death was what the priest wanted.

Deciding to wipe that gloating smirk off the Dingay's face, Nathan drew his sidearm and blew a hole in the wall across the room. And that got everybody's attention. Into the silence that followed his little demonstration, he said, "We aren't mutants from the other side of the Shallow Sea, Dingay. I have no knowledge about an Ancient Covenant with the Western Clans. If it's broken, then your Ghostland masters are to blame.

"We call ourselves the Speir'dina in our language. Loosely translated into Timornan it means people from the sky. Yes, the sky, we came from another world entirely. And yes, the Khutani makers called us here to host their symbiont children, but we also have with us our technology—a technology, or magic if you wish, that enables us to travel the Starry Void. Your masters may not find it so easy to defeat us 'savages' as they assume."

When Kashallan-Nathan saw the fear widen the priest's eyes, he nodded to Tobrach. "I've no need to taste that one. He's made it very clear where his loyalties lie." Grinning, the Warlinga drew his long Speir'dina knife and slit the man's throat.

Out of the others there were only two young novices who were free of the changeling taint. They were, like Neil, from a distant branch of the Dingay clan. They'd been sent to this keep to serve the Ima Matri's family only in the past couple years. Hair ornaments and all necklaces dropped into the fire, he took the traumatized youngsters' oaths, but resolved to send them back to Riath with the next runners going south. They could carry his message to have Ima Ngeal send some people to help harvest the fields before the Sorins came. They would need that extra food during the confinement even with this keep abandoned.

LATER THAT EVENING after a rest and his meal of lumpy masa gruel Nathan gathered the hunt leaders for a war council. "Our messages to Ticca should have reached hunt Leader Tizu by now," Nathan began when everyone had assembled and closed the door to one of the opulent Dingay audience chambers. "He should be well on his way back to our old base camp in the Broken Lands. From there, as a combined force we can head north into the Ghostlands."

"That is a good plan, Kashallan-Nathan," Tobrach said. "But I would like to take my hunters north to scout for a few more days. I want to assure myself that the changelings are still running north with their tails between their legs and not doubling back to attack us from behind."

The more experienced Varrod and hunt leader Warega dipped their head crests in agreement. Nathan grimaced, not liking the idea of descending into the dark again. But the underground tunnels offered the quickest and easiest way to reach their old base in the Broken Lands.

"Good idea," he said. "Follow the trail northward for a few days, just long enough to make sure they are really gone, and then catch up to us."

CHELKA PEERED THROUGH the shadows and mists, frantically searching for the way out. Always there was the dark in the waking world and within the Dream as well, heavy, oppressive. <<No escape,>> the voice taunted. <<You are mine, woman. Mine!>>

<<No! Never!>> Chelka screamed her defiance into the echoing blackness. Running, stumbling, turning down one passage then retreating to try another. She raced, looking for the light, for the way out of these endless underground caverns. *There has to be an escape—has to be,* she muttered to herself.

<<Run, go ahead,>> the voice mocked. <<It doesn't matter, there's no escape. I will have what is mine. Come to me; you know who is your true Master, Woman.>> Suddenly the mark carved into her forehead blazed with white-hot pain.

Chelka staggered, then whirling with teeth bared and claws extended she snarled, <<I'm not your property, Umwira Filth. Stop hiding in the shadows. Come out and fight me! Are you afraid, half-bred Umwira changeling?>>

The voice chuckled. <<Do you really want to fight me, Woman, are you sure?>>

Suddenly the stench of red kavay clogged her nostrils, triggering her inbred response to the Khutani's fertility compound her people needed to enact a sexual union. A phantom long tongue caressed the sensitive place under her jaw. Sensing her inner turmoil, he next gently licked the tender places on her wrists.

The soft spots, a break in her natural armor had been bred into her people to receive a kashallan's touch, but they were also deep wells of pleasure. Ghostly claws lightly scored her chest creeping closer to the elongating nipples in her breeding pouch. At the same time something long and hard thrust aside her tail questing for another opening. <<Mine!>>

<<No, damn you to the Black Pit!>> Chelka screamed her battle cry, formed a spear of etheric matter and whirled creating a circle of light about herself. <<I will never submit to you. I'll kill myself first, Foul Beast.>>

<<We shall see, Woman, we shall see.>> mocking laughter ringing in her head the voice faded back into the shadows. With a gasp Chelka flung herself into consciousness. Trembling she sat up and looked around.

Unfortunately for her peace of mind, they were still camped within the maze of underground tunnels that led into the Broken Lands. Beside her, Tobrach stirred, opening a sleepy red eye. "Chelka, is something wrong?"

"Go back to sleep, My dear One. It's just time for me to go on watch," she lied. Tobrach grunted and drifted easily back into sleep. It wasn't time for her turn at sentry duty, but there was no point trying to sleep. Drucas would only return to torment her again—it had happened before.

Not wishing to disturb her exhausted partner, who had just returned from a scouting mission, Chelka rose and moved quietly through the camp till she came to the sentry fire. Mar and a couple Speir'dina she knew by sight but not by name were there drinking the last of the evening's tea.

As she started to join them Nathan appeared suddenly out of the dark to block her way. Gasping, Chelka dropped into a fighter's crouch, then recognizing him she relaxed. "You startled me, Kashallan."

Nathan chuckled. "Keep alert, Warlinga." Then in a voice not his own but that of the Ancient that was often with him and the young symbiont, he said, "I sensed a ripple of disturbance within the river of the Dream just now. Does the Changeling trouble you still?"

Chelka felt her face color green and hoped the darkness hid her embarrassment. "I am sorry if I bothered you, Holy One. It is nothing. I can handle it." Can you? A tiny voice in her mind asked. His lures of both intense pleasure and pain were becoming harder and harder to resist, damn him.

No! It wasn't true. She was Warlinga, bred to fight the Hated Enemy. She would fight—kill—he couldn't make her do his bidding—ever.

Nathan studied her, his piercing grey eyes seeming to cut through the fabric of self illusion to the vulnerable core of her spirit. "Your bravery is commendable, but I can taste the tart flavor of your prevarication without forming the link. You would like what you say to be the truth, Warlinga, but we both know it is not," Qwaltamis chided.

Chelka felt the color of her shame deepen. Maybe what her family kept telling her was true. A woman wasn't suited for the life of a hunter of the ancient enemy. "I am sorry, Elder, my weakness shames me."

"There is no reason to be ashamed, Young One. The Enemy has wrought a powerful compulsion to master you. I doubt anyone of the hunters could have resisted his magic thus far any better."

Reaching out Nathan took her hand and formed the link. "Marti has already told us of your private torment. I kept waiting for you to come to me and ask for my help, but you did not, and this situation is becoming too dangerous to let continue."

Yes, she could understand that. As they traveled into the Ghostlands they couldn't afford to have her a possible—though unwilling—agent for Drucas and the wizards. "Maybe I should go back to Riath," she began.

"Only if that is what 'you' want," Qwaltamis said. "I can help you, if you permit. One of my descendants will guard your dreams when I am not able to do it myself."

Chelka let out her breath in a long sigh, feeling relief flood through her body. "Thank you, Maker, that would ease my mind. I don't want to go back, but I don't want to get anyone killed, either."

Sending a mild sedative down the link they shared, Qwaltamis said, "So be it, then. Now go back to your pallet and join your consort. We will have a long day tomorrow if we wish to reach this Speir'dina base in the Broken Lands my child speaks of."

When she was gone, Nathan took his own advice and went to lie down in his bedroll. <<Will she truly be all right, Amla?>> Corha asked, the sour taste of worry flavoring the symbiont's mental sending.

<<Not to worry, Young One, we will savor her dreams and keep them sweet. The Enemy will not have her.>>

Nathan detected a hint of smugness in the Maker's sending. Recalling what had happened to Dunnagh-Tani not long before, he privately wondered if the Khutani might be underestimating the Enemy's cunning and strength. <<Amla, Marti also was branded by the Changeling,>> he said. <<Though Drucas hasn't shown much interest in my Speir'dina hunter he might change his mind in future if he can't get to Chelka.>>

Qwaltamis rumbled a mental laugh. <<Hunter, is it now? I would have thought she was more than that to you, Chosen. Did I not taste the sweet flavor of a coupling the other night?>>

Damn, did the symbiont have to broadcast their business to the whole pod? Nathan thought. Of course his bondmate shared his pleasure with Marti when they played "the fucking game," and damn Tani anyway for teaching Corha about that. Now it would seem the big worm had shared their pleasure, too—or Corha had privately told it.

Unable to shield from the Maker as well as he would have liked, the gist of his thoughts only amused the Khutani more. <<Now, now no need to twist your tail in a knot, because I know about this, 'fucking game' the Little One boasted about.>> the Maker's amusement rippled down the Psy link they shared. Then becoming serious once more it said, <<And I savor your meaning about your mate. You are right and we will guard her dreams as well as the Warlinga.>>

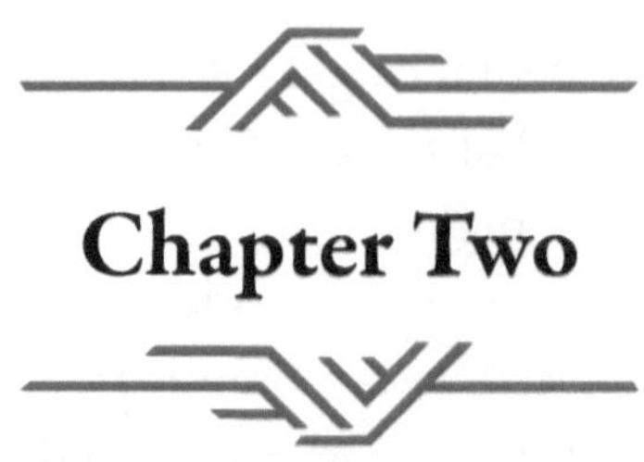

Chapter Two

Pausing on the cliff overlooking the beach where the clans' war canoes were being readied for their journey, Phillip-Yoey took in a deep breath and let it out in a long sigh of contentment. The morning air was heavy with moisture and rich with the scent of salt. The Shallow Sea at last. How he'd missed the cool sensuous feel of water against his skin! Oh, it wasn't the Great Swamp, but it was wet. He couldn't wait to plunge in, and be wrapped in the sinewy coils of his Khutani relatives swimming somewhere nearby.

It had taken them four days of hard travel to reach this sheltered cove on the coast from the healing springs where the clans had gone after the Ghostlander's surprise attack. After several war council meetings, and many heated arguments, it was decided that warriors from Blue Stone-Bitter Water, Sand Mountain, and Red Wind would go with him to join forces with the hunting packs coming from Ticca and the Yeyen Banai Valley. Together they would go into the Ghostlands to engage their common "Hated Enemy."

Rock Salt sent men to paddle one war canoe, but didn't formally join the Kashallan Alliance. They did, however, swear Blood-Oath to care for and protect the four warring clans' women and children while their men were absent.

Green Clay and Twisted Grass, whose territories bordered the Ghostlands claimed neutrality in the coming conflict and refused to favor one faction or the other. They did swear Blood-Oath not to give the enemy any information, but that was as far as they were willing to go against the Ancient Covenant, allying the West with the Ghostlands.

"You know once the Ghostlanders see us fighting alongside the Warlinga they may not respect your claim to neutrality," Phillip-Yoey warned Tego the night before they left for the coast.

Tego grimaced, but remained adamant that his people wouldn't get involved. "I expect you to keep them too busy to think about us, Grandson," the old warrior told him. At Phillip's frown he added, "If they do come, we will hide in the mountains as we did before. We will be all right."

"Well, if you change your mind, my offer to go East across the Shallow Sea still is open to you and anyone else who wishes to find sanctuary with my Speir'dina kin." Tego had given him a noncommittal grunt and Phillip had left it at that.

Defying the decision of their Elders, two young Twisted Grass warriors had joined them. Nytaka and Qwayku by name, they were cousins of Efosa. She had pleaded their case well to Yoey until the bondmates agreed to take them.

Fearing they would disobey their Elders and follow them anyway, he spoke to Tego on their behalf. He checked with Chang first, however, because it would be Chang who would supervise them for the most part.

The armachd agreed to take them under his wing, as long as they would submit to his discipline.The young men were about Timma's age, and Phillip hoped the youngsters would get along. Full of stories about heroes and their glorious deeds of war, the cousins could learn a lot from Timma, who had actually been in battles with the Umwira more than once. Yes, they could learn from him, if they could lose the arrogant superiority most Umwira had towards the Avairei.

Knowing that Phillip-Yoey and young Timma were bringing their women along, several warriors including Ogwy argued to have their own wives accompany them. To his surprise, the women, with the Elders' backing put up a united front to veto that idea. "We don't care what crazy Khutani and Avairei do," one matron was heard to shout. "Women have no place accompanying the warbands. You can cook your own food for once. They aren't going!"

Phillip supposed Ogwy's desire to bring Kelga was motivated partially by concern for how his new bride would be cared for in his absence. Knowing she was one of the last left alive in the traitor's family, his concern was valid, Phillip thought. Quietly he asked Masonja to speak to her witch friend, who belonged to the Rock Salt people, to determine if she would look after the girl as her pregnancy progressed.

Knowing the poor girl had no relatives to help her, Lesala agreed to the plan. When he told Ogwy that going to war was no place for a pregnant woman and Lesala of the Rock Salt people would care for his wife, he had reluctantly agreed to leave her.

Secretly the Kashallan wished Ogwy himself would stay on this side of the water with his wife and the Rock Salt men. He feared there might be trouble when Dunnagh-Tani and the rest of the Speir'dina and the Warlinga hunting packs learned of Sairsa's abduction. Unfortunately, Ogwy's unspoken competition with Tesulu wouldn't allow him to lose face by staying behind. So he was coming and they would have to make the best of it, dealing with trouble if, or when it arose.

Picking up the basket of medicinal roots and seeds he'd collected and hoped to plant somewhere on the eastern shore, Phillip-Yoey headed down to the beach. They were almost ready to go.

Ishka and Efosa met him as he stepped onto the shore. He handed Efosa the basket. "Can you keep this for me, Mother?"

"Yes, of course, my son," Efosa said, placing the smaller lidded basket inside her larger one, balancing the whole mass atop her head.

Phillip put an arm around Ishka's shoulder and gave her a quick hug. "Are you nervous?"

"A little," she admitted and smiled up at him. "But I'm excited, and maybe relieved, too."

He returned the smile. He felt all her emotions, but his feelings were spiced with a heavy measure of worry, as well. As they walked to the canoes, he murmured so only she could hear. "Have they decided which war leader gets the privilege of our exalted company for the voyage?"

She let out a low chuckle and hugged him back. "We are going with our Sand mountain relatives, in the fearless war leader Tesulu's canoe." Ishka giggled. "Along with my—other—spouse. Qwasigara is gracing us with his presence, as well."

"Mm, and what of the others?"

She did laugh more openly this time. "Much to his disgust, Ogwy is carrying Tess-weh and her household. My daughter and her man as well as Efosa and Masonja, and the Twisted Grass boys, are with the Blue Stone canoes—somewhere—with Noi or Lubwey maybe, and I'm not sure who agreed to bring the Demon's Loti slave, but he *is* coming with us."

Though Tess-weh was reluctant to confide in him how her recovery progressed, knowing that she had chosen to sail with them instead of using her power to transport herself and her protector across the straight told him a lot. It twisted his knot of worry a little tighter. He hoped she would be fully recovered by the time they encountered the Ghostlanders again.

The red sun was a shimmering pathway leading them home, Phillip-Yoey thought as they launched. Out of the shelter of the cove a stiff breeze came up from the south-west pushing them towards the eastern shore. Tiny caps of pale blue broke apart on the wave tops as their canoe's bow cut through the water. To the north the grey ridges of the Ghostlands were a threatening ribbon on the horizon.

As much as he would have liked to join the joyous pod swimming below them for play and a satisfying meal, Phillip-Yoey resisted their temptation. Tentacles extended, he dripped his regret into the water for the trailing pod to savor. So close to the Ghostlands they were exposed and vulnerable. They needed to hurry across before their presence was detected.

As the eastern shore drew closer, Phillip said to Chang, paddling alongside him, "Mah'lu, do you think you're close enough to be heard by some of our people?"

Chang stowed his paddle and reached for the waterproof bag at his feet. Pulling out a small black object he tapped some of the icons on its surface and waited.

The people in the canoe gaped as a loud hissing noise erupted from the object. Chang next tapped another part of the box and then held it close to his mouth. In Galactic Standard, he said, "Hey, Boyos, anybody out there; can you hear me, Lann Gheal?"

Only static was his answer. "Too far away yet," he said to Phillip. "Or maybe the amadans aren't keeping their comm-link on."

"Keep trying as we get closer. I'd prefer to give them some warning, before we just show up on their doorstep," Phillip said.

Chang snorted a laugh. "You got that right. It would be best."

Unable to hold back his curiosity any longer, Tesulu said, "What is that thing your warrior has, Brother-in-law, more Khutani magic?"

Phillip shook his head. "No, it's Speir'dina technology, actually."

"Not very good technology," Qwasigara snorted. "All it does is make a hissing sound. What good is that?"

"It's a communication device," Phillip explained. "Right now we are still too far away for the men who have a similar device to hear us. I'm hoping as we come closer to the shoreline they will answer."

The wizard snorted again. "Easier to use magic, Timornan technology."

Phillip-Yoey chuckled. "You may be right, Elder."

Chang tried three more times as they neared the eastern shore. The purple mounds of thorn were high ridges on the skyline by the time he got a hesitant response. "Hello? Who is this?"

Chang laughed and keyed his mic, "Who do you think, McLaren, you Amadan? It's me, Chang. Now let me talk to somebody in charge, somebody with a working brain cell."

McLaren laughed and swore at him in Caldoni. "I'll get Nathan. Will he do? Hold on."

Not understanding the words, but hearing a voice coming out of Chang's box at last, Tesulu slowed their pace. Some of the other canoes drew closer, knowing something was happening, even if they weren't sure exactly what.

It took a while, but at last Nathan's familiar voice came booming over the com. "All right, Chang I'm here. What's the problem? What does Hunt Leader Tizu want me to do now?"

Tizu? The Kashallan and Chang exchanged glances. "Uh, Nathan, I don't have any idea what the Hunt Leader wants. I'm not with the hunters coming from Ticca."

Sounding confused, Nathan asked, "Then where are you—and if not the hunt Leader, who is with you?"

Phillip muttered a curse, his knot of worry tightening a little more. There were too many pieces of the puzzle missing. Where was Tizu and why hadn't he let Nathan and the armachda know they were coming? And where, oh where was maker Tinguss?

"I don't understand, Phillip," Chang murmured muting the device. "Nathan is acting like he doesn't know about the alliance or that we're coming. Wasn't Hunt Leader Tizu supposed to be here already?"

"Be here to meet us, or send word of our coming," Phillip agreed.

"What should I tell him?"

Phillip grimaced, then gave a mirthless laugh. "This is an unexpected wrinkle in the fabric of our plan, to be sure. We tell him as little as possible but enough not to get us killed," he suggested. Chang nodded his expression solemn.

"Hey, Chang what's going on? Answer me."

"Sorry, Nathan, I lost you for a moment," Chang lied. "I'm with kashallan Phillip-Yoey, some new friends, and—uh— Tess-weh. We've been on a mission for one of the Makers. Didn't Hunt leader Tizu tell you?"

" Uh—no he isn't here yet."

Chang laughed. "Oh boyo, have we got a surprise for you then," he said in Caldoni.

"Shit. That's what I'm afraid of." Nathan said in the same language. "Uh, Chang, Phillip, nobody told us you were coming and bringing new—friends to our little party. Where are you exactly?"

"Not sure, but I can see the eastern shoreline clearly now. We should be coming ashore in..." Chang broke off to ask someone a question in another language; then he was back. "About a couple sun-marks maybe, the war leader thinks."

WAR LEADER? CHANG and Phillip were off the coast—in a boat of some kind—and there was a war leader? But there wasn't anybody out there but the Umwir—oh shit, oh shit!

In his middle, Corha picked up on his thought and flooded his senses with white-hot anger. Nathan staggered and would have fallen if Ross hadn't steadied him <<Umwira, Hated Enemy, how dare they!>>

<<Calm down, Shalla, I can't think when you flood my system with your anger,>> Nathan pleaded.

<<But the Enemy has captured our Amsi! >> Corha protested. <<We have to be ready we have to fight them.>>

<<Shalla, stop! Didn't you hear Armachd Chang say he was coming with 'friends.' He didn't say the kashallan with them was a prisoner. Phillip-Yoey is our Amsi, true, but I don't think Armachd Chang would have let anyone

hurt him. We need to wait and hear what they have to say, before we attack them. Maybe they really are our friends.>>

Oh, by all the gods of Caldon and Timorna he hoped so.

<<All right,>> Corha grumbled. <<I'll try not to be so angry, and I do want to meet our new Amsi, but the Umwira!>>

Damn. Did their Amla know about these "new friends?" why hadn't it told them? Damn! <<Yeah, yeah I know. I'm sure everything will be fine, Shalla, just stay calm. We will figure it out.>>

Opening his eyes Nathan stared at a worried Ross, and Aju'an. Several more Warlinga and Speir'dina hovered nearby attracted by the activation of the comm. "You all right?" Ross asked.

Nathan grimaced. "Yeah, now I am. Corha figured out who is coming for a visit and isn't happy about it, that's all." Ross raised an eyebrow in inquiry, but Nathan ignored him and returned his attention to the comm.

"Chang, where are you—and your friends coming ashore? We'll meet you there."

"We're supposed to meet the Hunt Leader and the boyos from Ticca at our old base on the mesa," Chang said.

Oh shit, most of the Warlinga hunting packs were near there. That would be a disaster in the making if they went there on their own without warning. "No, don't go there, plans have changed. Some of the guys are trying to see if there's anything left up there we can use. Between the Begta and the storms the place is a mess. We'll come to you. Where?"

There was some more garbled conversation on Chang's end, then he said, "I don't know how to explain it, but if you have some local Begta with you they'll know."

SPOTTING ONE OF DADO'S relatives named Brolo in the hovering crowd, Nathan beckoned him over. "Did you hear what Armachd Chang said?" Brolo nodded vigorously. "Do you know what place he's talking about?"

The Begta scratched his wooly head, thinking. At last he smiled, showing large yellow teeth. "It probably where Umwira mans always come when want food or slaves."

Nathan rolled his eyes and sighed. "Great. That's just great. We'll meet you there, over and out." Turning to Brolo he asked, "How far is it to this—place?'

Brolo shrugged. "We leave soon be there when sun high." Brolo raised his hand to where the sun would be about midday. About two hours, Nathan reckoned. "Ross put together a patrol—lot of Speir'dina with the Warlinga—we leave in fifteen min."

Newly appointed as his hunt leader and personal guard, Aju'an dipped his head crest and fell into step with him as he went back to his tent to gather his own gear. "What's going on, Kashallan-Nathan?"

"Good question. I'll let you know when I figure it out. Somebody forgot to keep us in the comm loop." Catching sight of the Warlinga's puzzled expression, Nathan stopped and turned to face him.

"I don't know how much of what was said back there you understood, but it would seem we have company coming. There's a kashallan—one you haven't met yet. He's coming with Chang and Moraga—and Tess-weh I think. There are some Umwira, warriors from the western clans, who are also with them."

As he saw Aju'an's head crest flatten Nathan held up a hand and spoke in a commanding voice. "They have a kashallan with them, a Holy One, Warlinga, get it, a kashallan! Chang says these warriors are friends—allies. I want no trouble with them. We wait, hear what they have to say and see what this is all about."

Damn, he wished the big worms or somebody had let him know what was going on. Keeping him in the dark could get somebody killed. Knowing how potentially dangerous this situation could become, Nathan rested a hand on the butt of his sidearm to emphasize his point.

"No trouble. Tell Tobrach, your brother—all the hunters, anybody disobeys and they will answer to me. We can't afford to be quarreling among ourselves right now. We will be doing the Ghostlanders' work for them if we do."

He could tell Aju'an didn't like it, but he dipped his head crest. "Your will, Kashallan. It will be as you say."

Chapter Three

Cresting the ridge, Nathan looked down and saw about twenty war canoes entering the mouth of the cove below. Arguing that for safety's sake, he should precede him, Ross was already crouched on the moss, day-scopes plastered to his face. Joining him, Nathan asked, "Can you see any of our people in those war canoes?"

Without removing the device from his eyes, Ross said, "it's mostly warriors in the canoes, but they have some women with them, and... a couple Avairei with them as well. I see Chang, I think in the lead canoe so one of the Avairei must be Timma... There's Moraga with some of the women in a canoe further back."

Nathan's heart gave a lurch. Tess-weh... It was hard to be around her even now. "If Moraga's there then Tess-weh must be as well. Do you see her with the women—or Cadrach?"

"No..." Ross played with the controls of the scopes, focusing in on the lead canoe. "There's another Speir'dina with Chang, but..." Ross let out a low whistle of surprise. "I think the other Speir'dina is Dr. Singey, but I'm not sure. He looks so diff—"

Nathan snatched the scopes away. "Let me see." He adjusted the focus and swore. It was indeed Phillip, a Phillip gone native. Along with his death strand were other carved necklaces. Hair confined in an Umwira topknot, he also wore some kind of tribal markings on his face and arms. Nathan swore again. Oh, everybody was going to love this! "That's Phillip all right," he told Ross, handing the scopes back.

Ross put them to his face, watching the progression of the canoes into the cove. "An Umwira kashallan," he mused. "I wonder what the Warlinga and the Imas are going to say. Who would have thought."

Nathan snorted a laugh. Never mind the Imas, what about the makers—his Amla? Damn! Who would have thought it indeed.

Then as if his thought had invoked the ancient Khutani, Maker Qwaltamis was suddenly in his mind. <<What is the Little One telling me, Chosen? It said something about Umwira capturing a kashallan?>>

Nathan sighed. Why did Corha have to call their Amla right now? <<It's Kashallan-Phillip down there, Amla, but I don't think he's been captured by them,>> Nathan said. <<I know it's hard to believe, but my armachd who is also with them said the warriors are 'friends.' He says they are coming to meet Hunt Leader Tizu, and that they've been on a mission for another Maker.>>

Sensing the Maker's flaring temper, he said, "Ross, give me the scopes back for the moment. Maker Qwaltamis just joined us. It wants to see them."

Hearing the tension in Nathan's voice, Ross passed him the scopes without comment. Nathan focused on the lead canoe the image much clearer, now that they were closer.

When Qwaltamis saw Tinguss's child relaxed and unbound among the Hated Enemy, it sent such a blast of uncontrollable rage down the link they shared that Nathan almost fainted, Ross hastily reaching for the scopes he almost dropped over the cliff.

<<Slimeworm!>> Qwaltamis roared.

In the choking heat of the maker's sendings that were threatening to drown him in its fiery broth, slimeworm and disobeyed the Council was about all Nathan could understand. But he could also taste that Corha was terrified by the Maker's reaction.

Feeling suddenly very protective of his symbiont partner, Nathan resisted giving into the Maker's rage. Before he was totally overwhelmed Nathan tossed what he hoped was a cooling balm into the Khutani's emotional whirlpool, <<Maker, please! I don't know what this is all about, but we won't find out if you continue to broadcast your anger. This isn't helping. Corha is very frightened right now. Please think of my young bondmate and calm down!>>

It took a moment, but finally the Ancient cooled enough to understand what Nathan was saying. Tasting both bondmates' distress, Qwaltamis dripped the soothing flavor of sweetness into its communication. <<I am sorry, my child. Seeing the evidence of betrayal before your eyes angered me beyond reason.>>

<<Betrayal? I don't understand.>>

<<That one's parent, Tinguss,>> Qwaltamis growled, its temper sparking again, <<was told by our Council not to proceed with its plan to make an alliance with the Western Clans while we savored the matter. Now it would seem the scabrous slimeworm has gone against our wishes and done it behind our coils.>>

<<Hmm, Amla, I don't know what's happened—and we won't know till we talk to my Amsi Phillip,>> Nathan mused, <<but from a tactical point of view, it would be better to have the Western Clans as our allies—if that's indeed what they are—than to have them as a menace at our backs.

<<We can't fight this war on two fronts, dividing our forces. We could lose if we don't take the help that's offered, and maybe maker Tinguss knew that.>>

<<The Dingay Changeling my Kasha interviewed before our Warlinga killed him, said something about the western Clans no longer being a part of the Ghostland covenant, Amla,>> Corha said. <<Something must have happened to change their minds. Maybe our Amsi can tell us. Please, Amla, I want to meet my new cousin.>>

The Maker grumbled a bit more, but finally agreed to allow them to land. <<I will stay with you for a time. I want to hear for myself this rebellious Child of the Wild Pools' story.>>

"THERE'S SOME PEOPLE up on the ridge," Chang pointed. "They've seen us, I'm sure."

Chang out of habit had spoken in the Western dialect. Tesulu and the other members of the crew stared in that direction. "Mm, I see them," Phillip-Yoey said. Turning to Tesulu, he smiled, showing lots of teeth. "War leader, Brother-in-law, isn't it time we let the people on the shore know who has come visiting?"

Tesulu laughed. "More than time, My Relative," he agreed. Glancing at Qwasigara he bowed. "Elder?"

The wizard nodded, unwrapped a hand drum and stood in the middle of the swaying boat. Pounding out a simple rhythm, he sang in a resinous voice, telling the watchers their clan, the deeds of their great men and asking to come ashore.

ON THE HILL THE MEN heard the chant, the sound deep and powerful, echoing off the cliffs in the sheltered cove. "Can you understand what they're singing about?" Ross asked, still with the scopes to his eyes. "They've stopped paddling. They're just sitting there."

<<They are telling us their clan affiliation,>> Maker Qwaltamis supplied. <<They are waiting for us to welcome them and give them permission to land.>>

"The Maker says they are waiting for us to welcome them ashore." Nathan's mouth curved into a sly smile. Welcome them, eh. All right, he'd welcome them—Caldoni style. "Ross, you bring those pipes of yours with you to this little party?"

"Yeah? Me and the Begta have been practicing away from camp when we can. I figured we might have some free time before Tizu gets here. The little furballs are getting quite good actually."

"Good, go get them quick-like."

Ross grinned. "Glad the Commander isn't here to hear you say that."

Nathan snorted a laugh. "Right, go get your pibroch."

Catching on, Ross laughed as well. "I will, and me and the Begta will announce your exalted self to our new—uh—friends?"

AS THE WAR CANOES HOVERED just off shore waiting for a signal to come ahead, they heard a strange wailing sound coming from up the slope. "What is that noise?" a warrior grumbled. "Has the hated Enemy sent evil spirits to torment us instead of welcoming us?"

"Be easy, My Kinsmen, there are no evil spirits here, truly. This is just a part of our welcoming ceremony." Phillip-Yoey called out to the people in the other canoes. He knew it was the Caldoni pipes they were hearing for the first time, but they didn't look reassured by his explanation. Some were getting angry, others looked frightened.

Then Moraga broke the tension by waving and shouting something in Caldoni her face alight with joy.

By that time Chang was laughing and pointing. "Look, Sir, there's Armachd Ross with Nathan coming down to welcome us."

Letting out his breath in a grateful sigh, Phillip smiled. "Yes, I see them now. Turning to Tesulu and his warriors, he said, "Be at peace. One of our Speir'dina leaders is coming to welcome us.

"His clan, the Caldoni, play their pipes to welcome newcomers and announce a leader. Nathan there," he pointed to the tall well-muscled man with a braided brown mane. "He is showing you and the warriors great respect in the traditions of his people."

Nathan walked solemnly behind the band, consisting of one Speir'dina man, and two Begta playing their hand-made pipes. Several more Begta pounding enthusiastically on hand drums followed in the pipers' wake. The sound was chaotic—jarring the entire tableau disconcerting—amusing?

Trying to keep a straight face, he glanced at Chang, eye brows raised. "Good thing Commander Tizu isn't here to see or hear this," Chang murmured.

Traditionally the pipes were also used to frighten an enemy in battle, Phillip knew, and suspected this display was a vailed challenge but kept that thought to himself. Phillip's lip twitched. "Definitely a good thing the Hunt Leader can't hear this," he agreed.

In the confusion of their arrival, Phillip leaned closer so only Chang could hear and murmured, "Since Tizu hasn't arrived or told anyone of our coming, we don't know what has happened on this side of the Shallow Sea. I think it wise to keep Tess-weh's presence among us a secret for now. Tell Moraga and Doyan. She is obviously still not at her best. Though unlikely, there may be spies here as well. No need to let the Ghostlanders know they didn't kill her."

"Good idea, I'll tell them. And I'll ask if her new protector can wear a headband to conceal his Wa'chassey'ul brand. Nobody will even dream of her now having an Umwira slave, so he won't give away her presence."

Then, not able to hold back his mirth any longer, he chuckled. "I wonder what Ima Sagas will have to say about this. Can you imagine him standing on guard outside Tess-weh's suite at Ticca?" He snorted a laugh. "Priceless."

Philip's own mouth curved into a thin-lipped smile. "Yes, quite."

Nathan and his entourage were on the beach now. To Phillip's dismay he saw there were a couple Warlinga with him. Praying for a peaceful arrival, he said, "Tesulu, run your canoe in. it will ease the others' minds if they see us being welcomed and not attacked."

Tesulu grunted and they rode a wave into the shingle. Everyone jumping quickly out the warriors lifted the bow further onto the sand. Phillip-Yoey with Tesulu and the wizard at his side walked to meet the people waiting for them.

AS THEY DREW NEAR, the band stopped playing and just stared at the newcomers. This was the first time Nathan, and he supposed most of the Speir'dina with him, had seen the people of the Western Clans. They were a wild-looking bunch, he thought. Well-built furred men with long ponytails hanging loose down their scarred backs, they also sported lots of bone ornaments and tribal markings on arms and faces.

The mixture of Avairei, Loti and Begta traits blended with the four arm torsos and long dog-like faces of the original inhabitants of Timorna, were evidence of the genetic mingling that had been going on for centuries between these warring peoples.

And right there in the thick of it was Phillip, Kashallan-Phillip, dressed in a loin cloth, death strand and bone-carved necklaces, his curly black hair twisted up in an Umwira ponytail and sporting his own set of tribal markings on face and shoulder.

<<Kasha, oh kasha, he is here,>> Corha said excitedly. <<I can almost taste him, he is so close now.>>

<<Calm down, Shalla, we'll taste him in a minute. We have other 'guests' to welcome.>>

"Well, Phillip, this is quite a surprise." Nathan said as he came up to them. "We had no idea company was coming." Nathan spoke in the language of the Khutani peoples and hoped the Westerners knew enough to understand him. He would have to ask Qwaltamis for the Western Umwira language patterns soon.

Phillip's mouth twisted into an ironic smile. "I'm not the only one full of surprises here, am I, Amsi. Did the Ce'awn finally convince you to join us?"

For just a moment Nathan's face clouded. Damn he wished the man hadn't brought up the subject quite so soon. "No—not exactly. Tell you later—"

Missing the significance of Nathan's words, Phillip babbled, "Is he here? I have so much to tell him—"

"N-no. Last I heard he was still in Riath. Tell you later."

Finally catching on, he sobered. "Oh, I can see we have much to share when there is time." Glancing over his shoulder he saw that more of the canoes were being waved in to the beach by Chang and some of Nathan's Speir'dina. Eilo and Goro from Red Wind had also joined them. And, Phillip took in a deep breath, letting it out slowly, here of course came Ogwy and Lubwey.

Waiting for them to join them, he said, "Forgive me, Elders, War Leaders, greeting an old friend has made me forget my manners. I'd like to introduce..." Phillip named the wizard and war leaders that had now joined him. "And this is Nathan—" he broke off raising an eyebrow.

"I'm Nathan-Corha," Kashallan-Nathan supplied. Turning to the warriors at his back he introduced Aju'an, Tobrach, and Ross.

The Warlinga and Clan warriors eyed each other warily, but nobody made a move for their weapons. That, he supposed was a good sign.

Then Qwasigara smiled showing lots of teeth. "A Maker come to greet us, how nice of you, Khutani. I feel so welcomed. Our kinsman didn't warn us. I feel so secure now knowing that you are here."

Phillip could see the Maker, probably Nathan's Amla coiled protectively around its child's etheric aura. He'd been so intent on trying to prevent a war from breaking out right in front of him he hadn't allowed Yoey's Khutani-heightened awareness to surface.

Using Nathan's mouth, the Maker said in its deep other-worldly voice, "I have warned my hunters to not start trouble. You are welcome as long as your warriors do the same, Wizard."

Then glaring at Phillip-Yoey with Nathan's iron-grey eyes, Qwaltamis said, "You, on the other hand, have much to answer for, Rebellious Child, as does your imprisoned parent."

Imprisoned? That explained why he and the pod hadn't heard from Tinguss all this time. Makers quarreling among themselves, he shuddered, Yoey sharing his fear. That was disturbing news.

Before the bondmates could stammer out a reply, Kashallan-Phillip was encircled by the familiar presence of his parent, Maker Tinguss. Somewhere hovering nearby he could sense other Makers swimming in the ether. Taking a deep breath, he let it out in a relieved sigh. <<Amla!>>

Tinguss took a moment to send him an affectionate squeeze, then focused its attention back on its peer. <<No, he does not, Amsi. My child did exactly what I charged him to do, make an alliance with the western clans. And if you had listened to all my story before imprisoning me, I would have told you and the others that it was too late to turn back what the Demon had foreseen in our future.>>

Taking control of Phillip's body, Tinguss considered the two wizards standing nearby. The Maker could see the amusement in their sharp dark eyes. They had definitely seen and probably heard the heated exchange between the two Khutani.

Using Phillip's voice, Tinguss said, "I am Maker Tinguss. Thank you for coming. I have just heard of your latest battle with the Ghostland warbands from another of my descendants. I'm sorry I wasn't there to give some assistance. It is I who sent my precious child to you to make an alliance. He has succeeded, but in a most unconventional way." The maker rumbled a laugh and Phillip's mouth smiled. "Shall I now call you my relatives, too?"

Qwasigara showed his canines. "We shall see, Khutani."

<<Who released you, Slimeworm?>> Qwaltamis growled, breaking in on the conversation, not caring if the wizards heard.

<<Maker Meyagus and I did,>> Gladdris said, the heat of its own irritation spicing their communion. <<There is no point to our Amsi's confinement now, don't you agree?>>

<<Do the others know?>> Qwaltamis grumbled, dodging the question.

Meyagus rumbled a laugh. <<They will now if they don't already.>>

Qwaltamis grunted. <<We need to talk.>>

<<Yes, we do,>> Gladdris agreed as they swam into the etheric mists.

<<I'm sorry, My Child, I have no time to explain now. I must council with my peers. I will come to you later. I am very proud of you,>> Tinguss said, sending a last burst of love to him as it uncoiled and swam away.

<<Be careful, Amla,>> Phillip-Yoey called, not sure if the Ancient heard him.

"I see that most of the boats are on the beach now," Phillip-Yoey said, returning his attention to the matter at hand. "I know we haven't given you any time to prepare, but do you have a place where we can set up our camp? I gather plans have changed since we last spoke with Hunt Leader Tizu."

Relieved by the change of topic, being also a part of that disturbing interchange, Nathan said: "Most of our guys are camped on the mesa seeing what the Sorins and the Begta left of our stuff. The Warlinga Hunting packs are—around, mostly trying to pick up the Ghostlanders' trail.

"You probably wouldn't know, Phillip-Yoey, but there were Umwira changelings in Riath, the High Matri herself was one as well as her hunt leader Drucas Segoi. We rooted them out and sent them running with their tails between their legs back North."

Qwasigara snorted. "I know that one. He thinks he is special—too great to talk to his relations along the Shallow Sea."

Nathan grunted. "Arrogant, he is that all right. He's right up there at the top of our shit list. He's a dead man for sure—if we can catch him."

Returning to the most pressing topic at the moment Nathan stroked his chin, thinking. "Now as to a good place to camp..." Without some preparation, he didn't dare bring the Umwira right into their main encampment. The problem was he didn't know the country around here well enough to suggest a good spot.

Canines showing in a wide grin, Tesulu said, "I know a place. There is a mossy clearing near a large Kavalpa grove up the hill to the north of here. We can go there and wait till this hunt leader of yours arrives."

Startled Nathan glanced at the Begta. Brolo nodded. "Umwira mans go there when come to raid. It good place."

Nathan rolled his eyes. "And you little furballs never thought to tell anybody about that?"

Brolo shrugged.

"Who were they going to tell, Nathan," Phillip said, "Gormach?"

Nathan sighed. "Point taken. All right, War Leader, let's find this camp site of yours and get you settled. I'll assign some of my Speir'dina men to see that nobody takes it into their thick skulls to settle old scores on both sides. If we're all friends now everybody is going to have to learn to play nice together—and that means everybody."

Ogwy folded his upper set of arms across his chest. "Where is your hunt leader?" He demanded. "He promised that he would meet us here."

Oh here we go, Phillip thought and shot him a dagger-look.

Nathan folded his own set of muscular arms across his chest and said, "A runner left Riath several eight-days ago. Hunt Leader Tizu should be on his way here by now."

Ogwy shook his head in disbelief. "He has no little box that talks like warrior Chang has, then?"

"He does, but since there's no satellite up there to relay the signal he has to be in range to use it." Nathan knew he was using words the Umwira wouldn't understand, but he didn't care. He didn't like this arrogant prick—and he'd bet the bacach wouldn't ask him for an explanation, either.

Phillip sighed. "Ogwy, I'm sure the Hunt Leader isn't here yet because he wanted to personally make sure the Blue Stone women and children were settled in safely with our Speir'dina kin before coming to meet us. He will be here soon."

At the puzzled look on Nathan's face, Phillip suspected he'd not understood most of that exchange.

<<I think we will have to help our Amsi and share with him the language patterns for the Western dialect,>> Yoey said. <<He looks confused.>>

A mental laugh. <<He does, doesn't he.>> "I'll explain later," he said to Nathan in Galactic Standard.

Nathan grunted. "Right then, let's get everybody settled."

As they beached and secured the canoes, Phillip decided he'd better have a little talk with the Blue Stone men, see if Lubwey or somebody else could curb Ogwy's self-destructive tendencies.

He'd witnessed Ogwy trying to provoke Tinguss into giving him the martyr's death he wanted when he wasn't allowed to keep Sairsa. Well, if he still wanted to die there were plenty of Ghostlanders who would love to help him out with that little problem, Phillip thought.

It was obvious no one here had heard what had happened to Sairsa and Briya, and he hoped to break that news only when necessary. Suddenly he was glad Dunnagh wasn't here for whatever reason.

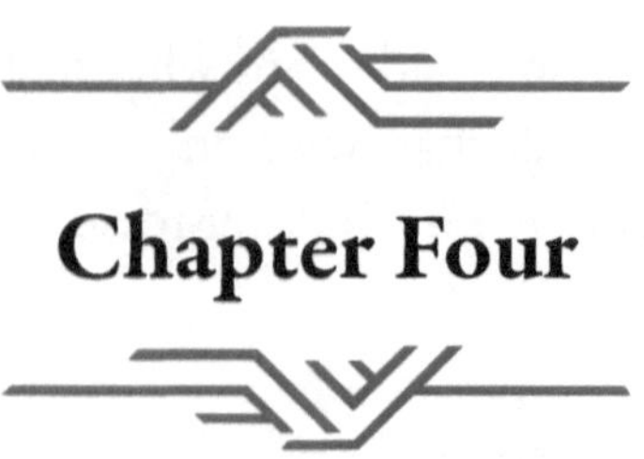

Chapter Four

As they strolled down the beach, Phillip said, "Yoey is excited to taste its new cousin. I'd like to swim into the cove and introduce you to some of my pod and share all the news, but I know that indulgence will have to wait."

Nathan's lip twitched. "You got that right. There'd be a lot of unhappy campers on both sides if that happened."

Phillip grinned. "Oh yes, there certainly would be unhappy campers, as you put it, but at least you can come with me over to the unloading canoes. Timma is over there, and I'll introduce you to some of the others while we're getting things sorted."

Nathan grunted and started to follow when he was stopped by his guards. "You aren't going over there without protection," Ross said. His Warlinga escort dipped their head crests in agreement.

Nathan scowled, folding his arms across his chest. "Really? These guys aren't stupid. No one is going to bother me—and I need you bunch to help coordinate this. Our new friends might need food and other supplies. And Ross, you are better at those kind of details than I am, as you keep telling me, right?"

"Yeah, I know I tell you that, but you're still not going anywhere without an escort." Ross folded his own arms, his face stubborn. "Take the Warlinga if not me, then."

Nathan rolled his eyes but gave in. "All right, all right, but only one man." He glanced at the two Warlinga silently watching. Who to choose? He knew Aju'an best, and they worked well together, but the Western Clans had raided in his family's lands for centuries—probably not wise to tempt him more than necessary right now. He was going to be pissed—

"All right Tobrach can come with me. Aju'an, I need you to help Ross. And while you're at it, send a runner back to our base to see if Hunt Leader

Tizu has arrived. Tell them what's going on down here. I'll be back to camp later this afternoon."

Aju'an was definitely pissed, but he only dipped his head crest and followed Ross, shouting orders as he went. Turning back to Phillip, Nathan saw that he was having a hard time controlling a grin. "What are you smiling about?"

Phillip laughed. "Why nothing, Amsi, nothing at all. Come on, let's find Timma." Nathan grunted and fell into step alongside him, a watchful Tobrach in their wake.

Coming closer to the unloading, they saw Timma by one of the war canoes, hands on hips glaring at two youths. Not wanting to shout or call attention to himself, Phillip-Yoey sighed. The cousins again. <<I'm starting to wish our mother hadn't talked us into bringing them,>> Yoey complained.

Before they could make the group aware of their approach, one of the young men, Nytaka he thought, took a swing at Timma. Timma grabbed his arm, kicked out, and the youth sprawled at his feet, gasping for air. As Qwayku charged in to help, Timma spun and knocked him flat as well.

Nathan chuckled. "I see our boy has been practicing."

Phillip grimaced. "Yes, unfortunately he's been getting lots of practice on our journey. During the battle at Red Rock, which I haven't had time to tell you about, he set up a medical station, and killed a Ghostland warrior."

The boys' scuffle had caught the attention of some of the Sand Mountain warriors who laughed, making rude jokes. Qwasigara, also walking by, stopped.

"You having trouble with these half-bred Begta, Nephew?"

"Nothing I can't handle, Elder. I'm sorry if we bothered you."

The wizard grunted, then he turned to the dazed youths picking themselves up off the ground. "If you Twisted Grass boys don't like taking orders from the priest, I know a warrior who would like a couple slaves to do chores and cook for him. Do you want me to ask Goro of Red Wind to trade for you?"

That was a real threat. Goro was notorious for abusing his women and slaves, and judging by the boys' wide eyed expressions they knew it.

Timma must have heard the gossip, too, and hastily said, "I'm sure they won't give trouble again, Elder. No need to bother the great Red Wind warrior in such a minor discipline problem. Is that not so, my students?"

Eyes cast down, the Youths nodded. "We are sorry, Sensei Timma," Nytaka murmured.

"I didn't hear you, Begta Puke, what did you say?" Qwasigara said, the menace still in his voice.

Qwayku repeated their apology, this time louder. Qwasigara grunted, nodded to the two kashallans and went back to helping with the unloading.

Returning his attention to his students, Timma folded his arms and said, "Now, do as I told you. Go help my wife and the other women get their things from the canoes."

"Wife?" Nathan murmured.

Phillip smiled. "Wife. And he's not the only one. You will meet my wife in a while."

"My you guys have been—busy."

Phillip laughed, then excused himself. "Say hi to Timma; I need to talk to 'the cousins.' They are some of my new relatives and partially my responsibility."

As the youths started to slink away down the beach, he called to them. When he was close enough so that only they would hear him, he said, "I just witnessed that little problem, but my wife has told me of other instances of your insolence. Lose the attitude, now!

"I know you've been raised on stories of war heroes and watched your elders show contempt for the Avairei slaves among the clans. But if you've noticed neither the wizards nor the warriors on our journey treat Timma with disrespect. Why? Because he has *earned* their regard.

"And I hope you appreciate how Timma stood up for you just now—in spite of your bad behavior. He could have agreed to let Qwasigara trade you to Goro. None of these warriors started out doing glorious deeds. They had to work for that honor. And along with weapons practice comes the discipline of service to the people—and that sometimes may include helping women or doing slave's work."

Phillip waved a hand to encompass the men joking and working all around them. "Ask any of them. If you have the courage, even ask the

Warlinga there; his name is Tobrach. They'll tell you the same thing, the warrior's craft takes work and discipline.

"I'm not going to repeat myself. We are done here. The next time there's a problem, you are traded, or on the next canoe heading home."

"Yes, Elder Cousin. We are sorry," they chorused and hurried off to find Efosa. Kashallan-Phillip was walking back to join an excited Timma and Nathan, when Ishka hailed him. Smiling he waited for her and threw an arm about her shoulder as she fell into step beside him. "I'm sorry I had to abandon you, My dear. I was just sending 'the cousins to help you and Efosa."

She chuckled and put her arm around his waist for all to see. "I saw them just now; they looked quite chastened. What happened?"

"A minor discipline problem, but the cousins shouldn't give you any trouble in future."

When they came up to a grinning Timma and Nathan-Corha, they were catching up, sharing the news. Niguiri was with them. Phillip had to inwardly smile. Nathan looked a bit glassy eyed, overwhelmed by their arrival and what the lad was telling him about their adventures.

Timma was starting to relate the story of how Tess-weh had invited him along when Phillip and Ishka joined them. "Nathan-Corha, I'd like you to meet my wife, Ishka," he interrupted before Timma could get very far along that trail—evidently Chang hadn't had a chance to speak to him yet

Ishka bowed. "Holy One, it is an honor to meet you," Ishka said. "I see you have already met my daughter."

Startled by her term of address, Nathan-Corha bowed in return. "Uh—thank you—Ima." He glanced at the young people. "Yes, I have." Sensing there was more to the interruption than Phillip just needing to introduce Ishka, he raised an enquiring eyebrow.

Including the young people in his next comment, Phillip-Yoey said, "For all our sakes, keep the information about the Spirit quiet for the moment. Timma, you can tell Nathan-Corha your adventures, but do it later, and do it where you aren't overheard—by anyone."

He glanced significantly at Tobrach, then in Galactic Standard, he added, "I'm sorry, Nathan, but I'm not very trusting at the moment. We've rooted out three Ghostland spies among the Clans. Many lives were lost because of their treachery. And you people may have a Ghostland agent or two as well, so be on alert." Nathan's color blanched, but he only nodded. There was a story there, too, he thought, but now wasn't the time.

Into the awkward silence that followed, Ishka said, "I'm sorry to interrupt you, Husband, but I could use your help for a moment."

"Of course, my dear, what's wrong?"

"It's your mother, she won't come; she seems very frightened."

Nathan widened his eyes. "Mother?" he mouthed. Then he scowled. "I hope none of my people are starting trouble already. If they are—"

Ishka shook her head. "No trouble in the way you mean." She bowed to Tobrach, acknowledging his presence with them. "K'San." Tobrach dipped his head crest in return. "Please excuse my kinswoman, Kashallan, K'San. She has grown up with stories about Warlinga Demons and now that she sees them for the first time she is afraid. Yoey, I was hoping..."

"Of course I'll come. Where is she?" Yoey said.

Ishka started back down the beach towards Noi's canoe. As they drew closer they could hear Noi and a few of his crew shouting. Phillip quickened his pace.

"Mother?" Nathan murmured.

"Yoey's mother officially." Phillip said and grinned. "You might as well come along, Amsi, and meet her and the rest of the family. You too, Tobrach. Good to see you again, by the way."

"Right. Mother, eh."

Wondering what he'd gotten himself into by accepting these new family obligations, Phillip hoped Efosa was able to settle in to her new life with a little reassurance from him.

As they drew near he saw a wildly gesticulating Noi, yelling at a huddled figure still sitting amongst her belongings in his war canoe. At several laughing men's encouragement, the cousins were trying to pull her baskets out of the canoe. Efosa kept shaking her head and swatting at them with one of the oars if they got too near.

"Crazy Twisted Grass Woman, get out of my canoe!" Noi shouted. "I don't care who your son is, I'm going to dump you onto the shingle myself if you don't get your baskets and go—and no Khutani will stop me!"

Unable to keep a note of amusement out of his voice, Phillip said, "Peace, Noi, the Khutani in question is here now. I'll get her out for you."

Crouching down beside the canoe Yoey said, “I’m here, Mother. What’s wrong; why won’t you get out? Noi needs to secure his canoe.”

Efosa sighed with relief. “Oh, my son, I’m so glad you’ve come.” She glanced around, then spying Tobrach hovering at Nathan’s back, she shuddered, clutching his hand, so tight he winced. “There are Warlinga demons here, Yoey, they might capture and eat us.”

Reversing his grip he extended his tentacles, sending a soothing balm down the link they shared. “No, no, Mother, no one is going to hurt you. Those old stories are just tales to make bad children behave.”

Thinking of that degenerate Warlinga Gormach, he acknowledged that there probably was some truth to those kind of stories, but he wasn’t going to tell Efosa that.

Phillip stood, forcing her to rise with him. Gently, he helped her out of the canoe and guided her away as the cousins leapt to unload her baskets. “Come meet our hosts.” Coming over to Nathan and his guard, Phillip said, “Mother, this Warlinga is my friend K’San Tobrach.”

Doubting the Warlinga understood much of what he’d been telling Efosa in the Western dialect, to his eternal gratitude Tobrach rose to the challenge and bowed to the frightened woman. “Sa, I am glad to meet you.”

“See, Mother he pays you respect and greets you in his language. He is a war leader here and he won’t let anyone hurt you.” Efosa shyly murmured a greeting, which he dutifully translated for Tobrach.

Then hoping to distract her Yoey said, “And this is Nathan—“

Efosa gasped, her eyes opening wide. “Oh, My Son, this is the new Amsi you’ve been telling me about, yes?” Then she reached over and patted a startled Nathan’s middle. “A’hei, Little One, I am so happy to meet you, My Yoey has been so excited. I am your Aunty Efosa.”

Under her touch Corha squirmed with pleasure. “I am happy to meet you, too, Aunty Efosa.” Then, <<Kasha, I have a new aunty,>> Corha burbled. <<The cousins at home will be so jealous when I tell them. None of them have an aunty.>>

Feeling like a deer caught in the headlights of an approaching air car, Nathan blinked. <<Uh, right, Shalla. I bet they will.>> “Phillip, wipe that smile off your face.”

"No, Mother," Yoey explained. "I was telling you about my Amsi Tani. This is a different cousin. We didn't know about this one."

Efosa giggled. "More new relatives, how wonderful! Now Yoey, your new cousin is much younger than you, so you must be gentle when you play together and be careful not to scare the little one with your stories, promise me?"

"Yes, Mother I will be careful, I promise."

Taking her arm and starting to lead her away, Ishka said, "Come, Mother Efosa, we need to find the cousins and see where they are putting our things. We should let your son and these men talk."

Efosa nodded, said her good-byes and followed Ishka back into the chaos of unloading.

Nathan scratched his head, a puzzled frown on his face. "How does she do that? You didn't finish introducing us and she knew about Corha—and even that it is younger."

Phillip laughed and walked back with him up the slope. "I have no idea. I think she may have a 'gift' but she maybe a little crazy, as well."

Nathan grunted. "What's her story?"

"We treated her son Mosi, who was ill from watching his father be tortured and then killed by warriors from the Ghostlands when they attacked the Western Clans during the Sorins. When we went into the Dream to retrieve Mosi's spirit, Yoey and the little boy formed a relationship.

"Later at Red Rock when we were attacked, the boy died and Efosa took it hard. She had already lost two husbands and all her older children. She's too old to have more and her family claimed she was cursed because she had defied her father's wishes and married a Sand Mountain man instead of his choice.

"Hoping to rid himself of a rebellious child and cause trouble for the Alliance, Tego, my new grandfather," Phillip made a face and pointed to the tribal brand on his shoulder, "adopted Yoey into the clan. As her son, she was now our responsibility to care for. They would have killed her or abandoned her otherwise.

"There's more to the story, but I'll tell you the rest another time," Phillip said as they came up to Aju'an and some of the others." Finished with securing their canoes, he saw that some of the Warriors were already disappearing up the trail to the warriors' hidden campsite.

Nathan stroked his chin thinking. "That's a sad story. What about that mark on your face; somebody else adopt you too?"

Kashallan-Phillip laughed. "Sort of." He pointed to his cheek. "I got this on my wedding night. Sand Mountain claims me as kin through my marriage to Ishka."

"Mm, does she know what she's gotten herself into? I wonder how she's going to like living with the Begta?"

He smiled. "She probably wouldn't like it. Though we've only had time to share bits and pieces of our stories with each other I'm sure you can tell by her command of the southern language that she's an educated Ima."

"Yes, I did notice."

"She's been through a lot living with the Clans. I wouldn't ask her to follow me when I go back to the Begta village, however. She can stay with her other husband at Ha'limra if Mah'lu Chang decides to settle there with our Speir'dina kin."

Nathan jerked to a stop, Tobrach almost bumping into him. "Chang?"

Phillip nodded. "Yes, Chang. His student is married to Ishka's daughter and of course the four of them spend a lot of time together. It's only natural for them to be fond of one another.

"I would have suggested he marry her, but there too, there were 'complications.' She gives good counsel and is a pleasure to talk to. I'm quite fond of her myself actually, but part of the year I will have to be away. I can't bring her or Efosa into the swamp villages. Mah'lu and I have worked it out. They will stay with him when I'm away. Most of the Blue Stone women and children are already with our people, so it won't be such a shock for Efosa and Niguiri especially."

Nathan shook his head to clear it and started walking again. "All this is so hard to take in."

"I'm sure it is, and there's so much more I have to share with you. Mah'lu's been invaluable to me on this mission; I'd like to keep him with me a while longer, if he's willing and you don't need him elsewhere. The Clan warriors trust him and Maker Tinguss gave him their language patterns before we started this adventure, so he can act as a translator, as well."

Still unable to believe it, Nathan repeated, "Chang... I thought he was never going to get over losing his wife and son."

"I'm not sure what happened to him during our stay in the mountains, but he's seems more—relaxed maybe—or a better way to put it, more content to be here on Timorna."

Nathan looked around then sighed. The beach was nearly empty most of the men with heavy packs and weapons on their backs were disappearing up the slope.

Following the warrior's progress, Phillip-Yoey said, "I should go or I'll get lost." His mouth twisted into an ironic smile. "Never having come here to raid, I have no idea where to go."

Nathan snorted a laugh. "I'm going to have to go back to our main base camp at some point today and there's so much to tell you. Why don't you come with me so we can relax and talk."

Phillip-Yoey reached over, took his hand and formed a link. "I wish I could. I would like nothing better than to do that. There is so much you need to know before we head North, and I suspect you have much to share as well, but I can't leave them—not now."

Nathan grunted and took Phillip's other hand, forming his own link, allowing the symbionts a brief moment to share in the way of their kind. "I know. I'll come back tomorrow and check in with you, maybe bring some fresh meat. Somebody said the Begta went hunting this morning." Reluctantly, Nathan-Corha released his portion of their connection and a moment later Phillip-Yoey did the same. "I see some of your guys are waiting for you, so I'll see you later."

Phillip-Yoey nodded. "Yes and my colleague Masonja is with them. Ishka or Efosa must have sent her and the Blue Stone men to find me." Waving his farewell he hurried to catch up with the waiting warriors.

Chapter Five

Nathan arrived next morning with a mixed band of Warlinga and Speir'dina. Trailing in their wake were several Begta loaded down with dressed-out obeylem meat. Their arrival was greeted with smiles by the lounging clan warriors, eager for the fresh rations. He heard them joking that it was nice to see Warlinga bringing them food like women. Some wondered if they would also cook it for them.

Chang laughed and told them, "Don't push your luck. I've eaten with them. Warlinga are terrible cooks." Everybody laughed at that.

Phillip was grateful for the distraction. Several of the men had wanted to go hunting that morning and that might have turned into a disaster if they'd been discovered by a Warlinga hunting pack that hadn't gotten the word they were allies now.

Later when the meat was cooking and Nathan had taken care of reassigning a guard patrol and all was quiet, the two kashallans sat together in the moss to talk. They could be seen by everyone, but Noi and Tobrach sat on their haunches a short distance away to guard their privacy.

After their symbiont companions agreed to carry on their own communication while their hosts talked, Phillip began speaking in Galactic Standard to add another layer to their privacy. "I'm sorry I had to spring this alliance on you, Nathan. I wish Commander Tizu had warned you. He and my Amla with the Sweh'an's urging arranged it. With the power of the storms behind them, Barak's warbands killed and tortured their way across the western shore, searching for the traitorous wizard that bred mutants to host Khutani."

"The traitors you're talking about are us, right?" Nathan said.

"Yes, I'm afraid so."

"Mm," Nathan grunted.

"That mistake cost a lot of innocent lives, Amsi. I saw firsthand how hard these people's lives are and how much they have to endure. True they are a brutal people, but they have to be to survive. I think that may be one of the reasons Maker Tinguss has offered sanctuary in the grasslands south of the great Swamp over which it has dominion, if they will stop warring with us."

"Wasn't that where our people were supposed to settle? There's an abandoned keep out there somewhere, I think."

"Yes, Ha'limra. And the Blue Stone women and children are there now. As our new kin they will stay with us if they wish even after their warriors return."

"New kin? You marry somebody else you haven't told me about yet?"

Phillip chuckled. "No, not this time. Tarla is married to the war leader's oldest sister Yannan."

"Tarla? How did he get mixed up in this?"

"To survive, Ogwy's band—including women and children—fled across the Shallow Sea. They were actually hiding in the caves near Ticca with Tess-weh's protection throughout the Storms.

"He was in the hunting pack Tizu formed when the blue stone presence was discovered so close to the keep."

Nathan shook his head smiling. "Damn... Tarla..."

"From what I observed before I left with the warriors he seemed happy, and Yannan adores him." As a thought occurred to him, Phillip added, "Getting them settled with our people is probably why Hunt Leader Tizu is late arriving here."

"Yes, well he'll be here tomorrow or the next day," Nathan said. "He's not in range for the Comm yet, but a runner was waiting for me when I got back to our main camp last night. Tell me more about our new 'friends.'"

"Mah'lu is probably the one to ask about their fighting skills, he's been holding practice bouts with them. But I do need to tell you more about the attack we suffered at Red Rock, because it has some significance as to how we proceed when we head North.

"The Clans had called a war council to discuss what to do about the Ghostlanders attacks. I was with Blue Stone at that time, but Sand Mountain and Bitter Water had also given me blood-oath and joined us. We went to gain support from the other clans. Just as we arrived, however, the Ghostlander sprung their trap and struck again."

Phillip shuddered, remembering. "It was total chaos, Nathan—terrible—they killed women, children, any and everyone they could. I didn't see much of the actual fighting. When Tess-weh disappeared, Cadrach grabbed me and Ata Doyan and half-dragged, half-carried us back down the trail where many of the women and children joined us.

"Where is Cadrach? I saw Moraga and the good Ata but I haven't seen him—or Tess-weh. Did they take off again?"

Phillip shook his head. "Cadrach is dead." Startled, Nathan blinked. "Yes, dead," Phillip confirmed, "and we almost lost Tess-weh, too. Chang and Moraga found their burnt bodies in the moss not far from the battle."

"Damn," Nathan said. "What happened?"

"While the clans and Speir'dina fought in this world, the Demon took on the Ghostland conclave of wizards. She managed to kill their leader, Barak, so she told me, but she was badly injured and burned in the process.

"As she recovers we've been trying to keep her presence a secret as much as possible. Qwasigara and Eilo caught a couple spies, and Masonja and I discovered another—somewhat by accident. They are dead but we feared that if the Enemy knew they hadn't killed her they might attack us again, before she'd recovered enough to defend us or herself."

"She's here with you now, then?" Nathan asked. "How is she doing?"

"She doesn't always let me attend her, but as best I can tell she's healing. But she and her protector came with us in the canoes, rather than using her power to transport herself and Cadrach as she did on the way over to the western shore. And that tells me a lot. She isn't ready to face them yet."

"Protector? Where did you find a Warlinga for her to enslave over there?" Nathan asked.

Phillip laughed. "Oh she has a protector all right, an Umwira protector. He's keeping his sigil covered with a headband but he's around. His name is Atahru."

Nathan swore, than burst out laughing. "Ima Sagas is going to be so—so... Oh, by all the gods of Timorna and Caldon, I can't wait to see her face when Tess-weh takes up residence in her suite at Ticca again."

Phillip grinned. "Yes, that would be something to see—provided we live that long."

Sobering, Nathan nodded. "You got that right."

"Now that I've filled you in on the basics of our journey, tell me what's been happening on this side of the water. I know Dunnagh and Tani were always joking with you about making a kashallan bond, but you seemed set against it. What changed your mind, Amsi?"

At the mention of Dunnagh's name Nathan blinked several times trying to hold back his tears. Through the link they shared, all felt his grief and sadness flooding their communication. Swallowing several times, he finally choked out, "Dunnagh... I don't know what I would have done if—we almost lost Dunnagh-Tani, Phillip." He took in a few shuddering breaths before he was able to continue.

"A changeling Warlinga K'San name of Drucas Segoi lured him and some of our people out of Shaden to aid nonexistent plague victims at Caltia Keep. We were at Shaden gathering Avairei and Warlinga houses to march on Riath. He was captured Tortured and held in a Riath prison. The changelings planned to put him on trial at the Solstice Fair.

The High Matri and her brother, also Ghostland changelings poisoned Tani with some foul Umwira drug and he almost died. Their plan was to show the people only Dunnagh and claim he was just another mutant not a kashallan as the alliance claimed.

"When we got the news of his capture, the council of Makers told the Ima Matri at Shaden that somebody would have to make the bond."

Sending a soothing balm back down the channel of their communication, Phillip said, "Oh, Nathan, how terrible for you. I know you two were close, so his capture must have been horrible, but was there no other way?"

Nathan shrugged. "I was already chosen. Back on the mesa before his fight with Gormach, Dunnagh laid a Geish on me. I swore Blood-Oath that if anything happened to him I would offer myself and make a bond."

"I remember you using that word before. You used to say, 'the Geish is off', when he teased you, but I never knew what it meant."

Nathan snorted a laugh. "Yeah, well now you do. It's an old Caldoni word; its power not invoked much nowadays on Caldon. I'd been trying to avoid it, but deep down I knew that someday the Gods would hold me to that oath." He smiled, sending his reassurance to the young symbionts that had been a part of their last emotional communication. "And besides I love my Shalla so it's all good."

"Mm, I'm glad. How is Dunnagh-Tani really?"

"When we left Riath, the bondmates were healing slowly but seemed well. Maker Gladdris was, I thought until yesterday, keeping an eye on him. I was told the Makers are a little worried about the long term effects of the drug the Umwira were giving him.

"It is a new substance they developed after the Makers lost contact with the Ghostlanders. The Changelings planned to toss it in the pools at Riath and elsewhere to stun the Khutani so their archers could kill them while helpless."

Phillip shivered at the thought.

"I know he wants to go home to be with his family but he's stuck in Riath at the moment taking oaths and checking for the changeling taint. I hope one of the other reasons Tizu wasn't here to meet you was that he was escorting his family to be with him. That will do a lot in helping him recover. Right now Amril Caltia is with him, but Amril was tortured too and isn't in much better shape than he is."

Phillip's face grew even more somber at this revelation. "I'm not sure about that. You see the reason I was with Tizu and the Ticca hunters in the first place was because Sairsa and Briya were captured by some of the Blue Stone warriors."

Nathan jerked upright, staring. "What! And you and your Amla made an alliance with them? I would have killed them all."

"It's complicated, Nathan—truly it is. I believe that was what the Commander and most of his hunters had in mind until they caught up with them. They thought they were chasing a warband out for booty, but what they found were starving women and children with their men making a desperate run back to their boats."

"Yeah, so some of the men just took a little detour to find some new women to play with before they left." He snorted his disbelief. "Yeah, right."

"Not exactly," Phillip said. "The women were food gathering near Ticca when Sairsa came across a Blue Stone woman giving birth. The witch bound

Sairsa with her dying blood magic to her newborn baby. The warriors were hunting nearby when they discovered the women."

Still angry Nathan growled, "If the mother was dead, they could have just left them alone."

"Nathan, I taste your anger for Dunnagh and for Sairsa—and yes, I am angry about it too, but as painful as it is for you to hear, I also know there is a deeper purpose at work here. Tess-weh saw it; she didn't stop it, but she summoned me to help."

Nathan snorted. "Help, oh yeah, you, the Demon and your damned Amla have done a great job with your 'help.'"

Phillip let out an exasperated sigh, wishing there had been a better place and time to let him know about Sairsa. But he also feared if Nathan found out another way—at a critical time—like just before a battle it could be disastrous. "Nathan, I know it's hard to see things from another point of view at the moment, but consider the warriors had two choices, they could kill our women, or they could bring the women with them."

"The Filthy Bacach could have just left them alone!" he repeated.

"No, they couldn't. The women when they returned to Ticca would have brought the baby—an Umwira baby, and that would have alerted the keep to their presence.

"With their own half-starved families with them, they couldn't run back to their canoes fast enough to outrun a well-armed hunting pack. For the sake of the baby bound to Sairsa, they took them. And yes, two of the warriors took them as wives, but they were saved from becoming brides to the entire warband, like my brave Ishka. At least they were spared that torment."

Nathan fell silent, but didn't break their link. Phillip-Yoey was aware of his churning emotions and the bondmates let him be, focusing their soothing concern on the young Corha.

Becoming aware of his bondmate's fear and distress at last, Nathan made an effort to control his own emotions. "You said Sairsa was caught in some magic spell. Why didn't you and your Amla break it and send the damned Umwira back across the Shallow Sea if you didn't want to kill them?"

"Because we couldn't," Phillip said, "Tess-weh said the magic between foster mother and child can't be broken without killing them. Her attachment to the baby's father, however, I did have Tess-weh break, otherwise she would have been in the canoes right alongside him. And how do you think Dunnagh would have coped with *that* blow?"

"Who is the man?" Nathan growled clinching his jaw.

"I'm not going to tell you that. We need this alliance too much right now to risk anyone, even you starting trouble. If we fight among ourselves we'd be doing the Enemy's work for them. It will be up to Dunnagh-Tani and Sairsa herself to decide if their love is strong enough to survive what has happened to them both."

"You and this damned alliance of yours that's all that's important to you, isn't it, Phillip?"

Feeling his own temper spark, he snapped, "Maybe it is, because I want us to survive this conflict with the Ghostland wizards! Stop thinking and behaving like a pamper Dymarian and more like a Timornan. We can't win with the Western Clans a menace at our backs—and it wouldn't take much to make them our enemies again."

Nathan swore and he and Corha released themselves from the link. Looking Philip square in the eye, he said, "You're so damned sure of yourself with this alliance. I wonder if you'll be so sure when Tess-weh ensnares you in her traps like poor Sairsa. What will you do then, hmm?" Seeing Phillip's stricken face Nathan let out a mirthless laugh. "It could happen, you know. I of all people know she can't be trusted."

That was a sobering thought, Philip-Yoey had to admit, and one he hadn't thought of before now. Taking a deep breath, he finally said, "I still believe in the alliance and what my Amla wants to achieve. And, as for me—I do trust that she has our best interests in mind. So I guess I'll have to take my chances like everybody else."

Nathan snorted his disgust, then his voice catching on a sob, he murmured Dunnagh's name, then swore in Caldoni again. Rising to his feet he turned his back on Phillip-Yoey and muttered, "Maybe you're right—I don't know—I gotta think about this for a while."

Nathan was hurting, and yes, angry at him and Tinguss for their part in the situation. Getting to his feet as well, Phillip pleaded, "I'm sorry Nathan. I can guess how much this must hurt and I know you're angry with me right now. But I wanted to be the one to tell you before you found out in another way." *And did something stupid,* he thought privately.

Nathan grunted and walked to join Tobrach. "I'll let you know when we hear more from Tizu."

Feeling choked with emotion himself, Phillip-Yoey trailed behind the two men, wanting to say something to bring back the comradery they had shared, but not knowing what to say to heal the wound.

As they reached the edge of the clearing and started up the trail, an unknown Warrior stepped out of the brush to block their path. Snarling Tobrach leapt in front of Nathan-Corha, with teeth bared and spear raised. The man watched the Warlinga impassively, but made no aggressive move towards either man.

Suddenly realizing who it was blocking their path, Phillip hurried forward, before Tobrach or Nathan threatened the Wa'chassey'ul further.

Under his breath, he murmured, "Wa'chassey'ul," as he passed them. Both men froze. To the Demon's protector, he said, "Hello, Atahru, does your Mistress wish to speak to me or these men? Does she need my assistance?"

The Wa'chassey'ul slowly shook his head. "No, Khutani; my Mistress is well." Then he focused his eerie stare on Nathan and the Warlinga. In a hollow otherworldly voice he intoned, "My Mistress sends her greetings." Turning to Nathan, the warrior's mouth smiled. "She remembers you fondly, Speir'dina."

Nathan blushed, turning red. Before things could get off track, Phillip said, "Atahru, do you have a message for Nathan or Tobrach?"

Atahru nodded slowly. "My Mistress says, Beware, Speir'dina, Warlinga! A stolen blade, a trust betrayed, the Guardian will die when the sigils of power glow with pleasure and pain. Sleep lightly, Warlinga, and My Jewel, for Chaos stalks you."

By the time the Wa'chassey'ul finished and had turned to leave a grim-faced Nathan was as white as a ghost. Glancing at the Warlinga's flattened head crest Phillip could tell they had understood at least some of Atahru's message.

"Wait!" Tobrach started to follow the Wa'chassey'ul, but Phillip stopped him. "Neither he nor his Mistress will give you more information. As Nathan can tell you, Tess-weh will only toy with you if you try."

Nathan grunted his agreement. "You got that right, Phillip. I take it that's her new protector, eh?"

"Yes, and it's obvious you two know—at least in part what he was talking about. Please tell me."

His grey eyes hard, Nathan muttered as he started walking. "Yeah, well you'll find out soon enough. Got to go."

Nathan was angry, but behind the rage Phillip-Yoey could taste his fear, even without sharing the link. "Oh, Mother Timorna, protect your children," Phillip breathed as he walked slowly back to his cook fire. After all that had happened he wondered if he could manage to choke down the meal he knew the women were preparing for him.

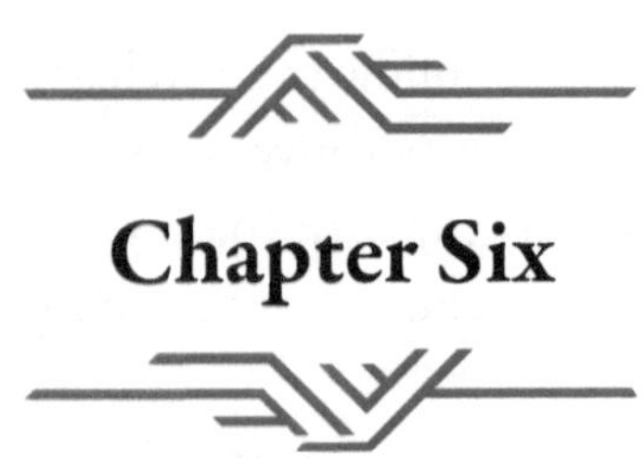

Chapter Six

A Speir'dina runner arrived next day to tell them that Hunt Leader Tizu and the hunting packs from Ticca had finally arrived. Everybody needed to pack up; they were moving the combined force north to a place near Tragar keep. Kashallan-Phillip could taste the clan warriors' apprehension without hearing the grumbling or putting anyone in the link. This would be a true test of "trust" for everyone on both sides of the alliance.

In early afternoon they climbed the winding trail up to the mesa where the Speir'dina shuttles had deposited the refugees from Dr. Bennett's wounded ship.

Walking beside him as they cleared the rise Lubwey glanced around with eyes wide. "Was this the place where you came from the sky to our world?"

Phillip grimaced and nodded. "This is where our ship came down, but it didn't look like this at the time."

Lubwey laughed. "I would hope it didn't look like this before the Sorins."

Nathan was right, Phillip thought as he surveyed the wreckage. The place was now nothing more than piles of unrecognizable rubble mounded around what had once been the open space of the quadrangle. Thanks to the storms and the Begta the base was just another galactic garbage dump.

Lubwey picked up a jagged piece of polli-fiber planking about as long as his arm that must have been part of one of the buildings' outer walls. He tested its strength by bending it between his hands. The plank broke with a loud crack, lethal shards spraying about him. Dropping the two halves with a hiss he jumped back.

Phillip's lip twitched into a faint smile. "The building from which that board came wasn't meant to be any more than a temporary camp. The Begta or the Ghostlanders probably took anything of value left here after we departed."

Lubwey grunted then bent to gather a few of the sharper pieces and wrap them in a leather cloth from his pack. “Maybe they did, but these might still have a use as darts for our bows if we can shape them.”

Phillip grew thoughtful. Spying Armachd Ross passing nearby, he called him over. Translating for the two warriors, Phillip said, “This Blue Stone warrior thinks pieces of this polli-fiber might serve as darts for his crossbow. Chang told me that one of the armachda was developing such bows for our people. Nathan said a team was sifting through the rubble for useful items. Do you know if they gathered any of this material to experiment with?”

Ross eyed the clan warrior speculatively, then shook his head. “I don’t think so, Kashallan-Phillip, but I will talk to Briyenn about it.”

On a planet where even the dead were mined for their usefulness to the living, nothing was wasted. Phillip was sure in time the mounds of garbage left there would be reduced to nothing but the shri moss underneath.

COMING DOWN OFF THE mesa after the noon’s rest break, the column headed north on a difficult rocky trail that skirted the worst of the reed-choked ravines. The refugees from Sulas and the base had traveled those canyons with difficulty on their journey south to the fortress of Ticca before the Sorin Storms. Philip was just as happy to escape a repeat of that experience.

They camped that night in and around a large kavalpa thicket with a good spring, which he learned was about a day’s fast walk from Tragar. Hunt Leader Tizu and the hunting packs from Ticca were there to greet them. Kashallan-Phillip was a little dismayed to see so many Warlinga among his hunters. When he had time to ask Tizu later about his choice, the man shrugged. “How could I refuse them? Fighting the Umwira is what they were bred for.” Then at Phillip’s frown he added, “Besides it was what maker Dievris wanted. And I wasn’t going to argue with it.”

Kashallan-Phillip bowed his head in acknowledgement. “I see your point, Hunt Leader. I wouldn’t want to argue with the Ancient either.” Suspecting Dievris was the Maker behind his Amla’s imprisonment, Phillip wondered if Dievris knew what a dangerous game it was playing.

Tizu, flanked by Nathan and the Warlinga named Aju'an, stepped forward to greet him and the clan leaders. His eye brows shot up when he saw Phillip's clan brands. "Well, you certainly took the Maker's charge seriously enough. I heard about your new bride, but nobody told me you joined the Umwira," Tizu said in Galactic Standard.

Phillip gave him a ghost of a smile. "It seemed like a good idea at the time."

Tizu grunted and turned his attention to the clan leaders beside Kashallan Phillip. Switching languages, Tizu surprised them by addressing them in their own Western Dialect. "Welcome, Clan Leaders. I am Hunt Leader Tizu."

As they walked to the place assigned to them to set up camp Tesulu voiced the concern that was on everyone's mind. "How can such a tiny man be the head of all the Khutani's hunting packs? I could break him in half with one blow."

Phillip snorted a laugh. "Great warrior you might be, Tesulu, but I doubt you could do that. Hasn't Warrior Chang taught you yet that small stature among us can be deceiving? Hunt Leader Tizu commanded many hunting packs of warriors among the star men. He is well respected here among the Warlinga and even the Blue Stone warriors. Isn't that so, Ogwy?" Ogwy growled a curse but finally dipped his head in agreement.

Qwasigara gave the Blue Stone man a probing look, knowing there was more to the story, but when Ogwy only cursed and left them the wizard dropped the matter.

Later that evening after their hurried meal Kashallan-Phillip was surprised when Marti and an unknown Warlinga female wearing a warrior woman's bone apron approached his fire. At the site of the unknown Warlinga coming into view from out of the darkness, Efosa gasped and almost dropped the cup of tea she was handing him.

Phillip-Yoey hastily took the tea, glanced up and smiled, motioning them to sit by the fire. "Marti! How nice to see you again. Nathan didn't tell me you were here. Did you just come in with Hunt Leader Tizu?"

She returned the smile and crouched on the opposite side of the fire, the Warlinga more hesitantly joining her. Marti, like Nathan and Ross, was dressed in a version of the uniform favored by the Speir'dina armachda of the former Lann Gheal Caldoni mercenaries. Over her black tunic and trews she wore a heavy leather vest, her belt of weaponry strapped on top.

"No, me and Chelka here have been with the hunters all along. We were in Riath—with Dunnagh-Tani before..."

Marti fell silent shaking her head no to the tea Ishka offered her. Around them in the darkness other small fires glowed, men talking and joking with one another as they relaxed from the long day's walk. "Ah, I see," Phillip said. "Nathan told me about Dunnagh-Tani's capture. But he didn't tell me you and Sa Chelka were also there."

Marti grimaced as if recalling unpleasant memories. "Yeah, we were there all right... We were a part of the guard detail that failed to prevent his capture," she added after a long pause.

Sensing how those memories troubled her, Phillip changed the subject by introducing the others sitting by his fire. "Warriors, let me introduce you to my wife Ishka, and my mother Efosa. Timma you already know, and the girl beside him is his wife Niguiri and those two," he waved a hand to the Twisted Grass boys sitting near Timma. "Those two scamps are 'the cousins, Nytaka and Qwayku.'"

Phillip sipped his tea considering them. There was something wrong with the women. Chelka especially seemed overly nervous in his presence. It could just be ambivalence to him personally and his allegiance to the clans, but he sensed something more.

Conveying his thought to Yoey, the symbiont said, <<I sense their wrongness too, Kasha. I wonder what they conceal under those colorful headbands?>>

<<Ah the headbands, I thought they were merely a new style from Riath. I remember seeing Tobrach and a few of the others wearing them. But now that you draw my attention to it I sense the bands are merely a concealment for something else...>>

<<Yes, a magical something else,>> Yoey confirmed, showing Phillip what it could see.

Hmm, his curiosity aroused, and hoping to draw them out, Phillip asked, "Sa Chelka, are you related to Aju'an Meh'gach whom I recently met? I see a certain family resemblance."

Shying away from staring at the clan brand on his cheek, Chelka dipped her head crest and blushed green with embarrassment. "Yes, Kashallan-Phillip, he is my brother."

Phillip smiled, hoping to set her at ease. "My bondmate Yoey informs me that It is unusual for a woman among your people to run with the hunting packs. I am glad to see you here. I hope in future other women will also take up the spear again as well."

Chelka bobbed her thanks, her green blush deepening. Marti's brown face brightened and she gave him a toothy smile of approval, then turned to her friend and murmured, "See, I told you. Here's another kashallan that approves. It's only the amadans in your family who are being stupid about this." Returning her attention to the group by the fire, she added, "It was Chelka here who discovered and killed one of the Changeling Umwira agents at Ticca—I killed the other one."

When Timma translated, relaying his own account of the events for the clan members unable to follow the southern Khutani dialect were suitably impressed, adding to Chelka's embarrassment.

Sensing her distress at last, Marti said, "Actually we only stopped by to see if you knew where we could find Moraga. We heard she was here—somewhere. But not speaking the language we thought it better to ask..."

"Mm, most wise perhaps," Phillip said. Turning to the cousins, he switched languages and said, "Will you go find Armachd Moraga for these warriors, please? Bring her here if she isn't busy." The cousins murmured their agreement, rose and slipped into the night.

"To save you stumbling about in the dark I've sent the cousins to get her for you. Now, while we wait can I interest you in that tea?"

The two women exchanged looks then Marti nodded and they settled back. Ishka rose and picked up one of Efosa's waterproof baskets. Bending down she murmured next to his ear, "I'll get some water from the spring and see if we have more seed cakes in our packs."

Phillip smiled and touched her hand. "Good idea. I'd prefer they didn't wander through our camp unsupervised," he said in the Western Dialect. She hesitated, wanting to asked more, but changed her mind and only nodded and hurried off.

When Phillip returned his attention to the people by the fire Timma was asking the women about his friend Amril. "He was captured by the changelings, too," Marti admitted, "But when we left Riath a few eight-days ago he was on the mend like Dunnagh-Tani." She glanced at Phillip, expression questioning." Nathan told you about the Ce'awn, didn't he?"

"Yes, he did."

Marti let out a relieved sigh. "Good. I wouldn't have wanted to be the one to tell you."

Phillip nodded. "I can understand that. I wouldn't have wanted to put you in that difficult position, either."

"Were you and Chelka treated as badly as I've heard he and Amril were?" Timma asked.

Once again the two women exchanged looks without answering the young man's question. Phillip scowled, hoping Timma would take the hint and be quiet. He didn't want to have them leave before he had a chance to get more information out of them if he could. Nathan still wasn't communicating with him more than the barest of necessities for the running of the combined camp.

Deciding to do some changing of discussion topics herself, Marti asked, "The Umwira woman sitting beside you, did I understand you a right? She is your 'Mother?'"

Yoey laughed. "She's my mother actually. The story is long and a bit complicated—which we can tell you more of later—but for now let me just say that she adopted me after her only son was killed in the Ghostlanders' attack on our encampment not long before we came back across the Shallow Sea."

Evidently Nathan and his Warlinga commanders hadn't shared that fact with them, because Chelka's head crest rose in surprise. Philip wondered why, and might have pursued more questions along that line of inquiry but Ishka came back at that moment and everyone's attention was diverted by the process of making tea and handing around the tea and seed cakes.

At the first sip of the clans' favorite drink, Sourwood Tea, Marti made a face then bravely took another drink. Ishka smiled. "It is an acquired taste, but as my husband can tell you, it's refreshing."

Phillip grunted and drank from his own refilled cup. "And just like kafa was in our old home among the stars, it's mildly addictive."

Marti laughed. "I'll have to take your word for that, Sir."

Overcoming her shyness at last Chelka asked, "Kashallan-Phillip, I've noticed your mother and wife have beautiful baskets. They are interesting, so expertly woven they even hold water like a gourd or clay pot. I have never seen their like. Can you tell me who made them?"

The kashallan smiled. "Why, yes I can." Switching languages he said to Efosa, "Mother, these warrior women are admiring your beautiful baskets. They want to know who made them. Care to tell them?"

Efosa dropped her gaze, then allowing a smile to curve her dark lips, she said in the Khutani people's language, "I make."

In the same language Ishka added, "My mother-in-law's clan, the Twisted Grass People, are famous for their basketry." Ishka picked up a small basket, empty now of seed cakes, and handed it to the women to examine. "They are famous for their four-handed weave construction. It is nearly impossible for those of us with only two hands to duplicate."

Marti dutifully set down her cup and took the basket. She looked at it for a moment then passed it on to Chelka for further scrutiny. Chelka took the basket in both hands, turning it one way then the other admiring its design and composition. "It is so beautiful. My aunt Eilith would love to have something like this." Cradling it in both hands she held it out to Efosa and Ishka. "Would you be willing to trade for this one or some other. My aunt would love a beautiful gift like this."

Startled, Ishka took back the little basket and seeing Efosa's puzzled expression explained, "This Warlinga wants to trade for one of your baskets, Mother."

Efosa gasped. "My baskets? But they are nothing special. Aunt Daylay can make much better."

Yoey laughed. "But Daylay isn't here, Mother, and you are. I think if Sa Chelka's aunty likes your work you could become very famous on this side of the water. Everybody will want them. You might even have to teach the cousins to weave just so you can keep up with the orders for your work," Yoey teased.

Efosa made a rude noise. "Those boys! Not likely." Then to Yoey she said, "Please tell this nice Warlinga that I will make her aunty a new basket as soon as I can gather materials and find the time to make it. It wouldn't be right to trade with her for an old basket we have been using."

When Kashallan-Phillip translated Chelka dipped her head crest. "Thank you, Sa Efosa, I'm sure my aunt will be most pleased."

At the sound of approaching footsteps the people by the fire looked round and stared into the darkness. In another moment Moraga's pale hair and face came into view, Masonja at her side and the cousins slouching along in their wake. When she saw who waited for her, Moraga let out a glad cry and opened her arms wide.

Marti rose laughing and hugged her back. Chelka rose as well but didn't join in the two women's embrace. She did smile and held her head crest high. "I didn't know you two were with the laddys come to join us," Moraga cried. "Who else is here from Lann Gheal?"

Steering them away from the fire Moraga guided her two companions back into the night. Phillip breathed a sigh of relief when he heard their voices heading for the Warlinga and Speir'dina encampment.

"What's wrong?" Ishka murmured as she cuddled up next to him. Phillip-Yoey hugged her close his hand with tentacles slightly extended brushing over her satiny fur. "You picked up on my unease did you?" She nodded, waiting for him to explain or not as he chose.

"Marti I know from our first days on Timorna when several of us were captured and enslaved by the Warlinga. Chelka I didn't know, but Nathan-Corha told me a little and they just now confirmed that they were held captive by the Ghostland Changelings in Riath.

"Our Ce'awn, the first kashallan among us was so badly tortured that he was left barely alive. Why are these women here—now? That troubles me, and we sense—there's something wrong with those two. I didn't want them wandering around our camp. And I especially didn't want them seeing Tess-weh."

Phillip had spoken loud enough to include the others sitting around his fire to hear. "But why?" Timma blurted. "Marti and Sa Chelka are our friends. They are the warriors that killed the Umwira agents at Ticca last Sorin Season. Why not tell them our story."

"Cause starwomans and Warlinga got Umwira magics." Masonja pointed to her forehead where the women had worn their colorful headbands.

Phillip felt a cold chill run down his spine. "Ah, that's what it is. Thank you, Masonja. I tasted something wrong, but I didn't understand what I sensed." Leaning forward to see her better in the dim light, he asked, "Can you tell me more about the Umwira magic?"

Masonja shrugged. "Better not wander round camp—better not find Tess-weh. I tell Speir'dina. Demon tell her, too maybe."

"Mm, good," the kashallan mused. Then as another thought struck him, he said, "Masonja, I've seen Tobrach and some others, Warlinga and Speir'dina wearing those headbands. Are they all infected with Umwira magic?"

The Begta shook her wooly head. "Naw, only womans got magics."

The kashallan sat back trying to make sense out of what he'd discovered. A few moments later his pondering was interrupted by more footsteps approaching. As they looked up Nathan's familiar features came into view followed by Tobrach wearing his colorful headband.

Nathan's sooty grey eyes looked tired and deep lines of stress and worry seemed to be carving new furrows in his pale Caldoni face. "Nathan, San Tobrach, this is a pleasant surprise. Won't you join us?" Kashallan-Phillip invited.

Nathan shook his head. "No, thank you, Phillip-Yoey. We were just looking for our women-folk. Have you seen Chelka and Marti?"

Well, well, well, she finally got her wish, Phillip thought.

<<The bondmates forgot to mention that little fact to us,>> Yoey mused. <<Would that explain their presence here, do you think, Kasha?>>

<<Not necessarily, Shalla. I think there's more to the story.>> Out loud he said, "They were here a little while ago looking for Moraga. I sent the cousins to look for her. Last I saw the three of them were heading for the Ticca encampment. Moraga wanted to visit with the armachda Tizu brought with him."

"Oh, that's good then. Thanks."

As the two men turned to go, Phillip motioned for the young people to leave the fire. Efosa understanding what he needed, hurriedly shepherded them into the night. Ishka too would have gone, but he placed a hand on her arm to remain. Masonja reached for the pot and poured herself tea. Before the men had gone too far to hear him, Phillip called out to them. "Nathan-Corha, Tobrach, what's going on?"

Nathan stopped but didn't come back to the fire. "Don't know what you mean, Philip? Got to go."

"I think you do know what I mean, and it's time to stop mucking about and tell me, Amsi. The old Phillip Singey may not have been able to detect the chaotic forces of Psy swirling about those two women, but Phillip-Yoey can see the Umwira taint—and so can Masonja. She sees it better than I can, and if those two come across the wizards in this camp they will see the power, too."

Nathan-Corha and the Warlinga moved closer as Phillip-Yoey continued to speak. "You'd better sit down and tell me what's going on. Why are they here, and what did the changelings do to them while they were imprisoned at Riath?"

Sighing Nathan came back and eased himself down by the fire, Tobrach crouching beside him. "They're here because they begged Maker Qwaltamis to let them join us," he began. "Drucas Segoi kept Marti and Chelka separate from Dunnagh-Tani and the others. He stripped Chelka and humiliated her, letting his men see and touch her without her apron, but what he really wants is to mate with her. Marti was just potential breeding stock in his eyes. He's marked them with his own personal ownership sigil. And at the end he tried to escape with them."

He glanced at Tobrach sitting quietly with head crest flattened during this recital. "If Tobrach here and her brother Aju'an and his hunters hadn't been so close on their trail that Drucas had to abandon them, they would be dead or in the Ghostlands now."

Phillip shook his head still not completely understanding. "But why bring them? Surely it would have been better for them—"

"They came for revenge, Holy One," Tobrach said, taking up the tale. "My Chelka and Sa Marti have sworn to kill him. And we as the members of her hunting pack have accepted the added burden Chelka brings to us as a woman warrior."

"And you agreed to this K'San? Aren't you afraid for her?"

"I am very afraid for her, but I respect her wishes in this matter. None of us may return from the North so I will treasure the time I have with her now and I will let the future care for itself."

"I am humbled by your devotion, K'San," Phillip said, "but do you truly understand the power coiling in those marks?" Turning to Nathan-Corha, he repeated, "Do you? Both women are a potential conduit for the Enemy to use against us."

"No more than some of your own pet Umwira could be potential spies for the Ghostlanders," Nathan snarled.

Phillip jerked back as if slapped. When he could speak , he said in a nearly calm voice. "I know you may still be angry with me, Nathan, but don't let your personal feelings blind you to the danger those women pose to all of us by being here."

Nathan stood, his mouth set in a hard line. Tobrach rose as well, his head crest still down, but looking more troubled than angry. "Well, I guess we don't see it that way and my Amla agreed to let them come and has set guardians from my pod to watch over them, so I guess you're out voted."

Phillip bowed his head in surrender. With an ironic quirk to his lips, Phillip said, "Your will, Kashallan." Nathan snorted and turned to go.

"Try not to forget what Tess-weh has told you, however," Phillip-Yoey said as a parting shot.

"Fuck the demon and you too, Phillip," Nathan muttered as the two men disappeared back into the night.

When they were gone Phillip-Yoey sipped at his now cold tea. Ishka took away his cup poured out the cold brew and handed it back with more from the pot warming by the hearth.

"Starmans mad at Kashallan," Masonja observed. "Him not think good—him like starwomans too much, maybe."

Phillip sighed. "Maybe, My dear, but there's more to it than that. He is angry with me because I told him about Sairsa and Briya being captured by the Blue Stone men. I think he is worried about Dunnagh and can't go to him right now, so I'm just an easy target for his frustration."

Ishka leaned forward and kissed him. "Knowing the cause of your friend's irritation doesn't make it easier for you to bear."

"No it doesn't," he agreed.

Chapter Seven

Tizu had the combined force up and moving before the watery Timornan sun had cleared the eastern horizon. With only a few short rest breaks throughout the day, they staggered down the trail into the narrow valley below Tragar Keep just before nightfall.

Looking down from the thorn-choked hillside into the valley where the first arrivals were already setting up camp, Phillip took a moment to gather his thoughts and allow the flood of unpleasant memories to dissipate and melt away. Drawing on his last stores of energy he had been near the end of the column today as they climbed the rocky trails leading to this isolated border post.

Coming back to his side, Masonja looked up at him, her concern plain in her worried yellow eyes. "Kashallan tired, need help?"

"I'm all right. I don't need your magical help, My dear. I can make it the rest of the way." He turned to stare out into the valley. "No I was just remembering the first time I was here. We were all paralyzed with your people's blowgun poison and totally at the mercy of that brute Gormach." He shivered and wrapped his cape tighter about his shoulders.

"Gormach very bad Warlinga," she agreed.

"Yes, he was." He patted her shoulder to reassure her then started walking again. "But Gormach is dead, and my memories need to stay in the past—where they belong."

Next morning after an uneasy sleep a messenger came to inform Kashallan-Phillip that Tizu wanted to hold a war council with all the leaders just after the noon day meal. To his surprise, they planned to hold it in the Khutani pools below the keep.

Chang who was also lounging by their fire with Ishka beside him snorted a laugh. "That's going to go over like a brick-filled balloon when we tell the

Clan Leaders," he said to Phillip, as the messenger disappeared up the trail to the keep.

The kashallan grimaced. "Yes, quite," he agreed. "I hope we can persuade them. I suspect the makers want to be present as well and it will be easier for Nathan and me to channel if they are nearby."

He hoped his Amla would be there and not back in some Khutani constructed prison again. The bondmates hadn't felt maker Tinguss in their awareness since that first day on the beach, and that also was disturbing. Phillip wasn't looking forward to the channeling, especially if another maker not his parent was asserting its will and controlling his body.

"I guess we'd better go tell them." He set down his tea and stood, Chang rising with him.

"Husbands, sit down," Ishka said in her best no nonsense Ima voice. "The wizards and war leaders can wait till you eat breakfast." The two men looked at each other, surprised, but dutifully resumed their seats by the fire. Phillip caught the gleam of amusement in Masonja's yellow eyes before she focused on her own bowl. Efosa, more nervous about defying men hastily served them each bowls of porridge mixed with slivers of dried meat stirred into the seeds.

A satisfied smile playing across her face, Ishka served herself and took her place between them. "You will think better if you aren't hungry when you try to convince them," she added and took a bite of her own meal.

"Very wise counsel, My dear," Phillip conceded and ate his porridge.

Chang was right. Nobody was happy about the place set for the coming meeting, some like Ogwy threatening not to go at all. Agreement was finally reached when Chang quietly appealed to their pride. Folding his arms across his chest, he drawled, "You know it's true the Makers will want to be there as Kashallan-Phillip suggests, but I also think that for the Warlinga it's a test of your bravery. If you refuse to attend it would show them that the Clan Warriors are cowards."

"Definitely something in that porridge to sharpen your wits, Brother-Husband," Phillip murmured for Chang's ears alone during the uproar that followed. Chang gave him a sly smile before returning his attention to the shouting men.

That remark challenging their bravery, of course tipped the balance in favor of attending the council wherever it was to be held, so just before the golden sun reached its zenith a group of grim-faced war leaders and wizards trudged up the trail to the open stone gates of Tragar Keep.

Tobrach, Nathan-Corha, Hunt Leader Tizu along with Aju'an and his brother Varrod were there to greet them. Rather than having to face a gauntlet of hostile but curious inhabitants of the keep, someone had wisely set most of Tragar's occupants to chores that would remove them from sight while the visitors passed through the main part of the fortress.

As Phillip-Yoey suspected, the pools below Tragar were about half the size of those at Sulas, and right then the rock walkway seemed quite crowded with all the extra men sitting or crouching in a tense half circle around the shallow lip of the keep's pool. Trailing ribbons of glowing fungi on the rock wall illuminated the darkness with an eerie yet magical green and purple light. The scent of copper and vanilla was strong enough to taste on the moist air.

Phillip's lip twitched, trying hard to suppress his amusement. Both the Clan representatives and some of the Warlinga were looking around discreetly, unwilling to openly display their curiosity.

As he and Nathan removed their clothes and stepped into the phosphorescent water lapping against the pool's edge, they could sense the massive forms of several Makers coming. The kashallans waded deeper into the warm liquid, stopping when they were about chest deep. Phillip glanced at Nathan. He looked pale, his skin oddly greenish in the fungus light. His eyes were sooty pools and there was a grim set to his jaw.

Suddenly anxious about the fate of his parent, Phillip-Yoey murmured, "Do you know who is here and what's going on?"

Nathan-Corha glanced sharply at him, then shook his head. "No. I don't know any more than you do at this point," he said under his breath.

In the next moment Phillip breathed a sigh of relief as Maker Tinguss wrapped him in its massive coils. Leaning his head against the sleek grey neck of that well-loved other, he said, <<Amla, I'm so glad you are here. We were worried—>>

Tinguss nuzzled him, its mouth tentacles playing gently over Phillip's face. <<I taste your concern, My Child. I am very sorry for abandoning you for so long, but you did well.>>

<<But what of the other Makers, Amla?>> Yoey fretted. <<Are they going to lock you away again?>>

Tinguss rumbled a laugh. <<No, no, Little One, the Council has talked. Everything will be alright now. No need to worry,>> it soothed.

Would everything be all right? Privately Phillip wondered if there wasn't just a hint of tartness to the sweet flavor of the Maker's sending. He hoped that reassurance was true and wasn't just meant to console and sooth the symbiont.

Wishing his Psy was stronger, and that he hadn't been such a stupid ass about Caldoni "magics" when he'd had the chance to learn from Dunnagh, he knew a shortened version of Caldoni training could have benefited him so much since his bonding—and right now was a good example. Phillip hoped the maker would try to speak to him privately before taking off again.

Inserting a mouth tentacle into a small cut on Phillip's shoulder Tinguss focused its yellow eyes on the group waiting uneasily on the pool's edge. Using Phillip's mouth, it said, "Thank you for coming. I know it wasn't easy for most of you to come into our sanctuary." It rumbled a laugh. "Nor was it any easier for some among us to let you."

Nathan snorted and using his mouth, Maker Qwaltamis said, "I am Maker Qwaltamis and I also welcome you. As my sibling has so eloquently argued on your behalf, if things are to change and our peoples redo the harm that has been done in ages past, we need to begin anew. No more secrecy. No more will the pools be allowed to be the private domain of the Avairei priests alone. Like it was in the past, *everyone* of good heart will be welcome to consult us at a heeling pool in future."

Addressing the wizards directly Tinguss continued, "I'm not sure how much about our underground water ways has been kept alive in your lore, but to show you this place once again was one of the main reasons I argued to hold this council here, as well as demonstrating once again our sincerity for the success of the alliance against the Ghostlanders. They are a potential danger to both our peoples."

"With so many Makers present here at the moment, it is also easier for us to shield our council from prying Ghostland eyes and ears. So be easy in your minds. No treachery is intended," Qwaltamis added. Qwasigara and Eilo nodded accepting the Maker's practical explanation.

At that point the Makers turned the proceedings over to Tobrach; he was K'San here and officially their host. Tobrach rose, hand on a short bone spear, and introduced everyone. He spoke in the Khutani peoples' language, everyone present familiar with it after so many years of warfare. As an added precaution against misunderstandings, however, Chang sat among the Clan members in case anything brought up was unclear to them.

Introductions completed he handed the spear to Hunt Leader Tizu. "I think we should begin by telling each other what happened to our peoples over the long Sorin Season."

To Phillip's surprise he began not with their time at Ticca, but with a brief biography of himself, and his leadership of the Caldoni mercenaries of the Lann Gheal corps. He spoke of how fleeing war among the stars the craft they were on had been damaged. They had been guided to Timorna because one among them had agreed to a kashallan bond.

Their galactic enemy found them and destroyed their ship, leaving them stranded here. Learning of the poisonous storms they made their way across the Great Swamp to Ticca Keep to wait out the Sorins. There they were discovered and recognized by a changeling Ghostland agent already placed in the keep.

"Some of my warriors had already fought a warband of the Ghostlanders, and our chieftain, the first among us to make a kashallan bond, fought their war leader with the mind magics, and won. As the Enemy ran this brave," Tizu smiled, "but maybe stupid kashallan, chased after the war leader and attacked him, physically biting into his flesh."

"That was the first time in living memory that a young Khutani had tasted the Hated Enemy," Qwaltamis said.

"Retreating into our Long Sleep after the Ghostlanders' plague killed so many," Tinguss added, "we allowed our stewardship to falter. Corruption and other misuses of power grew in our absence. That is how the Ghostlanders managed to infiltrate their changelings into so much of the Southern lands."

The kashallans caught the echoes of a tart exchange between Tinguss and other makers swimming in the shadowy depths beyond the light. A few were angry that it had revealed so much. Then, realizing that the wizards might be strong enough to understand some of what was said, as his Amla pointed out, the argument quickly subsided. Phillip caught the ironic gleam in Qwasigara's eye and suspected Tinguss was right.

When the silence dragged on long enough that he was sure the makers had finished, Tizu said, "We've given you a short summary of what has happened on this side of the Shallow Sea. Now I would like to hear what has happened to the Western Clans. It is my understanding that a covenant between your people and the Ghostlanders has ended. Do you know why they attacked you after all this time?"

"No, we do not," Qwasigara said, reaching for the bone spear. "Not at the time anyway. As their power peaked with the Storms the Ghostland warbands came down from the North killing and torturing as they came. No clan was left untouched. They sought out those of us with great magics for their 'special attentions'.

"It was only through the offerings of many Blood Gifts to the Unseen Ones, who heard our prayers—and the great power of those like myself and Eilo of Red Wind here," he bowed to his fellow wizard, "that with the aid of our brave warriors allowed some of us to survive that terrible time."

The war council fell silent when he finished, digesting his words. As he'd been recounting his tale, both wizards had also been conjuring strong Psy imagery for the Khutani and anyone else present with a strong enough ability to receive them.

After a suitable interval Tesulu rose and took the spear. "The Ghostlanders weren't through with us after the Sorins. They planted spies among us, because they hadn't found the traitors they claimed had betrayed the Real People to the Khutani."

Speaking without waiting for the spear, Goro snarled in his gravelly voice, "They said we broke our covenant with them first. We betrayed no one, the lying scum. They just don't want to share the southern lands they claimed belong only to them with their western cousins."

Tesulu growled and held up the bone spear. Goro grumbled but sat back, curbing his outrage. It was Tesulu's right to speak according to protocol.

"When we gathered to discuss how to take our revenge at Red Rock the Enemy had been warned by their spies and attacked us without mercy again. Many women and children died that day, as well as strong warriors. Maybe they hoped to wipe us out completely, but by then we had powerful new allies to stand beside us," he glanced at Chang and then at Kashallan-Phillip, "and we defeated them." Once again the Psy imagery flooded their minds along with the words Tesulu was speaking.

Though emotionally painful and hard on everyone present their accounting, Phillip realized was a far more moving testimony for his Amla's alliance than any amount of arguing he or the Maker could have mustered on their own

Taking back the spear at last Tizu held it between his hands for a long moment, studying its smooth alabaster contours. At last he looked up and said, "I am truly saddened by your news and moved by the bravery and courage of your people. War is terrible no matter if fought on a wounded world like Timorna or fought with powerful technology among the planets of the Starry River.

"To war against the kind of injustice your people suffered is what I pledged my life to fight against when I joined the company of the Caldoni warriors known in our language as Lann Gheal. Chang, whom you already know, and Kashallan-Nathan there were among my warriors before coming to your world."

Tizu allowed his gaze to come around the crescent of men, making eye contact with each one. Though not a Timornan custom to be so bold, most of the men met his stare and held it. "These Warlinga and Speir'dina have accepted that I have the greatest experience among them. They have chosen me as their hunt leader. I would hope your clan warriors will do the same. As a united force we will have a better chance than going off in small bands on our own. We would be too easily picked off and destroyed that way.

"And if the Ghostlanders have weapons left over from the old wars on this world, you will need my knowledge, for you won't be able to win with spears and bravery alone. Not even your expertise with what you call the 'War Magics" will be enough."

"We will need your expertise as you put it, that is true, Speir'dina, "Qwaltamis said, "but this conflict will be fought on many different levels.

We will war within the Dream as well as in the physical world. For the tactics and deployment of hunting packs and warbands I deferrer to your knowledge and skill, but as far as knowing about the powers manifest within the ether your skills are sadly limited. I taste that your Psy, as your people call it, is very weak. In those battles the wizards and my Khutani kindred will have the greater advantage."

"I don't doubt it and will bow to your will in such matters. I plan to be guided by you and," he bowed to the wizards, "our Clan Elders regarding all magics. And," he added, including both Warlinga and clan warriors in his next statement, "as the men from Ticca can tell you, I respect the knowledge of this world known only to a native Timornan. I will always give my full consideration to any advice you may offer before making a command decision."

There were grunts of approval when he finished. His willingness to learn seemed to both surprise and please them. Seeking to test him perhaps, Qwasigara reached for the spear and asked, "What do you know about the Ghostlanders and the land to the North? Before we can give you our allegiance we need to be assured that you will lead us true."

Tizu took back the spear. He tapped it on his palm, thinking. Finally he said, "I will be honest with you and say in personal experience not much. But Maker Dievris and Maker Qwaltamis here have shared with me through a mind-link a bit of their knowledge of the peoples and the lands to the north. However, during my time as a commander up there," he pointed upward to the unseen sky above, "I fought on many worlds and under many harsh conditions.

"I already know about the barren desert-like conditions up north. I saw them with our ship's technology before we even landed on the mesa. And, I know about the poisoned places still active from the old wars that can cause terrible mutations." He tilted a five-fingered hand back and forth, then continued, "some good, some bad. We have technology to detect them as well."

Eyes suddenly hard his voice grew rough with emotion when he said, "I also know about the raids into the Yeyen Banai to capture slaves for the Ghostlanders' foul monster breeding programs that create the unnatural creatures that trouble all our peoples now.

"A lot of the detailed plans will have to wait until we get up there and see what we face. As their former allies I would welcome your sharing any knowledge your people could offer on the matter."

Taking the spear Goro said, "I have fought with them a few times, but mostly we traveled south not north. I know little more than you. The Ghostlanders are very secretive." He glanced at his wizard Eilo, holding out the spear to him.

"As my warrior claims, Barak and the entire cabal of the dried up grey creatures *are* very secretive." A note of bitterness coming into his voice as he continued, "We are only their 'savage western cousins.' We are unworthy to be trusted completely with the mysteries of their power. When called upon by the old covenant we would go with them, spill our blood for them but never are we seen as more than slaves to be threatened with the old technology or placated with bootie when it suits them."

"Mostly we suffer and die without either their meddling or their help," Qwasigara said, taking the bone spear.

Tizu nodded. "I can see how difficult it must be for you. You live in a harsh land, caught between the jaws of two enemies. I honor you for your endurance and courage."

Reaching for the spear Tobrach said, "The hunters of Tragar are also familiar with the northern lands. It has been our duty to protect the Yeyen from Ghostland raids for many turnings of the yearly cycle. Though I am young myself, my hunt leader Warega is a veteran of many battles with the northerners. They fight with tooth and claw, spear and war club, but are also very skilled with the war magics. And this might be a problem for our Speir'dina hunters because many haven't been trained in the magics or are very weak in the power."

Tizu nodded his agreement to that observation. "I've already accounted for that weakness, K'San. Though you and your hunters haven't had much time to work with us, but over the last Sorin Season, as Aju'an or Fadir can tell you, we've worked on that.

"We developed a triangle formation to compensate for each other's strengths and weaknesses. A Speir'dina with his star weaponry is the point of the triangle. Then he is flanked by two Warlinga, protecting them all from both war magic and spear."

Tesulu and Lubwey nodded, seeing the wisdom in the plan. "Such a grouping of warriors would have an advantage over each man battling alone," Lubwey agreed.

Addressing the western clan leaders directly Tizu said, "Before we head north as an army I'd like to set up some training and practice bouts with your men. I need to see how they fight and learn how best to incorporate them into our overall battle plan."

"Ross tells me that we're expecting more supplies from the Yeyen, so we will have to wait for a time anyway," Nathan said. "Might as well make good use of the delay." There were grunts of agreement all around to that suggestion.

Tizu took a deep breath and continued, "There's one other thing, and I know from past experience that nobody's going to like my next proposal." Making eye contact with each man again, he said, "When the Speir'dina were stranded here we were not of one mind, or one people."

He pointed to his golden skin, then to the pale-skinned Nathan and next, to the ebony-skinned Phillip. "We came from different clans, you might say, what brought us together on that ship was that we were all fighting and fleeing war. Once on Timorna we were joined by many native Timornans, adding another layer to the disharmony we had to overcome as we fled across the Great Swamp to take Ticca Keep.

"Until the alliance rooted out the traitors among the southern peoples in Riath we were sought as outlaws by the Changeling hunting packs, so it was important that we achieve unity. Our Chieftain, the first kashallan knew we couldn't survive so divided. With Tess-weh's help we created new clan units we called a Teh'lach. These clans were made up of both Speir'dina and native Timornans." Tizu smiled remembering and Nathan and Chang laughed out loud.

Shaking his head still laughing Nathan said, "Everybody hated the new order at first. Lots of screaming and complaints. I thought Dunnagh was going to go crazy before everything was sorted." He laughed again, remembering.

"And how we achieved our unity," Phillip said quietly, "was by having councils every night to talk about and resolve our differences."

"And it worked," Nathan said. "By the time we reached Ticca and took the keep by force, we were of one mind, one people. Star men and native Timornans together—unstoppable."

"One mind, unstoppable," Tizu agreed, "and that's what we must do here. We are facing a dangerous enemy that already is of one mind with a powerful cabal of wizards to direct them.

"I know what I am asking won't be easy for the clans or the Warlinga hunters. Everybody has old scores to settle, I get that, but we have to set aside the festering hatred of many generations, because it's the only way I can see for all of us to survive.

"We don't have Tess-weh's help to make this easier, but we have to try. I propose we create some of these Teh'lach I mentioned mixing up our people, creating a new fighting force with new and unexpected war tactics to use against our common enemy."

Tizu was right; nobody liked his idea. There was a lot of grumbling as both clan warriors and Warlinga talked among themselves. Folding his arms across his chest Tizu waited, allowing them time to vent.

<<The wizards could help with this,>> Phillip commented to Maker Tinguss as they waited. <<When we attended a communal funeral ceremony after the Red Rock battle I sensed them doing something with their Psy like Tess-weh did in the Swamp.>>

Tinguss rumbled a laugh. <<I'm sure they could do something if they had a mind to do so.>>

Phillip sighed. <<I will try talking to my new relative Qwasigara, when I can catch him alone.>>

Dripping its amusement into their communication Tinguss laughed again. <<Do, My Child. Maybe I will try talking to my new relative as well. It may appeal to his pride to think a Maker might need his help.>>

It took a while but finally Tizu got the leadership he wanted, and their reluctant agreement to try a more watered down version of the Teh'lach.

In the morning they would begin the practice combats. Using that information they would decide whether to keep on with the triangle formations, substituting a clan warrior for one of the two Warlinga, or try a diamond pattern instead. With this information they would create the new teh'lachs.

Tobrach rose to close the meeting for the day. It was growing late and everyone was hungry. “My people have arranged a feast for us in the courtyard above,” he announced. “Please come join me.”

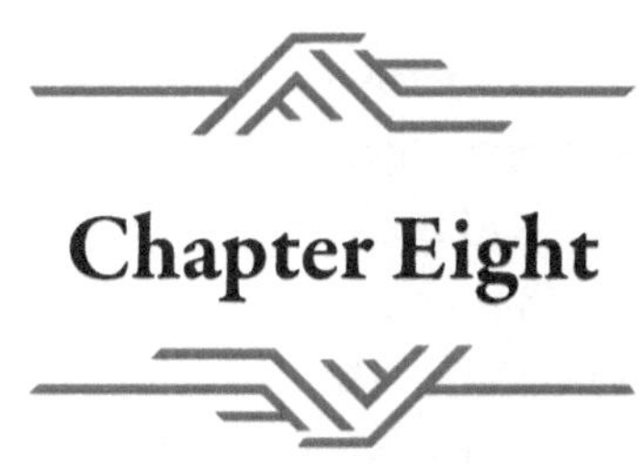

Chapter Eight

Phillip-Yoey blinked in the bright afternoon light as the council emerged from the open door of the keep. The outer court was awash with noise and movement. Long tables had been carried outside, now weighed down with steaming plates of food, Loti servants hurrying back and forth from the open-air kitchen in the far corner of the enclosure. The air was fragrant with the delicious smells of roasting meat, baking masa cakes and mushroom beer.

Phillip smiled, his worry subsiding for the moment, he was looking forward to the meal. Just behind him, Tizu and the Clan warriors were discussing the practice bouts for the morning when they heard angry shouting coming from somewhere nearby. Looking in that direction, the council became aware of a group of Warlinga and Clan warriors clustered together just outside the fortress gates.

Breaking off what he'd been saying, Tizu swore and raced for the gate the others not far behind. Once outside he shouldered his way through the circle of roaring hunters and warriors, where two men with bloodied spears circled each other, each side shouting their encouragement to the combatants. Rhys and a frantic Ross, their pleas unheard, were fingering their side arms and screaming for everyone to calm down.

Tizu took one look at the chaos, drew his weapon, aimed, and shot them both without warning. The two combatants sprawled motionless on the bloody ground in the next moment. Everyone fell deathly silent as he walked into the circle.

Coming up beside Phillip-Yoey, Tesulu asked in a low voice, "Are they dead, Kinsman?"

"No, I don't think so, just stunned maybe," Phillip murmured, then returned his attention to the men in the circle.

By that time the two combatants were waking up, dizzy and shaking their heads to clear them. Still unable to stand, they focused on the stern-faced

Speir'dina dressed in black before them. "Stay down," Tizu warned them. "If either of you shit for brains Begta get up before I tell you that you can, next time, you're dead meat." He held up his weapon.

His hard black eyes raking over the crowd, he said, "I am Hunt Leader Tizu, for any who don't know me. The combined council of both Clan and Warlinga have appointed me as the leader of this now combined force. From now on you will take my orders and answer to *me* if you don't."

Switching languages he repeated what he'd just said in the Western Clan's dialect. "This is a combined force now Warlinga, Speir'dina and Clan Warriors united as one, fighting our common enemy in the North together. I will tolerate no fighting or breaking of camp rules from now on. Got that?"

Turning in a circle he raked them with his cold stare once again. "I don't care who you think you are, hunter, Clan warrior, K'San or war leader you will comply with camp rules and I will deal with you the same if you break them.

"Fighting among ourselves to settle old scores will be punished with death. If you want to do the Ghostlanders' work for them, you will be treated like the spy you truly are—and killed—no exceptions. Do I make myself perfectly clear?"

Once again he switched languages and repeated his speech. The men remained silent, looking at one another shuffling nervously. Tizu raised his weapon again and drew a line of green fire in the dust at the onlooker's feet. Many hissed and hastily jumped back.

"I can't hear you, half-bred Begta? Do I make myself clear? No fighting will be tolerated!"

At the end of his second demonstration of Speir'dina weaponry, Tizu got the chorus of agreement he was looking for. "Good." He motioned for the two fighters to get to their feet. They rose warily and joined their fellows in the circle, keeping a safe distance from their fiery new commander as they did so. "Tomorrow will be a long day for everyone, so enjoy the meal our host K'San Tobrach has prepared for us and then get some sleep. We will begin practice bouts in the morning to test your skills and see how best to combine our forces."

As Phillip-Yoey started down the hill to find Timma and the rest of his household Nathan-Corha fell into step beside him. "Aren't you going to stay and join us?"

Phillip stopped and turned to him. "I was planning to come back. I just wanted to maybe check on Tess-weh and bring Ishka and the others back with me." His lips curving upward with amusement, he added, "I'm sure your new aunty would like to see you again. Care to come with me?" Nathan made a face then chuckled.

They walked along in silence for a while Phillip wondering what was really on his mind. At last Nathan got up his courage and said, "Those images—the ones the wizards and the war leader showed us with their Psy were pretty bad. Bad as any I witnessed with Lann Gheal. You were there at the last, right?"

"Yes, I was at Red Rock. I might have died there, if not for Tess-weh."

"Mm." he walked a bit further then blurted, "I can understand a little why you've chosen to defend them so fiercely, maybe. The Western Umwira aren't exactly what I pictured."

"No they aren't. They turned out to be different than what I assumed when my Amla charged me with making this alliance. That's why the teh'lachs and the nightly talking circles are going to be so important. If we ever hope to have true peace on this world after we fight this war in the North, we have to break down the walls of hatred and mistrust that have been built on both sides over the centuries."

Nathan grunted in agreement. Well, their little talk wasn't quite an apology for his earlier harsh words and blame, Phillip thought to himself, but it *was* a start in mending the rift tearing apart their friendship and he was glad of that.

When they reached the meadow where most of the combined force of warriors were camped the two kashallans saw that here too long tables had been erected, people already sitting around eating. When Phillip looked at Nathan eye brow raised, Nathan shrugged. "Makes sense to feed most of them here," he said. "Not everybody would fit into the keep's courtyard."

When they found his household, Phillip-Yoey was surprised to see Efosa sitting among several Loti and a couple Speir'dina women. Ishka sitting beside her seemed to be acting as a translator for them. The women were laughing and enjoying themselves Efosa demonstrating her four-handed technique for making baskets. A dark-haired Speir'dina woman was sitting between the folded forelegs of a Loti woman, each holding a part of the reeds needed for four-handed weaving. They laughed and struggled to duplicate working together what Efosa could weave so easily on her own.

Phillip looked at Nathan and grinned. "I'm glad to see her so happy like this," he confided. "Women aren't always treated well in the West. Because she dared to defy her family, she had a harder life than most when her husband and sons were slain. Maybe as a master basket maker among our people she can find a better life and the respect she deserves."

Phillip sighed. "And soon I'm going to have to find the time to give her the language patterns for the Khutani people's language. She will feel more at ease then, I'm sure. Right now she is still a bit nervous with so many Warlinga about."

Turning to Nathan as the thought struck him, Phillip asked, "And how about you? Do I need to share the language patterns with you as well?"

Nathan shook his head. "No, my Amla already did that. I understood what they were saying today." He scratched the stubble of beard on his chin. "But I suppose like you, my Amla and I will have to share those patterns with Ross and some of the others."

"That would be good. Let me know if you need my help with that."

They had almost reached the group when Nathan said in a quiet voice, "What are you going to do with your new family when we go North? Going into a war zone is no place for them, you know."

Phillip let out a long troubled sigh, wiping a hand across his face. "That I do know, but will they listen to me is another matter. I would like to send them south to wait for me at Riath—or Ha'limra—if that were possible. But they don't want to go, for a variety of reasons. When I was with the Clans I met people who had escaped, or were reclaimed by a hunting pack and returned to the Khutani-held lands. Most of them ended up going back to the Clans because of how they were treated by their 'families.'

"Right now Niguiri doesn't want to leave Timma. She's decided to become his apprentice medic. And Ishka... she doesn't want to leave her daughter—or her two husbands who have to go North."

Phillip thought about it a little more then added, "With the Sand Mountain brand on her face I think she, too, is afraid. She hasn't even disclosed to me her family name or the keep from which she was taken as a young woman. But she did talk to me once when we first met about the spite of the Avairei and she wouldn't allow her daughter to face their malice alone. She wanted Timma to marry Niguiri—to give her a better life on this side of the water, true, but she also begged me to take her with me.

"At the time I hadn't considered marriage. I was going to argue that Niguiri was too young to be on her own without her mother in a new place. Then Tess-weh told me Ishka would be dead within the year if I didn't marry her. Tesulu planned to wed her to that brute Goro, who has a reputation for abusing his slaves and women. Efosa told me he killed his last wife because she didn't give him a son. I couldn't let that happen even if the Demon hadn't told me to marry her."

Nathan-Corha nodded. "Yeah, I can understand that."

The woman in question looked up just then and spotted them. Leaning over to Efosa, Ishka said something and the woman looked up and smiled. "My son, you have brought my nephew to visit me. I am happy."

Turning, the other women saw them and scrambled to their feet bowing. Efosa hesitated, suddenly worried. "These nice women like my baskets and want me to teach them. Is that all right?"

Phillip-Yoey smiled. "Of course it is, Mother. I'm glad to see that my kin here appreciate you and your beautiful work. Teach them if you like." Switching languages Phillip-Yoey said to the Loti, "I'm Phillip-Yoey. I don't believe we've met."

"Not sure if you remember her from our journey across the Swamp, this is Anilah," Nathan supplied, motioning to the slim dark-haired Speir'dina. "She was a nurse back on Dymar. She came with Tizu and the guys from Ticca. Suyi and Bea here are volunteers from the Yeyen who came with me and the hunting packs from Riath. You ladies interested in baskets?"

"My mother was a weaver," Anilah said. "I've always loved doing things with my hands. When Suyi and I saw Efosa's baskets—" She shrugged.

Ishka chuckled. "They asked me if I would translate for them and ask my mother-in-law if she would show them how to make them."

"Members of my family are the basket makers for our village," Bea said. "When Sa Chelka mentioned that these Umwira baskets could carry water I, wanted to see them."

"Yoey, my son, these women say they know about a stand of grasses and reeds nearby that I could harvest. Could I go with them tomorrow while you are busy with the men, to gather some?"

Phillip glanced at Nathan. "Is it safe to let them go?"

Nathan shrugged. "Should be, but if you're worried I'll have somebody send a guard with them." Turning to Anilah he asked for more details about where the reeds and grass were. Satisfied with what she told him, he nodded and turned back to the other kashallan. "I'll check with Tobrach or Warega, but it should be all right."

Taking a deep breath, Efosa gathered her courage and asked, "Yoey, my son, can I borrow your Speir'dina knife for the day. It will be easier to cut the grasses if I use such a sharp weapon."

Startled, Phillip looked down at the often neglected knife hanging from his belt. He saw no harm in her request. He would probably be in the keep or down at the Tragar pool with the Makers all day. Taking it off his belt he handed it to her. "Certainly, Mother, but be careful with it. The blade is much sharper than a knife made of bone."

"I will be careful, My Son, and I promise to take good care of it."

"Take the cousins with you to carry your bundles," Ishka suggested. "That way you won't have to make so many trips."

Efosa laughed. "Good idea. Those two need to be doing something useful to keep them out of trouble."

In his middle Yoey dripped its amusement into a private communication to Phillip. <<With the practice bouts starting tomorrow, those two aren't going to be very happy chasing after women.>>

Phillip's lip twitched. <<No they won't, but it will be a good test of their warrior's discipline.>>

Catching a whiff of roasting meat on the breeze reminded Nathan of their reason for coming. Taking Efosa's hand he drew her to her feet. "We came down here to invite you ladies to have dinner with us," he said gallantly. Tucking one of her upper arms next to his side, he continued,

"So—uh—Aunty, will you do me the honor of accompanying me to the feast in the keep?"

Efosa stiffened when she realized he would be taking her among the Warlinga, then as he continued to talk to her in a soothing voice, she allowed him to lead her up the trail.

Falling in behind them Ishka took Phillip's arm and smiled up at him. "You seem more relaxed this evening. Did all go well today?"

He hugged her and chuckled. "That remains to be seen. There are going to be a lot of unhappy Warlinga and Clan Warriors tomorrow when we split them up and combine the warbands in a new way, but hunt Leader Tizu seems to have things in hand. After he gave them a demonstration of our star weaponry they seemed more agreeable. We shall see." He chuckled and hugged her.

"Mm, that's good, but I was also thinking of your friend Nathan-Corha. You two seem to have come to an understanding, perhaps?"

"Very perceptive of you, My dear, perhaps we have. During the council Tesulu and Qwasigara gave an account of the Ghostlanders' attacks on the Clans, complete with Psy visions for those with the skills to see them. Nathan, of course, could. Their account opened his mind, and maybe his heart to the suffering the clans have endured, and why I have worked so hard to include them in the kashallan Alliance.

"Oh he is still angry at the Blue Stone men for the abduction of his brother's wife, but he at least isn't blaming me or my Khutani parent for what happened. And I'm grateful for that, truly."

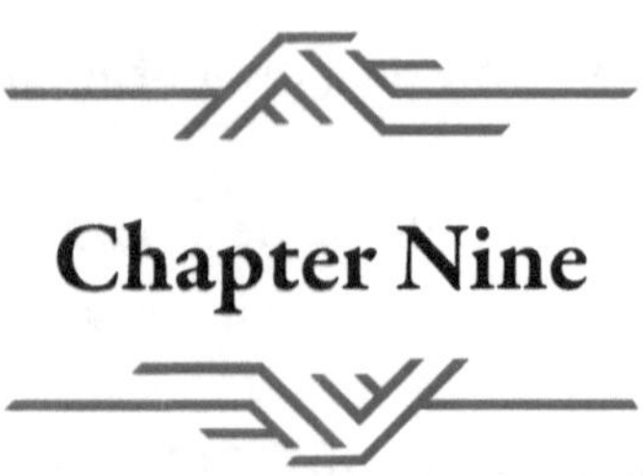

Chapter Nine

Next morning after breakfast Anilah and Bea showed up with two unknown Warlinga at their heels for the grass harvesting expedition. Smiling, Efosa rose to greet them.

"Do you need me to come with you to translate, Mother Efosa?" Ishka asked as she swallowed down the last of her porridge.

Efosa shook her head. "No, Daughter, I can manage. We are just cutting grass. You go on and help Niguiri and her husband with the medicines today like you planned. The boys are coming with me. They can run get someone if I need help translating."

Choking on his last spoon of porridge, Nytaka glanced over at the kashallan with pleading dark eyes.

"Go with your aunty today," Phillip said sternly. "The warriors will be practicing for many days yet. You can watch all day tomorrow if you like. I will tell the leaders so no one will make you their slaves for the day, running errands."

Dropping their gaze, the cousins nodded and hastily finished their meal, before he changed his mind.

When they were gone Chang laughed and poured himself more tea. "Nicely done, Brother Husband. I think Timma had in mind a few tedious chores lined up for them today and tomorrow."

Phillip halted with his own cup halfway to his mouth. "Does Timma need them? I guess I should have cleared it with you and him first before assigning them to the women. Sorry about that."

Chang shrugged and sipped his tea. "Don't worry about it. We mainly wanted to keep those two busy and out of the way today while Tizu gets everything set up. Your project will do as good as any."

Then after a short silence he added. "Rhys wants me to go with him up the valley this morning. So don't worry about the women, we will be around with a few of the boyos keeping an eye on the larger encampment while so many warriors are up at the keep."

"That does ease my mind," he admitted. "Nathan-Corha wants me to help him with giving some of our people the language patterns for the Western dialect. And I need to absorb the patterns for the Ghostlander's language myself. I suspect I will be at the Tragar Pool for much of the day."

EFOSA SMILED WITH PLEASURE when she saw the stand of tall orange grasses Bea and Anilah pointed out to her. She hadn't been sure the right kind of grass existed in this dry thorn-choked land so like parts of her home across the Shallow Sea. But just like in the higher parts of Twisted Grass territory, this tiny hollow surrounding the blue spring held the magic of life.

Seeing her smiling face Bea said, "Is good, yes?"

"Oh yes, is good," she agreed. She held up the Speir'dina knife and pointed. "We cut." Efosa glanced worriedly at the Warlinga, still uneasy with them following. Then she chided herself for being a stupid old woman. Hadn't her nephew Corha sent them? Surely her fears were groundless. Still... "You tell Warlinga wait, yes?"

"Yes," Anilah said as she joined them. "I'll tell them to wait for us here." Anilah spoke to the Warlinga who obediently squatted in the grass to wait for them.

The women decided that Efosa and Bea, being the more experienced gatherers would do the grass cutting, and Anilah and the cousins would follow in their wake, tying the grass into bundles and carrying them back to the open place where the Warlinga waited.

Often out of sight of one another in the tall vegetation, but always within calling distance, the women and the cousins spent an enjoyable morning singing, gathering and talking to each other in a combination of both languages.

As the sun climbed towards its zenith Anilah and the boys were hauling another few bundles of grass back to the clearing when Anilah suddenly stopped, the cousins almost bumping into her.

The ground ahead was empty, no hulking Warlinga waited to glare at them with their sullen red eyes. "Now where did those two grumpy hunters go?" Anilah said as she placed her bundle with the rest. Looking around she could see no one in sight. Calling out she heard no answer.

She didn't want to report them to Nathan-Corha or Hunt Leader Tizu, but abandoning them because they were bored was inexcusable. But had they abandoned them? Feeling a cold shiver run down her back, she surveyed the clearing with a new urgency trying to locate them.

"Maybe go for drink water," Qwayku offered.

"Maybe," she said slowly, "But if they wanted water only one should have gone at a time." No there was something wrong, she could feel it.

Keeping her voice calm so as not to scare the boys or alert an enemy, she said, "Boys, go get your Aunt Efosa and Bea. It's time to go—now!" To her relief, the boys didn't argue but melted back into the grass as silent as the hunting cats back in her home among the stars.

A moment after they left the screaming began. In Galactic Standard Anilah shouted at the top of her voice. "Lann Gheal Help! We are under attack!" Anilah shouted again and again till she heard an answering shout in return. The armachda were coming.

EFOSA HAD SPIED A PARTICULAR healthy clump of the orange grass on the other side of a cluster of boulders not too far away. Bea was still busy clearing out another patch so Efosa called and pointed to where she would be cutting next. Bea nodded and continued her harvest.

Efosa was engrossed in her work when a large hand closed over her mouth, blocking off her breathing. She bucked fighting for air enough to scream, dropping the Speir'dina knife in her struggle.

"Stop fighting us, Witch," one of the Warlinga growled next to her ear. "Or we will kill you right here."

They were going to kill and eat her anyway, Efosa thought. No point in making it easy for them. This was all wrong. Why were the Warlinga sent to guard them doing this?

"Grab her hands and tie them, Stupid Begta. The Master wants us to bring one of the traitors back to him alive."

Someone slapped her hard enough to black out her vision for a moment. When she slumped and would have fallen, one of the hunters held her while the other bound both sets of her arms. Half-dragging, half-carrying her they were heading off into the brush when Bea discovered them and started screaming.

Picking up Efosa's dropped knife one of the Warlinga bounded back and slashed at Bea's throat with the lethal blade. Bea leapt aside, the knife slashing her shoulder and arm instead. Screaming the alarm even louder, she ran towards the spring, a trail of bright purple blood staining the grass in her wake.

"We need to go—hurry! There are mutant hunters out here today," the man carrying Efosa shouted. "They will be following soon."

The one with the knife started to answer when his words were cut off by a well-aimed stone slamming into his jaw. In the next moment a barrage of rocks followed pelting both men.

One particularly accurate missile smashed into the arm of the man carrying Efosa. There was a loud crack, the Warlinga cursed, loosening the grip on his prize. Efosa woke just then and renewed her attempts to get free. The man snarled, trying to hold on, but couldn't with only one working arm. Suddenly she slipped out of his grasp, hitting the ground hard, gasping for breath. Before the other man could come back and pick her up, they heard a chorus of shouted questions from warriors heading up the trail of harvested grass straight for them.

"I told you we needed to wait and capture one of those traitorous Khutani-bound mutants. Now we've lost our chance," one complained.

"And I told you that taking a kashallan was too risky. No one would care over much about an old woman," the other snarled as they hurried deeper into the surrounding thorn brush.

"Well, we have nothing now. We can't go back to the keep and Drucas and the wizard won't be pleased with us when we reach home."

"At least we have the knife. Shut up and run, curse you!"

Showing themselves at last, the cousins continued to pelt the retreating Warlinga with rocks as Chang and the rest of the nearby Speir'dina warriors raced into view.

Waving the others on, Chang knelt by Efosa, untying her hands and checking her over for further injuries. She had a swelling on the side of her head and rope burns on her wrists, but didn't seem badly hurt otherwise. Bea on the other hand...

"How are you, Mother Efosa?" Still gasping for air, she clung to him, too badly frightened to speak. Shyly, the cousins came forward to stand nearby. Glancing up at them, he asked, "What happened; do you know?"

"When we got here two Warlinga Demons were carrying Aunty away," Nytaka said.

"They stabbed Bea, too," Qwayku added.

Chang sat back on his haunches staring. "Warlinga? Are you sure?"

They nodded. "Could you recognize them if you saw them again?"

The cousins looked at one another and shrugged. "Maybe—not sure."

Chang sighed. "Go on with your story."

"We threw rocks at them to drop Aunty," Qwayku said.

"I think I broke one's arm," Nytaka said proudly holding up his slingshot. "I heard a loud crack and he dropped Aunty. Then they were running away."

"Hmm, you did well today, My Warriors," Chang told them, making them smile with pride. "No one could have done better. Warlinga, eh..."

"I think they were the ones sent to guard us today," Nytaka offered. "When we took our grass bundles back to the clearing with the Speir'dina woman, they were nowhere in sight. She told us to get the Loti and Aunty, because something was wrong."

"We went to find the women, and then the Loti started screaming and ran past us bleeding," Qwayku said. "That's all we know."

That was more than enough, Chang thought grimly. Seeing that Efosa's breathing had slowed, he asked, "Mother Efosa can you walk, or do I need to send for a litter to carry you?"

"I think I can walk if the boys help me," she said. Then voicing her fears she said, "Why did those bad Warlinga want to kill and eat me? Just like the stories from home said they would. Do you think my Yoey is all right?" Glancing down at the ground around her she cried out with dismay. "Oh,

Warrior, I've lost my son's knife. He is going to be so angry with me!" Efosa started to cry. "I am such a stupid bad old woman. I've brought trouble and shame down on those I love once again. I should have let those demons eat me," she lamented. "Boys, please look and see if you can find Yoey's knife nearby."

"It's gone, Aunty," Qwayku said. "The Warlinga Demons took it." This statement made her cry even louder.

"It's all right, Efosa, it isn't your fault that the knife is gone," Chang soothed. "Phillip-Yoey is going to be more worried about your safety than a mere knife getting stolen. When we catch up to those men we'll get it back for him, so don't worry."

Chang put an arm under her shoulder and helped her to her feet, motioning for the cousins to walk on either side of her. "Those men gave you a bad knock on your head, so let me or the boys know if you feel dizzy. I don't want you to fall and hurt yourself more."

Efosa agreed and they started down the trail. Reviewing what he knew so far, as they made their slow progress back to the clearing, Chang said, "I don't think those were some of our Warlinga." *No, more likely they were Changelings sent here to spy on us—just like at Red Rock,* he thought to himself. "Can any of you tell me anything more about them now that you're calmer? Did they talk to you, Mother Efosa?"

Efosa snorted. "Those Warlinga demons called me a witch and a traitor. They said they would kill me if I didn't stop fighting them. I knew they were going to kill and eat me as soon as they got far enough away that no one would find them, so I didn't stop fighting." Wincing she touched the swelling on her head. "I don't remember any more."

"Hmm..." Chang walked along for a while then said, "You said those men called you a witch and a traitor, yes?"

"Yes they did."

"Mm, what language were they speaking when they told you that?"

"Why, my own language, of course, I couldn't have understood them otherwise."

Chang stopped on the path, turning to face her. "Mother Efosa, the Warlinga here don't speak the Western Tongue."

Efosa stared, frowning. "But they have to know my language. How else could they have spoken to me?"

How else indeed. "Maybe because they weren't true Warlinga, but Ghostlander spies sent here to learn our secrets."

"But why take me, warrior? I don't know anything."

No perhaps not, but you would make a good hostage, he thought. Out loud, he said, "I don't know, but we need to tell the war leaders as soon as possible."

Back at the clearing they found Anilah tying a make-shift dressing of wadded up grass over the still bleeding wounds in Bea's shoulder and arm. Finishing up she hurried over to them. "Efosa, are you all right?"

"She got a blow to the head," Chang told her. Glancing at the Loti applying pressure to the wound, Chang said, "We need to get back to the keep as soon as possible. Can you walk, Bea?"

"Yes, Warrior, I can if we don't go too fast."

Chang hoped she could, because there was no way any of them could carry her. "Good, then let's get moving."

They were nearly to the keep when Chang was hailed by Briyenn, hurrying to catch up to them. He waved the others on and dropped back to have a private word with the armachd. When Briyenn was close enough, he said, "Any luck in catching up to them?"

The armachd shook his head. We were following along; the sign as clear as day, then they just seemed to disappear into a rock wall. Rhys said to tell you he thinks those guys were using the war magics to confuse us. He's going to continue looking around see if he can pick up their trail again with his Psy, but he doesn't think he and the boyos with him can catch up with them after all this time."

When they neared the keep the sounds of the practice combats going on inside drifted out to them through the open gate. Putting a hand on Briyenn's arm, Chang murmured, "I'm going to take the injured inside and down to the pool.

"See if you can find Hunt Leader Tizu, Tobrach, and Nathan. Tell them what's happened, but don't make it obvious. In case those spies try to sneak back into camp I don't want the alarm sounded till we see what the brass wants to do about all this."

Briyenn saluted and loped off to join the crowd watching the current match, searching for Tizu or Nathan as he moved among them.

Ushering his charges hastily through the main hall Chang led them down the passage leading to the Tragar pool. When the cousins would have crept away to watch the fighting, Chang stopped them. "You can go watch later. First you need to tell your elder cousin your version of what happened."

"But, Sensei, there are Khutani—big Khutani down there," Qwayku said in a shaky voice.

Chang snorted a laugh. "Yes, there are, and you're going to be introduced to them real soon—now stop dawdling. Let's go."

Chapter Ten

Phillip-Yoey lay relaxing in the warm water, one of Maker Tinguss's coils looped companionably about his torso. The Maker had just finished giving him the language patterns for the Ghostlander's dialect.

<<It grieves me to have to share this language with you, My Child, for it means I will be putting you at risk again. If I could I would tuck you away in my wild pool in the Swamp forever.>>

Tentacles slightly extended Phillip-Yoey's hand stroked the Maker's sleek grey hide. Leaning his head against the Khutani's neck, he said, <<I love you too, Amla, but we both know that isn't possible.>>

<<No, alas it is not. Your bonding was created, it seems, to send you into the Heart of Danger in these troubled times.>> Tinguss allowed its mouth tentacles to brush across his face in a tender caress.

Suddenly Tinguss's head jerked up. Eyes flashing a gold fire, it hissed a warning. People from the keep above were coming. The smells of fresh cut grass, dusty fur and blood accompanied them on the moist air.

The kashallan sat up staring towards the rock ledge as they came into view on the walkway. Recognizing them a shiver ran down his spine.

<<Trouble?>> Tinguss asked.

<<It would appear so, Amla. I see my brother-husband Chang, my new mother Efosa, whom I told you about, and the cousins. I think they were going with Efosa today to gather materials for baskets.>>

Tinguss released him and nudged him towards the edge of the pool. Go to them. I can taste that the women are injured. I will be with you if you need me.>>

The kashallan rose out of the pool phosphorescent foam cascading down his torso. "What has happened?" he called as he waded into the shallow water at the edge of the pool.

"Oh Yoey, My Son, two bad Warlinga Demons tried to kill and eat me!" Efosa cried.

"Eat you, Mother?" Phillip glanced at Chang behind her and raised an inquiring eyebrow. Chang shook his head, promising more later.

"And then they stole your precious knife and ran away. I'm so sorry!"

Hearing her say his knife had been stolen sent a chill down his spine. Hadn't Tess-weh mentioned something about a stolen blade?

Well there was no time to ponder that now the women were both injured and needed his healing skills. He'd get the rest of the story later.

Bea seemed the most seriously hurt of the two. Anilah was removing the bloody wad of grass from her shoulder as he came over to them. The cut he saw was deep, still leaking dark blood down her flank.

."Bring her into the water," he said to Anilah. "The rest of you can tell me the story while I work on her."

The account came out in bits and pieces as Kashallan-Phillip stopped the bleeding and placed a healing seal of yellow kavay over the wound to protect it while it healed.

At some point during the recital Nathan-Corha joined them. Speaking to Efosa in a soothing tone he guided her into the pool where he and some of the young adults in his pod could examine her.

When they were done repeating their part of the tale, Chang took the cousins and Anilah up to watch the practice bouts, telling the kashallans he would report to Tizu and the Warlinga officers. "We need to begin a search for those missing Warlinga, find out who they were and who assigned them to the guard detail this morning," he said as he left them.

After they were gone all was quiet on the walkway, only the two kashallans and their patients left in the cavern. Giving Bea a mild sedative, Phillip-Yoey instructed her to stay in the warm water and let some of the younger Khutani watch over her while she rested.

Her eyes already heavy with sleep, she allowed him to lead her deeper into the pool where she could float with some of the pod to help keep her head and shoulders above water.

Turning away, Phillip looked up and froze. Standing in the middle of the walkway near the edge of the pool. Qwasigara stood with both sets of arms folded across his bony chest, glaring at them.

Nathan had his back turned to the ledge, still with his tentacled hands cradling Efosa's head. He was talking to her in a soft reassuring voice and hadn't noticed their visitor yet.

When Qwasigara saw he had Kashallan Phillip's attention, he said, "So, Khutani, what's going on?"

At the sound of his voice Nathan's head snapped round, the young adults by him hissing a warning. Qwasigara ignored their threat display and repeated his question.

Tinguss rumbled a laugh and raised its head out of the inky water, dripping its placating spice to sooth the young ones. Using Phillip's voice, it said, "Ah, Kinsman, that is a very good question and one we will be sure to share with you when we know ourselves."

"Kinsman, eh?" Qwasigara snorted, not sure he believed that explanation. "Not long ago I sensed someone using the war magics. It was a powerful working, so I ask you again, Khutani, what's going on?"

Hearing a familiar voice Efosa sat up and said, "Some bad Warlinga demons tried to kill and eat me, Elder."

"I doubt if they were our Warlinga," Phillip-Yoey hastily added. "I suspect they were more likely Ghostlander Changeling sent here to spy on us for the cabal of wizards." Turning to Nathan-Corah he added, "I tried to warn you. I hope now you will believe me."

Nathan sighed, the lines of worry around his mouth deepening with the added stress. "Yeah, maybe—but how? Dunnagh-Tani and I checked everyone coming on this mission for the changeling taint. I don't understand how a spy could get past our notice."

"Then you have a traitor among you," Qwasigara growled. Though he didn't say it, Phillip suspected he knew about Marti and Chelka's Umwira brands, judging by the hard look he gave Nathan-Corha. "You Speir'dina are too soft and sentimental to do what needs doing. All you Southerners are weak. You could never survive across the Shallow Sea."

"If we couldn't survive on that side of the water, why do your warriors keep stealing our people then?" Nathan shot back, his tone defensive and angry.

Oh here we go, Phillip thought. <<Amla help!>>

<<Enough, Chosen,>>Tinguss said into Nathan-Corha's mind, the tart flavor of disapproval in the sending. <<He knows about your mate obviously and though I don't agree with him, from his perspective, he has a point.>>

"Elder, I'm sure when we know all the facts these warriors will do what is necessary to insure our safety and rid this camp of Ghostlander spies," Phillip-Yoey hastily said to Qwasigara. "You saw how Hunt Leader Tizu dealt with trouble yesterday. He is a hard man worthy of our trust, do you not agree? He, I'm sure, will root out this evil among us."

"If you're so worried that we're keeping secrets," Nathan grumbled, "then why don't you come with me. I'm going to find the Hunt Leader right now to see what he's learned from the warriors sent to trail the spies."

Qwasigara nodded. "I will do that, Khutani."

Phillip-Yoey darted a look between the two men. He was torn. Someone needed to stay with Efosa and Bea, but without him there to cool Nathan down, he was afraid of what might happen.

<<Go with them, My Child,>> Tinguss said. <<I will stay here with the injured and Qwaltamis's children. You are right to go with them. And, I am curious about this woman who has adopted you as her son,>> the Maker added with a rumbling laugh. <<If she will let me, I want to taste her.>>

<<Thank you, Amla,>> Phillip-Yoey said. Turning to Efosa next, he asked, "Mother, I want you to remain here and rest till your head feels better. Will you be comfortable staying with our cousins and my Amla if I leave you and go with Nathan-Corha?"

Efosa was sitting with several young Khutani coiled about her, their mouth tentacles brushing against her wet fur. She was talking to them, and seemingly they were answering her in return. She looked up when he spoke to her and then nodded.

She waved a hand dismissively towards the ledge. "Go, My Son, you and my nephew do the man things you need to do. I will be fine. The babies are telling me such wonderful stories."

As they climbed back into the keep Nathan shook his head in wonder. "How does she do that? I've never seen anybody so at ease with our snaky relatives."

Phillip chuckled. "Neither have I. Like I told you, she has a gift."

"Or maybe she's a little crazy. You also told me that, too."

Phillip laughed. "So I did, but it's a harmless kind of crazy. And it's the kind of craziness that I wish more people had. It would make our jobs as kashallans easier."

Nathan grunted as they stepped into Tragar's main hall the wizard at their heels. Briyenn was waiting for them and saluted.

Chapter Eleven

The smells of fried mushrooms and porridge hit them like a hammer blow as the party from the pool walked into the main hall. Nathan frowned. He was suddenly hungry, but there was no time to go back to the pool and beg somebody for a meal. <<How much longer before we can eat real food?>> he asked his bondmate.

<<It does smell good, Kasha. I hope soon. Should we try some tonight?>>

<<Better not until our Amla or one of the other Makers says we can. We don't want to get sick right now. But it's going to be a real pain if we have to travel North still drinking that damned formula,>> he grumbled.

The hall was crammed with hunters loudly boasting about today's bouts. Loti servants carrying large serving trays drifted among them.

Hungry and still grumpy, Nathan barked, "All right, Briyenn, where is everybody? Have Rhys and the armachda reported in yet?"

Briyenn started to answer, then spying Qwasigara among them his eyes went wide. "Never mind him; he's with us. Just answer the question, armachd."

Briyenn saluted. "Uh—yes, Sir. Hunt Leader Tizu, Tobrach, Warega and the Meh'gach hunt leaders along with Rhys and Chang are in a private dining room. They told me to bring you to them when you came up."

Nathan motioned for him to lead the way. Briyenn hesitated, glancing once more at the wizard. "Get moving, Armachd—now."

Briyenn led them down a small corridor and opened the door to a chamber with colorful tapestries hanging on its walls. The men sitting around the table looked up as the armachd ushered them in and closed the door behind them.

Tizu's expression didn't change as he motioned the two kashallans and his unexpected guest to take seats at the table. No one was eating yet, though covered trays sat on a long stone bench against the wall.

A pitcher of mushroom beer and empty drinking bowls sat on the table. Nathan poured himself and the newcomers bowls before he flopped down on an empty stool.

When they were all seated, Tizu asked, "How are the women doing?"

"Shaken up and frightened, but their wounds aren't too serious," Phillip-Yoey said. "Did you catch them?"

Rhys shook his head. "They led us right into a stone cliff then disappeared. I tried tracking them with my Psy and eventually found the right sign, but they had too much of a lead on us. They were headed North as far as I can tell."

Qwasigara snorted, folding a pair of his arms across his chest. "You should have had one of us with you to see through their magics."

"Maybe so," Rhys agreed, "but there wasn't time to come back and search for you or one of the local Warlinga who know the area."

Qwasigara grunted, conceding the point.

"With everybody up at the keep today guess they figured it was a good time to grab somebody," Nathan said. Turning to Phillip-Yoey he added, "Lucky it wasn't you. Taking one of us north would have been a real prize for the Cabal."

Phillip shuddered and swallowed a drink of his beer. "That is a most unpleasant thought, Amsi."

"Yes it is," Tizu said. Turning to Qwasigara, he asked, "Can your warriors protect Phillip-Yoey and his household if he continues to stay in the main encampment or do I need to have Tobrach make arrangements for them to stay in the keep?"

"He is kin to us; we take care of our own," Qwasigara assured him. "They stay with the People."

Tizu nodded. "Good, then I'll leave their security in your hands. I got enough to worry about."

"So whose missing; do we know that yet?" Nathan asked.

"While you were at the pool, Kashallan-Nathan we conducted a search," Tobrach said. "Two men who claimed to be distant cousins of K'San Varrod's wife are now missing."

Varrod hung his head green with embarrassment. "To my shame, Holy One I may not have checked them out as thoroughly as I should have. When they showed up at our camp carrying the tokens that proved that Dunnagh-Tani or one of the Makers at Riath had tested them and found them free of the changeling taint I assumed they were who they said they were, and I accepted them into my hunting pack."

"Don't blame yourself, K'San Varrod," Tizu said. "They had the tokens; anybody could have made that mistake."

"Which brings up other questions," Chang mused. "Is someone forging those tokens, or are the real owners of those tokens lying dead somewhere between here and Riath."

"Or is the Khutani who gave them these tokens a traitor?" a grim-faced Qwasigara said.

"That isn't possible," Tobrach growled.

Qwasigara snorted and looked down his dog-like muzzle at the Warlinga. "Anything is 'possible.'"

Nathan swore in Caldoni, his temper sparking. "You dirty little Umwira bacach—I'll—" His face a dangerous shade of purple, Nathan jumped to his feet, his stool crashing to the floor behind him. "I should kill you for that!"

"Sit down, Nathan—right now,' Tizu roared. "Sit down before I'm forced to do something I'll be sorry for later!" Tizu drew his side arm. "I mean it, Armachd. Yes I'm talking to you, Nathan, because I give Corha credit for having more smarts than to act like a shit for brains amadan."

Catching the flattened head crest of the Warlinga in the room he growled, "And that goes for the rest of you, too. Nobody is starting trouble in here but me. So sit back and drink your beer till we finish—got that?"

Nathan stood rigid as a statue, breathing hard as he fought for control. At last he picked up his stool and sat. Pouring himself more beer he took a long swallow not looking at anyone.

Into the silence that followed Phillip said, "Qwasigara didn't know about Dunnagh-Tani, Nathan. I haven't told anyone about his capture and torture at the hands of Drucas Segoi." Phillip gave the wizard a hard look. "And, in his most irritating way, Wizard Qwasigara was just suggesting that we consider all the possibilities—that's all."

Throughout Nathan's display Qwasigara remain sitting on his stool, his face expressionless.

"As Phillip here just said, a traitorous kashallan is out of the question for many reasons, but forging the tokens or killing their rightful bearers is definitely a possibility," Tizu said.

Nathan put down his cup and rubbed a hand across his face. "And if they were forged that is going to mean a whole lot more work for me and Phillip-Yoey, because we will have to test everyone for the taint again."

"Maybe—provided the Makers feel that's necessary," Phillip said.

Changing the subject Chang asked, "San Varrod did the changelings take their things with them this morning?"

"I'm not sure; why do you ask?"

"It's important we know that—" Chang started to explain.

Tizu sat up with a jerk. "Damned right it is!" raising his voice he shouted, "BRIYENN!"

In the next moment Briyenn stuck his head around the door. "Sir?"

"Find out what happened to those changelings' personal items. If they are still here, bundle them up but don't let anybody touch them with their bare hands—got that?"

Figuring it out, Briyenn's eyes widened and he saluted. "Yes, Sir."

Qwasigara nodded his approval. "Most wise, Hunt Leader. If they left behind Ghostlander magics they could ensnare others among us."

Varrod's head crest rose at the wizard's explanation. Standing up, he bowed to the assembled men. "I think I will go with your hunter and make sure it is done as you command."

A tense silence enveloped the room after Varrod left. Before the wait became too uncomfortable, Tizu changed the subject by asking for some reports on the day's practice bouts. Tobrach and Aju'an gave their reports but it was clear to even Phillip that their thoughts weren't focused on the topic.

Tizu was about to suggest they break for dinner when a grim faced Varrod returned carrying a leather bundle. Crossing to the table he unrolled the leather, displaying its contents. There wasn't much, a half-formed knife blade, jars of resin and glue, some stone tools and a few bone beads half carved as if they were meant to be placed on a death strand.

"What about their bedding," Nathan asked. "They could have sewn something into a blanket or pillow."

Qwasigara gave Nathan a sharp look and nodded his approval. "Most wise, Khutani. It is the hiding place I myself would have chosen."

When Tizu inquired, Varrod said, "One of your Speir'dina hunters used his star weapon and fired their shelter with bedding and weaponry inside. There is nothing left but ash—and we scattered that."

"Good," Tizu said. He eyed the contents on the table, stroking his chin thoughtfully. "There's nothing in this mess like we found at Ticca, but we should burn it, too, I suppose."

The wizard snorted. "Yes, you should burn it. The items here may not look like what you have seen before but there is magic here." He glanced at the two kashallans a challenge in his eye. "Do you 'taste' it Khutani?"

Nathan-Corha turned red, but refused to be baited. Phillip-Yoey studied the items closely for a long moment, then said, "I am still young, Elder, I'm not sure what I am 'tasting', but there is—something wrong with the beads. I can't say exactly what, but I wouldn't want to touch them."

For just a moment Qwasigara's black lips curved into an approving smile. Then before anyone thought to stop him he picked up one of the stone tools and turned over the largest of the roughly carved beads. Hidden in a deep crack on its underside a dark crystal caught the light. When he was sure everyone understood its significance, Qwasigara flipped the bead over, concealing the crystal again.

Tizu swore one of Nathan's favorite Caldoni oaths. "That was cleverly done. Somebody might have thought it odd to see a Warlinga wearing a crystal pendent like an Avairei but nobody would have thought twice about another bone on a death strand."

"Elder, is that the only thing magic among these things?" Chang asked. When the wizard nodded Chang stood. Glancing at the Hunt Leader, he said, "Shall I get rid of this trash?"

"Yeah, do that," Tizu agreed. His mouth a hard line, Chang bundled up the items and left the room.

Into the silence that followed Tobrach said, "My kinsmen and I have been charged with the protection of these northern lands since the early times, but I can't recall any lore about such magics or tale of changeling spies among us."

"Nor have I," Varrod said. His voice taking on a note of smug satisfaction, he added, "We have discovered their evil and sent them running north with their tails between their legs. No more spies to tell the Ghostlanders our secrets."

Qwasigara snorted and stared straight at Nathan-Corha. "Are there no more spies among us—really?" Turning his intense glare on Tobrach, he repeated his question.

Muttering a curse under his breath, Nathan's face turned a deep red and the Warlinga in the room flattened their head crests and snarled. "Yeah, I'm sure," Nathan growled. "It's been taken care of, so drop it, damn you!"

Tizu scowled, glancing around the table at the angry men glaring at one another. "All right, you pack of mangy dogs, what's going on? Spit it out! What haven't you told me?"

Qwasigara folded his top pair of arms across his chest and let out a mirthless laugh. "I wondered if you knew, Hunt Leader. They haven't told you about the women?"

"What women?" Tizu folded his arms across his chest in an unconscious imitation of the wizard and raked them with a furious glare. "Somebody better start talking—now! What women?"

Nathan sighed and rubbed a hand across his face, then said in a colorless voice. "He's talking about Marti and Chelka. When they were captured along with Dunnagh-Tani Drucas marked them and claimed them as his personal property."

Tizu nodded. "So..." Then the significance of what Nathan said registered and he sat up, putting down his beer. Turning to Phillip-Yoey he asked, "Does he mean like Sairsa was marked by that damned Umwira magic?"

Phillip-Yoey nodded. "It's not quite the same, but yes, they've been marked with Ghostlander magic. We thought you knew."

"No, I did not," he glared at his subordinates, "and I don't like being blindsided like this either." Focusing on the wizard, Tizu said, "Elder

Qwasigara, are you saying that this Drucas or another Ghostlander could mess with these women's minds and use them as spies—or worse?"

"I am. They need to be killed."

"No!" Nathan-Corha protested. "You can't kill them or send them back to Riath." Nathan glared at the wizard. "And I'm not being a soft Southerner about this either. Chelka and Marti asked maker Qwaltamis if they could come. They've sworn Blood-Oath to kill the Changeling and the Makers and some of the Khutani cousins are guarding them in the Dream so they can keep their oath. So stop bringing it up; it's taken care of."

"And just when were you two amadans going to tell me about this?" Tizu snarled. When they didn't answer Tizu focused his glare on Aju'an and Varrod. "You being her brothers also knew and didn't tell me, eh?"

The Warlinga turned green with embarrassment but prudently kept quiet. Tizu swore and drummed his fingers on the table. When he was calmer he said to Qwasigara, "Well, there's no help for it now. I probably wouldn't have let them come if I'd known, but since they went over my head and got the Makers to agree to them coming I can't do anything about it now. But I would welcome your help and suggestions about this matter and anything else that comes to your mind in future."

Qwasigara seemed startled by Tizu's frank admission of needing his help. He nodded and rose. "I will consider your words, Hunt Leader." At the door he paused and looked back at Phillip-Yoey.

Phillip rose and addressed the men at the table. "I should go too. I need to check on my patients, before I go back to the main camp."

Tizu raised a hand in dismissal. Then turning to Nathan-Corha, he grumbled, "You might as well go, too. We're done for the day."

In the hall Nathan put a hand on Phillip's shoulder to stop him. "Go on with the wizard. I'll check on Efosa and Bea. I haven't eaten yet, so I'm going down there anyway. She can stay here for the night, if she wants, or I'll bring her down to the main camp if she doesn't."

Phillip-Yoey studied him for a long moment, then nodded. "All Right. Thank you, that does ease my mind." Tentacles slightly extended, Kashallan-Phillip brushed a hand lightly across Nathan's cheek. "And try to get some rest yourself, Amsi. I can taste you're not doing so well."

Chapter Twelve

N*ot doing so well?* Phillip was right about that, damn him, Nathan thought, as he rounded a corner and promptly threw up all the beer he'd drank at the meeting.

<<I'm sorry, Shalla, guess I should have asked before drinking so much of that beer when we were hungry. I wasn't thinking.>>

<<I'm sorry, too, Kasha, but that Umwira made me mad as well, talking about our amsi Dunnagh-Tani like that. I wasn't thinking about consequences either.>>

Nathan snorted a laugh and threw up again.

Like Dunnagh before him, Nathan's bonding had come with "complications." It seemed like they'd been fighting and always on the move ever since their birth as a kashallan. Corha was too young. They should be at home in the pools at Shaden, where he and Corha could grow and get to know each other, before being tossed into the middle of a war. It was too much, too soon, Nathan thought. But unlike Dunnagh who'd had little guidance from the enigmatic Makers, he had been able to form a link with his Khutani parent and had the guidance of Maker Qwaltamis from the very start, and that was a true blessing.

In a strange way, however, he sort of envied Phillip and his bonding to Yoey. Tucked away throughout the Sorin Season in the wild pool surrounded by his pod, that pair of bondmates had been able to grow and mature in a somewhat "normal" fashion—if a human-Khutani symbiont pairing could be called "normal," that is. And because of that uninterrupted time together, he could "taste" the difference. Yoey was mature, more mature perhaps than even Tani. And the host symbiont bond was strong between them, and he supposed their Amla, the rebellious Maker Tinguss.

WHEN HE ARRIVED AT the Tragar pool all was quiet. Both Bea and Efosa were asleep. Bea lay on her side, legs out stretched, her wounded arm slightly above the water's surface, a young adult hovered nearby dozing, as well. Efosa, on the other hand, lay in the shallows entangled in a snarl of his youngest cousins.

Taking off his clothes Nathan shook his head. The Umwira woman was a marvel to him. Trying not to disturb anyone he waded out into the water his hunger and turbulent emotions, tormenting him in equal measure. Where was his Amla? Corha's distress bleeding over into his consciousness, Nathan found he too wanted the comfort of his snaky parent.

<<Corha, can you taste our Amla nearby?>>

<<NO,>> the symbiont fretted. <<Only Maker Tinguss is here. Where is our Amla? Do you think the Umwira have hurt our Amla or—>>

Nathan swallowed the little one's growing panic and shook his head trying to clear it. Moving deeper into the darkness he stroked a hand across his muscular belly beneath which the symbiont coiled. <<Calm down, Shalla. I'm sure Amla Qwaltamis is fine.>>

In water over his head Nathan lay back and floated. Feeling somewhat like a parent himself, he had, not for the first time, more appreciation for Dunnagh's trials with the young Tani. The symbiont was a fascinating blend of child and adult. Corha in age was young but also had the encoded memories of its ancestors to draw upon. <<Do you think the Maker will feed us or will we have to wait—>>

Nathan felt more than heard Tinguss's rumble of a laugh as it encircled him with a coil and moved out into deeper water. <<No, you won't have to wait. I was left here to, 'babysit,' as your people might say, Chosen. And yes, this Maker will feed you. I can taste your distress.>>

<<But where's our Amla?>> Corha persisted.

Tinguss brushed a mouth tentacle affectionately across Nathan's neck and shoulders. <<Your Amla like you, Little One, was hungry and went hunting.>>

Hunting what? Nathan privately wondered. Tinguss must have swallowed a sip of his thought, for the yellow eyes that focused on him seemed to glow with amusement. Extending its feeding tube Nathan dutifully put it between his lips and began to feed.

Replete at last Nathan lay back in the Maker's embrace as Corha dozed. Tinguss inserted a mouth tentacle into Nathan's cheek to form a stronger link with a child not of its own making. Nathan squirmed, uncomfortable with the intimacy, and what such a probe might discover.

<<Be easy, Child, you have nothing to fear from me,>> Tinguss soothed. <<I remember you from your passage through the Great Swamp. Back then I could taste your loyalty and love for the one who still tugs at your heart even without forming a link like we share now.>>

Mentioning Dunnagh brought up a flood of memories and emotions he was powerless to control. Shielding Corha from the torrent, the Maker savored the feast of conflicted feelings that were tearing Nathan apart.

Such admirable and complex creatures were these children from the stars, Tinguss thought to itself as it dripped a soothing balm into its communication with the host. Dunnagh had been his anchor and now without the stability of his love's presence the host felt a drift in a sea of unknown currents and shoals. And Corha being so young, wasn't able to give him much guidance, needing stability of its own.

Tinguss wondered how much Qwaltamis knew about the stress its child was trying to cope with on their own. It would have to speak to its peer on their behalf—hopefully Qwaltamis would understand and help them. But right now... <<Rest now, Chosen, I will care for you and keep you safe until your Amla returns. You are protected and loved by all your new kindred. We will never abandon you. You aren't alone.>>

Choking back a sob Nathan brushed a tentacled hand over the Maker's satiny skin. <<Thank You, Elder.>>

Tinguss played a tentacle across Nathan's face in an affectionate gesture and rumbled a laugh. <<Now let me address one of your more practical concerns, before I put you to sleep. With the Blood Gift as a supplement, you are old enough to start eating normal food when you are away from us and need to.>>

Nathan let out a relieved sigh. <<That's good to know; I wasn't looking forward to drinking that formula on the trip north.>> He thought about it for a moment then hesitantly asked, <<If we're old enough, why did we puke up a while ago?>>

<<Stress,>> the Maker said. <<I know it's been hard for you since my child returned with the western clans. I taste that you feel caught in the middle with conflicting loyalties. When the wizard unknowingly attacked the honor of your old love you were enraged. A newcomer to our world you see merit in the alliance I charged my child to form, but you also are coping with encoded Khutani ancestral memories that flood your awareness at times, because Corha is too immature to sort and shield depending on the situation. This places an added burden on you as its host. And right now I taste that your own mental stability isn't all that strong. Is that not so?>>

Nathan stirred, ashamed and uncomfortable with the depth of the Elder's knowledge of him.

Tinguss tightened its coils then slackened its grip, offering the Khutani's version of an affectionate hug. <<No need for your fears and worry. Truly Timorna was blessed when your people answered our call.>>

<<Thank you for your confidence, Elder, I hope I am worthy of it.>>

<<You are most worthy, Warrior. I find your flavor very sweet. If I may make a suggestion, however?>> When Nathan grunted his agreement, Tinguss continued, <<As a test of your Warrior's discipline may I charge you with talking about your fears and concerns in these Teh'lach councils you have planned. Tell them, especially the Umwira about Dunnagh-Tani and what he means to you. Tell all of them about your training in Lann Gheal. Tell them your hopes and fears. Set them the example of what courage truly is, and dare them to match it.

<<Becoming so vulnerable won't be easy, not for you, the Warlinga, or the western clans, but as your love Dunnagh knew and tried to teach everyone it is important. With him as your guide and example you—and my child, too, must take up his burden and become the teachers and the healers of this wounded world. This is but another aspect of what it means to be a kashallan I would argue.>>

<<Hmm, I never thought of it quite like that before,>> Nathan admitted. <<Dunnagh always tried to tell me, but I guess I'm used to seeing my failings and not my *other* qualities.>>

<<And you have many admirable qualities. But enough talk for now you need to rest as much as the little one.>> Guiding him back into the

shallows, Tinguss nudged him towards a side ledge where he could rest his head. <<Sleep now. I will guard your dreams so have no fear.>>

NATHAN WOKE SOMETIME later not sure what had disturbed him. All was quiet. The dim light of the fungus trails on the rock walls showed only a dozing priest crouched on the walkway. Efosa and Bea were gone, collected by Phillip-Yoey, no doubt. Nathan yawned and sank back into the warm water. He guessed if he was needed someone would have come to get him. He was in no hurry to get up, enjoying the soft caress of the liquid against his sensitive skin.

Then becoming aware of another warm body curled up at his back, he froze. Who? Slowly turning he looked into Marti's dark eyes.

"Hi." She smiled showing lots of teeth and turned on her side to face him, one of her melon-like breasts brushing against his arm.

At the touch Nathan felt a shiver of rekindled desire. Fully awake now he asked, "Uh—what are you doing here?"

"Sleeping—just like you." She chuckled, then at his frown she sobered and added, "I was looking for you last night. Tizu said you seemed upset when you left the meeting. At first I thought maybe you'd gone back to the main camp with Phillip-Yoey, but when I found him he told me you went to the Tragar Pool to check on the injured women for him." She lifted one shoulder in a shrug. "So here I am."

"Mm, I see." Was everybody conspiring against him? "And the Khutani just let you come in and join me?"

"Pretty much," she said, then admitted, "When I stepped onto the walkway, that nice Maker Tinguss called to me and told me to come in and join you. We had a nice chat."

Nathan snorted a laugh. "I bet." In his mind he heard the echoes of Maker Qwaltamis's laughter and advice. *Give in gracefully, Chosen. She may not be the love that tugs at your heart, but she is a worthy mate—and this is Timorna after all.*

Detecting a note of bitterness in his voice, Marti's smile vanished and she became deathly serious. After a long moment she began in a low hesitant voice. "Nathan, you and I have both sworn the bond of the Ca'Companachda to others. I will always have special feelings and love for Carol just as you will for Dunnagh. I know I'm not your first choice; I get that and understand. I'm not asking you to give that up, but along with our other loves and obligations it doesn't mean we can't share something too. I do care for you."

She held out a hand to him palm down inviting the intimacy of the link. "Can't you—uh—taste what I'm saying is true?"

<<I don't need to taste her right now, Kasha,>> Corha said. <<She does care for us.>>

Nathan-Corha took her hand, but didn't form the link. Instead he kissed it. "I know you do. I don't have to form the link. We've already tasted that." He sighed. With Maker Tinguss's words about honesty and courage also echoing in his mind, Nathan took a deep breath and continued. "It isn't you, Marti, it's me. I'm, uh—afraid, I guess. I've lost so many I've cared about—it's hard to let go and love again." *Especially with the Ghostland threat and Drucas's mark coming between us*, he thought privately.

Being strong in the Psy herself, she must have picked up on some of his hesitation, because she pointed to her face. "Does this trouble you?"

"A little," he admitted. "But Maker Qwaltamis assures me the Khutani guard your dreams—and Chelka's, too. No...Oh, I don't know, maybe I'm scared if I love you I'll lose you, too—like Dunn—" he broke off swallowing hard. Gods of Timorna and Caldon what had that big worm done to him! <<Sorry, Shalla, I can't seem to stop falling apart—>>

<<It's all right, Kasha. You aren't falling apart—not really. And Maker Tinguss didn't do anything to you—except give you its permission to acknowledge your feelings. I love you, too, Kasha.>>

The image coming into Nathan's mind from Corha, of a human frantically trying to pick up and reattach falling body parts made him laugh.

Marti pulled back and stared at him. "What?"

Stifling another outburst he hugged her close allowing her glorious breasts to rub against him. "Sorry, Corha caught my thought about feeling like I was falling apart. The little worm sent me an image of a human trying to reattach body parts."

Marti chuckled and hugged him. "That is sort of funny."

"Yeah." It was, but he was tired of talking and self-revelation. Leaning forward he put his mouth over hers for what she supposed was a kiss. As she relaxed against him he surprised her by filling her mouth with an oily substance that had a faint vanilla flavor. Marti choked but managed to swallow quite a bit before she pulled away to stare at him.

"What the fuck! you Amadan?"

Nathan grinned, showing lots of pointed white kashallan teeth. "You want to make love to a kashallan, eh? About time you find out what that truly means."

"What did you do to me?" she growled.

Still grinning, he said, "You'll find out soon enough."

Marti scowled and punched his arm—hard.

"Ow! Stop that! I only gave you some green kavay," he said as he pulled her into deeper water and darkness. "You will understand in a short while. Trust me; I think you'll like what's gonna happen next."

Embracing her, he lay back in the water as she wrapped her legs around his waist. Sensing the couple's growing excitement, they were soon joined by other members of his Khutani relatives, eager to share with them in the experience.

Marti gasped; in the next moment the world exploded into a riot of colors and intense bodily sensations. The couple whirled in the center of smooth sensual bodies, touching, tasting. A kashallan's love! Well, it was something new—and wonderful. Should she tell Carol? With a choked laugh, Marti submerged herself completely in the experience.

Chapter Thirteen

Nathan-Corha strode through the Tragar outer courtyard, checking on the packing for their trip north. Thank all the gods of Timorna and Caldon that the supplies from Riath had finally arrived. They had taken longer to come than expected, but they had needed the extra time, he supposed, to get the Teh'lach groups up and working. As Tizu and the Speir'dina predicted it had been—and still was, a process with many bumps along the path.

Over to his left Armachd Ross, pad in hand seemed to be puzzling over some sort of list. He kept glancing back and forth between his pad and a mound of freshly unloaded supplies. Just coming out of the main hall the smaller figure of Ima Ishka walked between K'San Tobrach and Sa Chelka. Deep in conversation they seemed engrossed in whatever matter was under discussion.

Making Ishka his steward in Tobrach's absence had been a clever move on somebody's part. When Timma and Kashallan-Phillip learned Niguiri was pregnant, her male relatives—with Khutani backing—threw up a united front against her going with Timma as his apprentice.

"*A war camp is no place for a breeding woman*," was the Maker's final word on the matter. She was staying at Tragar. That, of course left Ishka with a dilemma. She wanted to go with her husbands, but also knew her daughter would need her love and support during this time, as well.

While she was still uncertain, Tobrach approached her with his proposition. "Ima, I need someone to remain here as my steward. I can't deny my experienced hunters the coming war with the Hated Enemy. They were bred for just such a purpose and it would be unforgiveable to leave them home.

"But there is still the care of the young Khutani left here, and the harvest to oversee, and the daily running of the keep to manage. I need someone trained and competent to take on that job."

She refused, pointing to the Sand Mountain glyph on her face. "Your offer is generous, K'San," she said. "But all your people and any southerner coming here with messages will see is an Umwira, over-stepping her place and trying to order them around."

"Not true, Ima, no one here thinks that. You are respected among my people in your own right. You are also educated, anyone talking to you can tell that, and as the wife of a kashallan no one will question your authority in my absence."

It took a bit more convincing from her husbands, but at last she relented and agreed to stay. When her appointment was announced at the evening meal, the Tragar folk accepted her with calm nods of approval. To Nathan's amusement, it didn't take long before everybody was now calling her K'Sa-Ima and taking her orders as easily as if she had always been a part of their lives.

Ishka laughed at something one of the Warlinga said, drawing Nathan's attention back to the packing in the courtyard. At the sound one of the newcomers who had come north with the supplies glanced round, staring at the three walking into the yard. Ross, too must have noticed the newcomers because he called out to Ishka, "Ima, if you aren't needed elsewhere for a while, I could use your help."

Ishka glanced at Tobrach, then said, "Of course, Armachd Ross. What seems to be the problem?"

Ross held up the tablet he'd been looking at. "I'm having trouble with these Avairei glyphs. I'm still learning, and either the hand writing is terrible or I'm just not familiar with the signs. Could you help me? Ata Thon is down at the pool right now and I didn't want to disturb him."

Tobrach said something to her and he and Chelka moved on to the practice field outside the gate where some of the younger hunters and clan warriors were practicing.

Nathan smiled as he heard Hunt Leader Tizu shouting a command for some "shit for brains amadan, to smarten up!" He supposed he should go out there and give the Hunt Leader a hand...

He was just about to do that when a disturbance caught his attention and he turned back to the activity in the courtyard. Over where he'd seen Ross and Ishka huddling over Ross's list one of the newcomers was gesticulating wildly and protesting whatever Ishka said to him.

<<I think our Amsi's mate is having trouble with that one,>> Corha said. <<Maybe we should go help her.>>

<<Yeah, Shalla, the practice bouts can wait.>>

Nathan-Corha walked slowly in Ishka's direction, his eyes focused on the newcomer. He was a tall Avairei with dark fur, his embroidered kilt and elaborate neck ornaments similar to that worn by the dandies Nathan had seen hanging around Riath after the take-over. He was a bit worse for the hard trip over the Jeban Pass his fur dusty and his mane needing a re-braid, but Nathan detected even from a distance that haughty air of superiority that many Avairei assumed when addressing peoples they thought inferior to their lofty status.

Ooh, how he hated that kind of attitude whether it was a Dymarian, an Umwira or the Avairei priests doing it. He'd been called a "Caldoni savage" far too often in his old life to put up with it now. As he came over he heard the man say, "Merba, Sister, please, you don't have to be afraid any longer. I'm sure the noble Warlinga in this keep will protect you from the foul savages. I can take you home now. I'm sorry your mother isn't here to welcome you, too, but Ima Urinia—we'd almost given up hope—"

Ishka broke in on his babble. "You are mistaken, Ata. My name is Ishka of Sand Mountain—"

"Merba, please, your terrible ordeal is finished; it's over now, you're safe. Don't be afraid to use your real name—"

"Ishka is my real name; I have no other. Please leave me alone!"

Ima Urinia? Oh shit! "Trouble, K'Sa-Ima?" Hardening his voice, Nathan gave the puffed up little shit a steely glare and said, "The lady said she doesn't know you." *And I wouldn't want to acknowledge you either, asshole.* "Move along, Ata, you're bothering the good Ima."

Straightening up to his full height the man glared at Nathan. The haughty stare might have been more effective if the Avairei wasn't nearly a foot shorter and at least 80 pounds thinner than the muscled warrior facing him. As it was, the impression fell a little flat, which the Ata tried to make up for with bluster. "I'm Crowis Nalev, son to Ima Matri Urinia of Shaden Keep, so be careful how you talk to me, Warlinga."

To his side he heard Ishka trying to stifle a hysterical laugh. Nathan folded his arms across his chest and glared right back. "Oh really?" Turning to Ross, he said, "I bet he made some over-worked Loti carry him in a litter over the Jeban Pass. Poor Urinia. Do you think we ought to send her a sympathy card?"

Ross laughed. "Maybe, but I think she just wanted to get rid of him for a while. I heard he wants to volunteer for the medic corps. Guess our boy Timma will smarten him up real quick if that's the way of it."

"How dare you speak to me like this!" Crowis blustered. "And not another mention of my mother's name out of your foul mouth, Warlinga!"

Ishka gasped. "Crowis, you fool!"

Crowis glanced her way then dismissed her warning out of hand. "I'm not a fool, Sister, these Speir'dina Warlinga just need to learn their place."

Ross glanced at Nathan a smile playing across his lips. "You want to turn the little brat over your knee for a good spanking or shall I do the honors?"

Nathan grinned showing white kashallan teeth. "You can do it." He held up a hand and extended his tentacles. "Don't want to damage these."

Ross smirked. "You could use a paddle instead of your oh-so-delicate pinkies. That's what me Da always favored." He glanced around the courtyard as if truly looking for a paddle. "I'm sure I could find something—how about a war canoe oar? That would do nicely, I bet. Want me to find Tesulu for you?"

Nathan laughed, but there was little mirth in the sound. "Better not. I hear he's looking for a new slave to cook for him and set up camp."

"Slave, eh? That would be another way this asshole could get some smarts, so keep all your options open, me lad."

Nathan chuckled, then seeing Ishka's horrified face out of the corner of his eye, he sobered. By this time Crowis had realized his mistake and had fallen to his knees, blubbering an apology. Nathan let him grovel for a time then said, "One of the first things you need to learn if you want to stay alive in this camp is, lose your Avairei arrogance, and don't make assumptions—about anyone. Until you prove your worth to me, the warriors, the women and even the Begta in this camp you're no better than a piece of dung in the privy hole—got that?

"Respect is earned, not granted by your family name. And as it happens Ross and I know your mother quite well. I made my bonding in the pools below Shaden, so don't you dare tell me—or anyone here who they can and can't mention."

Favoring Ishka with a ghost of a smile, he continued, "And this honored Sand Mountain woman is well favored among us—understand? She is wife to my kashallan kinsmen and related to the fierce war leader Tesulu of the Sand Mountain Clan of the People.

"If she says she doesn't know you—or wants to know you—then you will obey her wishes, respect her privacy and keep your mouth shut! Do I make myself perfectly clear, Ata?"

"Y-yes, Holy One, very clear."

Nathan motioned for Crowis to resume his feet. "Get up, you don't need to grovel." Turning to the dazed Ishka, he offered her his arm. "Ima, care to accompany me down into the main camp?" Ishka nodded and allowed him to lead her away.

"Hey," Ross called after them and tapped his pad with his free hand. "I still need this list deciphered."

Ishka stopped and would have gone back, but Nathan firmed up his hold and kept walking. "You got someone who can help you right there, Ross. I bet the stupid prick beside you can read. Get him to earn his keep for a change."

Crowis watched his sister and the kashallan walk out the front gate talking to one another. This was turning out to be a most disturbing experience. He'd come with the baggage supply on a dare from his friends, and to impress his intended, but the adventure wasn't turning out as he'd thought. And right in the middle of it all was his sister—oh Mother Timorna what was he going to do about that? He sighed. "Yes, I can read. What do you need, Warlinga?"

AS THEY WALKED DOWN the trail to the main encampment, Nathan could feel Ishka trembling, silent oily tears falling unheeded down her face. Out of sight of the fortress and the lower camp, Nathan guided her to a large flat boulder and sat, pulling her down beside him. He still held her hand, but didn't form the link.

After some time she took a shuddering breath and said without looking at him, "I guess my fate has caught up with me at last. I was hoping to avoid this—at least until after—when my husbands could stand beside me." Tears choking her voice, she continued, "But just like before when I was captured, I must face this ordeal alone."

Gently forming the link he put his free arm around her shoulder. "No, Ima, it's not like before, not at all. You are loved and respected by your husbands and many people, Warlinga, Speir'dina, me and the Khutani, to name some of your admirers. You're the wife of a kashallan and a fierce Speir'dina armachd now, and nobody—nobody is going to mess with you. We will make sure of that."

Ishka sniffed and wiped a hand across her face. "But what if they come for me while everyone is—away?"

"That's probably not going to happen, trust me. Between the Changelings scattered around the Yeyen inciting rebellion, and Speir'dina arriving to shake up the world order, things aren't like you remember—or fear. The Yeyen has its own troubles right now. Urinia and Ngeal Maveth, who is the new High Matri, by the way, have their hands full.

"And if your brother doesn't keep his mouth shut, or someone else recognizes you," he shrugged. "So what? As K'Sa-Ima Ishka, you will be in charge. Tell them to 'fuck off,' or put them in Tobrach's dungeons until we get back—your choice."

By the time he finished she was chuckling. "Though I don't know what the Speir'dina expression 'fuck off' means in your host's language, Kashallan-Nathan, it certainly has a satisfying sound upon the tongue. Even the clan warriors are now using it."

Nathan laughed and got to his feet. "Yeah, I guess we're a bad influence on everybody. Come on let's go find your family. Maybe you could make me a cup of that sourwood tea Phillip-Yoey is always raving about."

Chapter Fourteen

Crowis paused just inside the doorway of the main hall glancing around for a friendly face. The smells of frying mushrooms and masa cakes wafting out the open door all afternoon had been making his empty stomach rumble for sun-marks. But that awful Speir'dina Warlinga, Armachd Ross had kept him working at sorting and noting supplies till evening shadows made the light in the courtyard too difficult to see.

He wasn't sure how the news had gotten around about his trouble with his sister and a kashallan—probably the Begta he'd seen running about—but however it happened, he'd been getting angry looks and muttered comments about what they'd like to do to pampered brats if only the kashallans would let them.

And even just now when he would have like to retreat to a nice comfortable room in the inner keep he'd been told they were full. He was handed a raggedy blanket and told to find a place outside in the courtyard. In the courtyard—where only the Loti servant pens were! How could this be happening to him—him?

At last spotting a few Avairei Atas sitting at the end of a long table, he collected a plate and a mug of beer and wove his way through the boasting and laughing warriors towards them. Finally arriving intact, Crowis hesitated, suddenly unsure of his welcome even here. "Good evening, may I join you, Atas?"

The group consisted of a few middle-aged priests, an elder, and several young novices, talking and joking among themselves. All looked up at his request. There was a pause, then a grey-muzzled man in a ragged kilt, even more travel-worn than his own, motioned for him to take a seat across from him. "Evening, Ata. I'm Ata Doyan. Did you come north with the supplies this morning?"

Was it possible they hadn't heard about his disgrace? Maybe—or maybe the man was just being polite. "Yes, I came in today. I had hoped to volunteer with the hunters going North as a healer."

"Why, that's very admirable of you, Ata. I'm sure our Timma can use all the help he can get. Ata Fanon and I can tell you, Medics—as the Speir'dina call them—are a wonderful asset to the hunting packs. I've only been in one real battle, but I can testify from personal experience that we've saved many lives that would have been lost otherwise."

Real battle. Crowis took a big gulp of his beer. It tasted good. A bit stronger than he was used to, but so what, he'd had a bad day. He took another drink. "So you are a healer then?"

Doyan chuckled. "No, not really. Before I started my travels I knew little more than the basics any Avairei learns. No, my studies were mostly in our history and lore."

Crowis brightened. "That's my own field, Ata. Before coming here I was taking classes with Ata Pel the Lore Keeper at Riath. But if your studies are in our ancient lore, what are you doing at Tragar, Ata?"

"Right now I'm compiling an account of my journey across the Shallow Sea."

Crowis choked on the mouthful he'd just tried to swallow. The Ata next to him patted his back till he stopped coughing. "Go easy on that beer. The Warlinga here make it far stronger than what you're probably used to," he advised.

"Ata, do you mean that you went with a hunting pack to attack the Umwira across the Shallow Sea?"

"No, you misunderstand me. I was with the Western Clans when we were attacked by the Ghostlanders."

"So like my sister you were captured and made a slave. That must have been terrible for you. Who rescued you?"

A puzzled frown crossed the Ata's features as he said, "Slave? I wasn't a slave. And no one needed to rescue me I came back in a war canoe like everybody else." Taking note of Crowis's horrified face, Doyan set down his eating sticks and stared.

"Young man, don't you know we have an alliance with the Western Clans? I was with the delegation charged with making the alliance. Haven't you looked around this fortress today? There are Warlinga, Speir'dina and Clan Warriors training together right outside this hall. What, by the Blessed Goddess have you been doing all day?"

Reading supply lists, he thought glumly and gulped down more beer.

"Not paying as much attention as he should be, Ata,' came a voice from behind his back. "Ross kind of warned us he has shit for brains."

Crowis stiffened, but refused to acknowledge the insult. The cool voice mocking him mangled some of the sounds of his language as the Speir'dina did, so he already knew without looking one of his tormenters from the afternoon must have found him.

Doyan and the others at the table smiled and moved over so three newcomers could join them. To his dismay two of the black-clad men took places on either side of him. The other, wearing clan markings and an Umwira topknot took a seat across the table from him next to Ata Doyan.

"Ah Timma, there you are," Doyan beamed. "This young man just arrived today. He says he wants to volunteer for your medic corps."

To his surprise the man on his left wasn't Speir'dina as he'd assumed by the black clothing and long four-ply braided mane. No, he was an Avairei—but not like any priest Crowis had ever seen before. Another break in tradition. Did his mother and the High Matri know about this?

"What do you think, Son-in-law? Can you make something out of him?" the one with the topknot said.

The one called Timma shrugged. "Couldn't be any worse than dealing with the cousins, I suppose."

The Speir'dina on his other side snorted a laugh. "Oh yes, it could. He's older, more set in his ways, soft, and probably stupid."

That stung. "I am not stupid," Crowis protested. He was tired of people putting him down and talking about him like—like he was a Begta slave. He was Ima Matri Urinia's son. "I can read and have read all the old classics."

Ignoring his outburst, Timma said, "It might be a nice reward for the cousins to have someone else to boss around. I could put them in charge of his discipline."

Taking a sip of his own beer, the topknotted one snorted a laugh. "Oh, they would love that. You'd have to be careful that the cousins don't fall back into bad habits, though. You know how the Clans feel about the Avairei."

The one called Timma nodded. "Thank you for reminding me, Father-in-law. I'll watch them."

"I still like the idea of trading him to somebody for their slave. I need a good crossbow. Do you think he can cook?"

"Slave? Who has a slave to trade?"

Crowis slumped down on the bench, wishing he could suddenly become invisible. All this crazy talk had caught the attention of a passing warrior with a full plate. Sharp eyes above a pronounced muzzle studied him thoughtfully.

"Too soft, he doesn't look like much—but if he can cook, who would I speak to for the trading?"

The topknotted one chuckled again. "I guess that would have to be us, Noi. This one says he's related," Noi's eyes widened in surprise, "By marriage. He claims to be our Ishka's long lost brother."

"Lost, eh? Should have stayed lost." Noi moved away "Let me know when you're serious, Khutani." he said in the Western Dialect.

"Know anybody with a good crossbow?" Chang called after him.

Khutani? That was the only word Crowis understood in that last exchange. Was the one wearing Umwira glyphs another of these new kashallans? Oh Mother, were they serious about sending him into some sort of slavery among the western clans?

Looking him in the eye, the one with Umwira clan brands said, "You done with your meal?"

"Y-yes, K-kashallan."

Confused by the interchange, Ata Doyan said slowly, "I think I'm missing something here, Holy One, what's going on?"

The kashallan patted the priest's shoulder. "You are, Ata. We'll tell you later. Right now—" He stood up. Addressing Crowis, he said, "Yes, in spite of the clan brands I am a kashallan. Finally figured that out, did you. Maybe there's hope for you yet." Turning to Ata Doyan and the others at the table, who were trying not to stare, he bowed. "If you will excuse us, Atas. We have some family business to take care of."

As the kashallan was speaking, the two on either side of Crowis stood, pulling him up between them. With a vice-like grip on each arm they marched him out of the hall in the kashallan's wake.

ONCE OUT IN THE DARKNESS Phillip paused. Where to take the brat so they could have their "little talk?"

<<We could go to the pool,>> Yoey suggested. <<I don't think anyone but our Amla and Corha's pod are down there at the moment.>>

<<Mm, that's possible, but I'd rather save Khutani involvement as the big threat if we need it later.>>

"What are you thinking, Brother?" Chang asked.

"Yoey and I were just discussing where to have our chat. Yoey suggested going to the pool."

Chang snorted. "Gonna drown the little shit if things go sidewise, eh Yoey?"

"Hah, I hadn't thought of that, but it's an idea."

"Seriously, you two," Phillip said. "Mother Efosa might still be down there. And if she is, Ishka will be along to fetch her for the evening meal. I don't want to explain to her what we are doing if we get interrupted."

"Good point." Chang thought about it for a moment, then said, "I know several quiet dark places near the main camp that will do,"

"Please, let me go," Crowis pleaded. "I won't say a word about my sister being here—I'll just go back with the Loti—and keep my mouth shut like the other kashallan wanted—please."

Phillip-Yoey turned to face him. "Thing is, the Loti aren't going back. They are staying here to help with the Tragar harvest. So unless you think you can make it back all on your own, you are out of luck."

"And we aren't letting you stay at Tragar and bother my mother-in-law and my wife while she's breeding, either," Timma added.

Chang laughed and started down the trail. "No, it's the war path for you, me lad. As your sister's husbands and her new son-in-law, we are gonna see you cause no more trouble. Now it's up to you if you go north as one of Timma's medics, or a slave to one of our Sand Mountain relatives."

Chapter Fifteen

When they got back to their fire with a subdued Crowis in tow, only the cousins and a couple Sand Mountain youth about the same age or slightly older were there, playing a bone game.

Chang pushed Crowis down on the other side of the fire from the youths. "Sit and keep your mouth shut!" he warned.

Kashallan-Phillip crouched down nearby and reached for a sooty clay pot warming at the side of the fire. "What are you young warriors doing?" he asked as he poured himself some sourwood tea.

"Testing our war magic skills, Elder Cousin," Nytaka said. "Athala there," he pointed with his lips to the taller of the youths with a burn on one cheek, "He said we couldn't find the bone between him and Cho because being Twisted Grass Begta our magics weren't strong enough."

Pouring his own tea into the cup Phillip handed him, Chang looked up. "And was Athala right?"

"No, he was not," Qwayku said. "We saw through his illusions and picked the bone every time."

"Not every time," Cho said and then laughed. "But you did well—for little Begta."

Qwayku punched his arm and told him to "fuck off."

Chang's lips curved into a faint smile, quickly hidden behind the rim of his cup. Changing the subject before the boys argument could get serious, he asked, "Where are the women? It's getting late."

"They went looking for you," Nytaka supplied. "And to get Aunty."

Timma was back on his feet in a heartbeat and looming over the startled pair. "And you let them go up to the keep—alone—in the growing dark, while you sit here playing games like lazy Begta!"

The cousins shook their heads vigorously. "No, Sensei Timma, War Leader Tesulu and Juba were going up to the keep anyway so the women went with them. The War Leader told us to wait here—for you—and then Athala and his cousin came by and—"

"New fathers to be—all the same," Chang said to Philip.

Kashallan-Phillip grimaced. "I haven't had the pleasure, so have to take your word on that, Brother." Turning to the angry Timma, he added, "Calm down, Timma, and sit. I'm sure Niguiri is fine, and," Phillip motioned with a jerk of his chin to the slumped figure of Crowis sitting at Chang's side with a bowed head staring at the ground in front of him.

Noticing him for the first time the cousins stared. "Who is that?" they chimed almost in unison.

"That is your new student," Timma said, resuming his seat and picking up his tea.

"Our what?" Nytaka said.

"Student?" Qwayku echoed.

"Yes, you heard me, student. Starting tomorrow morning you will begin instructing him in the Warrior's Disciplines that Sensei Chang and I have been teaching you."

The four young warriors stared open-mouthed at the huddled figure of the bedraggled southerner. And Chang could just about hear the gleeful thoughts forming in their heads. "And before any of you get some bright idea about making him your slave, think again. He maybe a soft southerner right now, but he is also kin to us. He came here to volunteer for Timma's medics, so it will be up to you to toughen him up and teach him what he needs to survive as we go north into the Ghostlands. And that's all, understand me?"

"Yes, Sensei," they chorused.

"But can we beat him like a slave, if he is lazy or won't follow orders?" Qwayku asked.

"You can *discipline* him—within reason," Phillip said.

"Yes, Elder Cousin. But who is he?" Nytaka said, studying the newcomer more closely, "and what's his name?"

"He's our lost and newly found Brother-in-law," Chang said. "And as for his name..." Chang thought about it for a moment, then said with a twinkle in his eye. "You can call him, 'the Brat' for now."

At that Crowis's head shot up his eyes flashing with anger. "My name isn't Brat—whatever that means in your barbaric language. I'm Crowis Nalev, and my mother is Ima Urinia—"

Without even looking at him, Chang's hand shot out and cuffed him hard enough to send him sprawling. The young Clan warriors laughed. "As I said," Chang said without raising his voice or looking at Crowis. "This one's name, for the moment, is Brat. When he has earned it we will consider using another."

"What's going on here?" a woman's voice said from the darkness. In the next moment Ishka, Niguiri, Efosa and Masonja with two Clan warriors right behind them stepped into the firelight. When she saw Crowis sitting between Chang and Timma she froze, Tesulu nearly bumping into her.

"What's *he* doing here?"

Phillip-Yoey patted the ground beside him. "Come sit down, My dear." Then turning to their other guests, he bowed. "Juba, Kinsman, thank you for escorting our women while we took care of some other business."

Tesulu's black lips curled showing an impressive view of his canines. "This the new slave I hear you got?" He came a little closer to examine Crowis more closely. "Doesn't look like much. Can he cook?"

Though trembling Crowis mustered his courage and glared right back at the big brute. "No, I can't cook."

Once again Chang snaked out a callused hand and cuffed him. Crowis reeled back, but didn't fall this time. "I didn't give you permission to speak, Brat. You will remain respectful and silent when the adults are talking unless you are given permission to speak."

"Relative, eh, this Begta Puke?" Tesulu said, folding his muscular arms across his scarred chest.

Phillip-Yoey chuckled. "Get used to it, Tesulu. We had to. He came to volunteer for Timma's medics, so he'll be coming North with us."

"That supposed to make me feel better? Who's going to take care of him—wipe his backside for him and braid his pretty hair on the trip?"

"The cousins will be in charge of his discipline and training when he isn't helping Timma and me with the healing."

Tesulu's grin widened. "The cousins, eh?"

"I don't know if I would let him touch me," Juba said. "Does he even know what a jar of kavay looks like?"

"He knows the basics, all Avairei of his age and rank learn some measure of the healing arts," Phillip-Yoey said. "We can teach him the rest as we go."

Mustering his courage again, Crowis stared at Ishka with the tearful pleading look that had always been effective with her when he was a child. "Merba—Sister, please help me!" As her expression hardened, he realized his mistake in using her old name.

When she looked away and refused to answer Crowis cringed expecting another blow. The group around the fire fell silent, waiting her response. Ishka let the tension build for a long moment then finally stood. Without looking at anyone, she took a deep calming breath and said, "I want to talk with him."

"Would you like us to go so you can have some privacy, My dear?" Phillip-Yoey asked.

Ishka shook her head. Then spying the nearly empty water basket near the hearth, she poured the remainder into the tea pot and motioned for Crowis to get up and follow her. "It's late, and there's no need to disturb everyone. We will go to the spring and get water for the morning."

"If that's what you prefer, then so be it." When Crowis hesitated, Phillip motioned for him to go.

Chang put up a hand to stop him. "You will carry the water for her, Brat. Do I make myself clear?"

"I will carry the water," Crowis agreed and followed his sister back into the night.

When they were gone Chang turned to the boys still lounging by the fire. "Here is a better test of your war magics, young warriors. Follow them to make sure they are safe. Stay back to let them have their privacy, but don't let them, or anyone else, see you."

Grinning, the youths faded into the night as silent as hunting beasts.

CROWIS FOLLOWED ISHKA to the spring, suddenly shy and unsure what to expect. Uncomfortable with her silence he finally blurted,

"Mer—Ishka please. Can't you help me? I can't go North—my studies—Ata Pel—"

Finished with the water, she set down the basket and rounded on him arms folded across her chest, her voice rough with emotion when she answered. "Why did you come here then, Crowis? You're destroying my life—spoiling everything!"

Crowis sighed, feeling suddenly ashamed, and maybe as stupid as everyone had been telling him he was all day. "For all the wrong reasons," he admitted. "You probably don't remember my friend Adnim, but he and a few of my other friends dared me to go with the supplies heading North.

"I was just going as far as Tragar Keep, then heading back with the Loti and any messengers heading South. And," he added in a voice barely above a whisper, "I wanted to kind of impress my intended, Grasina Caltia. Mother thinks marrying into the family with ties to the first kashallan would be advantageous for us."

Ishka choked on hysterical laughter, "So, Little Brother, for the sake of a stupid dare and to impress a girl you've changed the course of your entire life. Oh, truly the Unseen Ones guide our lives down unknown paths."

"Unseen Ones? Ishka, please won't you help me? I have to go back—my studies—my marriage!"

Ishka cut him off with a negative hand gesture. "No, Brother, I can't help you."

"Can't or won't." Crowis grumbled, his voice taking on a petulant tone.

"Maybe both," she snapped, "and don't take that tone with me. Crowis, look at you—really look at what kind of man you've become. Arrogant, selfish, soft and pampered, you truly are what my Speir'dina mate names you, a Brat."

"I am not a brat—whatever that means," Crowis said sounding offended. Then, "What does the word mean anyway?"

"It's a word that refers to a spoiled child—and ever since you started this journey that's exactly how you've been behaving. Even bullying some poor Loti to carry your litter—a spoiled brat—"

"I'm not behaving like a spoiled child, Mer—Ishka, that's what they were meant to do, serve us—"

Ishka cut him off using one of the armachda's favorite curses. "No, they aren't here to be Avairei servants and slaves—ask my kashallan mate if you don't believe me.

"And if even an aging man like Ata Doyan can cross the Shallow Sea, walk from the Blue Stone Coast to Red Rock and then back to the coast without complaint, you can, as a much younger man, walk North to help our warriors who are sacrificing perhaps even their very lives to protect your sorry ass."

Cursing and hard, using language no Ima in the Yeyen would dream of repeating, this wasn't the sister he had grown up admiring—in memory at least. No, perhaps she was right. the Merba he'd known as a child was dead, replaced by a much harder version, an Umwira willing to hand over her own blood kin into the hands of mad men and savages, and for what, the sake of keeping her secret? Unbelievable!

This woman before him was—alien—unpredictable. "You're going to let them abuse me and take me north—where I might die, I might add—just to keep your secret?"

"Yes, I am. The question needing to be answered is whether you are strong enough and clever enough to survive your coming ordeal. And if you aren't," she shrugged, "then you will surely die."

At his horrified look she laughed, but there was no mirth in the sound. Her voice became as hard as stone when she continued, "What you will face with a kashallan and your new kin protecting you will be nothing—do you hear me—nothing, compared to what I endured when I was taken. I have no sympathy for your whining, Begta Puke. You are no relation to me—unless you *earn* the right to call me sister."

Stunned and overwhelmed, Crowis fell silent, unable to believe what was happening to him.

When it was clear he had no more to say, Ishka pointed to the full basket. "Pick it up; you were told to carry it for me."

Crowis picked up the basket, staggering a bit at its unexpected weight and started down the path after her. Before they reached the fire, he said, "Ishka, will you at least send a message back to Riath to let them know I am volunteering—sort of, with the hunting packs going North?"

"Already done," she snapped her voice still showing a trace of anger. "Kashallan-Nathan sent word with a runner earlier today."

"So there are people going South that I could go with," he said bitterly. "All of you have been conspiring against me. Were you ever going to tell our mother that you're still alive?"

Ishka stopped so abruptly he almost ran into her. "No one is conspiring against you, Foolish Brat. No one is going south at the moment. The Speir'dina have a system of polished mirrors that they use to communicate in their language over a distance, with a code made up of long and short flashes."

She began walking again, motioning for him to follow. After a while she said in a calm, emotionless voice, "And to answer your other question, I do plan to let Mother know that I'm alive. But I want to do it in my own way an in my own time. I refuse to be mocked, ridiculed, or pitied by the soft, ignorant people of the Khutani's southern lands. I will take my daughter, my unborn grandchild and my husbands and go back to our Sand Mountain kin across the Shallow Sea before I let that happen."

"Husbands," he grumbled. "So like that other kashallan with his three wives you have succumbed to the Speir'dina's perversions about mating. Are you even young enough, or able to breed, with one of them?"

Not expecting her quick response Crowis nearly dropped the heavy basket when she hauled off with claws slightly extended, and punched him on the jaw.

"Mind your tongue, Begta Puke! I am of the Sand Mountain Clan of the Real People and you will speak to me with respect, sniveling Brat."

In the night around them Crowis became aware of a rustling movement and realized for the first time that they weren't alone. He stepped back shuddering. No, of course they hadn't been alone in the dark. Someone—or someones had been sent to follow them.

"Keep out of this," Ishka snapped staring into the gloom. "I know one of my husbands sent you boys to guard my safety, but I will handle this—myself."

Boys? Did she mean those horrible Umwira cousins who would be in charge of bossing him around from now on? Shivering at what kind of reprisal might be in store for him if they told her husbands what his stupid tongue had said, he hastily apologized. "Sister, I'm sorry—I didn't mean—I"

"Shut up and keep moving, Begta Puke!"

As they were nearing the fire Crowis got up the courage to ask one more question. "Do you know what you will do after this—is over?"

She sighed. "No, not exactly. A lot will depend on what happens in the Ghostlands. K'San Tobrach has offered us a home here if we wish to stay. But Phillip-Yoey will need to spend part of his time with the Begta who live in the Great Swamp; that was where the host and symbiont were bound.

"So, we will probably go to Ha'limra. Most of our Speir'dina kin are settling there and my husbands tell me that there are Blue Stone and maybe some Twisted Grass people living there already."

"Umwira living in our territory? Surely you are joking, Sister!"

Ishka chuckled. "Oh, Crowis, you are so out of touch with how our world is changing. When the Makers called the Speir'dina to Timorna we got far more than just the new kashallans. Maker Tinguss invited the western clans to settle in the lands over which it has dominion if they would join the alliance and stop raiding."

BACK AT THE FIRE ONLY Ishka's husbands were still up and waiting for them. Several blanketed lumps clustered nearby quiet snoring issuing from the depths of one or two. As Crowis sat down the basket and rubbed his aching hand and arm, Phillip-Yoey motioned him to come sit by him on a folded Avairei-fur blanket. "It gets cold here at night and even colder as we travel north so mind how you care for that. You won't get another."

As he sat down, he saw the one called Chang leading his sister back into the darkness. As they drifted away he heard Chang say, "You look exhausted—and maybe a bit frustrated, too, Mo Gra. I've already fixed up a nest for us. You'll feel better after a good sleep."

The kashallan noticed a trickle of blood on Crowis's jaw, and a smile played at the corner of his lips. He studied him for a long time then asked, "How did your talk with your sister go?"

Crowis sighed. "Not as I'd hoped, but I'm sure you already know that."

Phillip chuckled. "I suspected as much. Now give me your hands."

Startled Crowis blinked. "M-my hands?" When the kashallan impatiently motioned again, Crowis held out his hands—palms up. Sighing Phillip-Yoey took his hands, turned them over and formed a link. Crowis flinched then relaxed.

"Surely you've felt a kashallan's touch before, so don't be afraid."

"Yes-s. the one called Dunnagh-Tani tested me for the taint." He stared at the kashallan's hands for a while his tentacles buried in his flesh. "What are you doing to me, Holy One?"

"To make it easier for you heading North, I'm giving you the language patterns for the Western Clans' language." He chuckled again. "Then at least you can understand when your new teachers and the warriors are swearing at you and calling you uncomplimentary names."

Crowis grimaced. "I'm not sure if that will be a blessing or a curse."

Phillip-Yoey grinned. "Maybe a little of both," he admitted.

"That's what I'm afraid of."

"Cheer up, Young Ata, things won't be that bad. And as my and Sensei Timma's student you are going to gain a wealth of new knowledge to rival any of the keep-bound Atas cloistered in the Yeyen three times your age."

Crowis snorted a mirthless laugh. "Provided I live long enough to return to the Yeyen, that is."

"Yes, there is always that—for any of us," the kashallan agreed. "But your survival will be, for the most part, in your own hands. If you are clever, and able to leave behind your old prejudices and accept the opportunity offered you to grow and learn a new way of being, you will do well."

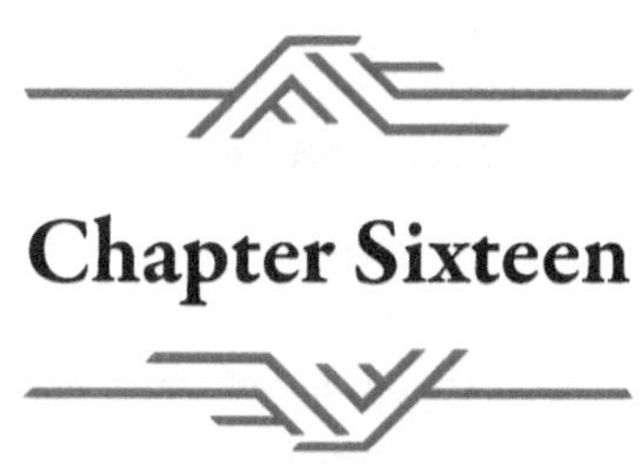

Chapter Sixteen

As Crowis feared and expected, the next day was one of the worst in his life. He'd been awakened at first light by one of the cousins giving him a rough kick in the side. "Get up, Lazy Begta."

Shivering in the morning chill, he was made to run with a band of the young warriors, back and forth to the keep twice. Keeping pace with him easily, the cousins whacked his buttocks with kavalpa switches every time he slowed.

Back in camp and hoping to rest, they next made him do a series of stretches and combat exercises till he thought his arms were going to fall off. Finally allowed to return to the family fire he was granted a rest, but when he ordered the Begta woman there to serve him some breakfast, assuming she was the family's slave he got another surprise. She threw a bowl at him and told him to get his own.

When he started to reprimand her for her insolence, she punched him, knocking him to the ground. "Stupid Mans, Masonja say get own food!" And then, of course, the cousins were there with their switches, telling him to mind his manners and be respectful to a powerful Begta Witch.

Begta witch? He didn't even know the little vermin had any admirable qualities, let alone could use magic! *Probably just used whatever power they had to become better thieves*, he thought, but prudently kept that opinion to himself.

Catching the last of that conversation Chang snorted a laugh and said to his sister and the kashallan coming with him up to the hearth. "It's as Ross warned us, Brother, he's a bit stupid."

His sister scowled, and the kashallan chuckled. "Definitely a slow learner. I would have to agree with Ross on that point. But let's not give up on him yet."

"Don't favor him on my account, Husbands. He's no kin of mine, I assure you," Ishka snarled as she took a bowl and served herself some of the morning gruel.

"Nobody will be favoring anyone in the Ghostlands, My dear," Kashallan-Phillip said as he sat down beside her. As he reached for an empty bowl, Masonja took it and filled it for him. "Thank you, My dear, but I could have served myself."

She nodded. "Masonja know, but already up so no problem."

"Well, thank you all the same."

The kashallan smiled as the older Umwira woman sat down on his other side. "Good morning, Mother, did you sleep well?"

"Yes, Yoey, My Son, I did." She looked up as Masonja placed a warm bowl of gruel in her hands. "Thank you, Sister."

Sister? And why did she call the Khutani her son? That was impossible!"

Swallowing a bit of her meal, Mother Efosa said, "Yoey, my son, I need some more Thuulla grass to make baskets while you men are away. I already have some orders after that nice Warlinga, Sa Chelka, sent my little basket to her aunt."

"I'm glad to hear it, Mother! Along with playing with the young Khutani in Corha's pod, I'm sure you will be very busy while we are away."

Playing with Khutani? Did they now let the Umwira go to the pool below the keep? Surely not! Not even the Avairei 'played' with the young Khutani! What was the woman babbling about!

The woman's face sobered, a tear falling unnoticed from one eye. "Yes—away.... I will miss you, My Son."

The kashallan hugged her. "I will you, too, Mother Efosa. But don't be afraid. You will be fine while we are gone. Ishka and Niguiri will be here and needing your advice about the new baby. And the people here at Tragar honor and respect you, both as my mother and for your skill with the basket making. No one is going to bother you. No more changeling demons, I promise. Your nephew Corha, my Amla Maker Tinguss and I have tasted everyone. You will be safe."

She patted his hand. "Ah yes, that nice Maker Tinguss, we have had such wonderful talks when the babies are sleeping. But I'm not worried about myself but you, my son."

"As best I can, I will keep safe and come back to you and my family, so don't fret, my dear." Giving her another pat, he asked Timma and Chang, "What are your plans for your students today?"

Chang shrugged. "The boys can make some time to gather some Thuulla Grass for her before weapons practice, right, Students?"

"Yes, Sensei Chang," the cousins said in unison.

"Take the Brat and show him what needs doing, because he won't know what Thuulla even looks like, but I want him back to work with me when you go for weapons practice," Timma said. Chang raised an eyebrow, so Timma continued. "I need to test his medical knowledge—to see how much time Kashallan-Phillip or I will have to spend away from our other duties teaching him. You can have him back after that, Sensei."

"Fair enough." He focused his gaze once more on the young men. "Students, why are you still here?"

The Cousins rose, grabbing their weapons. One of them stood over a bewildered Crowis. "You done?"

"No, I—"

Without allowing him to finish, the little monster snatched his bowl out of his hand, and gulped down the last few mouthfuls. As he set the bowl down he grinned at the astonished Crowis, slapping the switch across his palm. "You are now. Get up and get moving. You have Thuulla to cut and gather for Aunty."

AND THE REST OF THE day went downhill from there, Crowis thought, as he took advantage of the Cousin's distraction when they stopped to watch a particularly gruesome practice match between Aju'an Meh'gach and a brute the Cousins called Tesulu. Body aching and desperate, Crowis evaded detection and crept into the keep, searching for a quiet corner where he could rest for a moment and have some peace. Moving down a deserted hall, he came across an unoccupied room and slipped inside.

The room seemed to be a priest's tiny study, not much different than he might have found at either Shaden or Riath. Bright tapestries decorated the walls and a narrow bed was tucked into a far corner. In its center stood a large wicker table littered with several scrolls, an unfinished piece of bleached leather open with ink, pens and bits of smaller scraps of stained writing sheets in piles nearby. An open window let in a faint breeze and plenty of light.

Fascinated and also feeling comforted by familiar things, Crowis crossed to the table and sat on the stool. Unable to help himself, he pulled the manuscript towards him and began reading. Engrossed in Ata Doyan's account of his travels among the Western Clans he forgot about time and the cousins who would be looking for him by now.

He was just to the part where they were traveling up the coast and the Ghostland wizards had sent an unnatural storm to drown them. They were racing for their lives and then the Begta woman and Niguiri stood up in the canoes to chant spells to break up the storm, when a noise from the doorway caused him to glance up.

"Ata Doyan!" Crowis hastily jumped to his feet, dropping the scroll. "I'm sorry if I overstep—I was just—this is fascinating reading."

The priest laughed softly and came the rest of the way into his room. "It's alright, Ata Crowis. The scroll is meant to be read," he grimaced, "though perhaps in a more polished form than it is at present."

"No, Ata, it is perfect as it is. I glanced at it only out of curiosity, but once I started reading, I couldn't stop. It's marvelous. The story reminds me of the adventures of Benowin the Brave that I loved as a child. I wish I could write like this." Crowis tapped the manuscript with a finger.

"Benowin the Brave?" Doyan chuckled. "Well, I'm flattered, young man, but my scribbling is hardly that. And if you like such tales, perhaps when you come back you will have your own adventures to write about. None of our people have traveled into the Ghostlands and returned to tell about it in hundreds of years, you know."

"That is a thought, Ata." Crowis smiled, then sobering, he added, "If I return, that is."

"Yes, there is that possibility to consider." Then brightening, he added, "Of course if I give you paper and pens to take notes, your writing may become famous even if you aren't there to enjoy the notoriety yourself."

Doyan looked down at the spread out scroll in front of him. "I'm not trying to be morbid or wish you bad luck. That's the way I look at it for myself. I'm trying to put down as much as I can of our journey across the

Shallow Sea—in case I don't survive our trip North." Doyan sighed. "Perhaps you will have to finish my work for me, eh?"

Crowis felt a shiver of prophesy run down his spine. Shaking his head, he laughed nervously. "No, Ata, I'm sure that's not the way of it. You are still young enough to have many fine stories to tell before you feed the young Khutani."

Becoming embarrassed, Doyan looked down at his manuscript, and then changing the subject he asked in a lighter tone of voice, "Well, I need to get back to work. What exactly are you doing in here? Were you sent to get something from me?"

Crowis sighed and brushed his dusty braidlets oft his shoulders. "No, I wasn't sent to you. I guess you might say I'm hiding—from my tormenters."

Doyan chuckled. "Ah yes, The cousins, a bit mischievous but good boys at heart."

Good boys at heart? Well that wasn't how he would have described them. And as if mentioning their names had conjured the little monsters, here they were, standing in the doorway switches in hand.

"Hello, Nytaka, Qwayku," Ata Doyan said. "Do you need something?"

"Hello, Elder. Yes, we do." Nytaka pointed with his lips to Crowis and Qwayku slapped his switch. "Him, we need him."

"Oh my, I guess he didn't have permission to come here."

"No, Ata, he did not. Come on, Brat, Since you don't like watching our brave warriors practice so you could learn a thing or two, then you can dig new privy holes with the Begta."

"The Begta—me?" Crowis turned pleading eyes on the priest. "Ata, please, can't you make me your apprentice or something, so I can stay with you?"

"I'm sorry, young man, I can't interfere with what the Holy Ones have ordered. But perhaps as we travel north you and I will have time to talk more. I would like that."

"No more whining, Spoiled Baby, let's go." one of the cousins interrupted, shoving Crowis roughly out into the hall.

As the youths moved out of sight, Doyan heard Crowis pleading with the cousins. "I'm sorry, Sensei Nytaka, I won't do it again. Do I really have to dig holes with the Begta?"

Whack! "I'm sensei Qwayku, Stupid Brat! That's Sensei Nytaka. And yes, you're going to dig privy holes—and if the Begta tell us you were lazy or run away again—" Whack!

"Ow, stop that! I'll be good. I won't run away—I promise."

A smile playing about his lips, Ata Doyan took his seat and picked up his pen. He had a lot to write to finish his account, before they left for the Ghostlands in a few days.

FROM THE DIM CORNER near his bed came a soft chuckle. "Two children stolen away by the Umwira, poor, poor Urinia. She may not like what Sand Mountain returns to her." She chuckled again, but there was no mirth in the sound. "When the pampered little brat left his comfortable apartment in Riath on a dare, he had no idea what fleeing the shelter of his mother's kilt would mean. Do you think he will survive Ghostland wizards, fierce allied warriors and kashallans?" she laughed again. "I wonder."

Glancing around, he saw Tess-weh sitting on his narrow bed. How long had she been there, he wondered? Doyan rose to his feet and bowed. "Honored Spirit, Tessa, how may I serve you?"

Still dressed in the loose clothing that concealed all but her enigmatic dark eyes, she glided over to him and gently pushed him back onto his stool. "You may serve me, My Jewel, by continuing with your work. There is no need for you to rush your account of your travels. You have plenty of time to finish your narrative."

"That's very kind of you, Honored Spirit, but there are only a few more days until we leave and I have so much to copy from my notes before then."

She brushed a hand across his cheek in a tender caress. And this time it was the Speir'dina woman Tessa who spoke to him. "No, Ata, you misunderstand. You will have plenty of time, because you aren't going. We release you from this part of our service.

"You will stay here at Tragar, finish your manuscript, and help those who will take up your burden and go North in your place."

Doyan felt his heart skip a beat, oily tears pooling in the corners of his eyes. Taking a deep breath he said, "But I have sworn to serve and care for you as your Cha'Han, Tessa. I don't understand how I have displeased you and your bondmate?"

She shook her head and patted his shoulder. "You've done nothing to displease us—never that. You have helped me so much since you honored me with your oath. I will be forever grateful for your kindness and the insights you shared with me when I was still a lost and frightened newcomer to your world.

"In keeping with the oath you have sworn as my Cha'Han I am merely giving you a different task to perform in my service, that's all. Write your manuscript; it will be in part my legacy as well as yours. It will be a document of great importance to the healing of this world, my bondmate has seen it."

"But—" he began, then she cut him off.

"Moraga and Atahru will be with us, so don't worry about my welfare, Ata." She caressed his cheek once more. And this time it was Tess-weh who spoke. "Good bye, My Treasure." Turning, she stepped to the entrance and disappeared.

Doyan sat at his writing table, tears flowing unheeded down his face. Good bye, she had said, good bye. Did that mean she wasn't going to survive this coming war?

He feared it might be so. Unable to write anymore that day he crossed to his bed and lay down turning his face to the wall.

Chapter Seventeen

The next few days were a blur of activity for Crowis and everyone else at Tragar. Timma and the Cousins kept him busy with endless tasks that left him exhausted by the end of the day, leaving him no energy or time to visit with Ata Doyan and just relax. Each night he ate a hasty meal, crawled into his blanket and fell into exhausted sleep, till one of the cousins kicked him awake for the dawn run and weapons training.

In spite of himself, he was fascinated by his studies with Kashallan-Phillip and Timma, however. For one about his own age or even a bit younger, Crowis was amazed at the wealth of knowledge Timma had at his green-daubed fingertips. He'd always preferred the study of history and lore over more practical pursuits like the healing arts. But Crowis was intelligent and curious, so he grasped what they were teaching him—in theory at least.

Not that there weren't patients for him to practice on. Minor training accidents happened in abundance to the warriors, and after some supervision most of those patients were left in his care. The warriors often cursed him for his clumsiness, but Timma or Medic Williams told them to, "shut up, suck it up, and stop acting like pampered Southerners," when he was too shy or intimidated to tell them himself.

Today he'd been lucky and obtained a respite from the Cousins' tyranny. Armachd Ross needed his help with supply lists again. Ross had begged Kashallan-Nathan and Sensei Chang to let him have Crowis for the day, and—wonder of wonders, they had agreed. They had even told him Ata Doyan wanted to see him, and he could have a short visit with the Ata if he finished and didn't complain. Yes, and they would definitely check with the Armachd about his work and behavior.

Complain. It was a word with an ominous meaning among the Clan Warriors, Speir'dina and Warlinga alike. Crowis was coming to realize that the more he complained—about work assignments, exercise—or anything—the more tasks he was given to do and the more "discipline" he would suffer for his acting like a spoiled, soft, Avairei brat.

Brat! Mother Timorna, how he was coming to hate the sound of that word. Brat! Everybody was calling him that—even the Begta around here. And when they shouted it out, it usually meant that he was needed to do more work somewhere—like help dig a privy hole—or haul garbage to the midden with the Loti—or patch up somebody's bleeding arm.

So when he was engrossed in deciphering some Riath clerk's appalling scrawl, he was startled to hear someone shouting his real name.

"Crowis Nalev, is it truly you?" a tall slim Speir'dina with golden skin and curly red hair laughed and bounced towards him across the busy courtyard. "Adnim told me I might find you skulking around here if I looked hard enough—and here you are!"

Crowis dropped the list on a packed crate and hurried to greet someone from the world outside his current nightmare. Taking the man's hand he smiled. "Jojo, what, by all the Gods, are you doing here?"

"Why, dear Ata, I am a man charged with a mission," he burbled. "I came in with the last of the supplies. I'm going north with the 'troops' as we Speir'dina might say." Bending forward to whisper near Crowis's ear, he confided, "I'm glad I got to see you before you head back; you can carry my first report back to Tomas for me. He is dying for stories to create new performances for the coming season, you see."

Crowis felt his elation of a moment ago fade. He sighed. "I'm not going back, Jojo. I'm going North with everybody else."

Jojo mimed a horrified look on his expressive face. "Oh, Dear Boy, does your Mother know about this—or Grasina?"

Crowis grimaced. "They will by now. I was told a message went South days ago."

"Mm, that's good, I suppose, but, dear Ata, you don't seem very happy about the decision. Another impulsive act on your part, eh? Were you drunk at the time? As Ima Urinia's son you could tell them you've changed your mind. One of the kashallans here can speak to the commanders on your behalf, surely."

A kashallan speak on his behalf—his mother's son? Trying to swallow the hysterical laughter threatening to turn him into a jabbering idiot right in the middle of the courtyard, Crowis shook his head. "That's not going to work—no, oh Jojo, not in this case."

Jojo seemed puzzled, "But why ever not? I've met some of them—even worked with Tasheyna before her bonding. They are very understanding people; you don't have to be afraid—why not ask for their help?"

"Because-because—" Crowis could go no further with his explanation before the hysterical laughter he'd been trying to swallow came vomiting out his mouth and he doubled over laughing and trying to breathe.

Finally noticing that his helper was no longer working, Ross stormed over cursing under his breath. Noticing the newcomer for the first time and the choking Ata, Ross folded his arms across his chest and growled, "What's the matter with you, Amadan?"

Crowis straightened, still chortling. Taking a deep breath, he tried to force the words out before the hysterics took over again. "He-he wants me to ask a kashallan to send me home, Armachd Ross. Isn't that too funny? He wants me to ask a kashallan—" Putting a hand over his mouth Crowis burst into laughter again.

Ross swore a colorful Caldoni oath that made Jojo's eyebrows rise. "All right calm down, Asshole, you can laugh all you want while you're finishing that inventory. Get back to work, Brat, before I call for the cousins. I see Tesulu over there, so I'm sure they're around here somewhere."

Shame now adding to his misery, Crowis nodded and went back to the discarded lists. Brat! Jojo was here and would probably tell everyone back in Riath about his new name. Maybe he'd just find a convenient cliff to jump off in the Ghostlands rather than go home.

WATCHING TO SEE THAT Crowis actually went back to the job assigned him, Ross next turned to the foppish Dymarian still staring after the retreating Ata. Ross scowled. This one looked like another of the same kind of good-for-nothing as the Brat. What idiot in the capital let him come with the baggage? "So, Dymarian, what are you doing here—in a war camp?"

Jojo turned, smiled and gave Ross a theatrical bow. "Jo Tepring at your service, Armachd—Ross isn't it?" He held out a hand. "Most people just call me Jojo."

Ross ignored the outstretched hand. "Mm, I repeat; what are you doing here at Tragar?"

Jojo grinned. "Why I'm Timorna's version of the media, dear Armachd. I've been assigned by the Imas to report on the progress of the war. So as your, man on the scene war correspondent, I'll be sending back stories for the populace whenever runners head south."

Ross rolled his eyes and swore in Caldoni, telling Jojo just where he could stick his reports. Jojo's eyes widened. "Really, Armachd Ross, that's impossible—anatomically speaking."

When Ross's mouth dropped open, Jojo laughed. "Being part Caldoni myself, and an actor by trade, I'm familiar with all the best Caldoni curses. And I must say Lann Gheal has an amazing vocabulary. I've learned so much since coming to Timorna."

Ross grimaced then nodded. "Gods of Timorna and Caldon, didn't you get your fill of war back on Dymar? You said you were here for two reasons. What's the other one?"

"I'm also here as your bard and entertainer. I'm officially in charge of keeping troop morale up. And," he added suddenly becoming serious. "In keeping with Dunnagh-Tani's warning about creating a place for Speir'dina on this world, Dr. B and Tasheyna-Rinn sent me to gather accounts that Tomas and the Kashallan Players can use to create shows for our future employment among the Avairei and Warlinga houses over the Sorin Confinements."

Yes, that was important and an admirable goal, Ross thought. Maybe he was being too hard on the little twit... "Have you cleared all this with the brass?"

Jojo nodded. "I actually arrived a few days ago. I spoke to hunt Leader Tizu and K'San Tobrach right off. I have a room in the keep and I've been working hard with the women, the Begta and others on creating an entertainment extravaganza for our last night in camp."

He paused as if thinking of something, then beamed. "Ah Armachd, you're the one I've been needing to speak to. I was told that you play the pibroch. Some of the armachda I've had the chance to talk to have suggested we perform a sword blessing dance, in keeping with ancient Caldoni traditions.

"Oh, it won't be the same as back on Caldon, mind, but Anilah and that cute little Sand Mountain girl have some great ideas of their own how to enhance the blessing and truly make it a Timornan thing. I hope you will join us, Armachd, we need you, please!"

"My pibroch, eh?" *Oh, Tizu is going to love you for that,* Ross thought, wondering which amadan in the corps put Jojo up to it. "Sure, you can count me in."

Chapter Eighteen

Everyone was excited about the coming entertainment that Jojo was planning for their last night. As he went about the chores assigned to him over the next few days, Crowis heard the speculations, but paid them little attention. He was too tired by the end of each day to care. And besides, the performance would mean that the day of their departure was at hand, and he wasn't looking forward to going any further north.

In spite of lots of coaxing, the performers were being very secretive about their plans, sneaking off at odd times to "practice," strange noises and drumming coming from a guarded hallway deep in the keep.

At last the final day had arrived. It was a bitter-sweet time Crowis supposed. People were excited by the feast and planned entertainment, but all were saddened, knowing that on the morrow most of the people assembled at Tragar would be leaving for the North, many never to return.

After the feast when everyone was gathering for the show in the flat area where the practice bouts had been held, Crowis approached Chang and Phillip-Yoey with a request. "May I be excused so I can go find Ata Doyan? I was told a few days ago that he wants to talk to me. I didn't see him here and I haven't had the time until now to—"

The two men looked at one another, then after a silent communication Chang nodded. "You can go look for him and have a visit. There's no more work for you today." Then as Crowis turned away he added, "I don't want to send the cousins hunting for you tomorrow morning, so whatever you plan to do tonight be present at the assembly point at first light with everyone else. Do I make myself perfectly clear, Student?"

"Perfectly clear, Sensei, I'll be there." He promised. And he would be, Sensei Chang and the kashallan didn't have to worry about that. No point trying to hide in the keep and then facing the wrath of his sister and the rest of his new relatives when discovered. There was no escape for him now. It wasn't worth the risk—and the pain. He just wanted a break—a quiet time and a chance to talk to someone sane for a while.

Slipping back into the keep past the busy servants, Crowis headed down the quiet hallway that lead to Ata Doyan's room. He'd seen the priest at another table briefly during the meal, then he'd left with a covered plate and hadn't returned.

Arriving at Doyan's door he knocked quietly on the door frame and entered. "Ata Doyan? My Sensei and kashallan-Phillip have finally given me permission to visit. So here I am; what did you want to see—"

Crowis broke off finally becoming aware that the good Ata wasn't present. A lamp was lit on his work table; his manuscript spread out as before, but no Ata. Crowis came fully into the room, looking around. It was cold in here, dark shadows lurking in the far corners, twisting a knot of unease in his gut.

Maybe Doyan just went to the privy, or maybe he'd missed him and the Ata had gone to see the show like everybody else. He shivered, uncertain what to do. Should he wait? Hopefully Ata Doyan would be back soon. Still nervous he spied a scrap of leather on the table, he crossed and picked up a pen. He'd just leave the priest a note and then go...

Then he froze at the sound of a mirthless chuckle from the darkness deeper in the room. "No need to write the priest a note, My Jewel. Ata Doyan will be coming back—in a while. But first..."

A Speir'dina woman shrouded from head to toe in lose dark clothing stepped into the light from the shadows by Doyan's bed. "I sent the priest away for a time so we can 'talk.'" Her eyes glittered with a malicious gleam as she studied him thoughtfully. "A man of impulse and questionable bravery, are you sorry for the predicament in which your smart mouth and a desire to rival ancient heroes has landed you, hmm?" she chortled. "Cheer up, young Ata, in the Ghostlands you may get your wish for fame and glory—but at a price."

Who was this veiled woman, Crowis thought angrily. And how dare she talk to him like this! Past lessons in mind, he prudently kept his mouth shut and just glared, hoping she would leave.

She continued to watch him, finally she said, "You're beginning to learn, My Jewel, and you will learn even more under my tutelage."

Tutelage? Oh, Mother Goddess, not another crazy Speir'dina here to order him around! "I'm sorry, Sa, but my time is already taken up with duties assigned to me by my family—"

She snorted, her eyes sparkling with a dark amusement. "Yes, your new relatives have been keeping you busy, but along with your obligations to warriors and Khutani I require your service, as well, my new Cha'Han."

Cha'Han? Crowis racked his brain for the meaning of that ancient word. When the meaning finally came to him he barely managed to stay on his feet. A Sweh'an Demon, here? Oh, Holy Mother, nobody had told him these Speir'dina had made a contract with a Sweh'an Demon and now it wanted him—him!

She chuckled again and moved closer, caressing his cheek. The touch sent icy chills down his spine. He might have fallen to the floor if she hadn't been holding him up with her power.

"Y-you do me a great honor, Spirit," he finally stammered. "But I am not trained—"

Eyes hard she stared at him until he stopped his futile protest. "Trained or not, you have been chosen, priest. Your service will be needed on occasion in the North, but until that time you will continue your duties to the Khutani and the Teh'lach. Don't refuse the burden Ata Doyan will pass on to you, priest. You will not like it if I become cross with you, My Jewel."

"N-no, Honored Spirit, I will obey," he said through chattering teeth; he was sure he wouldn't like it, knowing now who and what she was. Not for the first time, he cursed himself for a fool when he agreed to take up Adnim's dare and come on this journey.

When Crowis had given her his oath the Sweh'an Demon stepped back, revealing Ata Doyan and an unknown Clan warrior waring a colorful head band in the doorway. "Come in, Ata, we are finished here."

Looking sad and unhappy Doyan came in and bowed. "Honored Spirit, is this really necessary? I am willing to go with you as before. There's no need—"

"Enough, Cha'Han, you may be willing, but I am not *willing* to let you go with us." Her voice taking on a tone of command, she said, "You will instruct my new servant in his duties while there is still time, My Jewel."

Doyan came the rest of the way into the room and sat heavily at his table. "Your will, Honored Spirit, I will do as you instructed me."

"Good." Then crossing to the door, she allowed the warrior to lead her away. "Come, Atahru, My Treasure, we have much to do while the rest of the keep is occupied."

"Yes, Mistress, much to do."

When she was gone Doyan sighed, rubbing a hand across his face. "Crowis, I am so, so sorry. I truly thought the last time we talked that I was going North in her service. I had no idea she would choose another and leave me—here. She commanded me to write my manuscript—Tess-weh says it's important in our future." He picked up a waterproof leather bundle from the floor by his stool and placed it on the table in front of Crowis.

"And your portion of the narrative, young Ata, will be meaningful as well. For whatever her reasons, this will be a big part of your duties in her service. She says our travels will have great significance in our future. But as I cautioned you before be discreet as you record your findings—to prevent any—*misunderstandings*. Now grab that stool over by my bed and come sit so I can instruct you in the other things you will need to know before you leave for the Ghostlands."

PHILLIP-YOEY TOOK HIS place next to Chang, Tesulu and Qwasigara on the benches set aside for the leaders of the alliance. Nearby on other benches sat Hunt Leader Tizu, Tobrach, Warega, and the Meh'gach brothers. More of Tizu's and the Warlinga's officers crouched or stood with the rest of the camp's interested inhabitants, forming a large U-shape around the open gates to the keep. Some of the shorter Speir'dina, Phillip noticed, had persuaded a few of the Loti to let them sit atop their backs in order to see over the taller Clan Warriors and Warlinga crouching in front of them.

Off to one side, near the entrance to the keep a fire had been built and several Begta and a couple Clan Warriors were warming up their drums. On the outer walls and on poles around the circle torches and oil lamps had been placed to illuminate the proceedings.

<<This is so exciting,>> Yoey burbled. <<Have you ever been to a show like this before, Kasha?>>

Philip chuckled, sharing a measure of his bondmate's excitement. "I occasionally went to an entertainment when I was a child or at university, Shalla, but I can honestly say I've never been to an event like this.>>

<<Oh good, then we will share it—for the first time—together.>>

<<Indeed we will, Shalla, indeed we will.>>

When it was time, someone from inside gave a signal to the drummers and they stood, beating out a strong rhythm to focus and quiet the assembly.

Then into the center area bounded an amazing figure dressed in a glittering costume of sequins and color. The crowd gasped, most Timornans never having seen the like. The tall slim Speir'dina took off his floppy hat and bent into a theatrical bow to his audience.

"Good evening and welcome. I am Jojo Tepring, your master of ceremonies tonight. We have a great show planned for all our brave warriors who are going North in the morning to protect our homes and families." As he was speaking he produced from his flowing robes several glowing balls that he tossed into the air and began to juggle...

Jojo was turning out to be a great showman, Phillip thought as the evening continued. He'd done a great job in the little time he'd had to prepare. Through the medium of story and song he managed to flatter the three very separate and unique groups of fighters making up the kashallan Alliance.

Jojo began by bringing out a small stringed instrument and in a resinous clear voice sang a ballad about the Speir'dina being called to Timorna and their long trek across the Great Swamp to take Ticca Keep.

"I've heard this in a shorter less polished version," Chang confided. "He started composing it when we were at Ticca over the Sorins."

"Mm, it's very moving, "Phillip said. "And it's a great way for the native Timornans to know our story."

Jojo followed with a change of costume and a humorous performance that had everyone laughing within moments. Two Begta crept in, one with a fake head crest atop his wooly head and the other wearing a ragged ponytail. They stalked across the cleared area, dragging rope tails and menacing everyone with their privy shovels held like spears.

Then Jojo strolled in wearing rope braidlets and an Avairei kilt. He flounced about, pretending to be unaware of the menace creeping up behind him. Eventually Jojo was caught and the hunters carried him back to an imaginary camp. While they were arguing over who should have him as their slave, Jojo managed to sneak away, and then the mighty warriors had to chase him all over again. The crowd was roaring with laughter by the time they all took their bows.

This act was followed by a couple of the Armachda singing a popular song from Caldon accompanied by the two Clan drummers. That too was met by cheers from the crowd.

When the assembly quieted, Jojo came back into the center dressed in his flowing robes again. "Thank you for your appreciation of our performance. We have had little time to prepare and everyone has worked very hard to send off our brave defenders, Warlinga, Clan Warriors and Speir'dina with our blessings and respect. So with that in mind, some of the young people have drawn upon Speir'dina and Timornan traditions to prepare a special blessing dance to ensure your victory.

Doffing his hat Jojo bowed, and waved his hand to the entrance where several drummers were lining up beside a few Loti women singers. Then three women, Timma and Briyenn stepped into the center of the circle. The three women were Ishka, Niguiri and Anilah. Chang and Phillip exchanged looks. "I guess we're finally going to find out what they've been up to the last few days," Chang said.

"Yes, I've been wondering why all the secrecy. Even mother Efosa wouldn't tell me," Yoey complained.

As the drums began beating out a slow haunting rhythm Niguiri swayed forward in time to the beat and stood in front of Tesulu. "Uncle, may I bless your spear?"

Startled, Tesulu blinked. Niguiri repeated her question. A puzzled expression on his face, Tesulu finally reached back and handed over the long spear that had been resting on the ground at his side.

Niguiri took the weapon and moved back into the center. While she had been collecting Tesulu's spear, Timma had approached Tobrach and obtained his weapon as well.

<<Kasha, what are they going to do?>> Yoey asked.

<<I'm not sure, Shalla. There's something going on. Am I correct that she has been tasting—>>

<<Green kavay, you are right—and Timma, too. I wonder why?>>

Knowing that green kavay if used recreationally could cause a type of intoxication, Phillip wasn't sure how he felt about the young people dosing themselves with it here tonight. Keeping his opinion to himself for the moment, he only said to Yoey, <<Mm, good question. Let's watch for now and see.>>

In the center the couple raised the spears high then as Ishka, Anilah and the Loti women began to sing they laid them on the earth in an X shape. As the song progressed, the couple swayed and moved their hips and feet keeping time with the drums. Those with the warrior's magic and the Psy could see and feel their trance deepening. With the aid of the green kavay Niguiri and Timma were building a spiral of power as they danced in and out of the crossed weapons.

As the couple swayed and hopped from one section to another of the cross, they moved their hips and bent occasionally to spread their hands over the lethal points of the weapons.

With a gasp Phillip sat back, seeing the lines of power they were implanting into the stone blades. "Damn, I wonder who taught our Timma to do that... Masonja maybe..." he exclaimed.

"Do what?" Chang asked. "He's always been quick on his feet and can learn movements easily. A dance isn't that different from a fighting kata."

Still staring at the couple, Phillip said without looking away, "No, their dance is one thing but the blessing is—something else."

Seeing the intense expressions on the Warlinga and Clan Warriors' faces Chang murmured. "All right, what are they doing? What am I missing?"

Tearing himself away from the dance with an effort, Phillip-Yoey said, "Kiss me, Mah'lu."

Startled Chang drew back and stared. "What?"

"Kiss me, if you want to see what everybody else is seeing. Hurry before they finish!"

Shrugging Chang leaned forward and kissed him, but instead of just touching lips Yoey filled his mouth with green kavay. Chang choked and swallowed. "Give me some warning next time, Amadan."

Phillip-Yoey grinned. "Sorry. Just give the kavay a moment and—"

And then it happened. The world exploded. Chang's view of the dance was still there but now a tracery of energy lines supplemented his normal vision. He saw Niguiri and then Timma draw up from the earth and down from the sky male and female lines of power. Then as the audience continued to watch, they twisted them together and spread them across the blades of the weapons they blessed.

When the song ended and they returned the weapons to their owners a great cheer went up and several more men held up their spears for a blessing. The young couple danced a few more rounds, but Phillip-Yoey could see that the pregnant Niguiri was tiring. Timma must have sensed it, too, for at the end of the next blessing, he led Niguiri out of the center and Anilah with Briyenn as her partner took their place.

This couple must have also been dosed with the green kavay, Kashallan-Phillip decided, because he could still see the lines of power swirling about the spears as before.

Chapter Nineteen

As the blessings continued Tizu watched, but it was clear he wasn't seeing what the kashallans and the native Timornans were viewing. Finally he gave in to his curiosity and grumped to Nathan, "All right what's the big deal here? Let me in on what's going on."

"Sure." Nathan grinned and leaned forward.

Tizu quickly held up a hand to stop him. "If you try to kiss me like Phillip just did to that amadan Chang I'll punch you, Nathan. I'm warning you—don't you dare!"

Nathan-Corha laughed. "Just trying to help, Hunt Leader."

"Nathan!"

"Oh, all right , give me your arm then."

"What, my arm? What for? Is Corha hungry and needs a snack? We just ate not long ago and now you want a Blood Gift?"

Nathan chuckled and grabbed Tizu's arm, rolling up his sleeve. Before the Hunt Leader could pull back he extended his tentacles and formed a link.

"You shit for brains Amadan, what are you doing to me?"

Sitting behind the men with Chelka, Marti chuckled. "You're gonna find out soon, Sir."

"Mm, that's what I'm afraid of," Tizu grumbled.

Grinning, Nathan said, "I just gave you a taste of green kavay to let you see the Psy fields, or the war magics as the Warlinga would say."

"Hey, Nathan," McLaren joked. "I'll kiss you; come over here."

"Ha, ha, McLaren, you're not my type."

"I just want you to give me some of that green stuff, so I can get lucky tonight."

Around them the Lann Gheal armachda laughed, and someone shouted, "Give it up, Boyo, even with a kashallan's help you aren't getting laid any time soon."

Then the green kavay kicked in and Tizu sat bolt upright. Eyes wide, he stared around the cleared area, taking in the dancers and the lines of energy flowing and swirling about the people gathered there.

Chin in his hands, he stared for a long time saying nothing, thinking. Finally he turned to Tobrach and asked. "K'San Tobrach, when you use the war magics, as you call them, are you seeing the glowing lines that I'm seeing right now when I watch the dancers?"

"I can't be sure if it is the same as what you see, but I suspect it is similar. If I watch the dancers right now I can see how they are drawing up power and placing the power on the weapons. But using this power to either send or detect the illusions we use when fighting is not quite the same. It takes training as well as natural talent to master the magics."

Tizu nodded. "I don't doubt that, K'San." Next he turned to Nathan and asked, "And these energies—this Psy is what you see as a kashallan?"

"With Corha's help I can draw upon that gift and see what the green kavay is allowing you to experience right now, yes. But mostly we just view the world with my eyes alone." Silent for a moment, he added in a thoughtful tone. "I was never into the old teachings like Dunnagh. I learned the basics, but he was a real student of the Warrior's Art. He could probably do with his talent and training—even without Tani's help—what most Timornans do naturally."

"Hmm..." Tizu continued watching the performance, but Nathan could tell his mind was also exploring a new idea. At last he said, "Corha, could you and Yoey give our Speir'dina fighters some of this green stuff just before they go into battle? If they could see what I am seeing now, that might give our people an extra advantage."

"That's an interesting idea," Nathan said, answering for them both. "It might work, but we would have to be very careful with the dose. Too much, and you'd have an amadan high and wanting to hug everybody in the Ghostlands. Too little, and the armachd might lose the sight at a crucial moment and get his entire triad killed."

Tizu grunted. "Forget it, then."

"No, it's worth considering, but we will have to think about it some more—maybe talk to the makers."

"Do that and let me know; will you?"

Before Nathan could answer, the blessing dance ended and Jojo bounded into the center again, holding up his hands for silence. When the crowd quieted, he said, "I know we haven't gotten to everybody, but we need to give the dancers and singers a rest."

When the angry growling started he held up a hand to placate them. "Warriors of the Alliance, I didn't say we were done. We are just going to shift our focus. The Speir'dina of Lann Gheal have a special way they prepare for battle, so we need to add their traditions to this Timornan mix, don't you agree, Armachda?"

With Jojo's question the armachda set up a great cheer. Tizu jerked and then looked down as someone dropped a set of headphones in his lap.

Puzzled he picked them up and examined them. "What's this for—" Then spying Ross walking into the center with his pibroch, he figured it out and shook his head. "No, no, no!"

Nathan and some of the other Speir'dina nearby laughed. "Give in gracefully, Hunt Leader," Nathan chortled. "You can't fight tradition—put the headphones on."

"They don't help," Tizu complained, but put them on anyway.

Glancing from one joking Speir'dina to another the Warlinga nearby exchanged puzzled looks, their head crests dipping in confusion. Finally Aju'an got up the nerve to ask Nathan-Corha, "What's wrong, Holy One; why is the Hunt Leader angry with us tonight?"

Nathan shook his head a smile playing with the corners of his lips. "Don't mind him. The Hunt leader isn't angry—not really," Nathan assured the native Timornans around them. "He's actually enjoying himself. He just doesn't appreciate good music when he hears it."

Overhearing that last comment Tizu took off the head phones and snorted. "Good music, my ass."

The armachda laughed, then fell silent as Rhys and a young armachd named Boughthy brought two wrapped bundles into the firelight.

"Damn," Nathan said his jaw dropping in awe. Turning to Tizu, he said, "You brought our corps icons with you?"

The Hunt Leader nodded, all serious now. "We are going into war after all. I figured we might need them—for their symbolic value if nothing else.

I'm not sure how the blades themselves would hold up in an actual fight—but they go with us all the same."

As Ross played *The Lann Gheal Honor Song*, Rhys and Boughthy marched into the firelight. In the center they unwrapped the corps' ceremonial swords and held them high. The gleaming metal caught the light and blazed as if made of fire. A gasp went up from the assembly as if the men had performed a miracle right before their eyes.

Metals were rare on Timorna, so the sight of a lethal weapon made of the precious material was—glorious—unbelievable.

As the tribute ended, Rhys and Boughthy laid the precious blades on the ground in the X shape like the women had done with the warriors' spears.

"The pipes you've been hearing and these mighty weapons are a part of the fighting traditions of the Speir'dina warriors that they brought with them when they came to Timorna," Jojo explained. "Bright Blade, or Lann Gheal in the Caldoni language. We hold here tonight the bright blade of our victory. We offer to Mother Timorna, The Great Hunt Leader, and the Unseen Ones the gifts of our sacrifice and blood. And so we will dance, call up the power and bless these fine blades as well. Do you not agree, My People?"

Loud cheering and roars of approval answered his question. Holding up his hand for silence Jojo continued. "And for this I think we need special dancers, steeped in the traditions of Caldon where the swords were forged." He bowed to Rhys, who bowed back.

As Boughthy left the center, Jojo theatrically scanned the circle as if looking for someone. Then finding Nathan, he threw up his hands and smiled. "Ah, I think we need some Kashallan power and blessings as a part of this ceremony." He bowed. "Nathan-Corha, would you join your armachd?"

Nathan shook his head. "No way. I'm out of practice get one of the young lads—like Boughthy there to dance."

"But Boughthy isn't a kashallan. Come on, Nathan, don't be shy," Jojo coaxed. "The armachda say you're the best."

Nathan said something in Caldoni that made the armachda laugh. "If you want a kashallan's blessing, get Phillip-Yoey to do it."

"Me?" startled, Phillip shook his head. "Nice try, Amsi, but I'm not Caldoni. The honor is all yours."

"Come on Nathan," Jojo begged, then turning to his audience, he said, "We really want to see our shy kashallan dance don't we? Come on everyone, let's show him how much we need his blessing!"

The crowd cheered, Phillip one of the loudest. Then someone started chanting, "Nathan, Nathan, Nathan," and soon the crowd took it up, the sound swelling to a great roar.

Tizu smirked and made a shooing motion. And finally Nathan acquiesced and joined Rhys in the center. Each man removed his boots and took places in opposite sections of the crossed blades, facing one another. As the Pibroch began to play they raised one hand to the sky and the other pointed down to the ground. Whirling and jumping in time with the drum and the wailing pipes the dancers moved from one section to another in unspoken unison, as one bare foot and then another lightly brushed the air just above the lethal steel.

Both men were skilled with the Psy, so as they flowed in and out of the pattern, they drew up a great well of power which they transferred into the steel. When the dance finally ended and they held up the Lann Gheal swords the weapons seemed to glow with their own radiance. A great cheer went up once more as the swords were rewrapped and carried back into the keep.

Still breathing hard instead of sitting back down Nathan came over and stood in front of Phillip with his arms folded. "Your turn, Amsi."

Phillip stared mouth agape. "Me? I can't dance like that! I was always a terrible dancer—and besides the swords are put away now."

Nathan smirked. "You're not getting out of your duty with that excuse. Up you come." Nathan made a lifting motion with his hands. The Clan warriors, catching on, added their own shouts of encouragement to the din.

Still feeling the effects of the green kavay, Chang chuckled and got to his feet bringing Phillip with him. Motioning for Ishka to join them, he took Phillip's hand and walked to the center. "Come on, Co-Husband, our turn."

"I think maybe I gave you too much of the green kavay," Phillip grumbled, but allowed himself to be guided into the light nonetheless. "Mah'lu, are you high?"

"Could be," he chuckled. "Come on, I got an idea."

Leaving Ishka to keep Phillip from sitting down, Chang went back into the crowd and brought back three spears from the Sand Mountain and Red

Wind warriors. He laid them down in a triangle, then gathered three more from the other Clans and made an interlocking symbol similar to the clan mark on Ishka and Phillip's cheek. The Clan warriors cheered.

When he saw what Chang had done, Phillip shook his head and clicked his tongue. "I've never done something like this before, and you want to make it so easy for me first time, Sensei."

Chang grinned. "Relax, Student, Yoey can follow me; just give over control and let it help you."

<<Kasha, our Mah'lu is right. We can do this. It will be fun,>> the symbiont burbled.

Putting Ishka between them Chang guided them to the space between the two peaks of the Sand Mountain glyph triangles. Facing the clans, Chang said, "For our victory and the honor of Sand Mountain and all the Clans, Elder Qwasigara, drummers of the People give us a song."

Qwasigara rose and in a deep powerful voice began to sing, the drummers quickly joining. Taking a deep breath Phillip let go and allowed his bondmate to dominate their shared body. As the music filled them the three flowed together as if they were of one body and mind. Weaving a pattern of male and female energies they danced between the spears, infusing them with the lethal power of the Unseen Ones' blessings.

As Nathan took his seat an excited Marti leaned forward and whispered next to his ear, "When they finish, let's you and I go up and do a blessing. I got enough Psy to follow your lead. A lot of the Warlinga from the Yeyen who haven't been around us much haven't taken part yet. They would probably like to be part of this, too—so let's do it."

Nathan thought about it then shook his head. "Nah, I'm too tired it wouldn't be good—might cut my dainty feet."

Marti scowled and punched him lightly on the shoulder. "You're feet are far from dainty and you're not that tired. Come on."

"Ow—yes I am." When she opened her mouth to argue further, he said in a quiet but firm voice, "Marti, no. we can't. Some here would see it as a bad omen."

Finally understanding that he was referring to the Umwira mark on her face, she sat back her expression grim.

Knowing that he'd hurt her, but unable to do anything about it, Nathan took her hand, brought it to his lips and kissed it. "Marti, I'm sorry, Mo Cri, I really want to, but we can't right now." Hoping to cheer her up he allowed his tongue to play across her palm. "But you can bless my spear all you want—later."

Setting aside her sour mood Marti chuckled and punched him again, this time harder. "You Amadan, maybe I will."

"Ow, Woman, stop hitting me—why you got to always be beating me up!"

She punched him again, but this time she accompanied the blow with a smile on her face. "Cause you're an Amadan—and you make me mad sometimes."

Later when the dancers finished, Tobrach rose, many of the other Warlinga standing with him. At the corner of his eye, Nathan had become aware of Aju'an and some of the others talking among themselves as the evening progressed, but thought little of it.

Addressing Jojo and the audience, Tobrach said, "If you permit, San Jojo, we have talked among ourselves and would like to share some of the traditions we Warlinga do to prepare for a hunt."

When Jojo bowed his agreement, he continued, "We don't sing or dance, but we chant our prayers to the Great Hunt Leader and conjure the power in the ways our ancestors taught us."

As he spoke seven hunters joined him, spears in hand. They stepped into the center, forming a circle. A low rumble starting deep in their chests it grew in volume as they raised their spears high then crouched and laid them upon the earth like the spokes of a great wheel, their tips forming a small circle within the larger one.

As the men rumbled, drawing up power from it seemed Timorna's very core, the ground itself began to vibrate under the assembly's feet. Before the rumbling could grow into a real quake the circle channeled the energy into a glowing tower in the small circle where the spear tips touched. As it rose and spiraled outward other spears held by the warriors in the assembly began to glow as well.

As this power spiraled, Tobrach chanted a deep-voice prayer to the Great Hunt Leader to bless the Alliance's hunt and keep safe and protect all the warriors of the alliance traveling into the Ghostlands to hunt the Enemy.

Jojo formally closed the evening's entertainment after that. Some of the audience drifted away to find their bedrolls, but many in the alliance remained gathered around the fires to sing and drum, not ready to seek their beds in spite of the late hour an the long day on the morrow.

As the assembly broke up into smaller groups to sing and talk, Ishka took hold of both her consorts' hands. A smile playing about her dark lips she hustled them into the shadows, and then back into the keep. "Come," she murmured, "before we are seen and someone stops us to talk."

"Where are we going?" Chang asked.

"You'll see, come on. Don't dawdle."

Chang and Phillip-Yoey exchanged looks, but dutifully allowed themselves to be drawn deeper into the quiet recesses of the keep.

Finally the kashallan figured it out and smiled. "We are going to the Tragar Pool aren't we?"

"Yes, but hush now; don't spoil it."

Having some idea of what she had in mind, Phillip said to Yoey, <<I wonder who suggested this to her?>>

<<Maybe one of Corha's pod or our Amla.>>

<<Mm, Amla Tinguss, eh... Guess we better give them more green kavay, Shalla. You know other people might come there as well.>> Phillip reminded his bondmate. <<I think Nathan-Corha has been bringing Marti to the pool. Mah'lu might be uncomfortable with the pod and—>>

<<It's a big enough pool—and dark,>> Yoey countered. The symbiont thought about it for a moment and then added, <<I suspect there is a more practical reason for coming here that I doubt our Ishka knows.>>

<<Mm, let me guess. The makers want our genetic patterns—especially our Mah'lu's in case we don't come back.>>

<<That would be my guess, too,>> Yoey said a taste of sadness in the mental sending.

Phillip stroked his middle. <<Let's enjoy our time together and not worry about the future, Shalla.>>

Realizing at almost the same moment that the pool was their destination, Chang hesitated slipping his hand out of Ishka's. "Maybe I should wait up here until—"

Ishka snatched his hand back and continued walking. "No. I want both my men with me on this last night. We stay together—this time. I know you two have been taking turns with me—being oh so careful not to offend each other and me, because in spite of Speir'dina talk to the contrary, it isn't any easier for you to share a wife than it would be for Clan warriors."

At their startled looks she laughed. "Men! You are so easy to understand. Of course I know what you've been doing. And now, according to Speir'dina custom and law, it's my turn to say what happens in our marriage—and I say we stay together."

Chang shrugged, the two men exchanged looks over her head, coming to an unspoken agreement. "All right if that's what you want, My dear," Phillip said. "We are yours to command."

She snorted a laugh. "I seriously doubt that, but for tonight I will hold you to that statement, Phillip-Yoey." Turning to Chang after a moment, she said, "Mah'lu, husband, think of us as just another triad—like the warriors you and the hunt leaders train. We work, make love and—fight the enemy together."

As they stepped onto the walkway by the pool she squeezed their hands. "And tonight I am sensei here, my students, so take off your clothes."

Chapter Twenty

In the evening shadows two warriors lay prone on a rock ledge. Below them the glowing fires of the Alliance encampment shown like tiny stars against the dark land. At the top of the rise across from them, the fortress of Tragar loomed, a menacing specter against the purple sky.

As the changelings watched, bright ribbons of silver and blue fire streaked across the darkness, enveloping the alliance army in a web of power. Even here, so far from its center of creation the tendrils of menace tingled against their scales.

"We should go," the older and wiser of the two said. "They conjure great magics; K'San Drucas will want to hear about the Enemy's preparations. The two Ghostland agents the Khutani worms missed can continue to send reports with the Master's crystal as the Alliance travels north into our territory. There's no need for us to take more risks now."

The younger snorted his contempt. Though still favoring his healing arm, he argued for a continued vigil. "K'San Drucas will only send us back, Lazy Begta. For whatever his reasons, he wants his own 'personal' report. And I for one, have no wish to feel more pain if he isn't pleased with what we bring him."

"I wish we would have dared use the potion the Cabal gave us to temporarily mask our true nature as well," the older grumped. "But we were recognized and so couldn't drift back into camp unnoticed, curse the Speir'dina to the Black Pit of Oblivion. It gets cold out here without a fire at night. We should go. They will be leaving in the morning and we need to be well away from here before their scouts find our trail. We've gained all the information we could—he won't blame us or punish us."

From the darkness behind them came a soft chuckle. "Are you sure of that, My Jewel? The changeling K'San isn't a man to let failure go unpunished. He is a master of the art of administering pain—as you both know—hmm?"

Startled, the two spies leapt to their feet and sprang off the stone, landing with their spears out and ready for battle. To their surprise, a lone shrouded figure stepped out of the thorn into the open where she could be seen. Seemingly unaware of the danger they presented, she continued, "Did you witness thc beautiful display of kashallan power? Are you afraid? Want to run North tell the K'San so he can protect you?"

She laughed, but there was no mirth in the sound. "Too late. Neither Drucas nor the Cabal of Ghosts can save you now. The Changeling will be so disappointed. Poor Drucas, be glad I will protect you from his wrath. Your failure will cost him his victory, do you know that? You should have gone north when you had the chance."

The youngest stepped forward snarling. "We aren't too late to go North, Speir'dina witch. And we will take you with us so you can personally admire his skills with The Art of Pain."

"Oh I doubt if the Segoi K'San could teach me anything—especially in The Art of Giving Pain." Her eyes above her veil glittered with menace as she stepped to meet him. "And as for taking me North, I'm already going there. I have my own escort and don't need another—especially not bumbling half-bred slaves like you two."

As he lunged for her, Tess-weh raised a hand and froze him with her power. Behind him he heard a strangled choking sound, then a heavy body fell to the ground. Turning his head the younger changeling saw a Clan warrior with a strange glyph on his forehead put his foot on his partner's back and pull his spear out of the man's dead body.

"Well done, My Treasure." She chortled. "I can see you enjoy killing the 'Hated Enemy.' Well, you can have this one, too—in a moment."

"Thank you, Mistress. I want only to please you."

"Yes I know, My Jewel, and you do please me—and you will please me even more—later."

Glancing at the dead changeling, the Clan warrior stared at the Speir'dina knife on his belt. Tess-weh noticed and smiled. "Take it if you want it, My Treasure, you deserve a little reward this night."

The warrior bowed deeply and took the knife, admiring its lethal perfection. "Thank you, Mistress."

Trembling the younger changeling begged, "Don't kill me. I will tell you anything you want to know about my K'San and his plans—I will tell you what I know about the Cabal, too—"

Impatient with his babbling Tess-weh silenced him with a flick of her power. The changeling let out a silent scream of pain. "Enough! I make no bargains with cowardly filth. You will tell me anything I want, no bargain needed." Turning to face the darkness, she drawled, "What say you, Khutani, do you have any questions for this garbage, before I let my slave have him?"

At her words two glowing eel-like creatures appeared in the air nearby. <<We have no questions. Do as you like with the changeling scum.>>

Tess-weh bowed. <<Your will, Khutani.>> She motioned for Atahru to kill the other one. Showing his canines, the Wa'chassey'ul did as she commanded, using his new knife.

An amused tone to her voice, she added, <<And have you discovered the two other gifts we left for you in the encampment?>>

<<We have found them, Spirit, but we don't understand the reason for them—please explain.>>

She clicked her tongue and shook her head in dismay. <<Oh, My dear Big Slimeworms, truly you slept too long. The world has changed while you traveled the Starry River in the Dream. Those two were also agents of the Ghostland Wizards and changeling bred.>>

<<That is not possible! We checked—again.>>

<<Ah, but it is possible, Khutani. Their masters have developed many poisons—with you in mind, I might add, while you indulged in the Long Sleep.

<<The two you missed had dosed themselves with a potion especially made to mask their true nature from your tasting. The effect is only temporary, true, but it has served its purpose many times over the years.>>

She pointed to the bodies on the ground. <<Have one of your children search them before the army goes north. You will want to taste the substance to know its flavor in future.>>

<<We will do that, Spirit. Your service to us is satisfactory.>>

<<Satisfactory, eh?>> Her eyes flashed with anger. <<Only 'satisfactory?' Have a care, Big Slimeworm, your arrogance and carelessness will get a few of you killed and maybe some of your precious children as well. There are already those hidden away in the North who cry for the kindred who have forgotten and abandoned them, never coming to offer them a release from pain and torment.>>

<<What are you talking about?>>

<<Go North and find out.>>

<<If you have seen that some of our children are in danger, then according to the provisions of your contract it is up to you to protect them.>>

<<My contract is with kashallans, Khutani—kashallans! It is not with you. The mess you've made of your stewardship of this world is of your own making and all will suffer for it.

<<In the future that is coming choices will have to be made. I can battle with only one enemy before my time among you is ended. Who to protect and save—the one—or the many. Choices, My dear Big Worms, death is hunting all of us.>>

The End

This story is continued in
Treacherous Campaign
Book Eight of *Tales of the Kashallans*

Don't miss out!

Visit the website below and you can sign up to receive emails whenever Celu Amberstone publishes a new book. There's no charge and no obligation.

https://books2read.com/r/B-A-YGQM-AEEHC

BOOKS 2 READ

Connecting independent readers to independent writers.

Did you love *Kashallan Alliance*? Then you should read *Taste of Memory*[1] by Celu Amberstone!

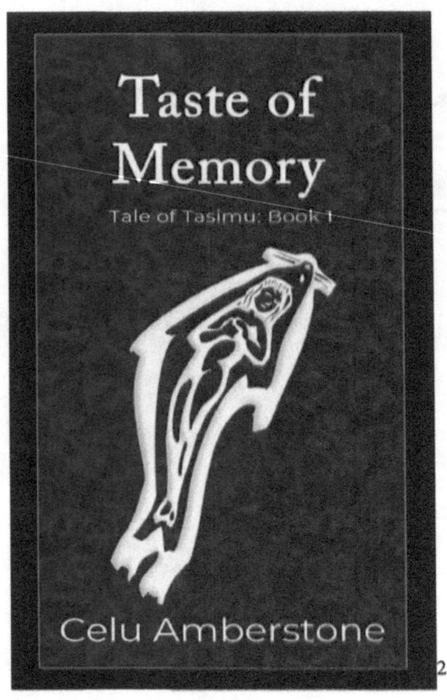

[2]

TASIMU is a youth who can call down the power of the northern lights to win a rock-throwing contest, but he is also a boy troubled by the mystery surrounding his birth. Others taunt him, claiming that he isn't truly human. Before he can discover the truth, gold is discovered on tribal land, and soldiers from the Empire come north with orders to remove his people from their northern home.

Taste of Memory deals with issues of family breakup, ritual abuse and cultural disintegration as these tribal people are forced to become refugees, stolen away from their ancestral land. But it is also a story where love for one's family and people triumphs over a need for selfish desires and personal power. This is the first book in the *Tales of Tasimu* series by celebrated author Celu Amberstone.

---

1. https://books2read.com/u/mgRD10
2. https://books2read.com/u/mgRD10

The Dreamer's Legacy is truly an interesting book. It takes a familiar story of the colonization of Indigenous people, and gives it a new and exotic twist. Celu Amberstone has fashioned a truly original take on aboriginal storytelling - it teaches, entertains, and mystifies.

- Drew Hayden Taylor (author of *The Night Wanderer: A Native Gothic Novel, Motorcycles and Sweetgrass*)

An original and gripping story. Amberstone transports us to a sad, wild land that is not of our world to tell a heart-warming story from another culture and another time.

- Dave Duncan (author of *The Seventh Sword, A Man of His Word, A Handful of Men*)

Merges the mythic aboriginal world with the grim realities of cultural disintegration. The Dreamer's Legacy is a compelling read.

- Eileen Kernaghan (author of *Wild Talent: a Novel of the Supernatural*)

Also by Celu Amberstone

Rituals

Blessings of the Blood: A Book of Menstrual Lore and Rituals for Women

Deepening the Power: Community Ritual and Sacred Theatre

Tales of Tasimu

Taste of Memory

When Memory Dies

Tales of the Kashallans

The Dream-Chosen

The Hunted Kashallan

The Outlawed Bond

Uncertain Refuge

Prey of the Umwira

Blood Magic's Snare

Kashallan Alliance

Treacherous Campaign

Standalone

Refugees and Other Stories

About the Author

Celu is of mixed Cherokee and Scots-Irish ancestry. Celu Amberstone was one of the few young people in her family to take an interest in learning Traditional Native crafts and medicine ways. This interest made several of the older members of her family very happy while annoying others.

Legally blind since birth, she has defied her limitations and spent much of her life avoiding cities. Moving to Canada after falling in love with a Métis-Cree man from Manitoba, she has lived in the rain forests of the west coast, a tepee in the desert and a small village in Canada's arctic. Along the way she also managed to acquire a BA in cultural anthropology and an MA in health education. Celu loves telling stories and reading. She lives in Victoria British Columbia near her grown children and grandchildren.

About the Publisher

Kashallan Press is an independent publisher releasing books by author Celu Amberstone. Among her books are critically-acclaimed works now re-released by Kashallan Press, and new works showcasing her talents in writing both fiction and non-fiction.

www.ingramcontent.com/pod-product-compliance
Lightning Source LLC
Chambersburg PA
CBHW030931260626
47169CB00002B/437

* 9 7 8 1 9 9 0 5 8 1 1 3 7 *